To Lou & June Cooper
with good wishes

Bob (LeRoy)

Where
Blood Runs
Black and White

A Novel
by

R. LeRoy Bannerman

Bloomington, IN Milton Keynes, UK

authorHOUSE

AuthorHouse™
1663 Liberty Drive, Suite 200
Bloomington, IN 47403
www.authorhouse.com
Phone: 1-800-839-8640

AuthorHouse™ UK Ltd.
500 Avebury Boulevard
Central Milton Keynes, MK9 2BE
www.authorhouse.co.uk
Phone: 08001974150

First published by AuthorHouse 9/1/2006

ISBN: 1-4259-4391-8 (sc)

Library of Congress Control Number: 2006905577

Printed in the United States of America
Bloomington, Indiana

This book is printed on acid-free paper.

To my son and daughter,

Mark and Jane

and my seven grandchildren

ACKNOWLEDGEMENT

This is fiction based on fact. In the fifties, the University of Alabama inadvertently admitted a black student. Aware of the error, the institution rejected her application and there ensued protracted litigation wherein the university was forced to accept her. On her first day of class, however, she faced a threatening mob and she was expelled for her "safety." After receiving her degree elsewhere, she chose to return to Alabama and in 1992 earned her Masters.

I am deeply indebted to Civil Rights authority Dr. Lauren K. Robel, dean and Val Nolan professor of law, Indiana University School of Law, for her assistance and advice in authenticating the development of this story. My appreciation also to Richard Hamlin for his contribution and expertise in the computer preparation of the manuscript.

RLB

Look now this land

Of furrowed fields and timber lines,

Of honeysuckled hedges and Southern pines,

Of resourceful folk who silently toil

The uncertain seasons of ethnic soil,

And once accepted this schism of day and night:

A world where blood runs black and white.

CHAPTER 1

"Abby..!"

She stopped at his call. This slender 16-year-old girl turned to see her boy friend coming toward her in long athletic strides. He was still some yards away. White dust puffed from his brogans as Joey Henderson jogged to catch up.

"Abby, wait!"

She smiled and, shifting her books, held forth her hand to him. He was breathing hard as he shuffled to a halt beside her.

"Hi," she said softly.

He beamed. "Hi there."

Up close, Abigail Price was very pretty. Her dimpled smile, her trim figure, and her soft cinnamon complexion made her one of the most attractive girls in Crestview's colored school.

Together, hand in hand, they walked slowly along a dirt, pine-needled path that snaked beneath a canopy of entangled trees. It was their shortcut home. And as they entered this quiet cloister of evergreens, oak, dogwood and sweet gum, they left behind the distant clamor of excited youth boarding yellow school buses.

"Where you been?" she asked. "Didn't see you after history."

"I know. I had to see th' principal."

"What about? Nothin's wrong, I hope."

1

"Naw," he answered. "Actually, it's good news I think. Abby, I think I got a chance to go to college."

"Really? When? How?"

He said hopefully, "If it all works out.."

"But Joey, when?"

"Soon, I reckon—maybe next fall."

"How'd it happen..! What did Mr. Johnson, th' principal, say?"

"Oh, he jus' called me to his office to meet a preacher. It was a Reverend Mortecai Ellison. He done most of th' talkin'."

"A—preacher?"

"Yeah, and he was very nice."

"You say Reverend Ellison—I think I've heard of him." Abby remembered, "He's th' pastor of th' Singletree Road Baptist Church."

"Yeah, but he's somethin' else too," Joey explained. "He's head of th' N-double A—C-P" here in Crestview, and he wants me to he'p them."

Abby looked at him quizzically.

"You see, if I do what they want, Mr. Ellison said they might be able to fix it so I could git th' money to go to college. And you know that's been my problem. Not enough money. But if he can handle that, it'd be great. Oh God, Abby, it's what I've always wanted—you know that."

She knew.

She knew of Joey's aching ambition, his intense desire to better himself, his frustration at having to exist in what he perceived a hopeless environment. He had told Abby many times how much he hated the farm, with its perpetual cycle of hard work, disappointment, and poverty. He wanted very much to attend college, perhaps even become a medical doctor one day, to gain a measure of prestige, respect. But his dream until now had eluded him. His family could not afford to send him to college. He was the son of a sharecropper.

"It's my chance, Abby," he breathed. "Don't you see? It's my chance..!"

Abby hugged her books, looking down as she strolled the path. She said quietly, "It's wonderful." Then, she added sadly, "But you'll be goin' away, won't you. I won't be seein' you for a spell."

Her concern was real. With one more year to go in high school and with Joey graduating within a few weeks, Abby feared any separation might jeopardize their relationship. Even though they had known each other most of their life, they had now become quite close and neither would wish their association to end.

Joey put his arm around her waist. "Oh, but that's th' good part—I won't be goin' away."

"You won't?"

"They want me to go here," he told her.

She was confused. "Here? What do you mean?"

He hastened to say, "They want me to enroll here in Crestview State College."

"But Joey, that's a—-a—"

"I know, I know…It's a white college."

For a moment there was shocked silence. Then Abby cried, "But you cain't! You know you cain't. Joey, they won't let you."

"What d'ya mean I cain't? If I got th' grades, they cain't stop me. That's it, they got to take me."

"Joey, I ain't talkin' 'bout th' college. It's *them* I'm talkin' about..!"

Joey instantly knew her meaning. Her fear of redneck reprisals was an indelible nightmare etched in an unforgettable childhood trauma. She had been only six at the time. But she would always remember that eerie night when raucous voices awakened her and, with wide-eyed wonderment, she saw shimmering light dancing on her newspaper-print papered ceiling. She quickly crawled out of bed, and kneeling on a chair looked out the window to see a flaming cross in their yard. And forever fixed in Abby's mind would always be the horrible sound of her papa's tortured cry as he was beaten and hustled into the darkness by white-hooded men.

Abby shuddered at the remembrance and her face was clouded in sadness. She and Joey now stood where the path skirted a freshly plowed field. The gray furrows could be seen beyond a hedgerow of tangled briers, honeysuckle, and a rusty wire fence. Standing in the shadows, they were silhouetted against the sunlit expanse.

"Look, Abby, I—I know how you feel." said Joey tenderly, awkwardly, recognizing the reality of her fear.

She had spoken to him only once about her experience. Once, angered by her insensitive stepfather, she had vented her rage and frustration on Joey. It was obvious that the hurt of her father's untimely death was deep and, scarred by the violent circumstances of the tragedy, she now saw only a world of hatred and ruthlessness—and a man who could never take her father's place.

"But it won't be like that," Joey assured her. "There won't be no trouble—not what you're thinkin'. My God, Abby, this is a college we're talkin' about; they're educated people—they won't let nothin' bad like that happen. There won't be no trouble."

"But you're th' one who's causin' trouble," she pointed out.

Joey, disillusioned at her reaction, walked slowly on, staring at the path thoughtfully. He finally spoke. "Okay, so some people won't be likin' it. I know that. And they'll probably cause a ruckus and th' whole thing will land up in court—and th' court'll decide. They explained it, Abby, it'll be whatever th' law says."

"But they don't respect th' law—and you know it!" she reminded him.

"Th' college will," Joey insisted. "They have to."

She stopped.

"You've got to listen to me, Joey. Like I been sayin', it ain't th' college that's th' worry. It's all th' people who won't be likin' what you're doin'—and there's a lot of them, and they don't stop at nothin'. You're bein' set up for a mess of trouble. You got to see that, Joey."

Disappointedly, he muttered, "Aw, Abby."

He walked ahead of her along the path. Then he stopped and held out his hand to her. She caught up, took it, and together they strolled through the afternoon splotches of sunlight filtering through the trees. Abby looked beyond, her eyes misting in memory.

She saw herself, a little girl, standing by a mother in mourning, gazing into the dark chasm of an open grave…She had longed once more to feel her father's embrace, to sense his love, his understanding. But the only lasting memory which lingered—then and for all time—was the painful sight of a crumpled corpse which had been him, her once gentle, loving father, being lifted from a wagon bed.

The woods now thinned and their path emerged into a patch of broom straw.

"Joey?"

"Yeah."

"Please don't do it," she pleaded.

"My God, Abby, it's my chance. There's nothin' wrong in at least tryin'..! It may not work out, but it's worth a try."

The girl paused and looked him full in the face. Her eyes shone. They were moist.

"When you cross that line, Joey, there are hateful people who'll do hateful things. I don't want nothin' ever to happen to you."

He turned away abruptly and, kicking a clod of dirt, snapped, "Damn it, Abby, I can take care of myself..!" He turned back, his eyes softening. "Look," he said, "It don't have to be like what you're thinkin'. They explained everything. All this is being handled by the N-double A-C-P, and they know what they're doin'..!"

Her body seemed to tighten in anger. "But they cain't handle th' rednecks, th' rowdies, those people who're out to kill! Joey, listen, please listen. You know as well as I do, somethin' awful can happen..!"

"Okay, alright, think what you want, Abby," he said, expanding his arms in a shrug. "It's a risk, maybe, but I know it's worth it. This is my chance and I'm doin' it! Hear me? I'm doin' it!"

"But Joey..!"

"Forgit it!" he snarled.

In the pause that followed, she hid her face from him. Then, to Joey's surprise, she suddenly broke down and began to sob. In that terrible moment, she bolted and ran down the path.

"Abby..!" he called.

On impulse, he started after her, but then he stopped abruptly and watched her run the curve of the path and disappear beyond a clump of myrtle bushes into a grove of pine trees. He looked for a long time, as if memorizing her short running stride, her billowing skirt, her white ankle socks, her pink blouse, her black hair. His cheeks stung with disappointment. He suddenly felt empty, exhausted, drained of the hope that had buoyed him only moments before. He now felt tentative, uncertain, even a little afraid.

CHAPTER 2

Neither Joey Henderson nor his ministerial mentor fully imagined the difficulty they might eventually face in the pursuit of their bold objective. Young Henderson knew not the motive of Reverend Ellison's plan, other than, as the local leader of the NAACP, he was exacting an intrepid effort to oppose Southern segregation.

This was first realized on an autumn Thursday in 1951. At dusk on that day, the pointed steeple of the Singletree Road Baptist Church was silhouetted against the orange oval of the setting sun. As dark slowly enshrouded the weather-beaten wooden structure, several people straggled in to find a pew. The minister, meeting them, smiled his welcome and regretfully noted how few had responded to his call to protest and organize against racial bigotry so rampant in their region.

The Reverend Mortecai Ellison was unsure as to how his effort would be received. He nervously saw his engagement in this controversial and perilous project as an antithesis of his personality and being. Yet, he had been moved to enter the cause in the hope that his race might appreciate his leadership in contending with the prejudice and injustice so prevalent in their community. He wanted to do something about it and he had taken this unprecedented step.

Now, almost a year later, the Reverend Ellison reached for his telephone to make a significant call. He felt the same sense of trembling expectancy which he had experienced back then on that warm fall evening. He recalled standing alone by the church chancel, hoping, silently praying that God and a goodly number of his congregation might give evidence that night of a deep concern for human rights and justice. It would take fortitude for these people to assemble, he knew, but he wished fervently that his Negro followers might banish fear and bind together for the important purpose of founding a local NAACP chapter. When it appeared that no other person would join the small group attending, Pastor Ellison feared the people there might begin to doubt the practicality of their purpose and possibly defect.

Ellison knew, of course, that a clandestine gathering like this might well bring the blazing terror of night riders. And it was not his nature to be bold. He was naturally compassionate and concerned, but not until this time would he have even dared assume any visible role as a reformer.

He had forever followed the pattern of his upbringing faithfully, and in the quiet manner of his parents had accepted the social status of colored people as something universally expected, inevitable. As a boy, he was puzzled, but he soon learned that "to get along" he had to adhere to tradition, harness his feelings, be passive, be pliable. In this way, he became what was called a "good" Negro and, by example and by thought, he lived his life of compromise.

Even later, as an ordained minister, the Reverend Ellison saw his mission as a mitigator, a man of the cloth who might keep the peace, who would forever counsel his people to be patient, law-abiding, docile, before the pressure of a white power structure. In his sermons and his daily discussions, he always advised his flock to follow a gentle path, to avoid confrontation, to live a Christian life, to steer a wide course and give white folk little cause to be upset or angry. In short, to "turn the other cheek."

With World War II, however, this philosophical approach soon soured for Mortecai Ellison. He witnessed the return of Coplin County's black sons from overseas, who would again face racial bigotry—familiar but forgotten—and find it hard to take. They had, after all, worn the American uniform with pride and distinction, so they felt they deserved a measure of respect and equality. Moreover, they had been received freely in the liberal cultures of war-torn Europe and now expected similar treatment at home. But most devastating of all was the harsh reality that, although they had fought gallantly against the racist principles of Adolf Hitler (some of them dying), they were to find the same oppression at home awaiting them. And the bitterness that they had endured before began to quietly simmer.

Reverend Ellison felt a personal sensitivity to all this as he observed the distress of these returning veterans and the conflict within their families. He became acutely conscious of an unjust world about him. "Turn the other cheek" simply did not apply. And as he saw impatience build into a pyramid of frustration, his anger underscored an urgency to do something about it. No longer could he mentally distance himself from the plight of his parishioners.

Mattie's son, for instance.

He remembered the Sunday he had looked out over his congregation to see a khaki-clad, beribboned black youth seated beside his mother. It was Mattie's boy. And Reverend Ellison deviated from his text that Sabbath to express joy at seeing the young man back, alive, and he passionately projected his voice in prayer to praise the Lord—and he heard an echo of loud "amens" resounding throughout the church.

Mattie's son had earned a Silver Star, having served in England, survived the Normandy landings, and had been wounded near the border of Belgium. And his mother, happy to have him home, sat close and held tightly his arm as the pastor intoned his blessings.

Afterward, at the door, Mattie had her son shake the minister's hand, at which time, smiling broadly, she pointed out the significance of his decorations. The young soldier, although embarrassed, willingly submitted to his mother's pride. Reverend Ellison then saw them walk away, the widowed mother holding onto her son's arm, and the boy, tall and strong—-except for a noticeable limp.

But it was not a happy homecoming. Even though Crestview's climate of racial prejudice had always been a part of his life, Mattie's boy felt it more upon his return than ever before. He said little, tried to ignore the small incidents of racial bias, but he nevertheless seethed at what he saw. Then, one evening, Mattie came pounding on the preacher's door.

"Mattie, my dear, what on earth—!"

"Pastor, pastor! My boy! He's been arrested!"

"But—but why?"

"He didn't do nothin'!" she cried. "They jes' put him in jail..! Oh, Pastor Ellison, please—can you please go see him?"

The reverend had no stomach to go near the county jail. It was, to all his race, a fearful place where burly officers looked with disdain upon all black people—whether inmate or visitor. It would be, he knew, an uneasy, intimidating experience.

But out of duty, Ellison suppressed his dread and, mustering his nerve, asked to see the young man. It was then that he learned the particulars of the soldier's problem. Three arrogant, white teenagers had challenged him downtown, called him an "uppity nigger" and shoved him from the sidewalk. Mattie's boy fought back. But when the deputy arrived, he ignored the Negro, asked the white youth if they desired to press charges.

The boys, bloodied and shaken, said yes.

In his dingy cell, seated, his head bowed, the soldier in soiled khaki told his pastor that all he regretted was the agony he had caused his mother.

"She raised me right, Mr. Ellison. Honest to God she did," he said. "It jes' don't figure that she should be troubled by this heah mess."

The reverend assured him that that he had done his Christian duty. And they then knelt down and prayed together.

The minister left, indignant, disconsolate, determined.

In the months to follow, the Reverend Ellison abandoned his idealism and preached fiery sermons about his forsaken race. He urged his flock to seek justice and dignity—not tomorrow, but now. And he assailed a system which condoned hatred, mayhem, which denied basic human rights, which denigrated the good in all men. He told his people to stand tall, be proud, show courage and conviction, and face misfortune with faith and with strength.

"Ye are the oppressed!" he told them. "Be strong in the name of th' Lord..!"

In 1950, while attending a regional Baptist convention for Negroes in the state capital, Reverend Ellison happened to meet C. D. Daniels, the state director of the National Association for the Advancement of Colored People. In their talk, Ellison was quite vocal in his complaint about his community's attitude toward Negroes. The NAACP official leaned back in his chair and said, "Reverend Ellison, the need in your community is obvious, I think. And you're the right person to establish a local chapter of the N-double A-C-P."

Ellison thoughtfully replied, "I don't know."

"But you said that you didn't like what's happenin' in your town."

"Yes, I know, but I'm a minister and—well, that makes a difference, I think."

"You're a leader, my friend, and you must do all you can for your people. You want to eliminate injustice and inequality, don't you?"

"Yes. I suppose so."

A week later, Ellison announced his intent from the pulpit. He stressed the need. His voice thundered within the sanctuary, as he called upon his congregation to "Stand up for Jesus! Strike a blow for righteousness!"

He then asked them to meet to consider action.

Wide-eyed worshippers, awed by this brazen attack on white supremacy, looked up at Reverend Ellison's perspiring face, now rippling with anger and emotion. It was a charge and an anguished appeal they did not like. They were afraid. Yet, with emphasis and undeniable conviction, the minister prevailed upon them to step forward and be counted.

"Now! Now! Th' time is now!" he shouted.

The congregation stirred uneasily.

"Like th' Lord said unto Moses—*let my people go!* And you must say likewise—and do likewise—*now!*"

Reverend Ellison then announced his intention. He urged them to pass the word, to enlist all to join together at a church assembly on a designated night to discuss and plan an organized effort to fight racism in their community.

Five showed up.

This, a far cry from the fifty people required to start a NAACP chapter, was disheartening. But Ellison wearily understood. He had observed those who had shuffled in to take their seats—the man down front in a faded suit; behind him, two young girls who sat together; and in the third pew, seated apart, an elderly woman and a worker in grimy overalls. It had taken real courage to come.

"We'll..uh..jus' wait another minute or two before we start.."

He waited. But no one else came.

Mortecai Ellison, nevertheless, optimistically considered it a beginning. He was confident that they would eventually reach their goal. He explained the possibilities and purpose of a local chapter, and he exhorted his small gathering to persuade others to join.

So, in the months to follow, the membership slowly increased to qualifying strength. Sadly, though, there were no professionals among them. Teachers, lawyers, and doctors dared not risk the inevitable reprisals which would surely come if they participated.

For almost a year, the chapter struggled without any apparent influence or impact. They met regularly at Ellison's church and tried to muster an aura of importance, but Mortecai was dissatisfied. He drove to the state capital one day to confer once more with Daniels. He openly expressed his despair and disappointment. Even though the membership seemed eager to bring about hopeful change, a failure to see noticeable results was demoralizing. The minister feared that his people might lose faith and abandon the cause.

"I'm worried, C.D."

Daniels sympathized. "Things move slowly," he pointed out.

"But I feel we've got to do something to spark new life in the movement."

"I agree. What you need, Ellison, is something big," said Daniels.

"Big?"

"Something that'll impress th' hell out of th' national office."

"I'm not interested in impressin' th' national office," Ellison maintained. "I just want to impress th' colored people in my county."

"But my dear man, it goes hand in hand. Don't you see?"

Ellison did see. It was patently obvious that if his chapter were to succeed, grow, attract attention, achieve results, gain support, it would have to tackle a project of substance, of significance. But what? He and Daniels discussed several possibilities.

Always, a key objective of the NAACP—desegregation—seemed to surface as a viable motive. After a pause in their conversation, Daniels said, quite casually, "I believe you've got a college down there, don't you?"

"Yes, but—"

"It's a state institution too, I gather."

"Yes, sir. It's a small college, located on th' edge of town," Ellison explained.

"And—traditionally white?"

"Yes, it is."

"Good," said Daniels. "Integrate it."

Ellison blinked. The suggestion, uttered with such aplomb and innocence, shocked the minister. Did Daniels really understand the difficulty, the danger involved? Did he truly know what he was saying?

"You're kiddin', of course."

Daniels chuckled. "I most certainly am not."

"But—how?"

His swivel chair squeaked as the state official of the NAACP leaned forward. He nodded and smiled as he reached for the telephone and placed a call to New York. He spoke to Avery Anderson of the NAACP Legal Defense Fund and asked his advice as to the possibility of their suggestion. He grunted several times in response to Anderson's remarks, then turned the phone over to Ellison.

Anderson was not encouraging. He cautioned that such strategy would necessitate meticulous planning. It would be costly, he said, and it would undoubtedly take time. But if he saw merit in the scheme, Ellison was told, the organization would take it under advisement. What the minister needed to do first, Anderson explained, would be to recruit a suitable black candidate who would dare enroll at an all-white institution. And of course it would have to be someone who might have both the academic credentials and the perseverance to endure endless disappointments, duress, and intimidation.

"Not an easy task," Anderson commented, then added graciously, "But when you've found someone who meets those qualifications and you think you're ready, then call me."

Ellison conceded that this would not be a simple endeavor.

Back in Crestview, the Reverend Mortecai Ellison pondered the task ahead of him. Who could be asked to brave this hazardous assignment? After all, to face the fury of white dominance would take unprecedented courage. Yet, he had to find some black youth who might dare challenge segregation, who would have the gumption to withstand criticism and threats, who could envision an urgency to seek racial equality.

Some days later, he visited the Negro high school to speak to Elias Johnson, the principal. He explained the NAACP plan and wondered if the principal might recommend a capable graduating senior who would willingly volunteer to apply to a white institution. Johnson appeared reluctant.

He asked, "Do you realize what you're asking this young person to do?"

"Yes, I do," the reverend replied. "I know, it's not going to be easy. But you know it's important. We've got to take a stand; we cain't put it off no longer."

Johnson looked at the minister. "I—I don't know," he said slowly. "I doubt you'll find anyone ready or willing to risk what you're suggesting. Pastor Ellison, you know this place as well as I do."

"I do. And that's all the more reason why we must do it. We don't want to jeopardize anyone's welfare or safety, believe me."

"But I think you are," said the principal.

"Look, sir, for too long we have succumbed to the abuse and atrocity imposed on us by white people—and we deserve better. This is a reasonable plan. The very worst that can happen is for the student to be rejected by the college—which could bring about a lawsuit. For you see, being a state institution, they are subject to constitutional law which forbids bigotry and inequality. Don't you see," implored the minister, "we have every chance to win and do away with this shameful indignity to our race."

The principal sighed. "I do believe all that you say, but—I cannot bring myself to urge anyone to endanger their life."

"Not if doing it he'ps them?"

"What do you mean?"

"We are prepared to arrange payment of expenses for this young person, if he'll apply and attend Crestview State College," Ellison told him. "Now, surely there's a good student who would like to attend college, but cain't really afford the tuition."

Elias Johnson leaned back in his chair and looked off. Then he said, quietly, "There is one young man."

"Good."

"He's an honor student and the son of a sharecropper. I know he would like to go to college, if he had a chance. But unfortunately, his family cain't afford it."

Ellison brightened. "Can I talk with him?" The principal arranged an interview.

To Joey Henderson, the minister explained the function of his interest. Ellison was candid, as he promised the principal he would be, and he made sure the young boy fully understood the future he would face. The young Negro carefully considered the prospect before answering. The Reverend Mortecai Ellison smiled as he shook Joey's hand.

Now, the minister seemed satisfied. He saw a way to preserve the existence of his local chapter of the NAACP and accomplish notable results. The Reverend Mortecai Ellison reached for his telephone. He awaited a call to NAACP Headquarters in New York. Anderson answered.

"I think we got our man," Ellison said.

CHAPTER 3

The college in Crestview, despite its paradoxical image as an academic entity in a small agrarian community, existed as the dream of public-spirited citizens who believed its presence might bring prosperity and a possible cultural renaissance to their community.

Founded first as a boy's academy in 1850, it eventually became coeducational—a pristine, socially accepted prep school for proper offspring of white, well-to-do families. And as it endured the difficult days of the Great Depression, Crestview College survived to attain a respected and laudable reputation. Its success was credited to Dr. Jasper Morton, a brilliant leader who actually acquired a four-year accreditation for the institution. It then became Crestview State College.

In 1940, generous alumni gifts and contributions from a consortium of concerned industries enabled the college to relocate from its original, decaying, ante-bellum structure near the railroad tracks to a site at the edge of town. There, in what was once a peanut field, a cluster of brick structures became a monument to Morton's legacy.

For over 48 years, President Morton led the institution with unrelenting determination and uncompromising tenacity. He became the icon, the architect of Crestview State College, the idol of whom everyone spoke with awe and endearment. He was known and revered by many people-from the occupant of the governor's mansion to the habitués of Al's Barber Shop downtown.

But the attribute most admired by people of the region was the obvious fact that President Morton was a firm advocate of Southern principles and traditions.

He once told a Rotary Club meeting, "Under no circumstances would I evah dilute the quality of education or the future of our society by accepting anything other than the finest of white young people to meet the challenges of the South and the world..!"

Jasper Morton continued to head Crestview State College long after age and infirmity made difficult his duties. No one dared suggest a successor. The board of trustees, the students and alumni, even the citizens of the town, could not envision the institution without him. And he would not resign, although illness and advanced years soon forced him to limit his presence and participation. The deans and faculty daily endured his absence. Occasionally, of course, the old man could be seen tottering about the campus with a cane, pausing now and then to exchange greetings or inanities with a student or a member of the staff. To some, it was a pitiable sight. But although wrinkled and wizened, Dr. Morton offered an affable and confident facade until the day he died.

In 1950, at the age of 83, Jasper Morton passed away in his sleep. His body lay in state in the lobby of the administration building for three days. It was the largest funeral ever recorded in Coplin County. And at graveside, several distinguished people—including the governor—paid homage to this venerable man.

Called upon to say a few words, the senior member of the Crestview board of trustees, Henry P. Hartley, arose from his folding funeral parlor chair. Known for his acidulous personality, this crusty, elderly man conceded in his customary unvarnished manner, "Th' sonavabitch was a legend."

No one present seemed shocked by the remark.

So, in this climate of closely guarded esteem for Jasper Morton, the next president of Crestview State College arrived. Dr. Byron McAndrew, in accepting this important position, was unaware that he would undoubtedly be entering the most treacherous interval of his career.

Mrs. Gardenia O'Neal peered over her pince-nez, as she poured tea for an assembly of distinguished guests. She was in her element as she presided at this important function sponsored by her ladies club, in conjunction with the college alumni office. It was a reception in the ornate luxury of the old McDaniel mansion to welcome the new president of Crestview State College.

15

The gilt-edged panels of the large room resonated with the shrill chatter of the many people who, out of curiosity or duty, were in attendance. There were college personnel, state and town leaders, and the social elite. They mingled in clusters beneath the crystal chandeliers of the cavernous hall.

The guest of honor, tall, lean, Lincolnesque, was quite visible. Dr. Byron McAndrew was encircled by several ladies, the mayor, an alderman, and he smiled with self-assurance as he balanced a thin cup on its china saucer. He was at the moment politely picking his way through a minefield of intimidating questions.

"I do declare," piped up Mrs. Humphrey, capriciously, "I nevah thought a man so *young* could *evah* be our president!"

Byron laughed, good-naturedly. "If that's flattery, ma'am, I like it."

"Well, suh, I suspect th' job will age him quick enough!" interjected the mayor with a loud chuckle. McAndrew nodded and smiled.

"But—I reckon you cain't beat experience."

The remark, with its caustic overtone, was reinforced by penetrating eyes contemplating the new president. The unsmiling speaker, Eli Hanson, was not only a town alderman but also a member of the Crestview State College Board of Trustees. McAndrew remembered the man's solemn, discerning face during his interview. Hanson obviously held doubts.

"What Eli's referrin' to, I think," said Crestview's mayor, Lonzo Butler, "is that anyone comin' in—like you, f'instance-has got some mighty big shoes to fill."

Byron looked at the mayor. "I understand."

"You see, we simply *adored* Dr. Morton," bubbled Mrs. Humphrey.

Eli Hanson picked up the conversation and talked as if McAndrew was not even present. Looking past Byron at Mayor Butler and Mrs. Humphrey, he said, "Now, President McAndrew here's no fool I reckon. I jus' know he'll be leavin' things well enough alone. I figure he's goin' to run things purty much as Dr. Morton set 'em up. I mean—it's jes' common sense now, you cain't improve on success.." Only then did Hanson acknowledge Byron. "Can you?"

"That's true," agreed McAndrew, amicably.

"What exactly do you plan, Dr. McAndrew?" asked one of the ladies.

"For th' college? It's a little early to say for sure," he replied, "but I would like to do everything I could to maintain the basic character of this fine institution."

The lady smiled.

"That's good to hear," said the mayor.

"You do have a lovely wife," cooed Martha Humphrey.

16

Byron followed her gaze to an auburn-haired lady at the far end of the room. He saw that she was standing with two women and a man, and they were engaged in cordial conversation. And he wondered how she was faring.

Florence McAndrew was well aware of her responsibility as a college president's wife. And as she discussed her husband's appointment, she was mindful of a need to be both diplomatic and discreet. With a sense of caution, she tried to be interesting and engaging.

Maureen Spivey, fiftyish, cocked her head inquisitively as she stated what seemed a subtle insinuation. "I do understand that you and your husband spent some time up no'th."

"Yes. My husband received his doctorate at Harvard," Florence answered, with a gentle smile.

"Now, isn't that interesting," purred Mrs. Spivey.

"Yo' husband sure is a brilliant man, Miz McAndrew," offered Ben Stanley, hovering nearby.

Maureen hurriedly added, "But I was wonderin'—what you thought of th' Nig-rers up there.."

"I beg your pardon?"

"Was there any trouble? Did you have to mix with them, or anything like that?"

"We didn't have much opportunity," replied Florence McAndrew, and she turned to Ben Stanley. "You know, of course, that my husband was born and raised not too far from here."

"Yes, ma'am," said Ben. "That was a mighty big thing in he'pin' us decide to bring you folks here. You see, we feel a whole lot more comfortable havin' somebody who's familiar with our ways around here."

"Oh, my, yes, that is so important," responded Mrs. Spivey.

"Yes," agreed Florence, quietly, glancing at Byron beyond a group of overdressed ladies. "I think he'll do just fine," she said.

Stanley agreed. "I'm sure he will."

"You and Mr. McAndrew will be needin' house he'p, I'm sure," suggested Maureen Spivey. "If I can be of any assistance, dear lady, don't hesitate to ask. Ben here will tell you that I know th' Nig-rers 'round town pretty well. And I'd be happy to put you in touch with th' good ones—you know, who know their place and will work really hard."

Florence suppressed a grimace and quietly said, "Thank you."

Joey tossed fitfully in the darkness of his bed, fully awake, his mind filled with confusion. Through a thin partition of his wall, he could hear his father snoring in the next roam. He stared up at a ceiling he could not see, his hands clasped behind his head, his brow damp with perspiration, thinking. He was only faintly aware of the spring storm brooding beyond his bedroom wall, its grumbling thunder, its quick waver of lightning.

He thought of Abby. An image of her distress still consumed him and he wondered how truly prophetic were her feelings. He told himself over and over again that he was not afraid, that it was right and proper and that everything would turn out well. He wanted to believe that her emotions were merely an agitation of feminine weakness. Why should her concern bother him?

Yet, he knew that she spoke of a remembrance that to her was a vivid reality. He was well aware that he was trespassing on the proprieties of white society and that his actions might likely draw the wrath of indignant citizens. There could be anger. There could be trouble. Even danger.

His mind, however, refused to dwell on negative thoughts and embraced instantly a vision of what might be, what could be. He would of course be accepted, he thought, as the first Negro to enroll in an all-white educational institution within the state. This would bring him instant fame and he would be lauded for this bold and courageous endeavor. He would be known and respected; he would *be* somebody..! And as he lay there in bed, he felt a quiver of excitement which titillated him, energized him, made him perspire.

But what if he failed? What if his actions made difficult the future of his own race? What if he fostered resentment among blacks as well as white people? Was he being stupid, culpable, used as a pawn for the self-serving interests of the NAACP? He wondered. He knew he had agreed, but perhaps it was not too late to back out.

He wanted someone to help him make a decision, to talk it out, discuss the possibilities, the merits and dangers of the move. He needed advice. He would not ask Abby, not now, and he was not yet ready to face his family.

He heard a peal of distant thunder and the walls of his bedroom shimmered in a flash of subsequent lightning. He turned to the wall. He listened to the guttural snoring, like endless surf, pounding from the other side of the partition. He pictured his pa—stout, tough, a strong-willed patriarch, bearish in both looks and manners, holding the whip hand in his family, unyielding in his simple and stubborn determination. And Joey tried to imagine how this man might accept the news of his son's impudent act.

Joey turned again in bed, and the dilemma revolved with him. The air of the room was charged with a sharp, uneasy expectancy —the imminence of the storm, the agony of choice. He somehow felt drawn to the challenge, as if bewitched by its risk and enthralled by its adventure. He was, of course, motivated by more serious ideals as well—goals of personal development and racial equality. But what if the dream was only that, a dream, with dire results to follow. What then? The agony of choice. He weighed his chances. He vacillated. And he pounded the pillow in frustration.

There was a loud crack of thunder and the storm seemed nearer now. It began to rain. His eyes opened wide and, quite suddenly, he sat up.

Of course!

Silhouetted against the instant radiance of lightning which illuminated the room, he remembered. Uncle Nat. He could help. He was the one person who could lift him from this morass of mental anguish.

Joey had often visited the old man over the years. Uncle Nat, in his seventies, lived alone in a small cabin at the edge of the woods, a field's width from Joey's house. And the boy used to stop by on Saturdays or after school to talk and listen to his elderly friend, as he sat in a cane bottom chair, his wooden leg stretched before him, reminiscing about his nomadic adventures long ago as a fireman aboard an Atlantic Coast Line locomotive.

Joey suspected that many of the old man's tales were exaggerated and no doubt expurgated for the ears of his youthful audience. Nat enjoyed Joey's interest and always took time to explain the conditions of life back when he was a young man.

One story which Uncle Nat reluctantly told was how he lost his leg. It was a railroad accident long ago and the old man related it only because he felt its moral implications might assist others in reaching the same righteous deliverance he had personally experienced.

In the telling, some details had to be omitted.

It had happened early one morning, shortly after midnight. Nathaniel, then a young buck of twenty-one, was wending his way homeward between the interlacing tracks of a railway yard. The sound of crashing couplings and chugging engines reverberated crisply in the damp, foggy, night air.

Nat, on this night, was inebriated. He stumbled across the tracks, singing loudly, and the watery lights of the rail yard glinted in the gathering mist. The standing boxcars seemed shadowy apparitions. He stepped on a track, slipped, and slid beneath the grinding wheels of a shunting freight. His scream slit the air and, simultaneously, the eerie cry of a switching engine ironically echoed in the distance.

His right leg had been severed.

19

The tragedy lingered long afterward. Nat became a recluse, embittered, enmeshed in a trauma of self-pity. But one day he was befriended by an Afro-Methodist minister, who persuaded Nat to attend a revival meeting. It was then, as they say, he "got religion"—and his faith became his obsession. It was the turning point in his life.

As he grew older, Nat—affectionately called "uncle"—settled in a small, unpainted house at the edge of the woods, not far from Joey's place. He did odd jobs on the farm, read his Bible, and was seen as a quiet, respectable Negro, who went his own way, unnoticed. Joey stared at the ceiling and smiled.

Uncle Nat. Of course.

The old man liked him, enjoyed his visits, and felt a fatherly interest in him. Besides, Uncle Nat had the age, the experience, the adventurous soul to understand what Joey really wanted to do. He would explain to the old man the principles involved, his intent, his ambition, and Uncle Nat would offer him the encouragement he needed. Joey knew that this man was the one person who could make him comfortable with his decision.

The boy breathed a sigh of relief and turned over in bed. But thoughts still lingered in the confused matrix of his mind. And he could not sleep.

CHAPTER 4

Dr. McAndrew's first year as president of Crestview State College seemed as if it was the eye of a hurricane—eerily quiet, yet uncertain, uneasy, apprehensively expectant. He was constantly aware of being closely observed as he tried to handle the preconceived notions of how the college should be administered. He wanted to be his own man, yet he was sensitive to the prevailing mind-set which dictated that the institution's operation should not veer too far from the venerated policies of Jasper Morton.

McAndrew applied himself diligently to the challenges which faced the college. He worked hard to develop closer alumni relations, to manage budget allocations and elicit greater state support. He gave much attention to the faculty and sought to encourage high standards of teaching and research.

But he was also mindful of problematic situations which, unseen at the moment, hovered near like impalpable ghosts. One which bothered him most was the likelihood of desegregation. While most thought it inconceivable, McAndrew accepted it as an imminent development, even inevitable. Each day brought evidence of a growing struggle for ethnic equality, a movement which seemed to be gathering momentum and attracting support from high quarters.

If integration should be mandated, he wondered how the college might cope? It would be a traumatic experience, Byron knew, and it would befall his responsibility. He wondered if it might be best to intercept the problem, even prepare for its eventuality.

He summoned his assistant.

Joey sat jackknifed in the jamb of the open door, looking out at a scrim of rhythmic, slanting rain.

He sat, hugging his knees, and pondered the pastel spell of a watercolor afternoon. He saw a forlorn pullet huddled in the puddled shadows of an ancient pecan tree—and he saw himself a like image of dejection.

Behind him sat Uncle Nat, slumped in his cane-bottom chair, his denim-draped wooden leg stretched before him, a limp open Bible on his lap. The room was dark and the old man looked beyond the young boy at the falling rain. Joey heard the vibrato of an aged voice as Nat assessed the weather.

"Looks like it's goin' to set in," he said.

The young boy looked back and searched the aged, gentle face, but the filmy eyes of the old man were focused far beyond the boy as he gazed at the sullen scene outside. Uncle Nat had listened with apparent interest as Joey carefully detailed his desired endeavor. But the elderly man had expressed no opinion.

"What d'you think, Uncle Nat?"

Nat looked down at the boy. "I don' rightly know," he said.

"But I tol' you about Abby and how she was."

"I kin see that—she bein' upset and all fer you."

"But she's actin' like a woman. She's jes' scared."

Joey found little assurance in his words, even as he said them, for he knew that Abby's fears were decidedly plausible, that danger did exist.

"Ain't you?"

"Suh?"

"A little skeered?"

"Naw," Joey lied. "I kep' tellin' Abby, nothin's goin' to happen. We're talkin' about college and court trials and such, not th' kind of stuff that used to go on, like lynchin's and things like that. This is different."

The old man rolled a quid of tobacco in his cheek and leaned over to spit into a coffee can by the side of his chair.

"And you thinks that's all ther' is to it," offered Uncle Nat.

"Sure! I—reckon. Don't you?"

"Maybe. But ther's one thing that bothers me." Uncle Nat looked down at the boy. "You're messin' in wher' you don' belong. You know that, don' you? White folks don' like that."

"But that's th' whole point, Uncle Nat," Joey maintained. "It's high time they be told that we do belong, that we got rights too. And somebody's got to stand up to 'em sometime. Why not now? Don' you think that's th' way it oughta be?"

Uncle Nat chuckled. "Lan' sakes, boy, you sure got vinegar in yo' veins."

"I don't know, Uncle Nat. But I keep thinkin' about this thing and, well, I kind of think it's important."

"You wants to do it, then," Uncle Nat assumed.

"Yeah, sure, I think so."

"Come hoot or holler, you're gonna do it..!"

Joey answered quietly, "Yessuh."

"Have you tol' yo' pa?"

Joey looked out at the pecan tree and the pullet. "Nawsuh," he said, "not yet."

"Don' yo' think yo' oughter?"

"I reckon."

Uncle Nat spit again and brushed his hand across the stubble of his chin. "But you wants to know what I think."

"Yessuh."

Uncle Nat passed a wrinkled hand over the tissue pages of his open Bible and said, "Th' Lord God made us strong and gave us th' good sense to know that as long as we walk in th' paths of righteousness for His name's sake, goodness and mercy shall follow us all th' days of our life. And if we trust in Him, we'll git along, we'll git along. Lord, yes, we'll git along."

The knarled fingers of his right hand clutched the Bible to keep it from slipping from his lap, as the old man leaned forward to touch Joey on the shoulder. "I know you wants to do this thing, son—and maybe you ought to—but you bes' be careful. You bes' think about it fer a spell. And remember, jes' pray to yo' good Lord and He'll he'p."

Joey had hoped for something more substantive, more encouraging, something more decisive, something drawn from the life of this aged man which might cut for him a clearer, more convincing future. He was not satisfied. He pleaded, "But it's important...Don' you think so?"

Uncle Nat nodded. He thumbed a few pages of his Bible and read aloud, from Isaiah: "Cry aloud, spare not, lift up thy voice like a trumpet, and shew my people their transgression, and th' house of Jacob their sins."

23

He looked up from the Book, smiling. "You is that voice, young man; you is th' voice in th' wilderness, and you'll be heard, Joey."

In the frame of Uncle Nat's open door, Joey shifted uncomfortably. He felt the chill of the damp air outside. "But, do you really think there's goin' to be trouble?"

"Son, what you're doin'," said Nat, solemnly, "ain't goin' to set right with nobody, I 'spect."

"But should I be doing it?" asked Joey.

"It's up to you, son." said Nat simply.

Joey was disappointed.

The old man suggested that Joey wait "...and see what'll happen— wait, and..."

Uncle Nat leaned over to spit tobacco juice into the coffee can. He then wiped his mouth and, looking down at Joey, completed his advice. "...and trust in th' Lord," he said.

Dr. Charles Cartwright, as the presidential assistant, was a willowy, eager individual of medium height. He moved quickly, almost with feline grace. He smiled often, was oppressively polite, personable, seemingly insistent on pleasing everyone. Yet, his glib style and guarded demeanor might have caused many to suspect his sincerity.

"Have a seat, Charlie." Wright eased across the room to take a seat in a leather-bound chair before the large executive desk. He held a clipboard, which he carried with him always, often consulting its sheaf of dog-eared documents to scribble down notes or retrieve facts.

Byron McAndrew relied on Dr. Cartwright's judgment. He had retained Charlie as an assistant, for he had served as a key advisor to Jasper Morton during the final four years of the former president's active administration. Indeed, it had been thought that Cartwright might be Morton's logical successor, and that if denied the position he would surely depart in disappointment. But when Dr. McAndrew was installed instead, Charlie elected to remain on as a link and a liaison with the past. And Byron was grateful.

After all, Charlie was a Morton man, a member of the old guard, one well entrenched in the orthodoxy of the region and who might know best the expected course of McAndrew's presidency.

"Charlie, as you know, there has been increasing civil rights activity which might well affect a radical change in our social mores and standards. Negro groups in particular have elicited the support of the government and

24

the judiciary in forwarding their cause. Now, I have conferred with college administrators throughout our area and the consensus is that court-ordered integration of schools and colleges may well come —and perhaps sooner than we think. Now.."

Cartwright's smile faded.

"Now, given the likelihood that we may have to face this situation," continued the president, "I feel it imperative that we develop some plan to deal with the matter."

"Oh, come now, Mac," chided Cartwright with a slight smile. "You know as well as I do that such a thing could never happen—not here."

Byron shook his head. "I'm not so sure."

"Mac, believe me, it's all talk," said Cartwright. "You know the coloreds in these parts. All over, in fact. They know their place. They're not about to risk requital for any bold or stupid move like that."

"Perhaps. But if it's a Federal mandate, a court-ordered decision, Charlie, we'd have no choice."

"Nevertheless," declared Dr. Cartwright, "I think it would be most unwise to even presume that desegregation is likely—even possible."

"Why not?"

"Look, sir, Jasper Morton dedicated his life to upholding a tradition of separation of the races. He saw it essential in order for Crestview College to survive and prosper in its Southern setting. And he was respected. Now, it seems obvious to me that for the sake of the college the less said about separation of the races, the better."

McAndrew shook his head. "I disagree."

The president's assistant was silent as he studied his clipboard.

Byron insisted, "Charlie, I feel we should be prepared, no matter how remote it might seem. Should it come, it would be best to have some operative plan to make the transition go as smoothly as possible."

Cartwright scribbled a note on his clipboard, then looked up. He was smiling. "Mac, I think you're worrying needlessly. My personal opinion is that it will be a long time coming. Believe me, this issue has no urgency."

"Maybe. Maybe not."

Charlie shook his head, as if to dismiss the president's apprehension. "If you're really concerned about the future of our institution, Mr. President," the assistant said, "I think you ought to be devoting more time to a far more pressing problem facing us."

"Yes? And that is?"

"Communists."

McAndrew's face reflected surprise. But before he could comment, Dr. Charles Cartwright hastened to explain, "Even our alumni, with whom

25

I talked yesterday, were quite vocal in expressing their concern over our failure to initiate measures which might protect our institution from the vulnerability of communist infiltration. As you surely must know, Mac, the threat is an ever-expanding danger." He added, "It's widely known that no institution, especially a college, is immune to this growing menace."

It was clear to Byron that Charlie was responding to the national phobia, fanned by the likes of Fulton Lewis, Jr. and Senator Joseph McCarthy, of a perceived communist conspiracy enveloping the country. He did not share the belief and he reserved judgment.

"Surely, you don't believe communist influences actually exist here?"

Dr. Cartwright said soothingly, "Mac, my dear friend, this Red menace is not limited to Washington, D.C., or any large city for that matter. It can be right here—in our small town—in this very college. And our supporters—the alumni of this institution—are worried and wonder why we are not taking essential measures to seek out undercover subversive activity affecting our youth and our democratic principles."

President McAndrew toyed with his glasses as he contemplated Cartwright's warning. It was difficult for him to believe in the veracity of this paranoia sweeping the country. Yet, he could not dismiss the expressed concern of valued supporters of the college.

"Okay. If you see it as a threat to our college, what do we do?"

"Perhaps..." Cartwright drummed his fingers on his clipboard. "Perhaps we need to implement the oath."

"The oath?"

"A lot of colleges and universities are requiring it these days. And I think we have every right to ask our faculty to sign sworn statements that they are not now, nor have they ever been, members of the Communist Party," Charlie contended. "It's quite acceptable."

"No," said the president, firmly. "I will not do that. The introduction of this—oath—appears to me an Orwellian approach which could very well undermine the morale of our faculty."

"But Byron," said Charlie in a soft, insinuating tone, "wouldn't you rather risk that, than expose your college to the evils of communism?"

Dr. McAndrew arose and slowly walked around his desk to lean against it. He looked down at his assistant and said, solemnly, "I do not dismiss your concern lightly, Dr. Cartwright. But, until we have substantive evidence that this so-called conspiracy actually exists and is a threat, I am concerned first and foremost with another impending problem which I feel certainly may occur in the not too distant future."

"Integration, you mean."

"Yes."

26

Charlie shrugged.

"So for that very reason," said Byron McAndrew, "I urge you to assist me in the development of a reasonable plan to either postpone or accommodate the acceptance of Negroes in this all-white institution."

Charlie stood. "If you insist, sir." He turned, then looked back. "I still think you're jousting at windmills. Desegregation must never be— not here. And my fervent advice is that we must fight it. Yet, if you are truly anxious about Negroes forcing their way into our college, then I think you had better look to the root problem."

President McAndrew eyed him curiously.

"This is exactly the sort of thing these communist conspirators would like to do—exploit the Negro to undermine our democratic principles." At the door, Cartwright glanced over his shoulder. "Think about it, Mac."

CHAPTER 5

The sunset silvered the green, young blades of knee-high corn, as its acres undulated slightly in the early evening breeze. Joey looked out over the expanse, standing at the edge of his back yard. It had been a week since his talk with Uncle Nat. A lot had happened.

Today had been graduation day. And after the ceremony, he had stayed only briefly to see his family and Abby before hurrying home. He had quickly doffed his coat and tie and now, in white shirt and best trousers he stood nervously at the end of the long rows, awaiting the return of his father from the fields. He faced a duty he did not relish. No longer could he delay telling his parents of the decision he had reached. And he thought it best to discuss it with his father first.

Even when his mother, Hannah, having returned from the graduation exercises, called from the back porch, he had shouted to her he could not come in, that he was waiting for his pa. She assumed that Joey wanted to tell Elijah about the graduation, so she went back inside the house.

As dusk settled, the air came alive with a low, steady drone of insects, and the darting silhouettes of skittering martins flitting across the sky. Joey stood, with arms crossed, watching, waiting, in the waning light. His pa would be working late, of course, but he knew that as soon as he turned the mule into the lot by the large stables near the white landowner's house, his old man would be trudging wearily homeward, his heavy feet kicking clods of dirt between the rows of corn.

28

Nervously, he mentally rehearsed the story he had to relate. It would be difficult, he knew. After weeks of wrestling with the propriety and pragmatism of the NAACP proposal, he at last had decided.

So now, he waited. It was almost dark.

His thoughts drifted to Abby—and they were not happy thoughts. A strain in their relationship had developed over his involvement with the NAACP scheme. She considered it an unwise and dangerous pursuit. And while they continued to see each other upon occasion, it was not quite the same. He missed her fervor, her commitment, her support. And now, feeling alone, he felt he needed her more than ever.

He saw her briefly at the end of the graduation exercises, but he had hurriedly excused himself and rushed away without an explanation. He imagined that she might have been disturbed by his abrupt departure, but he wanted desperately to see his father alone. And to catch him at the end of the day before entering the house was of course his best opportunity.

So, he waited.

His pa had not really mentioned his son's graduation. He had left it to Hannah and the children to represent the family at Joey's commencement. His work in the fields took priority. It was difficult for Joey to tell if his father really wanted to attend or not. And now, with his pa returning weary and hot from his long day's labor, Joey began to wonder if this was indeed the best time to speak to him.

His reverie was broken by the sound of footsteps, and the clump of a heavy stride suddenly brought the figure before him. The man loomed large, muscular, breathing hard, perspiring.

"Hi, pa."

The man stopped, startled.

"Joey. Whut'n th' hell you doin'?"

"Waitin' fer you, pa. I wants to talk to you."

Elijah Henderson removed a crumpled straw hat and mopped his glistening forehead with a dingy, sweat-stained bandanna. He looked beyond his son at the silhouette of the house and the pale glow that was its kitchen window. He imagined supper waiting on the back burners of Hannah's wood stove. He was tired and he was hungry.

"Cain't it wait?"

"No, suh, I—" Joey cleared his throat. "I figured I bes' speak to you first, pa—before we see th' family, I mean."

Elijah responded quickly. "You ain't in no trouble, I hope."

"Oh, nawsuh," replied Joey, with a nervous laugh. "Aw, no, nothin' like that. Fact is, it's sort of good news—and, well, I wanted to talk it over with you first."

Elijah expended a weary sigh. "Awright, whut is it?"

For one quick moment, Joey's tongue stuck to the roof of his mouth and the young boy could not utter a sound. He swallowed hard. He could only stare at the stocky man before him. And then, he heard himself saying, weakly. "I think I got a chance to go to college, pa."

The farmer looked at his son, then turned away, impatiently.

"Joey," he sighed, "We've done gone over this damn thing so many times.."

"But this is different, pa!" the boy contended.

Elijah stopped. He drew a deep breath. "Look, I tol' you I simply cain't afford it. I jes' ain't got th' money!"

"But that's jes' it!" Joey explained, "They's goin' to pay my way." Elijah had not listened. "It's jes' too damn much money."

"But listen, pa—it's them! They's going to pay my way."

There was a pause. "Who is?"

"Th' N-double A-C-P."

"Who?"

Joey moved beside him. "It's like this, pa, th' preacher who's in charge of th' N-double A-C-P here in Crestview—well, he talked to me. And he told me that if I wants to go to college, they'd he'p pay my way."

"Pay yo' way? A—preacher?"

In the fading twilight, Elijah's expression was dark, uncertain. He did not understand.

"Whut d'you mean? Whut's goin' on?" Elijah asked.

Now came the hard part. Joey looked down at his dusty shoes. Then, after an eternal moment, he looked up into the white, inquiring eyes of Elijah, who repeated, "Who you say's doin' this, a preacher? We ain't wantin' no charity."

"No, suh, it's nothin' like that." The boy felt for the right words. "This preacher talked to th' principal at my school, Mr. Johnson, and was tol' that I was a good student."

Elijah stared at his son, feeling that he had heard this before.

"Mr. Johnson tol' him that I really wanted to go to college. And then th' preacher talked to me and said he could he'p."

"He'p? How?"

Joey hastened to explain, "He tol' me that if I he'ped them, they'd fix it so my tuition and expenses would be paid."

There was a pause before Joey's father said, "Look, nobody don' give nothin' fer free; you know that, Joey."

"Yessuh, I know that."

Elijah started walking slowly toward the house, with Joey beside him. "I don' know 'bout this.." His father sighed. "Joey, it ain't that I don' want whut's bes' fer you. Lord knows, if yo' can find a way to go to college, I ain't about to stand in yo' way. Yo' ma and me—well, we only got pas' th' third grade. And we ain't proud of that. I reckon we know better'n mos' folks whut it means to git an education. 'Cause we didn't git it and it ain't been easy fer us. We wanted it diff'rent fo' our chil'lun."

It was almost an apology. Joey had never known his father to show such personal feelings and he was struck by the tenderness of this strange confession.

"I wanted it good fer all of you. Even Derek."

This surprised Joey. Elijah never spoke of Derek, Joey's older brother, who was then serving his eighth year of a 15-year sentence in the state penitentiary.

"But Derek, he was no good from th' start," observed Elijah, bitterly. "And thank God you turned out better. I wanted you to finish high school. And you did."

Then, Joey heard him say, "I was hopin' you'd be he'pin' me on th' farm. But if you see fit to go to college, and can, well.."

A sense of sudden guilt welled up within the boy and he stopped to stare at the weary, departing figure of his father. He called after him, "But pa, ther's somethin' else..!"

Elijah, his thumbs hooked in the pockets of his grimy overalls, turned once more to face his son.

"There's more to it," Joey told him. "That preacher's head of th' N-double A-C-P, like I said.. Well—he wants me to do somethin' fer them."

The man waited. "Whut?"

"They want me to go to a—certain college."

The man still waited.

Joey swallowed. "They want me to go heah—heah—in Crestview."

"Whut d'you mean?"

"Crestview State College—th' college heah in town."

There. He had said it.

Elijah glared at the vague figure in the gathering gloom. His voice came in a guttural gasp. "You—cain't—do—-that!"

"But I've got to, pa. They's goin' to take care of everything—th' application, everything. And they'll see to it that my tuition's paid."

"But you cain't—! That ain't no colored college!"

"I know, pa—but that's th' point! They figure there oughtn't be jus' whites goin' to better schools, that colored people ought to have a chance

31

too. They want to make it happen. So they want a colored person—me—to try. And if I do, well, that'll prove that we're jus' as good as they are..!"

There was a ghastly pause. Only the sounds of the night.

Then, a low, pained, guttural reaction. "It's dark," breathed Elijah, "but I tell you, boy, I can see one damn fool.."

And with that, he stomped off toward the house. He moved quickly up the rickety steps of the back porch and stood before the rusty hand pump. He rocked the handle and filled a cracked enamel basin with water. He then let down the suspenders of his soiled overalls, unbuttoned and removed his shirt. Joey watched his pa roll the bar of lye soap around in big, callused hands, saw him lather his face and muscular chest, and then, as he scooped up cold water to rinse his face and body, the boy stepped back to avoid being splashed. Bent over, his eyes closed, Elijah reached blindly for the cloth towel. Joey handed it to him.

"I want to do it, pa," said Joey, simply.

"Why?"

"I want to be somebody," the boy said.

"You are somebody..!" growled his father.

Elijah twisted the towel in his ear, drying himself. Looking at his son, he asked, "Have you tol' yo' ma?"

"No, suh."

Elijah then reached up to the nail by the back porch pump and took down the tattered clean shirt his wife had put there. He slowly buttoned the shirt and lifted his galluses.

"Let's eat," he said.

They sat around an oilcloth-covered table, its worn, faded surface centered by a smoky, kerosene lamp. In the dim, flickering arc of light were bowls of food with wisps of smoke spiraling upward the smell of fresh boiled vegetables. There were steaming white potatoes and snapped green beans—cooked in bacon fat, of course—and a platter of whiteside pork.

Emma, Joey's 12-year-old sister, brought the hot biscuits straight from the oven. And as she seated herself, the family joined hands in their customary ritual of grace. Elijah mumbled a few words of thanks and in unison they voiced an "amen" conclusion.

Hannah was seated at the end of the table, across from her husband. She was a wiry woman of uncertain age, perhaps even younger than her frail, haggard countenance conveyed. She was immediately occupied by her two young boys—Cleo, age 5, and William, 7—urging them to eat, be less boisterous, to stop picking at one another under the table

Emma chatted about her friends and what they would be doing, now that school was out. Elijah, his head bowed, his brow beaded with perspiration, seemed oblivious to the commotion about him and ate voraciously. Joey watched furtively, awaiting and dreading the moment he himself would become the center of attention. He did not have long to wait.

Hannah was now looking at her husband, and she was smiling. "You oughta been ther', 'Lijah," she was saying.

He looked at her, his cheeks undulating as he chewed.

"If you'd of seen yo' boy marchin' down in his cap 'n' gown today, you'd of been a mighty proud man," she glowed.

Elijah grunted.

"Ther' were lots 'n' lots of people ther'. Lot o' people you'd know."

Elijah nodded and kept on eating.

"It was really nice. Ther' was music and speeches and—" She looked at Joey. "Tell 'im, Joey."

Joey glanced at his father, then down at his plate. "Ther' ain't much to tell."

"Oh, but ther' is," insisted his mother. "Yo' shoulda seen th' people clappin', 'Lijah, as soon as they—"

"Now wait a minute!" growled Elijah, interrupting her. "Don' keep sayin' I oughta been ther'..! I warn't ther', and you know damn well why! God knows, I wanted to be. But somebody's got to work them fields out ther'. I need he'p. And now that school's finished, I'll be wantin' you out ther' with me, Joey."

"Yessuh, I—"

Hannah interjected, "You don' be botherin' Joey about no farmin' or field work, not now, not after whut he's done. Our son's jes' graduated. And he's th' first in our family to do it!"

Her husband glowered. "I know! You been tellin' me! But that don' give him no right to be th' high and mighty one! And let me tell you, all th' schoolin' in God's green earth ain't goin' to bring in my crop..!"

"I'll he'p, pa," promised Joey. "Honest I will."

"Leave him be," ordered Hannah. "Our boy made us awfully proud today; ther's no two ways about it. I purt nigh cried, jes' seein' him up ther' on that stage gittin' his diploma.." Suddenly, her face brightened. "Go git it, Joey; show it to your pa..!"

"Aw, ma.."

"Go git it," she urged.

"Pa ain't interested."

"Who'n th' hell says I'm not interested?" snapped Elijah. "Of course I want to see it!"

Joey, assuming this a request, started to rise, but his action was suspended by a brief gesture from his father.

"Later. Better eat first."

Hannah reprimanded the boys and again returned to the telling of Joey's graduation ceremony, including details of the program, the names of friends she had seen, what they had been wearing, and that moment of particular joy— "When Mr. Johnson, th' principal, stood up and talked about Joey, and how smart he was, and—"

"Aw, ma..," muttered Joey, embarrassed.

"—ever'body clapped!" she concluded, triumphantly. Emma added, "They like to tore th' house down!"

"I clapped too!" shrieked William.

At that moment, Cleo punched William and a tussle ensued at the table.

"Stop it!" screamed Hannah.

Elijah had had enough. Irritated by an exuberance he could not share and filled with the frustration of what he now knew of his son, he dropped his fork with a clatter.

"Dammit!"

All eyes were riveted on the man at the end of the table, who planted his huge hands on either side of his plate, his arms akimbo, his face furrowed in anger.

"You keep yabberin' 'bout th' boy, and whut he's done..! It's whut he's goin' to do that bothers me! Tell 'em, boy; you tell 'em..!"

Like an electric current, consternation coursed through Joey's body. He cast a baleful look about the table. He felt the palms of his hands grow moist. In the long moment that followed, Hannah watched, expectantly.

Her voice was small. "Joey?"

"I.." His eyes met hers across the table. "It's just that—well—I think I'm goin' to git to go to college."

The family, suspended in stupefied silence, stared at Joey and then at the father. What could be wrong with that?

"That's—good," Hannah said; then, looking at Elijah, "Ain't it?"

"It might be," muttered the man at the head of the table, "if it warn't fer th' simple fact of wher' he's got to go to college."

Hannah, puzzled, asked, "Wher'?"

Elijah, his mouth full, nodded. "Tell 'em, Joey."

Again, he felt their searching eyes. Again, he was on display. And again, he tried to explain without igniting concern. "There was this preacher, you see.." He thought it best to begin at the beginning. They waited.

"This preacher—a Reverend Ellison, I think his name was—he's head of th' local chapter of th' N-double A-C-P. Well, Mr. Johnson had me meet him, and we talked about college and stuff. And this preacher said that they'd fix it so I could go to college."

Hannah clasped her hands. "That's wonderful!"

Elijah's reaction was a derisive snort, as he busied himself eating the final morsels of food on his plate.

Joey shot a quick glance at his father before explaining, "Only—I got to go where they want me to go."

Hannah said, "But that's all right, ain't it? College is college."

Elijah put his fork down. "That's jes' it. They ain't th' same."

Joey informed her, "Ma, they want me to try to get into th' college here—Crestview State College."

"Real-ly?" piped Emma.

Hannah, still confused, mumbled, "But—that's a—a—"

"You're damn right," snarled Elijah. "A *white* college!"

She ventured, "But—they won't let you do that, will they?"

"Hell no, they won't," answered Elijah, firmly. "Ther'll be all hell to pay!"

After an awkward silence, it was Emma who asked the pertinent question. "Why? Why do they want you to go to a white college, Joey?"

Joey did not answer instantly; instead, eyed his father with a half hope that he might be the one to offer the explanation himself. But Elijah was mopping his plate clean with a biscuit. So, with a deep sigh, Joey tried to point out the significance of the endeavor and the mission of the NAACP.

"You see, it's not only a big chance fer me, but a chance fer all of us..!"

His mother was uncertain. "It—ain't dangerous, is it, this thing you're doin'?"

"No, ma, I don't think so."

His father's face tightened. "You don' know a damn thing!"

Joey looked at Elijah.

"Anytime you start actin' smart alecky, kickin' over th' trace chains, like you're doin', ther's bound to be trouble," his pa warned. "You jes' watch. Ther's goin' to be trouble."

"It's not like what you're thinkin', pa—we're dealin' with a college, not some redneck rowdies. Either they take me in or they don't. It's worth a try."

"Son.." Elijah shifted in his chair, leaned back, and folded his arms. "Yo' ma and me wants whut's good fer you, like I tol' you. And we work awfully hard to git it, fer all of you. And whut you can git on yo' own, that's all right too. But I tell you, it bothers me how you git whut you git. Maybe we ain't got yo' book-larnin', but we been around and we know a thing or two about whut's goin' on. And we know it's allers bes' to mind yo' own business. We tried hard to teach you young'ns that—to respect other people and grow up to be good God-fearin' Christians. But this.. This thing you're doin', Joey, it ain't right. And I don' like it. I don't like it nary a bit, I tell you."

Joey started to speak, but there was really nothing to say, so he looked down at his plate and toyed with a strip of whiteside pork.

"Besides," continued Elijah, "whut's it goin' to mean if you don' git to go to college? I mean, hell, a lot o' folks don' go, and they make out all right. Look heah, boy, I got a farm out ther' that's almost paid off. Now, it's goin to be your'n one o' these days. If you work it right, it can be a purty smart livin' fer you and yo' family."

"But—I—don' want to farm."

Elijah frowned. "Why'n th' hell not?"

"I'd—just like to do somethin' else," said Joey. "I'd like to be a doctor, maybe, or somethin' ."

"You think yo're so damn big you cain't git yo' hands dirty!?"

"No, suh."

"Oh, ho, I hope not," scoffed Elijah. "'Cause come tomorrer mornin', yo're gittin' up wit' th' chickens, heah? And I tell you, boy, yore goin' to be lookin' up th' ass end of a mule, from sunup 'til way after sundown."

Joey tried not to show resentment.

"School's one thing, Joey, but ther's a lot o' larnin' to be done out ther'," said the man with a vague gesture, as if indicating the fields beyond the walls of his house. "You understand whut I'm sayin'?"

"Yessuh."

"Good." With a deep sigh, then, Elijah pushed back his chair.

"Well, I reckon I'll be turnin' in. I'm right tard."

They saw him struggle to his feet, stand humped over, his big hands gripping the table, his head bowed. He stayed there for a moment, then slid slowly back into his chair. Joey watched him, warily.

"Like I tol' you, Joey—yo' ma and me, we wants whut's bes' fer you. But-I'd as soon mortgage ever'thing I own, lock, stock, and barrel, than fer you to be doin' this damn fool thing yo're plannin' to do."

"But pa, there ain't nothin' wrong with what I'm doin'. All th' N-double-A-C-P's tryin' to do is get a little respect for us colored people. I mean, my God, how long can we go on suckin' th' hind tit of them white bastards out there..!"

"Joey!"

He looked at his mother. "Sorry, ma."

"Joey.." His father drummed his fingers on the table. "You're too damn stupid to go to college if you cain't see whut's in it fer you when you start meddlin' in wher' you don't b'long..!"

Elijah, stiff with fatigue, turned away angrily from the table. And when Emma called "'Night, papa," he gave only a flick of his hand to acknowledge her. He walked on wearily toward his bedroom door, his heavy brogans clopping on the wooden floor. The door rattled shut behind him.

The two young boys had scampered out to the front porch to play with Slag, the old hound dog. And Hannah, heaving a heavy sigh, slowly got up from the table to assemble the supper dishes. Joey was still eating and Emma watched him. As Hannah stood, she looked soulfully at her son.

"Joey?"

"Yeah, ma?"

"It'll be all right, won't it?"

"What I'm doin'? Oh, sure."

"I mean.." She sank into her chair again, her hands resting in her lap. "Ther' won't be no trouble, now, will ther'?"

"No, ma," replied Joey. "There's nothin' to worry about."

"I ain't so sure," said Hannah, pensively. "I sort o' feel like your pa. I don' rightly know if you should be doin' this thing."

Joey reached over the table, as if offering his hand to her. "Don't you be worried about nothin', ma. Ever'thing's goin' to be jes' fine."

Her eyes enveloped him with a tenderness that made him somewhat uncomfortable and self-conscious.

"Oh, it'll be all right, ma. Don't you be worryin'."

He heard her sigh. Her hands left her lap to grip the edge of the table as she raised herself up again. She lifted the stack of dishes and she quietly said, "Jes' th' same—I wished you warn't doin' it."

Without giving Joey a chance to answer, Hannah turned and moved toward the kitchen. Joey watched her leave, wishing he could allay her fears—wishing he could strengthen his own will.

Emma, who had been listening curiously to the conversation, leaned forward and whispered, "Are you really goin' to do it, Joey?"

He looked down at the table.

"None o' your business," he said.

CHAPTER 6

On this summer's day, the shoreline water of Quintock Lake mirrored green foliage and the reflection of a large, rustic building. Owned by the college, Quintock Lodge was a rambling log structure which served as a seasonal retreat for institutional affairs.

From its porch, President Byron McAndrew watched the arrival of the men in whose trust hinged the future of his institution. He looked on as members of the board maneuvered their large automobiles and trim sports cars along sandy ruts leading into the Quintock Lodge parking lot. He saw them get out, stiffly, after the ten-mile drive from town, some stretching, absorbing the fresh air and scenic splendor of the place. Others appeared eager, bringing both overnight bags and a buoyant mood of boyish enthusiasm, laughing loudly, joking. Several brought fishing gear.

Byron had requested this meeting, vaguely indicating that its purpose was to consider a matter of grave importance. He did not reveal the topic, however, for he knew that his concern would not likely be taken seriously by any member of the board. Yet, he felt strongly a need to broach the subject, to at least discuss, however distasteful, the possibility that their college might one day be enjoined to accept Negro students. If this became a reality, he wanted to have in place contingency plans to counter the move, or, at the very least, minimize the consequences. Or could it be that his fears were groundless and that, as Cartwright had suggested, he was simply "jousting at windmills"?

President McAndrew watched the men arrive, sensing that soon he would be entering a "lion's den" alone. He had wanted someone of influence to support his theory, but he could not bring himself to approach Henry P. Hartley, the elder member of the board. While his support would have been invaluable, McAndrew knew him to be an avid segregationist. The old man, Byron feared, might quash his ideas before they were given a full and proper hearing. It was best, thought he, that the issue be presented before the entire board. So he had requested a special meeting and, because he wanted quiet meditation and the earnest involvement of all participants, he had suggested that they assemble at Quintock Lodge.

This suited the board. The agenda mattered little to them as long as they could enjoy the serene and natural setting of Quintock and its well-stocked lake. To them, it was to be a fun weekend.

"Hope th' meetin's not goin' to last too long, folks, 'cause there's a bigmouth bass out there jes' callin' me!"

Byron recognized the voice of Russ Carver, real estate, as he brushed by, struggling with a suitcase, his tackle box, and an assortment of rods and reels. Eli Hanson, lawyer, slapped him on the back and chortled, "Talk 'bout a big mouth!"

Carver turned. "A shyster like you sure cain't talk!"

This got a laugh, typifying the light, congenial air that pervaded this privileged group, as they hustled about, selecting their assigned rooms, sorting out their luggage. Everyone seemed loose, happy, impervious of any problem or issue which might have brought them together.

Quintock Lodge had been built only three years before by money from wealthy alumni. Although rustic in appearance, it was well appointed to comfortably accommodate short visits by officials or guests of the college. Its sleeping quarters included four large rooms with multiple beds and a number of single rooms for VIP personalities. On duty for these summer occasions were usually two cooks and a houseboy.

As they observed the men settling in, Byron benevolently engaged old man Hartley in conversation. He was, to Byron, a cantankerous but interesting man. His brittle perceptions of life seemed cut and dried and conclusive. McAndrew actually admired his sinewy character, although he seldom agreed with his obstinate manner.

The bourbon was poured and, as the men selected comfortable seats in the lounge, the banter gradually dissipated into quiet conversation. Byron, himself, helped H. P. Hartley into a deep cushioned chair by the brick and stone fireplace.

E. Braxton Edwards, a textile magnate, assumed his position as chairman of Crestview's board of trustees and rapped his gavel. "Gentlemen, gentlemen!"

A hush followed, as eyes centered on him.

"Gentlemen, as you probably know, we're meetin' here today at the request of our president, Dr. Byron McAndrew. Now, I believe he has a matter of importance to bring before th' board, and—while I know you guys have got your drinkin' and fishin' to do—I do hope you will give Mac your undivided attention." He turned to McAndrew. "Okay, President McAndrew, th' floor's yours."

"Thank you, Braxton."

The president cleared his throat and surveyed the room. The pause was long and deliberate. All eyes were riveted on him. He began: "I've been giving a great deal of thought, gentlemen, to a matter that, frankly, bothers me. And because it could affect th' future of our institution, I need your advice, and—possibly—your action." He looked down, but he could still feel their piercing eyes. He looked up. "It has to do with our status as an all-white institution."

A restless tremor rustled the air and a low murmur speculated the meaning of the president's comment.

Byron continued: "It's obvious, if you've been in touch with developments, that minorities are becoming more active, more militant, more insistent on changing th' status quo. Now, up until now, most of us have ignored this—because, until now, most efforts like this have been ineffectual. But frankly, I see things changing—and not the way we'd like to see it, I think. More and more, gentlemen, these groups are bringing to bear considerable influence on our government, on the authorities, even the judiciary. And who knows what imperatives may soon arise from these actions.."

The men were stunned. After a moment of silence, a tentative voice was heard.

"Uh—'scuse me, Mac."

It was Eli Hanson.

"Jus'—what is it you're drivin' at?"

"Simply—that we could, by law, be forced to change our traditional requirements."

The deep voice of B. H. Bellinger, a banker, muttered, "You're talkin' about Nig-ras?"

"Well—yes, yes I am," Byron responded.

"Now, dammitt, stop pussyfootin' around," the banker growled. "You're talkin' about Nig-ras getting into our college, right!?"

Byron was hesitant. "Perhaps. Well, yes."

"Nevah!"

This outburst from Hartley, sharp and biting, reverberated within the room and was simultaneously accented by the crack of his cane. The old man, flushed and trembling with emotion, had plunged his stick onto the polished pine floor. Everyone turned to see him leaning forward in his chair, eyes blazing, his chin resting on knarled hands which cupped the rounded head of his hickory staff. "Nevah..!" he hissed.

Byron shifted uneasily. A sudden silence hung heavy and intimidating. The president searched their faces.

"Please. Don't misunderstand," Byron said. "I'm certainly not abandoning our long-established tradition here at Crestview. I'm really only tryin' to protect it."

"Good Lord..!"

It was only a gasp, hardly intended to be audible, but Russ Carver now realized that his spontaneous expression of dismay had been heard throughout the room. Seeing everyone looking at him, he smiled sheepishly and explained, "Sorry. It's jus' that I didn't really expect anything like this. I thought we came here to talk about th' new gym."

"Yeah," agreed Bellinger in his deep bass voice. "All this is pretty far-fetched, if you ask me. My God, I can think of a lot more important things to take up our time, Mac."

"Really, Mac," insisted Jim McCall, a CPA, "aren't you kind of blowin' at straws? I mean, let's face it, there ain't a chance in hell this little college of ours is ever goin' to be integrated."

"Not if I have any say-so!" snorted Bellinger. "Admittin' Nig-ras is pretty much a dead issue, as far as I'm concerned."

"More likely, if he tries it—a dead nigger!" quipped McCall, chuckling.

Several laughed at this, but McAndrew's face hardened. "I understand how you feel. And I agree, to a point. But believe me, gentlemen, we cannot assume that all things will remain th' same, that we will never be confronted with this issue. And all I'm sayin' is.."

Concerned chatter now reached a crescendo.

"All I'm sayin' is..," repeated McAndrew, as the group quieted again. "..We must try to anticipate even th' improbable. And it's vital that we organize and be prepared. We want things as they are, yes, but it's up to us to offer that assurance. We need to talk, we need to plan. That's all I'm askin'."

"But Mac, my friend.." It was Russ Carver again. "What's there to talk about? We got a policy."

"But our policy is vulnerable, Russ. If we should ever be challenged in court, I really don't know how we'd stand. Mr. Hanson could probably give you a better assessment than I could. He's th' legal expert. I'm a college administrator—and, as such, I am very much concerned about th' future development of our institution. I certainly don't want to be faced with any unexpected crisis which might disrupt our progress or endanger our existence."

They looked at Hanson. "What about it, Eli?"

"I don't know if I can be of much help," said Hanson, as his face assumed a sober mask. "But, considering it from a legal standpoint, I really don't think we need worry about Nig-ras challenging our long accepted social status."

"Maybe not now," admitted McAndrew, "But what if th' Supreme Court decides to overturn some accepted opinions on the basis of the Constitution, say.. What if—th' political and legal climate changes?"

"Those are mighty big ifs, my friend," said Hanson.

"Nevertheless," continued Byron, "I feel it would be wise for us to be in a position to convincingly meet all opposition and criticism with some proof that we favored the Negro without prejudice, even though—and I stress this point—even though our policy remained the same."

More than one trustee noted the antithesis of McAndrew's comment. How could one have his cake and eat it too?

Continuing, Byron said, "Now, for us to offer this evidence, I feel that we have to provide some positive, practical assistance which might assure the Negro a full and adequate education."

Bud Timons, a farmer, spoke up. "I don't see that it's our responsibility to see that these black people are educated."

"Maybe not," McAndrew conceded. "But it would offer a convincing argument that we are concerned about equality of education among all races."

Bellinger groaned. "I jus'—don't like th sound of all this.."

"Yeah, it sounds like you're askin' us to take in Nig-rers."

Byron looked at Jim McCall. "No, of course not. We don't have to. Not yet. But I do think we should take steps to counter that possibility. Now, what I am suggesting is that we sponsor a class to tutor qualified Negro high school graduates, a sort of—prep course to help them meet entrance requirements for college. Th' class would be conducted off campus, but team taught by our faculty."

"Now, wait one damn minute!"

Al Spivey was a bullish, deep-tanned construction contractor. He had half risen from his chair to point his finger at McAndrew. "Sounds to me like you're invitin' damn colored kids to apply here!"

"Yeah, you got 'em in already!"

"You're askin' for trouble!"

"Hell, yes!"

A sudden, tense, and awkward silence followed this montage of emotional outbursts. Then, quickly, the void was split by the crack of Hartley's cane. He had again punctuated the troubled air with disapproval.

"Don't be a fool..!"

All eyes enveloped the old man.

"Don't be a fool, Mac!"

Byron blanched.

"If you think we're goin' to spend money tryin' to educate some damn niggers, you've got another think comin'..! My God, man, do you know what you're doin'? You're prejudicin' our position! How'n th' hell will we evah convince anybody that we cain't abandon our accepted, traditional stand if you start mollycoddlin' colored people? Hell, man, niggers have no place in th' scheme of things. This is an all-white college and will always remain so—that's our policy, now and forevah!"

A murmur of approval coursed through the assembly.

But Hartley had not finished. "It's a damn fool notion, if you ask me, to be organizin' these heah classes.. C'mon, Mac, we ain't goin' to put our white teachers in a position where they have to mix with niggers—no suh, nevah!"

There was almost applause as members of the board, now relieved, reacted appreciatively to the old man's tirade. Some were even standing, as if the meeting had ended. It seemed as if Hartley had won the day. And now, helplessly, McAndrew turned and silently appealed to Edwards. The chairman stumbled to his feet and gaveled the meeting to order again. He tried to take a vote, but no one was interested. The meeting, rather than being adjourned, simply disintegrated—leaving Byron alone, dispirited and heartsick.

After dinner, some of the members decided to return to town. Byron did not try to dissuade them. It seemed so futile. Several, however, stayed overnight to fish.

In the fading glow of twilight, President McAndrew watched from the porch the several automobiles wend their way around the lake toward town. As he watched them disappear, he saw the distorted shapes of twisted oak and scraggly pine silhouetted against the white, sandy terrain. And he wondered of man and of Almighty God.

In the ensuing weeks, the trustees resumed their belief that integration was no threat and that, if evidenced, would never be accepted at their college. But they had to be vigilant, they knew. The trustees simply did not trust their new president. He would bear watching.

Meanwhile, the Reverend Mortecai Ellison stood on the gravel path close by the railroad tracks several hundred yards from the depot platform. He knew that the Negro coach, always positioned in front, would stop well beyond the concrete stage created for the convenience of disembarking white passengers.

He craned his neck to see the tiny speck on the horizon as it appeared at the apex of converging rails. Then, he heard the distant moan of its diesel whistle and the speck loomed larger. And then it was upon him. He stepped back as the locomotive rushed past him. He felt a flush of heat as he saw the windows flash by and the train squealed to a stop.

Ellison searched the opaque windows for a stirring which might signal the arrival of his visitors. He saw a black porter swing down easily and put in place a heavy metal stepping stool, then assist a woman and her two children to the ground.

Avery Anderson and his two attorney colleagues of the NAACP Legal Defense Fund, having arrived from New York to investigate and evaluate Ellison's plan to integrate a local white college, now looked out the murky Pullman window at a somnolent small town setting. And they sensed some hesitancy in stepping forth into what they perceived a precinct of racial prejudice.

Then, at last, they appeared. The three men emerged and stepped down stiffly, with white shirts rumpled, ties askew, clutching suit coats and briefcases. Ellison hurried forward to introduce himself.

Later, in a cafe across the tracks, they became acquainted. Anderson, a lithe young lawyer, was obviously the principal NAACP representative—and it was he who put most of the questions to the Reverend Ellison.

Brushing a fly from his perspiring brow, Anderson asked about the racial climate around Crestview and he listened as Ellison described the demarcation of attitudes. The minister stressed the sincerity and determination of the Negro population, and he assured Anderson that the black people of Coplin County would stand solidly behind any effort to integrate the college.

"You'll see—at th' meetin' tomorrow night. They'll be there."

45

CHAPTER 7

The four men crowded into Ellison's '48 Dodge sedan for the short ride to the preacher's house out of town. But the reverend purposefully drove his guests slowly by Crestview State College to point out the target of their intention. Anderson and his two compatriots saw the red brick buildings, the spacious campus, several students—all white—hurrying along its sandy paths.

Then, under a big shade tree in the back yard at the Ellison home, the minister's wife served the men lemonade and the reverend told them about Joey—how he desperately wanted to attend college, what a promising student he had been, and how much he was devoted to their cause. "He'll do jes' fine," was Ellison's conclusion.

As they relaxed, Avery seemed quiet, thoughtful, but his two associates talked incessantly about New York, the activities of the Legal Defense Fund office, and the dire struggle of the National Association for the Advancement of Colored People to obtain Negro rights, equality, respect. At length, Anderson interrupted. "This boy.. I 'd like to meet him."

"You will, of course," Ellison answered.

"I mean now—right away."

"You—want me to drive us out to his place—now?"

"If it's possible."

It was a little after four o'clock when the four men crawled into the rust-spotted Dodge and Ellison headed for the Henderson farm. Avery sat up front with the reverend, while the other two slouched in the back, grumbling quietly about the oppressive heat. Even with the windows down, the breeze was hot and stifling. And as they looked ahead, the asphalt highway seemed awash in a watery mirage of heat waves.

The automobile eventually turned onto a clay, corduroy road, which rattled the car and its occupants as they rode past endless farmland and wilderness. Red dust boiled up behind them and the air became acrid and suffocating. One of the men on the back seat succumbed to a spasm of coughing.

After a few miles, Ellison swerved into a narrow, rutted road, and pulled up into the barren yard at the Henderson house. The reverend got out. As he started to walk slowly toward the house, Hannah, who had heard the car, stepped onto the porch. He tipped his hat and asked if they might see her son.

"Joey ain't heah," she said. "He's down yonder in th' fields he'pin' his pa."

Ellison, who had introduced himself, asked, "Will he be back soon?"

She shrugged. "Yo' kin walk down ther', if'n you want," she suggested.

Ellison looked back at the men. One sat slumped in the back seat of the car, his legs dangling from the open door. The other two stood leaning against the car, watching the slender woman on the porch. They were obviously hot and exhausted.

"No ma'am," Ellison told her. 'We'll jes' wait around out heah. 'Spect he'll be comin' in soon, you think?"

She shrugged again and walked back into the house.

The torpor of the late afternoon ticked off time slowly. One man paced a little. But mostly, they stood by the car as the sinking sun lengthened the shadows and burnished the landscape with a luminous glow.

They heard the tinkle of a cow bell and the cackle of a protesting hen. Avery looked at his watch, and one of the lawyers lit a cigarette. The other stretched and yawned. Ellison fidgeted.

"I tol' my wife we won't be long.. She's fryin' up some chicken for supper. But I reckon th' boy oughta be back pretty soon now."

Avery sighed with a hint of impatience. "Yeah."

Long, interminable minutes passed. The sun sank slowly and the vagueness of evening enveloped them. Then, suddenly, Joey appeared, bounding off the porch in long strides to meet the men who were waiting. As he saw him, Ellison exclaimed, "At last! He's here now!"

The boy slowed as he approached, eyeing the strangers standing there. He knew these important people would be coming, but why should they be here at his house? The reverend stepped forward quickly to greet him. "Joey, I want you to meet these heah gentlemen—they've come heah all th' way from New York. They're from th' national headquarters of th' N-double A-C-P..!"

Before Ellison could introduce them by name, however, Avery Anderson stepped forward to announce, "Hi, I'm Avery Anderson. Heard a lot about you, Joey."

Joey forced a pallid grin and took the outstretched hand.

"Now, Joey, we are most grateful for your acceptance of this special mission," said Anderson. "But there are a few things we have to know. Do you fully understand the particulars of your participation?" Joey looked at him quizzically.

"Let me put it this way, do you realize the personal risk involved?" Another reminder. For one brief moment, Joey saw again the fears and fleeting image of a girlfriend, as well as his own undeniable doubt.

"I—think so," he said, tentatively.

The lawyer with the cigarette stepped forward to say, "Joey, I think we need to know how truly conscientious you are in pursuing this plan that has been mapped out. We've had too many unfortunate situations where the volunteer seemed eager to help, yet disappeared when the going got rough."

The other attorney quickly added, "This is no walk in the park, Joey. We want you to understand that. Once this matter gets underway, you're going to be the center of attention. There may be delays, intimidation, even threats. It's going to take a lot of guts, I can tell you."

Ellison was concerned. They were supposedly here to help, and yet they seemed intent on scuttling the scheme. Could they not realize how difficult it was to persuade a young person like Joey to participate in an uncertain activity as this?

Avery Anderson, smiling, then said, "We're really not trying to frighten you, Joey. It's just the simple fact that—well, we want to be sure that you'll stick it out, that you'll follow through with your promise. The success of this campaign is really up to you. And if we have anything to do with this, we've got to know that we can depend on you. So, if you have any misgivings or questions, now is the time to get them out in the open."

Joey Henderson, having been silent during this inquisition into his motives and mettle, now shifted nervously, his hands jammed in the back pockets of his soiled overalls. He said quietly, "No, I've been told about as much as anyone could tell me, I guess. I reckon nobody really knows exactly what'll happen. But I said I'd stick it out and I will, if I can get to go to college. And, uh—well, there is one question I'd like to ask. If they turn me down at Crestview State College, if this whole idea ain't successful, will your offer to pay my tuition be good for another college?"

Anderson, surprised, stared at the Reverend. "What's all this?"

Ellison stammered, "Well, we did tell Joey here that we'd manage to pay his expenses if he would only do this for us."

"What are you saying!? My God, Reverend Ellison, man, we can't do that!"

"I know," affirmed Ellison, "I know th' N-double A-C-P cain't—but my church can."

The associate with the cigarette tossed it aside, as he said, pointedly, "But you represent the N-double A-C-P."

The Reverend Ellison wiped his forehead with his hand. "But I'm also pastor of the Singletree Baptist Church. We help people who need help. And Joey heah needs help. He needs money to go to college."

"I don't know," said Anderson. "I don't know about this. It has an uneasy appearance of suggesting bribery. It looks as if you're paying off a black kid to get into a white college. Now, that won't look too good if it comes to legal push and shove."

"But it's not bribery!" Ellison insisted. "Joey knew exactly what was going on. He wanted to help our cause. All he wants in exchange is a college education. And ain't that agreeable to the goals and purposes of the N-double A-C-P: to advance the people of our race?"

Anderson looked off contemplatively. "Yes, but it does complicate matters a bit."

"Can I say something?"

They looked at Joey.

"I do want to do this for th' good that'll come of it. And I'm willing to trust my luck that nothin' will happen to me—or anybody, for that matter. But I want a college education and I can only get it with your help. I don't know about you, but it seems to me that's a small price to pay for me sticking my neck out."

For several seconds, no one said a word. Then, Avery Anderson quietly asked the minister, "Are you sure this fund raising for Joey's tuition cannot in any way be traced to our organization?"

"I'm certain," Ellison assured the NAACP attorney. "In fact, my church has enlisted the aid of an outside committee of outstanding black citizens to handle the collection of contributions."

One of Avery's associates, who had paced several steps, turned back to ask, "But for what purpose have you given for soliciting this money?"

"The contributors know it's for charity," said the Reverend. "And we're right up front in explaining that its use is to make it possible for a capable young man to attend college."

The same lawyer pointedly persisted, "But reverend, do you tell them that's it's to pay for a black boy to enter a white college? "

Ellison looked at Anderson. "No. "

Then he added, "If they want to know, sure, but it's enough to say that it's an opportunity to provide a college education for a promising young man of our race. Because, like Joey mentioned, we'll be sending him, even if the college happens not to be Crestview State College."

Anderson reluctantly seemed satisfied. He stepped forward to shake Joey's hand. "It was good meeting you, Joey, and we'll look forward to seeing you at the meeting tomorrow night."

Without further comment, Avery Anderson wheeled and walked to the car. Reverend Ellison bade farewell to the boy. And Joey stood and watched the old Dodge back up and head down the lane to disappear in the gathering dusk.

The men were quiet as the automobile moved past barns and trees that were silhouetted against the charcoal sky. Avery, up front with Ellison, was mesmerized by the car's flickering headlights and dozed fitfully. He then became aware of the reverend speaking. Clearing his eyes, he saw that they were now on the asphalt highway, with darkness closing in. He turned to see the profile of the minister in the brief light of a passing car. The reverend was asking, "What d'you think, Mr. Anderson?"

"Hmm? What did you say?"

"I was wonderin' what you thought about our chances."

"To integrate Crestview? Oh, I don't know. Good, I'd say—very good—if th' pieces fall into place. A lot depends on how your meeting goes tomorrow night," answered Anderson. Then, he added, "It's really up to you folks, you know."

Ellison cast an inquisitive glance at Avery Anderson.

"So much depends on local support," Avery explained.

"I hope we're goin' to be gettin' help from th' N-double A-C-P headquarters, though," said Ellison, concerned.

"Oh, we'll be around," assured Anderson. "But, as I said, a lot depends on your meeting. If we can give a favorable report to Mr. Thurgood Marshall, then you can count on the organization backing you all th' way."

Lights whisked by as they heard the crescendoed whine of a passing car.

"Will you or someone else go with us to enroll Joey?" Ellison asked.

"No, I don't think so," said Avery.

"Why not? Don't you think it's important for us to have a lawyer from th' N-double A-C-P with us when we do this? I mean, after all, you carry a lot of weight, you mean somethin'."

Anderson shifted in his seat. "First of all, I don't think it's wise to show up at all to register the young man. Do it the usual way, by mail—send in the application with all the essential items, transcript, and so forth. In that way, you'll avoid a needless confrontation. If they're to refuse him—as they most likely will—let them do it on their own cognizance. They'll then have to support their denial in writing. And while it will likely be vague and inconsequential, it'll give us something to go on. We'll know our next move."

Ellison nodded.

Avery yawned. "There's nothing magical about the N-double A-C-P in New York. It's th' N-double A-C-P down here that's counts, that really makes it all work. Because, you see, down here—right here—is where it's happening. You folks know better than anyone else how to deal with th' people and th' situations of your own community. You know because you're part of it. And that's why we rely on you."

The Reverend Ellison stared ahead at the unfolding ribbon of highway. As his headlights feebly probed the darkness, he also tried to see beyond the perimeter of the present. He so desperately wanted to look beyond the reality of the moment, to envision the future, to know more of what was expected of him. He felt a clamminess of perspiration. He felt a little sick, a little queasiness which he interpreted as fear. But then, he reminded himself, he had not yet had supper.

The following evening at twilight, a goodly number of black men and women—some with small children, even babies—filed into the small church to hear the NAACP lawyers from New York.

It was like a revival meeting.

Indeed, the Reverend Mortecai Ellison wished it to appear as a church service, if only to explain the cluster of vehicles parked outside. Hymns had been selected, so that the group might break into spontaneous song should there be an appearance of any unwanted white visitor. Several men carefully screened the people who entered and then inconspicuously stood guard to watch for intruders.

The Reverend Ellison opened the meeting with prayer, and Joey, sitting down front, felt the nerve-ends of a caged animal. As he listened to the expected procedure of this daring transaction, he began to have uneasy regrets and wondered if it was truly too late to renege. Each time his name was mentioned, he felt exposed and vulnerable. With sweating palms, he glanced about him apprehensively and saw the expectant faces of neighbors and people he did not know. The voices of the speakers droned on and his head began to hurt.

Avery Anderson was telling the congregation, "It's up to you. If we're to be successful, it's up to you. Don't think this young man here is going to do it all. We're all needed—you, me, all of us. And each of us has an important part to play. We're facing the formidable opposition of white bigotry."

He enumerated the challenges facing them. *Money.* "We'll need funds to foot the cost of transcribing briefs, to pay for clerical expenses, as well as court and other organizational costs." *Visibility.* "It's important for us to be seen supporting this effort. It's vital for each of us to be involved. And if it should come to a trial, believe me, you need to be there. We need to convince everyone that it's local people, not outside troublemakers, who care the most about the outcome." *Housing.* "I don't have to tell you about the need of lodging for any visiting colored person who would come here to the South. Most of the hotels and boarding houses are run by white people. So, it's up to you to provide rooms and places to stay for any Negro lawyers or consultants or witnesses brought into our case." Anderson concluded, "There is so much to be done, and we need you. So, if you can type or file, make acquisitions, run errands, do anything to assist, we need you."

There were questions and comments and several expressions of doubt. A few faces reflected an ancient mistrust, even apprehension, but there was also a consensus of commitment, an obvious emotion that a new life was being rekindled. There was, Reverend Ellison noted, a rebirth of hope, of confidence and determination.

So he ended the meeting in song.

CHAPTER 8

Bernice Tutwiler, unmarried and particular at 59, sat primly at her desk examining the morning mail. She neatly slit the envelopes with a silver letter opener, extracting student application forms or letters of inquiry concerning the college. She hummed lightly to herself.

Bernice had been Crestview's director of admissions since the fall of '43, when she succeeded Caleb Jones after he had been drafted into the service. The appointment at first was only temporary, since the college intended to hold the position for Caleb upon his return. Indeed, she was accepted only because of a shortage of male applicants. But when the news came that Caleb had been killed at Anzio, she was asked to stay on.

The job suited her, and she approached it with a preciseness common to her character. She soon reduced to routine the task of managing student records, keeping track of degree credits, and enforcing admission requirements. She felt it was far more significant and challenging than garden club socializing and contract bridge, the two principal pastimes of her sister Ethel.

The two spinsters lived together in a large, frame, Victorian house fronting Pinckney Street. It was a stark white edifice of ornate gingerbread and wide verandahs, having been left to them by their late father, a long-time, respected doctor of the community. They seldom had visitors, but neither was reclusive. Ethel was active in social circles of the town, while Bernice, of course, had her duties at the college. They were very close,

53

and people tended to cower before their spunky, outspoken independence. Citizens of the town referred to them—surreptitiously, of course—as "the sisters."

Having resided in Crestview all their life, they lived by the rules of their church, their social standing, and their personal prejudices. They considered themselves Southern "ladies" with values irrevocably entrenched in a heritage which nurtured pride and dignity and an enduring perseverance. Both were long-time members of the UDC (The United Daughters of the Confederacy).

Ethel, the elder, was tall, lean, austere, and by her aloof, erect posture always exuded a sense of aristocracy and discipline. A former school teacher, she still maintained a severe, no-nonsense facade. She minced no words and in a dialect thickly Southern, yet edged in brittle directness, she always spoke her mind.

Bernice, on the other hand, was a squat individual, more gentle in her demeanor and far less formidable. But she could be direct, too. She, like her sister, was fastidious, fiercely loyal, and opinionated. Better organized than Ethel, Bernice was more appreciative of details and therefore attended to all the household records and did most of the shopping. Merchants watched her carefully count out her change after each transaction, amused at such frugality in the face of what many assumed a sizable inheritance left to them by the good doctor. The sisters' wealth was always a subject of intense speculation.

Bernice, at her desk, sighed as she opened the envelope. She was pleased to see the familiar admissions form filled out completely in ink. And yes, there were all the essential documents, including a high school transcript. She expertly perused the sheet. Reasonable grades, she noted. And, at first, her eyes slid past it; then, darted back in disbelief. The name of the high school registered. Bernice stared through her pince-nez with wide-eyed amazement. "Good lord," she breathed, "it's a—" She bit her tongue. "It's a Nig-ra!" Nervously, she reached for the telephone.

"I—really, I—" sputtered Ethel, "cain't believe it!"

"Well, I can tell you, I was shocked, too"

"But are you sure, Bernice?"

The two sisters were having dinner, and Bernice had just informed Ethel of the startling news that a Negro had applied for admission at the college.

"Are you certain?" Ethel asked.

"Of course I am!"

Of course, she was sure; after all, Bernice had been the first to see the young Negro's application. Now, in relating the story to her sister, she felt a certain titillation in telling what few people knew. But she did slightly resent Ethel's implication that she might have been in error.

"I saw his application; of course I'm positive," she insisted.

Ethel shook her head. "But what Nig-ra would do a thing like that? I mean, good Lord, doesn't he know that Nig-ras are not permitted? That it's a college for our kind, not his?"

"Of course he knows."

"Then, why? Why would he want to be where he isn't wanted? Cain't he see he doesn't belong?"

Bernice sighed. "I really don't know, dear, but I think we'd better talk about this later." A young Negro girl had just entered from the kitchen with a hot casserole.

It was Abby. She worked three afternoons a week for the sisters, as housekeeper and cook. On these days, she would serve them dinner, quickly clean up the kitchen, and depart for the long walk home.

"I declare," breathed Ethel in dismay and, completely ignoring the presence of the young girl, firmly asserted, "I jes' don't know what's come over colored folks these days—they jes' don't know their place any more."

"Ethel!" hissed Bernice sharply, glancing at Abby.

"Oh, fiddlesticks," Ethel answered, irritably, "I know."

Abby had heard and was aware, but she tried to ignore the racist implication and attend to her duty.

Ethel now turned and said sweetly, "Abigail, dear, would you pour me another glass of tea?"

Abby, having set the casserole on a hot mat, reached for the pitcher of tea on the sideboard behind her.

Ethel watched Abby fill her tumbler with tea and continued, "There are some—and I count our Abigail here as one of them—who certainly know how to act properly." She lifted her glass. "Thank you, dear."

"Yes'm," responded Abby and promptly departed for the kitchen.

Bernice looked across the heavy oak dining room table at her sister. "Really, now, Ethel, I do think we should be a little more considerate of that girl."

"Fiddlesticks, she knows that we appreciate her," replied Ethel. "And that's more than a lot of them do of us, I tell you."

Bernice started to speak but then she saw Abby returning with a platter of hot biscuits. The girl placed it before the ladies and backed away.

"Is this young colored man from around here?" Ethel asked boldly, ignoring the presence of the young girl.

Bernice glanced at Abby and quietly answered, "Yes."

"Well, that does surprise me. I would nevah have thought it possible. You can mark my word, there's going to be trouble. Nobody's going to let that boy enroll in our college! I can tell you *that!*"

Abby cringed. It was Joey they were talking about. He had done it! Like being touched by a hot iron, the realization stung and singed her mind with sudden fear. Oh, God, she thought. But she tried to show no emotion and busied herself at the sideboard.

"How sad, how very, very sad," Ethel was saying. "You'd think that if he came from around here, he'd simply know better."

"I—suppose."

"Well, it jus' cain't be..! It's a horrible thought; it's—it's unthinkable! Bernice, dear, you're the registrar—you got some say as such."

Bernice said, "Yes, well, the president has called a meeting the first thing tomorrow morning to discuss it."

"Then speak up!"

If there was panic, it was not evident in the several concerned members of the Crestview administration as they assembled in President McAndrew's office. Ed Blair, athletic coach and dean of students, walked in with Cartwright, the two conversing in casual tones. Bernice Tutwiler followed, a little flustered, her arms filled with manila files, college bulletins, and other pertinent records. They took their seats at a small conference table at the far end of the president's office beneath tall, gauze-curtained windows. The mahogany table reflected the slanting rays of morning light.

McAndrew, who had been conferring with two attorneys, arose from behind his desk and motioned the men to follow him to the conference table. One, a familiar face, was Eli Hanson; the other, a governmental attorney from the state capital, Rob DeWitt. Byron seated himself at the head of the table and began. "By now, you all know what we're up against."

"Do we ever..!" breathed Blair, shaking his head.

"—you know Mr. Hanson, of course, and by his recommendation I've asked the advice of Mr. Rob DeWitt here, a very distinguished lawyer and the assistant attorney general for the state. I feel we should discuss the consequences of this recent development and decide our proper course."

Cartwright observed, "Our first step is quite obvious, it seems to me. We reject th' boy's application."

"On what grounds?" asked Byron.

Cartwright eyed President McAndrew curiously. "Why—come on, Mac, it's obvious. He doesn't qualify."

Miss Tutwiler spoke up, quickly, "Oh, but he does—doesn't he?"

"How do you figure that, ma'am?" asked Blair.

"I mean, academically speaking, of course. He's well above average, I'd say."

"But my dear," whispered Cartwright, smiling. "He's black."

"Now that..," said McAndrew softly, with a slight, nervous cough, "..is a matter we need to consider quite carefully."

Charlie agreed. "I would hope so."

"The point I'm trying to make, Dr. Cartwright," said Byron, "is that because it is a volatile issue, we simply must be certain of our legal position." He looked at DeWitt.

Before the man could speak, Hanson muttered, "No problem there, I'd say; wouldn't you say so, Rob?"

Rob DeWitt was a stocky man of medium height, sloe-eyed, with slate gray hair, and a congenial face which bore lines that revealed a mature, considered nature. He answered, "It is, of course, state law—th' separation of th' races. But, as Dr. McAndrew is sayin', we—should proceed with some caution. Supersedin' state statute, of course, is th' constitutional guarantee of individual and personal rights under th' Fourteenth Amendment. So, you see, it jus' wouldn't be wise to make race or color th' principal issue in rejecting this young man."

"But he's a Nig-ra—and we don't accept Nig-ras!" insisted Cartwright. "It's policy!"

DeWitt smiled. "I know. But we must avoid, at all costs, any position that can be interpreted as prejudicial. My advice is that you rationalize your denial of th' boy on grounds other than th' fact that he is colored."

"I don't get it!" hissed Coach Blair. "Why cain't we call a spade a spade?"

Bernice glared at him, not knowing if he meant it as a scurrilous pun or an innocent point of philosophy. Eli Hanson stepped into the breach of brief silence to explain. "A precaution, Mr. Blair. Should this go to court, it would be most unwise to jeopardize our case with any implication that our action has been associated with racial bigotry."

Charlie Cartwright expended a long, deep sigh. He was not smiling. "It'd be a sad day," he said, quietly, "if we were ever forced to take 'em in."

"If you remember," McAndrew reminded him, "I tried to warn all of you that this might happen."

Hanson remembered the Quintock proposal by the president, but said nothing. Cartwright resented the reminder.

"I know, I know," he admitted, "But Mac, it's not meant to be. This college was founded on that principle. And—quite frankly—it'd be th' end of everything. Think of th' disruption, th' disgrace, th' loss of our reputation—"

Ed Blair leaned back in his chair. "Charlie's right. It would be one helluva mess 'round here.."

Bernice felt much the same as her colleagues, yet she sensed the need to justify her rejection. She thought of something. "Maybe it'd be unfair to th' boy, even if it was possible for us to take him in."

She was thinking of the social isolation and ostracism that would certainly be inevitable. But no one asked her meaning; instead, McAndrew sighed impatiently and commented, "Obviously, there is a greater magnitude to this problem than we might imagine. It's no longer a simple matter of maintaining th' status quo, or adherin' to traditional standards; it's far more complicated and complex than that. I think there is little doubt that this young man is being advised by some well-organized group, maybe th' N-double A-C-P. And while we've come to believe that a colored person has very little clout—around here, at least—we really shouldn't underestimate his influence in the context of current feelings. We must make a decision—but make it with caution."

Cartwright winced. He wished his president would be a bit bolder, firmer, more forthright—at least, openly express a distaste for the mixing of the races and assure them that integration was impractical, indeed impossible. He had to believe that it could not, should not, must never, ever happen. Oh, if Jasper Morton were only alive…!

Morton. Cartwright remembered something. He turned to Bernice Tutwiler. "Did you—tell me, Miss Tutwiler, did you say that this boy's application was complete in every way?"

"Yes. I believe so."

"Everything?"

"Yes, he even enclosed a deposit for his room. Oh, my, yes, his forms were properly filled out, I'm sure, and he included all the necessary documents."

"Such as—a high school transcript.."

"Yes, of course."

"And—letters of reference?"

"Yes."

Cartwright was smiling now. "But—not any of these letters were from a Crestview graduate, were they?"

Bernice opened her mouth to reply, but, instead, shook her head. She looked puzzled. All eyes focused on Dr. Charles Cartwright. The presidential assistant sat comfortably secure, fondling his clipboard.

"Charlie, what are you driving at?" the president asked.

Ignoring Miss Tutwiler, Charlie said, "I think, gentlemen, we have th' means to end our little crisis before it even gets started. We have the answer."

"What do you mean?" asked Hanson.

A smile tickled Cartwright's features, as he said, soothingly, "Our dear Jasper Morton, in his infinite wisdom and great vision, had the foresight to introduce a stipulation in our entrance requirements which jus' might do th' trick. I don't think he was talkin' about Negroes—he didn't have to. This was a white institution and he was goin' to keep it so. But what he was really concerned about was maintainin' th' character and standards of his college and its student body. And he figured that th' best way to do this was to have each applicant submit six letters of recommendation or support from—and get this—from graduates of this institution. It's in th' book, right there, still in th' catalogue."

"It is?" An astonished Bernice hastily rifled through the Crestview State College bulletin.

"But Charlie," said Byron, "even if it is, I don't believe this has ever been enforced, has it?"

"No, perhaps not. But it's there."

"Here it is," acknowledged Bernice, and she read aloud, "'Six letters testifying to the applicant's good moral character and aptitude for entrance at this institution may—'" She paused, looked up, and repeated, "'may—be required—and such letters should be from former graduates of Crestview State College'."

"Sounds like an option," muttered Blair.

"But it's there—to be used," maintained Cartwright.

DeWitt nodded. "I agree. This, I think, would certainly give substance to any denial and therefore place th' onus on th' candidate."

Eli Hanson placed a hand, palm down, on the table, as a gesture of finality. "That should do it, then"

"I'm not so certain," said Byron.

"What do you mean?"

"If this young man is bein' counseled by an organized effort to end segregation, can we not expect further legal action to counter our decision?"

59

DeWitt nodded. "Of course. But we'll cross that bridge when we get to it. Right now, we must take it step by step."

Hanson straightened in his chair. "So, Miss Tutwiler," he advised, "I think you can write that letter of denial at your earliest convenience, specifyin' th' inadequacy of this boy's application."

Cartwright leaned toward Bernice. "I'll help you draft that letter, Miss Tutwiler," he said. His smile then encompassed the men. "It should be diplomatically vague, and not too hopeful," he added.

Hanson echoed DeWitt's chuckle and turned to hear the senior lawyer say, "Perhaps it would be best if you had Mr. Hanson's input, as well, in constructing this letter. Purely from the standpoint of legal advisement."

Charlie nodded his agreement.

McAndrew still seemed uncertain, but he sighed and said, "Well, that's about it, I suppose—for now. But I must express a hope that we handle this matter discreetly and with as little antagonism as possible. I think it behooves us to say as little as possible, to be circumspect and sensitive to th' volatile nature of th' problem. In this regard, I don't have to remind you that there should be no action or comment without my direct approval. Is that understood?"

No one commented except Blair, who suggested, "Keep us posted, Byron."

CHAPTER 9

Bernice Tutwiler felt quite uncomfortable. As she waited in President McAndrew's office on this quiet Sunday morning, she nervously kneaded her lace handkerchief as she watched the pendulum clock on the wall. It was almost half-past eight o'clock. She sighed. She wanted very much to be in Sunday School.

Dr. Cartwright and Eli Hanson entered, speaking quietly, nodded a greeting to Bernice and took their seats. The president was conferring with his secretary in the outer office.

"I don't like this one bit," Cartwright muttered.

McAndrew had consented to an unprecedented meeting with the young Negro applicant and his attorney, against the advice of his assistant. Cartwright felt the college should not accede to this minority request, that they should remain aloof, indifferent. But Byron insisted that it was the fair thing to do, that young Henderson deserved an official face-to-face explanation of their action in rejecting his admission into Crestview State College. Cartwright bitterly claimed that, as an interloper, the young man deserved no such courtesy.

"Mac, it only makes us look weak," Charlie told the president. "And besides, I don't know whether you've thought about it, but it's highly irregular permitting that colored contingent on campus to enter our administration building. It could cause contemptuous talk and the wrong impression."

Dr. Byron McAndrew admitted that appearances were important. So he purposely arranged the conference at an early hour on Sunday morning, reasoning that there would be few people around at that time to witness the arrival of the young Negro and his attorney.

It was October,1952. Joey Henderson walked between the two men and, as he climbed the steps of the college administration building, he felt a queer, uneasy sensation. He observed the white fluted columns which fronted the entrance to the red brick building. So this was it. An exclusive college for white people. As he moved up the steps, he sensed he was treading consecrated, unnatural territory. Maybe one day this would change. He would enter this place then without any feeling of intimidation. He would belong.

Joey quickly stepped forward to hold the door for the Reverend Ellison and Edgar Hall, the Negro attorney retained by the NAACP to represent him. They were welcomed by President McAndrew who, in turn, introduced Bernice Tutwiler, Dr. Charles Cartwright, and Eli Hanson.

Hall, dusky black, was a portly individual with a fat face that radiated warmth and congeniality. He had driven down from the state capital early that morning. Placing his worn, leather briefcase on the floor beside his chair, he now smilingly acknowledged his gratitude for the opportunity to discuss the situation—even at "this unusual hour," he laughed. Cartwright eyed him cautiously with instant dislike.

Byron McAndrew officially opened the meeting. "You gentlemen must understand that we might welcome Mr. Henderson as a student at Crestview, if —if he had been able to comply completely with the stated admission requirements of this institution. But, as Miss Tutwiler here, our registrar, has repeatedly written to Mr. Henderson—"

"Beggin' your pardon, President McAndrew," interrupted Joey's attorney. "But it's precisely these 'requirements' that happen to be at issue here. Particularly one. You know, as well as I do, that it would be impossible for our young man here to obtain acceptable letters from six graduates of your college."

"Why not?" asked Cartwright, pointedly.

Hall glared at the presidential assistant, then smiled. "Why, Dr. Cartwright, I don't think I have to tell you, sir, that in these parts, it would be nigh impossible for my client to get six letters from *any* white citizens—much less alumni of this college."

"Why not?" Cartwright repeated. And he returned the lawyer's smile, as he said, "White citizens—-as you call them—are as accommodating as anyone else."

Hall looked at Cartwright. He then laughed. "I agree, I do agree..! I'm simply pointing out how difficult it would be for Mr. Henderson to even locate graduates of Crestview who know him well enough to write letters of recommendation."

"But that is of course the requirement," insisted Cartwright.

"But it's unfair!" countered Edgar Hall.

"Are you suggestin' that we change th' rules just to accommodate this young man?" asked Cartwright.

"No! Not jus' for my client, only. For all qualified people tryin' to enter this college here. But you've got to understand that, in the particular case of my client, or anyone else of his color, there is imposed an unduly harsh and impossible obstacle—one that's beyond bein' reasonable."

Charlie Cartwright was almost ready to retort, to tell this black bastard, in no uncertain terms, that Negroes were never intended to be at Crestview State College in the first place! And whether unreasonable or not, there would always be an obstacle, as far as he was concerned, to make damn sure that such a travesty would never occur. But he gripped his clipboard and said nothing.

"It's important to understand, I think," Eli Hanson was saying, "that there is indeed a reason for the stipulation requirin' those six letters. Our college heah takes pride in th' fine young men and women who come here to graduate. And, as a member of th' board, I can tell you, we intend to make sure that every person who considers comin' heah meets th' highest standards of character and upbringin'."

"I can appreciate that, sir, and I do understand," said Edgar Hall, leaning back in his chair and crossing his arms. He then added, "But what I cain't understand is why six letters from respectable colored citizens of this community cannot serve equally well to testify to Mr. Henderson's fine character."

Byron tried to answer him. "Well, now, we feel that anyone who has been to Crestview, been a part of us, understood our traditions, and met our requirements to graduate—only they truly understand what we expect of our students and what is demanded of them."

"But..," suggested the Reverend Ellison, slowly, "Cain't you see that, in th' case of Joey's application here, such a demand is really unfair?"

Cartwright smiled and said, "But a rule is a rule."

"But cain't you waive this rule, at least on this occasion?" asked Hall.

Cartwright still smiled. "Why should we?"

"Because—"

Hall's attempted rebuttal was swallowed up in a realization that was all too clear, that rationality and logic had little to do with either the issue or their discussion. A prohibitive obstacle had been erected and his client was forced to comply—or, otherwise, gain relief through recourse to litigation and the courts. The latter option, obviously, seemed their only alternative.

Bernice Tutwiler had said nothing as she sat there during the long morning, listening. She noted the silence of the young man who like herself seemed uncomfortable and out of place. She had not been called upon to answer for, advise, or even comment about the policy she exercised in the performance of her job. She felt remote, inconsequential, like a leaf floating in some aimless current. And often, during the discussion, her mind drifted. And she was in church again, seeking divine guidance, and praying—for this boy, perhaps, this college; indeed, beseeching fairness for all mankind.

The news soon spread.

The Evening Gazette took casual notice of the occurrence in a single column, page two account, and while it was titillating news few people put much stock in the successful outcome of this rather boldfaced act.

The local garden club, of course, was intrigued and shocked that any young Negro boy would even dare seek admittance to a white college—especially their college. And Ethel Tutwiler, sister of the college registrar, quickly became the club's resident consultant for evaluating rampant rumors.

The men of the town also shared the same concern and curiosity. Inside Bobby Ray's Bar and Grill, glum figures, perched on stools, slumped before brown bottles of beer, murmured forlorn opinions as to the boy's chances.

No one believed it possible.

At Oliver's Dry Goods Store, a customer ended the conversation with the defiant conclusion, "It jes' cain't happen.."

But it was happening. And to Joey, it suddenly seemed to be happening fast. It had only been a week since their meeting with the administrative officials of Crestview State College, and already a hearing had been scheduled before a Federal judge.

As Joey walked between the Reverend Ellison and Edgar Hall to climb the marbled steps of the U.S. District Court in the state capital, he felt a tremor of exhilaration and expectation. He had been informed of the procedure. The hearing would determine if a temporary injunction would be granted to force the college to accept him; that is, until such time a trial might otherwise decide. For now, there would be no jury, just the judge, listening, as the attorneys argued the case and offered witnesses to justify their respective cause. The judge would later render his decision.

As he entered the huge hallway of the building, Joey felt a tightness in his throat. He sensed an awful tension as he walked through the marbled labyrinth, hearing the reverberate sound of voices and footsteps, and feeling the significant presence of this place. He tried hard not to be nervous.

In the courtroom, a few people had gathered and were waiting. The colored and white sat separately, in clusters. There appeared obvious interest in these proceedings and a low murmur seemed to intensify the suspense. The two men escorted Joey down the aisle and through the swinging gate of a balustrade enclosing the well which separated the audience from the bench.

Hall indicated a seat for Joey to sit beside him at the plaintiff's table. Ellison then retired to a front seat behind them.

On the other side, Rob DeWitt and Eli Hanson sat at their table, their heads together in deep conversation, while Dr. Cartwright stood, leaning over, listening to their strategy.

The bailiff silenced the crowd and opened the court. Judge Collins, bespectacled and wearing a flowing black robe, quickly took his seat and gaveled the session to order.

"This hearing is for action to enjoin a state institution of higher learning from limiting admissions to white persons only, and has been brought by one Joseph E. Henderson against the officers and trustees of Crestview State College," said the judge. He then said, "If the counsels concerned are ready, we will now proceed."

Edgar Hall struggled to his feet and carefully detailed how his client, seeking to obtain an adequate education, had properly applied for enrollment at Crestview State College and was unlawfully denied admission on grounds perceived as prejudicial and without due cause.

On the other hand, Rob DeWitt argued that the college was clearly within its right to refuse the plaintiff for the simple reason that the candidate for admission had not complied or conformed with all the stated requirements for enrollment. DeWitt denied any prejudicial intent and maintained that Henderson's case had been carefully reviewed by the college, before and after the young man's non-acceptance. He pointed out that a special conference had even been arranged by the college to fully explain the inadequacies of the subject's application, for the benefit of both the plaintiff and his counsel. Moreover, the assistant attorney general questioned the sincerity of Joey Henderson's intent.

"Otherwise," the lawyer offered, "if he was truly interested in an education, the plaintiff would certainly find it easier to enter and matriculate at a qualified Negro college or university."

Hall vigorously objected to what he called a malicious effort to discredit his client, and, perspiring profusely, he emphasized the fine qualities and dedication of the young man. This brought him to the issue of the alumni letters, a requirement which he said was being used as an evil instrument to deny the rights of a Negro.

"If th' function of these letters is to provide testimonials of good character and ability," Attorney Hall pointed out, "then the plaintiff, your honor, has more than fulfilled his responsibility by providing—not once, but twice—th' letters required. Granted—they were not from white graduates of Crestview State College, but they were from well-respected colored people of our community—people who know this young man personally, who know him as a fine, upstanding, hard working, Christian boy."

To prove his point, Edgar Hall called to the stand a parade of witnesses who spoke for Joey's character and good will. Some were elderly, faltering, but firm in their support for the young man. Mr. Johnson, Joey's principal, testified to the young man's scholastic aptitude and his intense interest in education. Joey's minister told of his church record and his good moral character.

Judge Collins, meanwhile, listened with restless unease as the hearing extended well into the afternoon. At length, about mid afternoon, he interrupted the proceedings and called the two attorneys to the bench.

He leaned over and whispered, "This whole affair's goin' on longer than I anticipated. Cain't you two fellas wrap it up?"

DeWitt shrugged. "As far as I'm concerned, we've made our case."

"But no one from th' college has been questioned yet," Edgar Hall reminded the judge. "I do think they need to answer for their actions."

"Well," sighed Judge Collins, "if you insist on draggin' this out.. I have to tell you that I set aside only one day for this hearing because of a crowded docket. Obviously, it's goin' to take longer than that. So I see no alternative, gentlemen, but to continue this case at another time."

"But your honor," pleaded Hall, "Could you not rule for a temporary injunction, in order that my client might not be further delayed in starting the new term?"

"I would object to that, of course," muttered DeWitt.

Judge Collins said, "I'm afraid we have not progressed sufficiently in these deliberations to attest to the feasibility of such an order. No, Mr. Hall, we'll just have to wait."

The hearing was reset for the following month, the second week in December.

Joey's mind was of mingled thoughts, as he swung the bush axe in vicious strokes. He was helping his father shrub the ditch banks of the farm. As he whacked away at the weeds and underbrush, he pulled the entangled twigs and vines into a pile; whereupon, Elijah gathered them up in his arms and tossed them onto a burning fire. Each armload smothered the flames and white smoke boiled upward into a gray, wintry sky.

Elijah was not happy with his son. He just could not understand why his boy was so stubbornly insistent on pursuing what, to him, was obviously a risky and foolish notion. He resented the time demanded of Joey by these people who thought they could change the world. A waste, he thought, and he needed Joey for more useful tasks. He wished for it all to be over, done for, ended.

As he wielded the sharp instrument, young Joey thought of the ordeal ahead. He would have to face the court, he knew, and he wondered how he would react.

And he thought of Abby as well. He had spoken to her in church. And although she had seemed friendly, there appeared a strange and obvious awkwardness in their relationship now. He wondered if, by this personal struggle of his, he had ended by losing her.

His mother as well, he thought of her—and his pa, also, who labored silently in an ambition to do well in his knowledge and wisdom of the land. Joey knew that his commitment had created considerable worry for them both. And he felt badly, for he knew he had no right to do this.

As he whacked away at the saplings which were whips along the ditch bank, he recalled the confused feelings he experienced yesterday when the Reverend Mortecai Ellison informed him that their case had been delayed yet again. The assistant attorney general had taken ill and due to the impending Christmas holidays, the hearing had been postponed until after the first of the year.

Joey now, more than ever, felt the pressure of events. He leaned against the handle of his bush axe and wiped his brow. He felt weary.

Weary of waiting. And he wondered what Christmas would possibly bring that year.

In the cold, January morning, the silent town anxiously awaited the fate of the coming event. The streets were empty. And between the railroad tracks a coil of dust was seen, swirling, dancing over Main Street. One could hear the whine of a swaying, creaking Coca-Cola sign.

Inside the warmth of Al's Barber Shop, men spoke freely. As Al moved the whirring clippers up the nape of Dr. Neal Ogden's neck, he paused to survey the several men who sat on a line of chairs awaiting their turn. He had just finished telling them of his conversation the night before with Charles Cartwright, the college administrator, who had stopped in for a haircut. It had been just before closing time and no other customer was in the shop at the time, so Dr. Cartwright was quite talkative. He told Al about the Negro boy who had applied to enter Crestview State College and of the hearing that would determine if the college might be legally forced to admit him.

"When's th' hearin'?" asked Lester Dykes.

"It's goin' on right now," Al answered.

Aldo Fennick said, "I thought that hearin' was months ago."

"It was," said Al. "But they never finished. They're startin' ag'in today."

Jeff Carlyle was seated next to Dykes. Snapping his newspaper, he growled, "Hell! I'd end it damn quick."

When the hearing first began, many curious white citizens of Crestview and the region had crowded the Federal district court to see justice rendered in accordance with accepted Southern dogma. But the frequent delays which followed had dulled interest and now hardly anyone seemed aware that the case had resumed. Al enjoyed relating this bit of news and he looked around to relish the response.

"Th' bastards'll never learn!" Carlyle added.

Aldo Fennick, who was a plumber, sat one down from Carlyle in the line of cane-bottom chairs. "So they're goin' to try it ag'in, eh, Al?"

Al nodded. "Yep."

"It's about time. I hope they git on with it and teach that little bastard a lesson," snorted Carlyle.

"Don't be so sure."

Jeff turned toward the voice and sized up Lester Dykes, who was waiting patiently his turn. Lester returned a half smile as he explained,

"Th' way them damn lib'rals in congress are playin' footsie with th' coloreds, well—I jes' ain't surprised at nothin', really. Jus' wait and see how this whole thing turns out."

Randy, the other barber in the shop, paused in the process of trimming Murdock Faison's beard. He straightened to look at Dykes. "I hope to God you don't mean we'll be havin' to mix wit' niggers.."

Titus McDivett chuckled. He was next for Randy's chair. "Yep, you'd better git your wire cutters out and another pound of lard, Randy. You'll be cuttin' their hair next..!"

Over the laughter, Randy muttered, "I'll be damned if I will!"

Jeff Carlyle did not laugh. "I don't think it's so damn funny myself," he snapped. "Fer God's sake, men, don't you know what it'll mean if that damn court says th' college has to take that boy?. That—nigger?"

Aldo Fenrick, acutely aware of Carlyle's concern, breathed, "Yeahh.."

There was only the click of Al's scissors in the vacuum of silence that followed. Then, Lester said, quietly, "I keep thinkin' of those little girls that go to school up there. I cain't see them havin' to associate wit' Nig-ras. I really cain't."

"Think th' court will take that into consideration?" Titus asked.

"A fed'ral court?" responded Lester, "Don't make me laugh."

"Well, he ain't there yet," said Murdock Faison from the barber's chair.

"Mr. Faison's right," spoke up Randy, "I cain't see him gittin' in ther' neither."

"Well, like I told you, Dr. Cartwright was of th' opinion that it would not likely be a favorable decision for th' boy," reported Al. Then, handing the physician a hand mirror, he asked, "What do you think, doc?"

Dr. Ogden scrutinized his image, as he held the mirror so he could see the back of his head reflected in the wall mirror behind him. "I jus' hope there'll be no trouble."

"Yeah, you can say that again," agreed Al.

The doctor struggled out of the chair and was reaching for his wallet to pay Al. He eyed the barber shop assembly and said, "I guess we haven't had any racial problems here in—what?—twenty years?"

"Easily," said Al. "Long before th' war."

"I personally don't see that it'll do us no good startin' trouble like we had back then. Remember, Al? Th' Klan was running wild and there was house burnings and killing and—God knows what. Ever'body was scared back then. Remember, Al?"

"I remember."

Jeff Carlyle spoke up. "Wait one minute, doc. You talk about trouble. There's one thing you ain't lookin' at. We ain't th' one that's causin' it."

"Jeff's right," stated Murdock, as he stood up from Randy's chair and stretched. "If I know anything, it's that damn N-double A-C-P that's behind it all."

"Hell yes," Aldo declared.

"And if they want trouble," added Murdock Faison, "I say let's meet 'em half way."

The doctor shook his head slowly. "That's just it. We cain't be takin' to the streets with axe handles and burnin' torches, like they did in th' old days. It's jus' counterproductive; it don't get us anywhere. No. No, that's-not th' way. That's why there's a court case. And that's where it's got to be settled."

Jeff Carlyle shrugged as he moved past Doctor Ogden to climb into Al's chair. "Yep, you're right, doc—that is—if they settle it th' right way."

Murdock Faison, rubbing his newly trimmed beard, brushed past the doctor on his way to the door. He took down his mackinaw from the coat rack and hunched into it. As he paused to put on his gloves, he raised his voice to say, "Whether ther's trouble or not depends on that court, I'd say!" At the door, he looked back. "I figger they know a thing or two. 'Cause th' day that little pip-squeak gets into Crestview College, that'll be a cold day in hell!" Then, with a parting gesture of farewell, he opened the glass-paneled door and departed. Before he could close the door behind him, however, a gust of chilling air swept in.

Titus McDivett shuddered. "Or a cold day in Crestview, you mean," he quipped.

Everybody laughed.

CHAPTER 10

Bernice Tutwiler was nervous as she took the stand. She had been told over the Christmas holidays that her testimony might be necessary, so she had conscientiously reviewed the tenets of her job, hoping her knowledge and presence would prove convincing for the college and its cause. She tried to walk with confidence to the witness chair, stood staunchly to take the oath, sat primly in the chair, and even nodded to the judge.

Edgar Hall approached her slowly. She could not get used to having to answer to a colored person. It just didn't seem right. And as she watched him incredulously, he circled thoughtfully without looking at her. Then he stopped pacing. Their eyes met.

"Your name, please."

"Bernice M. Tutwiler."

"Er..Miss..Tutwiler?"

"Yes," she answered in a tone of resentment.

"Miss Tutwiler, you are the official registrar for Crestview State College, I believe."

"Yes I am."

"And you've been the registrar for—how long?"

"About ten years," she answered quietly.

"Please speak up for the court," prompted Hall.

"Ten years," she said loudly.

Oh, how she hated being ordered about by this dark skinned man. She didn't care if he was a lawyer; it just didn't seem right. And she being a respectable white Southern lady too.

"Then we can assume you know your job well," Hall surmised.

"Of course."

"You understand the policies of your institution and, indeed, you carry them out in accordance with your duties as the registrar of Crestview State College—is that correct?"

"I believe so."

"You—corresponded with Mr. Henderson here, th' plaintiff, on several occasions, did you not, explaining th' policies of your college and what you perceived as deficiencies in his application?"

"Yes."

"And what were those deficiencies?"

"He did not have the letters of reference required of candidates for admission, for one thing."

Edgar Hall rubbed his chin. "You mean, Mr. Henderson did not submit any letters of reference at all?"

"Oh, he did submit some letters, but they were not suitable. They were not from alumni of Crestview."

"Oh, I see. Each prospective student at Crestview State College is required to submit—six, is it not?—letters of support from former graduates of the college before he or she can be considered for admission, is that correct?"

"Yes."

"Everyone?"

Bernice paused. "Most everyone, I believe."

"But not everyone, right?"

"Well—not everyone—because some—"

Hall interrupted. "And how do you determine who will, or will not, have to submit such letters of reference?"

Bernice drew a deep breath. "I was about to explain, when I was interrupted. I was going to say that some candidates are known to the college by family ties or other relationships, which makes it unnecessary to have this sort of proof of good character."

"You know them, in other words."

"Yes, that's about it."

"Miss Tutwiler, tell us, how many students within the last five years have been required to submit such letters of reference before being accepted by you and the administration of Crestview State College?"

"Practically all of them," Bernice replied.

"All of them?"

Bernice stared at him.

"Remember, Miss Tutwiler, you're under oath," Hall reminded her. "Let me repeat my question, so there'll be no doubt as to what I'm askin'. I want to know how many students accepted at your college within th' last five years were required to provide six letters each from graduates of Crestview State College, testifyin' to personal knowledge of that candidate's moral character?"

"Well, I—er—cain't rightly say," said Bernice, hesitantly.

"You're th' registrar, aren't you?"

"Of course I am!" replied Bernice, indignantly. "But you got to understand, I have to review the applications of many students, and you're askin' me to remember each one of hundreds of people—and I cain't do that!"

Edgar Hall looked at her with a slight smile, rubbing his chin contentedly. "But surely, Miss Tutwiler, you can remember to what degree this particular requirement has been enforced over the years—if, indeed, it has been required at all—until now."

Bernice glared at the dusky figure before her, her lips tight with anger and embarrassment. Why did they permit this black person to speak to a lady like her in this way?

"I don't remember!"

"Come now, Miss Tutwiler, you surely remember that this particular requirement has not been imposed for years!"

"Objection!" Rob DeWitt had risen from his chair. "The counsel is badgering the witness. She has tried to answer that question..!"

"Your honor, I'm sure it's a matter of record. And if we have to subpoena those records, we will, but—surely Miss Tutwiler can apprise us of these facts without goin' to that trouble."

Judge Collins ruled for the plaintiff. "I think Mr. Hall has a point. I believe the issue has some credence, and I feel Miss Tutwiler should provide some expertise in the matter. The objection is overruled."

"Then, would you answer me, Miss Tutwiler—has this regulation been applied recently?"

"No," answered Bernice, weakly. "Not recently."

"Your witness," concluded Hall triumphantly.

Ellison smiled. Things were going well, he thought. Hall had boxed them into an admission that the rule had not been applied with consistency and soon, he thought, they would be able to prove that its application in Joey's case was vindictive and prejudicial. So, for Joey's advisors, the first day of the hearing ended on a high note.

73

But on the second day, the court had hardly opened when a gathering at the bench indicated some confusion. After a lengthy deliberation, Judge Collins explained that on this day it would be necessary for Rob DeWitt, the attorney for the defense, to absent himself in order that he might appear for another case as the assistant attorney general. Therefore, the Henderson hearing would have to be continued, said Judge Collins, and its resumption was reset in three weeks.

A disappointed Edgar Hall wearily left the courtroom. Just when he felt he had the momentum, time might now reverse the advantage. Hall's dismay was reflected in the faces of those around him. And Joey, too, sensed their disillusionment.

There always seemed a delay, thought Joey. Why couldn't they seek a hurried settlement? Three weeks slowly passed and Joey was present as the trial resumed.

"Dr. Charles Cartwright!"

Charlie eased out of his chair and moved quickly to the stand. He took the oath dutifully and sat down to eagerly await the first question from Rob DeWitt.

The sloe-eyed lawyer began: "Dr. Cartwright, you're the assistant to the president of Crestview State College, are you not?"

"Yes, I am," said Cartwright, forming his familiar smile.

"And you've been a college administrator for some time now," suggested DeWitt.

"Oh yes, for the past seven years—as a presidential assistant, that is. I was first appointed by Dr. Morton."

"The former president.."

"Yes. And a very good man."

"Then, Dr. Cartwright," asserted DeWitt, cupping his chin, "you know when certain rules came into effect and how they have been implemented."

"Oh yes."

"About the entrance requirement in question, then.. I'd like for you to give us a few particulars about its origin and its implementation. When was the rule requiring six letters of reference from alumni of the institution first established?" asked the assistant attorney general.

"At least ten years ago, I would think," Charlie replied. "President Morton was instrumental in the development of that rule."

"Why?"

The smile, which occasionally gave way to brief moments of solemn consideration, now returned. Cartwright answered, "Dr. Morton firmly believed that Crestview, as an institution, should always meet the highest standard of morality and conscientious learning, and should, by her constituency, uphold a long tradition of Southern excellence. And to assure this, he decided that the approval of those who knew, who had actually attended and graduated from Crestview State College, would be most helpful in judging the quality of any new applicant."

"So this regulation, which has been on the books for same time, was for the purpose of selecting good, conscientious students, and not, as some infer, as an instrument of cruel, vindictive partiality."

"Heavens, no! It was never intended to be a deterrent or obstacle to any candidate desiring admission to this college."

"Now, as regard to the plaintiff, Dr. Cartwright," continued the attorney for the college, "did this rule have any particular significance?"

"What do you mean, sir?"

"Well, he's a colored person," stated DeWitt.

Cartwright smiled. "We have no stated policy of separatism. The fact that the candidate is colored made little difference."

At this, Edgar Hall grimaced. Such hypocrisy! He was eager for an opportunity to cross-examine. But, for now, he could only fidget and listen.

"So, as far as your stated admissions policy is concerned, this requirement is as applicable to Negroes as it is to whites."

"Of course."

"But the college has never admitted Negroes," observed DeWitt. "Is there a reason for this?"

Cartwright smiled. "Well, it is rare, indeed, for a colored person or even anyone from a foreign country to make application to matriculate at our college. But if they should, and they qualify, I can assure you they'd be properly considered. But of course, everyone must meet the standards we expect and demand at Crestview State College."

"Thank you, Dr Cartwright."

The hearing continued for yet another day, with each side struggling to offer evidence which might influence a favorable decision. In the summing up, Edgar Hall insisted that the college had been unfair and unreasonable and inconsistent in their admissions policy. He claimed that Joey Henderson had been willfully denied his constitutional rights as a citizen of the United States, that he was wrongfully rejected on the basis of his color and race. Joey, Hall maintained, was serious in his desire for an education, that he was eminently qualified, and that as the plaintiff in the case, he should be granted the injunction asked for, and thereby force Crestview State College to admit him immediately.

The assistant attorney general, however, pointed out that Mr. Henderson had been refused on the technicality of an inadequate application only, that there was no bias evident in the action, and that the institution had made every reasonable effort to communicate with and assist the candidate. He stressed the importance of the regulation and why there should be no exception. Further, DeWitt expressed a belief that the plaintiff was not seeking admission in good faith and, therefore, was not being denied an opportunity for a proper education.

The hearing was over. And the long wait began. The chilled, final weeks of February passed slowly as the participants speculated about the outcome. On the first of March, Judge Collins handed down his decision:

> *The plaintiff's motion for a preliminary injunction is hereby denied, for it is the opinion of the court that the overwhelming weight of the testimony is that the plaintiff was not denied admission because of his color or race; rather, by an admitted failure to qualify on the basis of stated entrance requirements of the college. It would seem, however, that some rules imposed by the institution are inconsistent and may be, for the plaintiff in particular, unfair and discriminatory. A full trial on the merits is needed in order for the plaintiff to have a fair, unfettered, and unhurrassed opportunity to prove his case.*

The citizens of Crestview read the verdict with misgivings and doubt. They were, in general, happy the black boy had been denied the privilege of invading the sanctity of their all-white institution, but they were deeply disturbed that a United States court would even consider granting a Negro the right to contest the propriety of accepted social principles long established as community law.

"It's a shame!" gasped Ethel Tutwiler, as she indignantly tossed aside the Evening Gazette.

But three days later, Ethel would be even more upset as she read that, in filing his complaint, the Negro boy had dared to name her sister as a codefendant in the case. There it was, in the local paper—her name—their name—associated with this distressing, contemptible racial controversy. She was mortified.

When Bernice came home from her office that evening, Ethel was sitting upright in her wingback chair. Ethel's head swiveled as Bernice entered the room and the elder sister glared at her.

"My, but it's brisk outside!" said Bernice, and then she saw her sister looking at her. "Why, Ethel, dear, what's wrong?"

"This!" she snapped, raising the crumpled evening paper from her lap. "Have you read this?"

Bernice's face softened. "Oh. Oh, my, yes, yes."

"But this is horrible!"

"Oh, now, Ethel, it's nothing to get upset about."

"Upset! When you see our good name dragged through the mud of this miserable Nig-ra trial, how can you not be embarrassed!?"

"But sister, I'm not the only one listed, you know. And after all, I am the registrar."

"I don't care about anyone else—it's you I'm thinking about."

"I'll get along all right," Bernice assured her.

"But, but," sputtered the elder sister, "To be connected with this awful, despicable affair—how can we live it down!?"

Bernice stood before her sister. "Oh, Ethel dear, don't make such a mountain out of a molehill. It's a formality. And people understand that."

"Hmmff!" snorted Ethel. "I'm not so sure the garden club will," she grumbled.

Mic Purvis listened, saliva dripping from the corners of his mouth, his eager eyes wide. He listened intently as Jeff Carlyle, seated on a nail keg, leaned forward and stealthily explained his idea for the men assembled in the back room of Aldo Fenrick's plumbing supply shop.

"It's damn clear. Th' court ain't goin' to do a damn thing. You know what that judge had to say—it's all in th' Gazette. Now, I think th' time's come when we got to take things in our own hands. Now, we've let bygones be bygones fer too long. I say we ought to put a little scare into those sonsabitches and teach 'em a lesson or two. It's time we showed these niggers they cain't run over us and that by God they'd better toe th' line. They'd better damn well stay in their place! Now, what d'ya think, fellas? Are you with me?"

"Damn right!" said a man standing by Fenrick's workbench. "What you got in mind?"

Carlyle grinned. "I figger a bunch of us ought to take a little night ride and raise a little hell around heah..!"

"I'm fer that!" affirmed the man sitting by a pile of copper pipe.

"Good. We ain't done nothin' like this fer a long time. And our niggers have jes' plain forgot. So I say it's 'bout time we took 'em down a notch or two, made 'em remember where they ought to be in this town of ours. Le's drive on down yonder by th' branch on th' other side of Crestview—y'know, wher' a whole bunch of them nigger sharecroppers live-and jes' let 'em know this heah's white man's country!"

"Yeah!"

Purvis felt a fever of excitement as Carlyle outlined his expedition of terror. Life's horizon for the little man was a limited view. Mic Purvis was a weak, lonely man, who needed the company of his cronies at Bobby Ray's Bar and Grill. He drank a lot and never held a job for long. He had worked as a laborer for a construction company, then delivery boy, and most recently as a handy man for several citizens of Crestview. At the moment, he was out of a job.

But as a simple-minded individual, he never seemed to worry. He wandered about the town, slovenly dressed, panhandling for food and drink, always anxious to join the camaraderie of troublemakers who stirred up racial strife. He hated Negroes. He relished a thought that they were beneath him.

"When do we do this?" someone asked.

"Next Tuesday. It'll take that long to round up enough men."

"Ain't we enough?"

Jeff Carlyle replied, "Look, I want a whole bunch of us—th' more th' better—to scare th' hell out of these black bastards!"

"You want us to bring guns?" someone asked.

"No, no—better not," advised Carlyle. "Let's keep it simple. We ain't out to hurt nobody. Jes' burn a few crosses, scare th' shit out o' 'em—so that they know they'd better toe th' mark."

Mic Purvis giggled. He rubbed his rough hands together. He was ready.

Ellison's Dodge swirled into the yard and Joey alighted, looking back at the preacher, who smiled encouragement and nodded a brief farewell.

Then the boy watched as the car moved away, splashing water in the deep, rutted road.

It had cooled off after the heavy rain and Joey noticed dark clouds in the west. It might yet storm tonight, he thought, as he entered the house. He saw his father sitting by the empty fireplace, repairing a leather harness. It was too wet to plow, or otherwise Elijah would have been out breaking ground for the new crop.

Elijah looked up as Joey entered. "How'd it go?"

"Okay, I reckon," Joey answered, shrugging off his suit coat.

"Whut happened?"

The day-long episode had begun early that morning when the Reverend Mortecai Ellison stopped by to pick up Joey for the long ride to the state capital. Attorney Edgar Hall had asked for the Henderson boy to be present at a meeting which he had arranged with NAACP officials.

Joey had been up early and was waiting for Ellison's Dodge as it pulled into the yard. The minister leaned over to open the car door for the young man. "How you doin' this mornin', Joey?"

"Okay."

"Well, we ought to be knowin' a lot more after today," Ellison told him. He explained that they would be discussing courtroom strategy.

"When do we go to court?" Joey asked.

"We don' know yet. They got twenty days to answer th' complaint, I understand. When they do, they'll set a trial date," the reverend replied as he turned onto the highway leading past town toward the state capital.

They rode in silence for awhile. Joey then muttered, "I reckon I won't be makin' it to college this spring.. Or maybe even this summer."

Ellison smiled. "Maybe. But it'll be soon. You can count on that."

They had little else to say during the one-and-a-half hour drive. And as they rode the long miles, Joey viewed a panorama of bleak sharecropper shacks and barren fields along the way. He looked out the misty window of Mortecai Ellison's Dodge, as he thought of life and a reason for him to be doing what he was doing. His mind merged into fantasy and he saw himself in heroic dimensions, remarkably restoring respectability to his race, bridging the gap between whites and blacks, single-handedly building a utopian society which no one had thought possible. And although it was without essence or truth, his imaginings saw a glorious moment when he would be lauded for his boldness and his courage. The dream seemed real. But then, suddenly, the fantasy faded into the sound of a car motor. He was back into the present, sitting beside the Reverend Ellison, who stared ahead at the highway, tight-lipped and silent. At that instant, a familiar fear returned for Joey.

And this anxiety never left him, even after arriving, and followed him up the wooden stairs to the lawyer's office. He heard the heavy breathing of the preacher as they climbed the steps together. And when they entered the attorney's office, Joey recognized the familiar face of Edgar Hall, who, with a broad smile, stepped forward to greet him. C. D. Daniels, state director of the NAACP, also stood to extend a welcoming hand to the Reverend Ellison. There was another familiar face, as well; that of Avery Anderson, the NAACP lawyer from New York, who had half risen from his chair, smiling.

Quite a gathering, thought Joey, and then he noticed another man. He had not moved, this stranger, his lanky frame coiled in his chair. Behind his tortoise-shell glasses were heavy-lidded, sleepy eyes, which gave him a dour, awesome appearance. There was, nevertheless, the hint of a smile below his beaked nose and unobtrusive mustache."

"Pastor Ellison, Joey," said C. D. Daniels, "I'd like you to meet Mr. Thurgood Marshall."

Ellison was obviously impressed, but the name meant little to Joey. The boy, however, understood that the man had to be important and this meeting significant. He sat, jiggling his knees nervously, and looked about him. He saw the crack in the plastered ceiling and the several black-framed photographs on the walls of the office. And he heard them talking, as they began immediately to discuss the impending court action. They seemed to ignore Joey as they spoke of plans and procedures and tactics, often using legal language the boy could not comprehend.

"Obviously, you've made major inroads in our case against the college," said Marshall, "And I feel you're definitely on the right tact."

"I think we have 'em worried, all right," agreed Hall, smiling.

"But we're not there yet," Marshall cautioned, his tone grave and reflective.

Collectively they felt that the court's recognition of the college's inconsistent application of enrollment procedures, particularly the requirement of alumni letters as being occasional and perhaps prejudicial, was something they should pursue. To reinforce their case, it was suggested that they secure—subpoena, if they must—records which might support their accusation that the college had applied a little-used regulation to deny the admission of Joey Henderson. After all, if the admission procedure had not been applicable to all white students, then there was ample reason to believe that its practice in this instance was decidedly prejudicial.

"Much will be made of Joey's motive for attending Crestview State College," said Daniels.

"Of course."

Thurgood Marshall pointed out that it was necessary to prove damaging discrimination regarding Joey's freedom and right to choose for himself the education he deserved. And Marshall cautioned care in the stratagem to be used. For one thing, there were two Negro colleges in the southern and western parts of the state. It would be argued, of course, that these institutions were founded and supported to provide educational opportunities for the Negro race and that there was no need for this young man to enroll in any all-white institution.

"Th' same 'separate but equal' crap," muttered Daniels.

"Precisely," said Marshall, and then he added, "But while we know the fallacy, we've got to do more than simply point it out. We've got to prove it—at least to the satisfaction of the court."

"It seems then," said Hall, thoughtfully, "that Joey's decision to study medicine makes a valid case for attending Crestview. After all, it's th' only institution around here, other than the state university, that offers anything close to what you'd call pre-med training."

"But—is that sufficient cause for him to enter this particular college?" asked Anderson.

"Why not? It's accredited, it's close—and if, indeed, th' administrators of Crestview claim they are not prejudiced, then our young man has every right to qualify as a candidate for admission."

As the lawyers talked, Joey wondered if his decision to become a doctor was too ambitious. It would be difficult to attain, he knew, for his financial dilemma would still prevail.

Yet, he felt he would make a good doctor. He was not squeamish at the sight of blood and had always been present each fall, helping, at hog-killing time. In high school, he made good grades in biology and chemistry, and once, with a friend in the eighth grade, he had even operated on a dead cat, using a razor blade as a scalpel.

The meeting at last ended and the participants stood, content with their plan and their prospects.

But now, Joey's reverie was suddenly erased by the familiar voice of his father. His pa asked again, "Whut happened?"

"Huh?"

"I said, whut happened?"

"Oh, nothin' much, I reckon," said Joey. "Mr. Thurgood Marshall was there."

"Who's he?"

"Some big lawyer with th' N-double A-C-P," answered Joey.

"Hmmff," snorted Elijah, pushing the leather through a metal clasp. He paused, put down the harness, and looked up. "They still goin' ahead with this heah court business?"

"I reckon."

"It's a damn waste of time, I say," muttered his father.

"Maybe, pa, but they don't seem to think so."

Elijah grunted, and picked up his leather harness again.

Joey remembered the resolute faces he had seen that day and, in spite of their steadfast confidence, he could not help but question his own conviction as to how it might turn out. His pa's skepticism did not help. He stared into the empty fireplace and contemplated the passion and heat of public pressure he must soon face, and he wondered if he was really up to it. He wished it to be over soon. Very soon.

CHAPTER 11

It was almost midnight as the men assembled beside an old abandoned textile mill. The brick-crumbling wall of the building was splashed with darting arcs of headlight as vehicles maneuvered into place. Shadowy figures of boisterous participants prowled the perimeter, laughing, shouting, eagerly awaiting the start of their nightly mission.

Mic Purvis climbed into the bed of a pickup truck to settle beside a can of gasoline. He slapped the hand of a buddy and grinned.

"We gonna git black meat tonight!"

The man snorted as they heard others in the back of another truck let out a whoop. The dew-damp, spring night chilled Purvis' body, but he felt exhilaration as the vehicle moved to gather speed. The procession careened through streets of the town and now burned rubber as it raced along the asphalt highway. Mic squinted his eyes against the night wind. He tingled with expectation.

Soon, the line of automobiles and farm trucks swerved onto a rutted, country road, driving at a wild and reckless pace. Then, at length, the lead car slowed and pulled over. Uncertainly, the procession ground to a stop. The still of the night was filled with the sound of idling motors and the babble of men who seemed confused by the delay.

Jeff Carlyle slammed the door of his car and swaggered back, pausing beside each vehicle to give instructions.

"Keep close. Don't wander off. And for God's sake, remember why we're out heah. We ain't out heah to hurt nobody—jes' scare th' livin' shit out of 'em!"

The men nodded, gripping steering wheels or rifle barrels.

Yes, some had not heeded Carlyle's caution. They felt comfortable with firearms. Besides, what better way to show that they really meant business.

"Maybe we could take a pot shot at one or two," suggested one man.

"No!" Carlyle was adamant. "If we start trouble like that, then we're done for. It'll backfire, men. All we want to do is scare 'em, teach 'em that they'd better watch out—or they could be in for big trouble. That's all. That's all we need to do. You hear me, now?"

The men murmured and Carlyle added, "Now, stick close. We're gonna do this together. Jes' you stick close to me."

And with that, he wheeled and marched back to his car with a determined step.

The caravan continued.

By chance, they came onto Abby's house. She was asleep. But the distant din of racing motors and loud yelling aroused her. For several thick moments, she was disoriented. She lay there, listening, unsure of the cacophony which raged outside. Then, a thunderous realization dawned. And she was frightened.

She saw first the flickering light dancing on her window. She quickly leaped from her bed to see outside the evil image of hatred burning brightly in her yard. Beyond the flaming cross, she saw the movement of men. And for one fearful, agonizing moment, she saw again as a little girl her father being thrust into the darkness. She screamed. The horror of the past had revealed itself this terrible night.

The men clamored aboard, intoxicated by their riotous escapade, and the wheels of their conveyances churned dirt as they ran their route over rutted roads from one Negro house to the next. It was now after two in the morning.

To Purvis, it was exciting. They would arrive in wild abandon, shouting, shining spotlights on the gray, silent house, and immediately spring into action. Several men quickly erected a crude cross in the middle of the yard, then dousing it with gasoline and setting it afire. The flames would flare and its brightness illuminated objects around the building—a hayrake, a well house, a hanging tire that was a child's swing—all in white, ghost-like images. And the men would lean against their trucks or cars, staring at the burning cross, laughing obscenely or yelling threats.

And almost as quickly, they were gone—leaving behind the crackling, dying blaze, burnishing the clapboard walls with flickering light, while inside, a family hovered in whimpering fear.

Then, at last, they came to Uncle Nat's place.

"Who lives here?"

"Hell, I don' know. Who gives a damn? It's a darky's house. Let's give him th' works!"

The cross was planted next to the house and Purvis sloshed a pail of gasoline over it. He snickered gleefully as he wheeled the bucket. Much of the liquid splashed against the side of the house. A match was tossed. The cross blazed in brilliant heat and light.

They departed quickly, unaware that their fire had caught the worn, resinous siding of Uncle Nat's house. The commotion outside jarred the old man awake. He heard voices and was annoyed that it could be young boys on a nightly binge. He slowly raised himself from his bed and he became aware of a frightening glare of light in the next room. He heard the crackling, smelled the smoke, felt the heat! His house was on fire!

He searched for his wooden leg, tried frantically to buckle it on, but nervously fumbled it and helplessly saw the artificial limb clatter to the floor. Clutching his walking stick, he struggled toward the door, hopping on one leg. But he lost his balance and fell. Sprawled on the floor, he pitifully raised his head as if to ward off the onrushing tide of flame. He knew he was doomed!

"Oh, Jesus!" he cried.

As the pickup truck bumped along, Mic Purvis and his companions were silent. It was late and they were tired. But they knew it had been a good night. They had set out to strike fear in the Negro neighborhood and their mission had been a success. As Jeff Carlyle had commanded, they had issued a warning and no doubt had convinced them all that they had best maintain a place of subserviency in this white society. Purvis and the men, now weary and content, sat back and pondered the excitement of the evening. It had been a good night.

They were not far down the road when they looked back to see the sky aglow. They were puzzled. Dawn was yet an hour away. Someone muttered, "My, but that's a mighty bright one."

"Yeah," giggled Mic Purvis.

"No, wait," exclaimed the third man in the back of the pickup truck, "That house—it's th' one we were at—it's on fire!"

"By God, I believe you're right."

"Wonder who lived ther'?"

Purvis snickered. "Only a nigger," he said.

The hour was late and Florence McAndrew lay abed, fully awake. Her bedside reading lamp was on, the evening paper by her side. She had just read the unsettling news of the attack on a community of colored residents the previous night, and of the elderly black man who had died in the flames of redneck violence. Florence was worried.

She wistfully watched her bedroom door, awaiting the return of a husband who was working late. She wanted to discuss with him the tragic implications of the event. It concerned her that mob violence could actually occur in Crestview and she wondered what it might mean for the safety of the college and, most especially, her Byron's welfare.

Hearing his footsteps, she sat up in bed. As he entered, she observed that he appeared weary and dispirited. But she saw his eyebrows arch in surprise upon seeing her. "Hi, you still up?" he asked.

"Yes," she answered.

Byron shed his coat and stooped to give her a light kiss upon the cheek.

"You look exhausted," she said.

As he released his tie, he breathed deeply. "Yes..yes, I guess I am. These meetings go on and on. But here now, what are you doing awake at this hour?"

"I couldn't sleep. I waited up for you."

"Well, that's nice, but.." He looked at her.

"Have you seen this?" she asked, raising the newspaper.

"Th' Evening Gazette? Not really. Haven't had time." He sat down on the edge of the bed to pull off his shoes. "Like I said, these meetings are so tiresome. And especially tonight. Everybody's really uptight about this Negro applicant and his litigation." He reached for the newspaper. "Why? Is there something in here you wanted me to see?"

Florence told him, "There's a story about some horrible racial trouble outside of town. Some awful men burned crosses and set fire to several colored houses—even killing one poor old colored man."

"Yes," Byron sighed. "Yes, I heard about that."

"Well, it—distresses me."

"Yes," he conceded, quietly.

"It frightens me to think that if this can happen here and now, what might happen if that young Negro boy is admitted to our college."

He stood up to take his shirt off. "Well, let's not worry about that right now—he hasn't been accepted yet."

"But you know there's a good chance he will be. And if the college has to take him, you know there'll be trouble, serious trouble. This—this article in tonight's newspaper tells us surely that this community will not stand for this young man's intention—not here, not in Crestview. And it worries me to think what might happen—to our college, to us, to this town, to you, Byron..!"

He sat on the bed and leaned over to touch her cheek. "Now, darling, let's not start imagining things that really do not exist. As I said, he hasn't been admitted yet—and should he be, who's to say th' transition will not go smoothly, quietly, without incident."

She turned her face from his hand abruptly. "Don't treat me like a child, Byron." She angled her eyes at him. "You know as well as I do what it'll be like if that Negro actually enters this college.. The people around here will stop at nothing!"

He drew a deep sigh and slowly, wearily, stood up, unbuttoning and removing his shirt. "Well, lawlessness will have to be curbed, for sure. But I think it can be handled."

"Aren't you even a little bit concerned?" she asked.

He turned to face her. "Of course I am! My God, Flo, didn't I try to warn them? I've been concerned for a long time..! But no one listened—so —here we are."

"I hate him for what he's doing," muttered Florence.

"Who, th' boy?" Removing his trousers, he looked at her and his features softened as he said, "That doesn't sound like you, Flo. I'm a little surprised. I always thought we were pretty tolerant."

After a slight pause, she added, "But this is different."

"Different?"

"Oh, you know what I mean. I think he's acting irresponsibly. He should have the sense to know that what he's doing is threatening himself, the college, the community, everyone! And I worry about you and your job." She then muttered, "He's a menace."

"No, my love," said Byron, gently. "No, it's not him. If anything, it's th' blind racial intolerance of the area that's th' real threat. But this is nothing new, and we shall have to deal with it. I—feel we've got to believe that our country, this region even, is growing a little wiser about human relationships." He looked up. "Uh—why are you looking at me that way?"

"Oh, Byron, don't be naive," she said.

Byron nodded. "It may sound like that, but I really mean it. We've got to be optimistic, my love. Bigoted people will have to learn." He looked at his wife and smiled. "And there's never been a more challenging mandate for education than this, my dear."

She saw him retrieve his pajamas from his drawer and move toward the bathroom. Florence of course trusted her husband and wanted very much to believe in his commitment, his intelligence, his ability. But a feeling of foreboding—and confusion—still possessed her. Her natural instinct, of course, had been to empathize with the Negro; yet, seeing so vividly the impending trouble she knew was inevitable, she could not dispel an anxiety which threatened her peace of mind.

Joey Henderson sat down on the porch steps and buried his head in his arms. And he cried. He had tried hard to hold back the tears all through the funeral. Even though his eyes welled with tears during the church eulogy and at the graveside service, he had bravely fought them back. But now, alone at hone, he sat down and let himself go. He sobbed fitfully.

Elijah, coming around the house, heard the boy and stopped abruptly. He stepped back and looked furtively past the corner of the house to see his son bent over, the boy's body trembling with smothered sobs. In that one instant, irrevocably, his heart reached for his young son. But he remained hidden, silent. He wanted to say something, to help, sympathize, to sooth his son's grief. But it was difficult. Not given to such personal empathy, Elijah found the feeling strange and awkward. He turned back.

Joey was all alone with his thoughts, his anguish. And as the afternoon wore on, he felt empty, exhausted. There were no more tears now, only a sense of an unconscionable loss, about which he could do nothing. And it lingered like a bitter taste and made his mouth dry and his throat hurt. Looking off at a sky streaked with the blood and lavender of sunset, he tried to fathom feelings that were painful, confusing, incriminating. Uncle Nat had died at the hands of unscrupulous men, this was certain. But had they not been motivated by recent events? Provoked, possibly, by him? The troublesome thought that he might have been the cause, even indirectly, of this terrible tragedy tortured his mind and compounded his grave despondency. He swallowed hard.

He tried to tell himself that the incident had little to do with him, that it was, of course, a crime created by the bigotry of cruel white people. He told himself that the violence which occurred on that horrible night had been inevitable, that it was the natural consequence of racial hatred which existed in their divisive society. He even tried to rationalize that Uncle Nat had lived a full and useful life, that he could be content with the goodness he had given the world. But such thoughts only affixed a feeling of guilt and made Joey even more aware of his inestimable loss.

That night, at supper, little was said. A pall pervaded the family gathering and Elijah, who had been among the men who had found Nat's charred body, seemed untalkative and unusually distant. Joey hunched over his plate, picking at his food, and the others about the table observed a respectful silence. Only the tempered chatter of the two small boys was heard, but even they seemed to sense a strange, somber atmosphere.

At last, Elijah got up from the table, almost angrily, and stalked out onto the back porch. The boys ran outside to play, for it was a mild March evening. Emma helped her ma with the dishes and Joey sat, mired in his own personal misery.

Time passed and Joey, deciding to go to his room, was about to stand from the table when, suddenly, the back screen door slammed shut and he heard a guttural oath. Elijah brushed past Hannah and the girl and, standing between the kitchen and the table, fixed his eyes on Joey.

"I hope to God you're satisfied, boy..!" he hissed.

Joey, uncertain, startled, sank back in his chair. He looked up at his father.

"What do you mean, pa?"

"You know damn well whut I mean!"

Hannah, looking at her husband's broad back as he loomed over her son, inquired anxiously, "Whut is it, 'Lijah?"

Without looking at her and still staring at Joey, he growled, "You damn well oughta know. It's 'bout Nat."

Joey stammered, "Uncle Nat..?"

"Yeah, damn right—and you!"

"Me?"

"You know damn well whut I'm talkin' about..!" snapped Elijah.

Hannah thought she knew. "Lijah, please.."

"No, th' boy knows. Don' you, Joey? You know damn well that it's all your fault. If it hadn't been that mess you started tryin' to git into thet college wher' you don' belong, Uncle Nat would be alive today..!"

The accusation stung.

"Don' you see it, son? Ther's goin' to be trouble from now on, as long as you keep on doin' whut you're doin'. I said from th' very start there'd be trouble. But you wouldn't listen."

"But pa.." Joey choked, close to tears.

"Lijah!" sobbed Hannah.

He glanced back at his wife. "I know. I know—Joey thought a lot of Uncle Nat—we all did. But that don' change nothin'..!" Facing his son again, he said, "I don' want to be hard on you, son, but you got to damn well know that you cain't go on wit' this notion of your'n. You see whut it did? You see?"

Joey sat, his head bowed. His worst fears had been resurrected, confirmed. He both regretted and resented its implication.

"Oh, 'Lijah.." whimpered his wife. "Joey ain't done nothin' to make whut happened to Uncle Nat happen, you know that."

"Don' you see whut I'm tellin' him, woman? I'm sayin' he's got no right to carry on wit' this crazy idea of his'n! It's got to be stopped now before ther's more trouble!" Elijah shouted. "And there will be!" he emphasized.

Joey's face revealed a sheen of tear-moistened cheeks in the light of the kerosene lamp, as his eyes beseeched his father. He pleaded, "Pa, I didn't do nothin' to Uncle Nat—they did..!"

Elijah looked down at Joey, menacingly. He retorted, "But you damn well started it!"

"But pa—"

"Look, Joey, hold it! I nevah made myself plain before. But I'm tellin' you right now, I allers thought somethin' like this would happen. And still, I nevah thought it'd be—really like this." Elijah looked off as if viewing some veiled memory, and his voice reflected the image he perceived. "When I stepped into whut was left of Uncle Nat's house t'other day—and found his burnt body—and I saw and smelled th' death of him.. Oh, God, I hope I nevah have to see nothin' like that evah ag'in in my life..!"

"Don't say no more, pa," Joey pleaded.

"No, you got to listen," insisted Elijah. "We cain't have nothin' like that happenin' evah ag'in, not here, not now." He eased into a chair next to his son. "You got to see, you got to listen, Joey, it ain't right. You're makin' trouble fer all of us."

Joey mumbled, "I—didn't mean to."

"But that's th' way it is, son," said Elijah. "Now, th' only thing to do now is give it up. You got to see that's th' only thing that makes sense."

There was an instant of silence before Joey raised his eyes and said, quietly, "But really, pa, I—don't think I can."

"You cain't do what?"

"Quit."

"Th' hell you cain't..!"

"It's too late," said Joey.

"Th' hell it is..! You'll do it."

"I gave my promise.. They're countin' on me."

90

"Hell, boy, I'm countin' on you!" Elijah folded his arms defiantly. "Look, Joey, it's th' right thing to do. You got to give it up—fer your sake, fer all of us..!"

"But pa, we're half-way there," Joey insisted. "It's bein' tried in court. We can win!"

"Win what?" Elijah waited for a response and, receiving no immediate reply, asserted, "You'll win yo'self a peck of trouble, that's whut! You got to realize you cain't win—even if you think you do, you don't..!"

"I—know what you're sayin', pa," Joey conceded. "But—you got to believe, pa, it's somethin' that ought to be done. We can do it, I know we can. And it'll mean a lot to all of us."

Elijah unfolded his arms and sat up in his chair. "If you don' make trouble for us, it'll mean a damn sight more. And that's exactly what you're doin'. Look, Joey, ther's no need fer you to stir things up like this. Your ma and me's got to face people 'round heah, and we sure as hell don' want to be shamed by whut our young'ns are doin'." He paused. "It was bad enough wit' Derek." He cleared his throat. "So, tomorrer, you bes' tell that preacher-man that you're quittin', that you're through—that you're not goin' through with this damn fool scheme of his no more. You hear whut I'm sayin'?"

"But pa... "

"Tomorrer, you hear me?"

Joey nodded.

CHAPTER 12

The first evidence of the morning sun illuminated the horizon with its palette of pink and pale magenta, gradually pushing back the dark shroud of night. The mourning dove and bobolink signaled the coming of day and the cottontail scampered between the beanpoles of Hannah's garden.

It had been a restless night. Neither Elijah nor Joey had slept well. They were awake in the early morning hours to hear Hannah moving about preparing breakfast. Perhaps she had not slept well, either.

The two men did not speak as they sat down at the table. And minutes passed with only the clatter of breakfast utensils marring the morning silence. Hannah busied herself in the kitchen. Emma and the boys were not yet up.

At last, Elijah mumbled, "We're goin' to be turnin' ovah that ground down by th' branch today. I think we'll plant cotton ther'."

"Yessuh," Joey answered.

Joey, hunched over his plate, awaited the inevitable order for him to see the Reverend Ellison sometime that day to end the NAACP effort to integrate Crestview State College. He nervously contemplated what he might say to Ellison.. He was not at all sure he could back out, not now, not with the trial in progress. How could he abandon a cause so well conceived and underway? Yet, he could not deny a concern which bothered his father—and him!—that he might yet be the subject of further reprisals, equaling the loss of an Uncle Nat. He felt uneasy, confused, and more than a little uncertain as to what should be done.

Elijah grunted, pushed back from the table and stood up. He stretched and yawned.

"I ain't forgot whut you ought to be doin' today. I said last night you got to talk to that preacher man 'bout quittin' this fool idea of tryin' to git into thet white college. And I meant it. You're goin' to do it like I tol' you, ain't you, Joey?"

"I reckon so, pa."

"Only thing is, I cain't spare you today. We got too damn much work to do, and I need you in th' field. So you can see him tonight, tomorrer fer sure."

Elijah turned to head for the privy out back. Emma and the boys were up now and Hannah tried to maintain order and serve them at the same time. Joey, now deep in thought, wandered out onto the front porch. He stood there, perplexed, watching the growing light glisten the dew on the grass beyond the yard. It was a hard choice, for he knew not how to liberate himself from the responsibility he had undertaken. How could he go back on his word? He remembered his vow before Anderson that he would stick it out. What could he say to Ellison? And what would be his reaction?

Then, he heard it.

The clatter of a car coming up the road. He saw it turn into the curving lane that led to the Henderson house and immediately identified it as a Ford V-8. Joey quickly stepped inside to watch through the front window. He saw it pull to a stop in the front yard and two black men got out slowly. One was slender, the other big and muscular.

The slender one started to walk toward the house, but he stopped when he saw Elijah coming around the house. He seemed to know him, greeting him cordially with "How you doin', 'Lijah?'

"Rufus..! Rufus Rudimeyer—ain't seen you in a coon's age!"

"Been right smart busy, like you, I reckon," Rufus replied.

Rudimeyer was one of the more fortunate blacks who tilled his own tract of land. His farm was located beyond the branch which separated the fields that Elijah sharecropped.

"Oh," said Rufus, "Do you know Obidiah Wesley? Obie farms a piece up th' road from me."

"Howdy," said Obidiah Wesley.

"Pleased to meet you," said Elijah, shaking the big man's hand.

"I know it's kind of early," acknowledged Rufus, "but Obie and me wanted to catch you 'fore you took off for th' fields."

"What's up?" Elijah asked.

"Well, you see, 'Lijah, it's like this—we're—well, sorta upset."

"'Bout whut?"

"About what happened t'other night," stated Rudimeyer.

Obidiah added, "Yeah, you see, we was hit by that bunch of redneck rascals that ran hog wild through our place, burning crosses and scarin' our folk. And thet made us—well, purty damn mad."

Rudimeyer said, "Yes, and well we know why they did it."

It seemed clear to Elijah that their visit concerned his son. He shifted nervously and spit tobacco juice in the sand of his yard. He looked Rudimeyer in the eye. "You don' need to worry none, Rufus. I've had it out wit' my boy and we've done decided whut's right. Joey's goin' to see them people tomorrer to tell 'em he's quittin' this cockeyed scheme of him tryin' to git into thet white college. It was trouble from th' beginnin', but, well, th' boy didn't see that. But I talked to him and—well—he'll be mindin' his own business from now on."

The two men stared at Elijah and, for a moment, there was an awkward silence. Elijah sensed that something was wrong.

Rufus cleared his throat. "I don't think you understand us, 'Lijah." He paused, then said, "We ain't here to ask your boy to quit."

Obidiah Wesley added, "Fact is, we're here to support him in what he's doin'. We wanted to let you know how proud we are of him. We know it takes a lot of gumption."

"You see, 'Lijah," said Rudimeyer, "most of us feel that it's time we all stood up for our rights and not knuckle under to redneck threats like t'other night."

The big man folded his arms and said quietly, "We had a neighborhood meetin' and talked about it. That's why we're here. We want your boy and you to know that we're behind him."

Elijah was speechless. He jammed his fists in the pockets of his faded overalls and thoughtfully stepped off a circle. "I don' know," he muttered. He repeated, "I don' know. Meddlin' into white folk's business ain't a good idea, I'm thinkin'."

"To hell with white folk's business!" snapped Obidiah Wesley.

Rudimeyer, seeing Wesley's anger, stepped in immediately. "All we're sayin', 'Lijah, what your son is doin', my friend, is buckin' the tide and we're here to he'p him."

Elijah spit again and stared down at the brown splotch in the sand. "But it cain't change th' way things are. Th' kind of trouble you and Mr. Wesley faced t'other night will crop up again. Ther's no stoppin' 'em, Rufus. And don't forget, a good man was killed."

"I know..," said Rufus, solemnly.

"But that's th' risk we take," Obidiah insisted. "And ain't it better to take a risk doin' somethin' right for our people, than to give in and do nothing'? We cain't go on hopin' thing will get better. They won't. "

Rudimeyer said, "I know what you're thinkin', 'Lijah, and it's right of you to be a little concerned 'bout your boy. We know th' risk he's takin'. But he's got an organization behind him—and th' law."

Elijah was skeptical. "Th' law's been controlled by white men."

Rufus then said, "Maybe. But you talk it over with him and decide. But be sure to tell him that we're behind him. Tell him that we happen to think that what he's doin' is kinda important."

"You'll tell him for us, won't you, Mr. Henderson?"

Elijah looked at Wesley and nodded.

"Well..!" breathed Rudimeyer. "Reckon we've taken up enough of your time, my friend."

Rufus smiled and shook Elijah's hand. Henderson watched them get into their car, saw the Ford make an arc to enter the lane which led to the road. Elijah looked a long time in the direction of the departing automobile. Then, almost wearily, he clomped onto the porch to enter the house.

"Who was that?" asked Joey.

"Jes' some farmers up th' road," Elijah answered.

"What'd they want?"

Elijah looked at his son. "Nothin' much. Look at th' time! Le's git goin', boy..!"

En route to the stables near the landowner's house, they walked in silence. After awhile, however, Henderson recounted his meeting with the men that morning and reluctantly revealed their conclusion that any action to eradicate segregation was admirable and that Joey's effort was appreciated.

Joey, elated but uncertain, asked, "What—do you think, pa?"

Elijah did not speak for awhile. Then, he muttered, "I don' know."

Later that morning, as Elijah hitched the trace chains to the coupling of his mule's collar, he looked across at Joey on the other side of the mule's neck and muttered, "I still think it's a damn fool thing you're doin'."

It was now a season of beginnings, the promise of new growth, the smell of freshly turned earth, the essence of planting and the pursuit of new life. And Elijah, content with a future so common to his outlook, did not press his son further. Joey accepted the moratorium and awaited developments. The trial date was set and the presiding judge appointed.

Judge Grooms was a tall, sharp angled Southerner with deep set, hollow eyes, and firm convictions. He had been a regimental commander during World War II and, soon after early discharge, returned to the bar, became a superior court judge, and was quickly named to the U.S. District Court. Everyone knew him as a strait-laced jurist who conducted his proceedings with dispatch and efficiency. Partial to the prejudices of the Deep South, he nevertheless tried to take a dispassionate, universal view in the interest of his court deliberations.

The trial date was set for May 18, 1953, some nine weeks away, but the date became doubtful when Edgar Hall issued an immediate appeal to Judge Grooms demanding acquisition of the college's enrollment records. He argued that they were essential to determine the frequency and extent to which the incriminating reference letter rule had been applied. Although Judge Grooms appeared reluctant, he set a hearing for the following week. DeWitt demurred.

The counselors for the college were visibly annoyed as the principals gathered in a courtroom before Judge Grooms. DeWitt argued that the petition was unreasonable, that it would be both cumbersome and expensive, that an assemblage of such data would take an undue amount of time and trouble, and that its provision was unnecessary in view of the fact that the pertinent information could be obtained through direct, sworn testimony at the trial.

"But, your honor," implored Edgar Hall, "it is our contention that these records are absolutely essential to establish culpability on the part of the college regarding its unfair enrollment procedures, and, unless my esteemed colleague has something to hide, this information should be made public. The plaintiff is deserving of these important facts."

"Your honor," spoke Rob DeWitt slowly as he struggled to his feet. "I have already explained that Crestview State College, in it's normal mission of educating our youth, has neither th' time nor th' money to engage in what amounts to nothing more than a fishin' expedition, as my opponent here well knows."

Judge Grooms at first questioned the relevancy of the request, then ultimately decided that the records might be significant and ruled that the defendant should produce enrollment documents for the academic year preceding, both fall and spring semesters, the summer session, and the fall semester recently completed. His order established a deadline of three weeks, or by April 27th, with the expressed hope that the trial might begin as planned the early part of May.

The counsel for the defense protested, arguing that three weeks was too little time to fulfill the court's order, that it was a burden on the resources of the college. But Judge Grooms was adamant—three weeks, only.

After two weeks, however, the college forces requested an extension of time, claiming filing difficulties and an inadequate staff. Judge Grooms granted an additional two weeks, but firmly emphasized that this would be an absolute deadline. The judge, further, continued the trial to provide time for attorneys to review the records and he established a new starting date for Monday, June 8, 1953.

The weeks passed slowly.

Then, on the Monday following the first week of June, the event which had attracted widespread attention, not only in this country but abroad, commenced in a Southern-based U.S. District Court. The media and all involved participants, plus a limited audience of interested citizens assembled for a momentous showdown in the case of Henderson versus officials of Crestview State College. The trial had far-reaching implications. The future of segregation in the South seemed subjugate to its outcome.

Charlie Cartwright had talked with the attorney. And he confided in Eli Hanson. He was disappointed.

"I had rather hoped DeWitt would press th' point of a possible connection with communism. You know, Eli, there's little doubt in my mind that this ridiculous mess is just another example of how we're bein' dangerously undermined by subversive elements. Obviously, th' N-double A-C-P is a communist front organization. We need to nail them on that issue."

Hanson drawled, "Yes, well, I'm sure Rob understands how best to handle this. We'll leave it up to him."

Charlie persisted, "But don't you see, Eli, we have to expose them. That's the surest way to get to the root of th' problem." Hanson looked around him. "Yes, well, we'd better take our seat."

Rob DeWitt watched the black-robed figure of Judge Grooms stride confidently into court to take his place behind the bench. The assistant attorney general for the state then sat and sorted several papers before him. He looked over at the young Negro seated at the plaintiff's table. A defense of the college position should not be too difficult, he surmised.

They began the process of jury selection, wherein a man was asked, "Do you feel any prejudice or animosity toward the Negro?"

"Oh, no, suh," he replied, "They got their rights, and we got ours."

He was dismissed.

Another ventured, "There are, of course, bad colored people, like we got bad white people. And there'll always be. Th' trick is to tell which is which!"

He was accepted.

There were not many peremptory challenges and by mid-afternoon of the second day the jury was set. Then, opening arguments established the parameters of conflict, and the case of Henderson versus B. Tutwiler, registrar, B. McAndrew, president, and the Board of Trustees of Crestview State College, was underway.

Edgar Hall did not waste any time. He was quick to strike at what he considered the defendant's most vulnerable posture. On the morning of the third day, he called Bernice Tutwiler to the stand.

She was nervous, as she arose to move starchly to the front of the courtroom. She was determined this time, however, that she would not be flustered. She took the oath and sat there, eyeing the paunchy midriff of the Negro lawyer as he approached her, smiling.

"For the record, Miss Tutwiler, would you state your position and your responsibilities at Crestview State College."

"I am the registrar."

Edgar eyed her with avid intent.

"And your responsibilities?"

"My job is to receive and process student applications and, once they are admitted to our college, I keep the record of their grades and monitor their progress in meeting the qualifications for graduation," she replied.

"Tell me, Miss Tutwiler, did you alone decide that Mr. Henderson did not meet the standards of entrance at your college?"

"Yes."

Bernice flushed noticeably, for she wondered if she had just told a lie. She had not intended to, of course, and her mind raced forward through circumstances which surrounded the refusal of the boy's application. Although she had officially sent the letter of denial, it had been, after all, a collective decision of the college administration. How could she tell him that?

"I wrote the letter," she explained.

"You—wrote the letter—knowing that your regulation requiring six letters of reference from alumni of Crestview State College would of course be difficult and even impossible for the plaintiff to fulfill.."

"It was the requirement!" asserted Bernice.

"I see. But not always applied in every case, right?"

"I told you before, there are instances when it isn't necessary, when applicants are beyond reproach, when prior knowledge is sufficient to ascertain the applicant's moral and academic character."

"How frequently—or better yet—how *infrequently* has this rule been applied?" asked Edgar Hall.

"Objection!" DeWitt did not even bother to rise, as he added, "That information has already been provided counsel."

"Sustained."

Hall nodded. And then, he said, "Let me put it this way, Miss Tutwiler—having looked over your records for the past year and a half, I cannot find any successful applicant who, as part of his application, found it necessary to submit six letters of reference from alumni of the institution."

Bernice blurted, "That's not true!"

"No?"

Bernice paused. She simply must not allow this man to fluster her. She drew a deep breath. "All candidates for admission at Crestview State College are expected to furnish letters of recommendation."

"But must these letters be from graduates of your college?" Hall inquired.

"Many of them were."

"But not all of them—correct?"

"Most of them."

"Yet, the regulation states specifically that six letters must accompany every application and that each one of these letters of reference must be written by an alumnus of the college. Now, I would remind you, Miss Tutwiler, that you are under oath and I would wish you to explain precisely why it is permissible for some candidates to get around this particular requirement."

"Your honor!" interrupted DeWitt, standing. "Miss Tutwiler has already explained, I believe, the very legitimate rationale for variously interpreting different candidates, as well as the appropriate rules."

The judge said, quietly but firmly, "I rather think that, in the context of this inquiry, it would be helpful for the registrar to explain more fully her guidelines for determining acceptable candidates, so I shall permit her to answer the question. Mr. Hall, would you restate the question for Miss Tutwiler?"

"Thank you, your honor, I will. Miss Tutwiler, please explain why you can be so lenient with some candidates and so strict with others?"

`Bernice glanced at the judge, then at Hall. "I've tried to explain that there are many conditions to be considered in the acceptance of good, promising students. There can be no hard, fast rules, even though there are requirements. We do try to be human in our approach to the selection process. Sometimes, if we feel it warranted, we may waive a particular regulation or—or modify it—according to the circumstances of the person involved."

"Very interesting," mused Edgar Hall. He looked into Bernice's eyes and, cupping his chin thoughtfully, said, "You say there are many conditions which may decide the acceptance or refusal of a candidate.."

"Yes," she answered.

"Would—being a *Negro*—be one of those conditions?"

"Objection!"

Rob DeWitt's shocked, angry voice rang out, and Judge Grooms leaned forward quickly. "Mr. Hall..!"

Hall raised his arms. "I'm sorry, your honor, I'm sorry." DeWitt was furious and assailed the black attorney as being disrespectful of the court's decorum and demeanor.

"I said I was sorry," said Edgar Hall and added, "Your witness."

CHAPTER 13

"Joseph Henderson! Please take the stand..!"

The summons severed the young boy's mind like a scythe. It was a surprise. Edgar Hall knew of course their intention, but there had been no time to prepare his client.

The bailiff held out the Bible to Joey.

"D'you swear to tell th' truth, th' whole truth, and nothin' but th' truth, so help you God?"

Joey mumbled "Yessuh" and, at the bailiff's command "Take a seat and state your name," the young man eased into the heavy wooden chair and muttered, "Joey Henderson."

He nervously glanced up at the black-robed magistrate. Judge Grooms looked stern, but he granted the boy a slight smile before directing his attention to the assistant attorney general for the state who at the moment was moving forward to pose his first question.

"When you applied for admission to Crestview State College, Mr. Henderson, you did understand, I'm sure, that it was a college for white students only?"

"Yessuh."

"Then—might I ask why?"

"Suh?"

"Why did you apply?"

Joey cleared his throat. "I thought maybe if I qualified—"

"But you didn't."

Joey swallowed. "I mean, if my grades were good enough, I figured there might be a possibility that they'd take me in. I was told that I was a good student and I heard it was a good college. And, well, they offered th' kind of courses I wanted."

"And what courses are those?" asked the lawyer.

"Well, you see, sir, I would like some day to be a doctor and—"

"A medical doctor?"

"Yessir."

DeWitt tried to suppress a sardonic grin and, looking upward, assumed a serious demeanor as he suggested, "That's a pretty difficult course of study, isn't it?"

"I—reckon so, sir."

"And you believe you're up to it?"

"I think so—I—well, I hope I am."

DeWitt sidled in front of the witness stand, looking off contemplatively. "And so you thought of Crestview State College as a possible choice—right?"

"Yessir."

"But not your only choice."

"My—best choice," ventured Joey.

"For your information, my friend," said the assistant attorney general, "there are a number of colored institutions here in the South which offer pre-med training. Fisk University in Nashville, for instance, or Morehouse College in Georgia. Perhaps Florida A & M or Dillard College in New Orleans. Ever consider any of these?"

"No, sir."

"Why not?"

"Objection!" interjected Hall. "A leading question with little relevance to this case. Mr. Henderson's options are not germane to th' principal issue in dispute. The significant fact is that Mr. Henderson did apply for admission at Crestview State College, was rejected, and it is to be determined if—!"

Grooms growled, "Please, Mr. Hall, you don't have to belabor the issue before this court. We know why we're here. I would say, however, you do have a point."

"Thank you, sir," said Hall and sat down.

"But your honor!" DeWitt pleaded, "If it pleases th' court, I am only tryin' to ascertain if th' plaintiff has entered into his objective in good faith and with full recognition of its eventuality."

"Well, if there's a substantive point to be made, get on with it," ordered Judge Grooms.

"Yes, your honor." Bob DeWitt then turned to the witness. "Admittedly, Mr. Henderson, this effort of yours to enroll in an all-white institution like Crestview State College obviously took a lot of thought and nerve. In deciding to do this, I'd like to know if you considered all circumstances surrounding the position in which you're placing yourself."

Joey did not answer.

DeWitt continued. "After all, you'd be th' only colored person among an entire campus of *white* people..! Did you not think of that?"

"Yessir, I did, sir," said Joey quietly.

DeWitt crossed his arms and looked at young Henderson. "And yet, you decided to go against tradition and take this unprecedented step." DeWitt looked down, then raised his eyes to pierce the demeanor of his nervous witness. "Or did you?" he asked.

Joey shifted in the big, wooden chair. "Suh?"

"Decide for yourself."

Joey looked puzzled.

"Or did perchance th' N-double A-C-P decide for you!?"

"Objection!"

Judge Grooms peered at Edgar Hall.

The black lawyer stated, "Unfounded assumption and argumentative."

"Sustained."

DeWitt spread his arms as a gesture of helplessness. "But your honor, it's important for th' court to know if th' plaintiff made th' decision on his own volition, or was he unduly—even unlawfully—influenced by others!"

The judge removed his spectacles and with a wide handkerchief polished the lens. "Are you suggesting impropriety?"

"Possibly, your honor."

"The witness may state, under oath, whether or not he was coerced into making his decision."

Rob DeWitt then asked Joey, "Did you understand the question? I am asking you if th' N-double-A-C-P in any way influenced you in making your decision to apply for entrance at Crestview State College?"

Joey paused before he answered. "No, suh, I—I don' think so."

"You don't—*think* so!?"

"They helped me, for they knew I wanted to go to college—but it was my decision, really."

"Why? Why then, Crestview State College?"

Joey cautiously conveyed his thoughts, as he explained, "It's close to home, for one thing. It would help if I was close to home."

"Why is that important?"

Joey answered, "If I had to go off, it would cost more, I figured."

"If money is an issue, what hope have you to pay your tuition here?"

"I don't know. I —"

"Objection!"

Judge Grooms sighed and eyed Edgar Hall.

"Irrelevant."

DeWitt spoke quickly. "If the plaintiff's ambition is a reasonable expectation, then how it is to be achieved is significant and quite pertinent to these proceedings, your honor."

Judge Grooms began to show annoyance. "Mr. DeWitt, you persist in speculating about what the plaintiff might have done. We are dealing only with facts of what has been done and how it relates to the issue involved. Now, we are here to determine if, in seeking acceptance at Crestview State College, the action of the plaintiff is within the bounds of his constitutional right—and, similarly, if the denial of his application has in any way violated those rights."

"Yes, your honor, I understand," said DeWitt. "But I would point out that, given the alternatives, the plaintiff has not been denied his rights, or an opportunity for an education..!"

As the judge was listening to DeWitt, a young man in a gray suit was seen hurrying down the aisle to approach the defendant's table. The judge saw the man lean over to confer with the assistant attorney general.

Judge Grooms gaveled for order. He and Edgar Hall watched as Rob DeWitt listened attentively to what the young man was saying. Apparently he was an assistant from DeWitt's office.

Judge Grooms once more sounded his gavel. "Mr. DeWitt!" snapped the magistrate, angrily. "Can you explain this intrusion and interruption?"

DeWitt turned and slowly walked toward the bench. "I beg your pardon, your honor." As he came closer, he said, "I have just learned of a most shocking and incriminating development which may well terminate this trial."

The judge directed Hall to approach the bench.

The two attorneys moved close as Judge Grooms leaned over to ask, quietly, "Now, what is this all about, Rob?"

DeWitt said, "It has been revealed that th' N-double A-C-P is even more involved than we suspected. I have just found out that this organization is illegally using this young man as a pawn to violate our standing state law of segregation by subsidizing his tuition to attend Crestview State College!"

"But that's not true!" exclaimed Edgar Hall.

The judge muttered, "This is a very serious charge, Mr. DeWitt."

"I know."

Judge Grooms was disturbed. "I hope it can be justified."

"It can, your honor."

"Well, then, I think we'd better discuss this in my chambers." He glanced over at Joey and said, "The witness may step down."

Judge Jeremy Grooms moved behind his huge, highly polished desk, and extracted a cigar from an ornate humidor. With a small knife, he cut the tip and rolled the Havana along his tongue. As his teeth clamped down on the cigar, he muttered, "Have a seat, gentlemen. Let's get to the bottom of this." Then, he seated himself and lit the cigar.

DeWitt said, "I think Edgar here will confirm that what I've heard is of course true."

Hall protested. "I certainly will not, for it isn't true."

"You mean, you deny that a promise was never made to subsidize Joseph Henderson?" asked DeWitt.

"No, I would not deny that. It's just that I think you have your facts wrong. The N-double A-C-P had nothing to do with it."

"But we have th' word of a contributor," DeWitt informed him.

Judge Grooms removed his cigar and leaned forward. "Are you saying that the young man out there was bribed into submitting his application to enroll in this white institution?"

"No, sir, certainly not. Not bribed," Hall replied.

"Edgar, for God's sake, what else is it?" DeWitt demanded.

"The effort to assist the young man was only intended as a means to provide a way for him to attend college, to get an education, to be a doctor, as he said. The Reverend Mortecai Ellison helped raise th' money —not from th' N-double A-C-P, like you say, but from private, interested contributors."

"Ah, but the Reverend Ellison, your honor, happens to head the local Crestview chapter of the N-double A-C-P," pointed out Rob DeWitt, with a triumphant gleam in his eye.

Hall smiled. "The Reverend Ellison also happens to be pastor of th' Singletree Baptist Church, so he'pin' people's not out of th' ordinary for him."

Grooms expended a wisp of blue smoke and asked, "But there was a deal, was there not, encouraging Henderson to enroll in Crestview State College?"

"No, sir, not to 'encourage' him," Hall offered. "Merely to assist him. To apply at Crestview State College was his idea."

"Balderdash!" exclaimed DeWitt. "Who you trying to kid, Edgar? That young man's bein' led around like a yearling with a ring in his nose."

"Gentlemen!" interjected Judge Grooms, "It'll be up to you to prove your position in court. I simply wanted to clarify your contention, Rob. For the N-double A-C-P organization to intervene in this manner would have been highly irregular. According to Edgar here, I gather this is not the case."

"Let me assure you, your honor, that the N-double A-C-P is interested only in the issue of unlawful segregation and the denial of a Negro's rights under the fourteenth amendment, and has not and will not be involved in Mr. Henderson's college expenses or arrangements," stated Edgar Hall.

DeWitt wanted very much to say that there had been a conspiracy, that the NAACP and the young plaintiff were in collusion to violate social principles of the region and the college, with malicious intent even to disrupt the operation and threaten the existence of Crestview State College. He was never so sure, as now, that the boy was not seeking admission in good faith. He wanted to reveal this knowledge to Grooms, but, remembering the charge of the judge to prove it in court, he remained silent.

Judge Grooms ground the end of his cigar into an ashtray and, arising, said, "Well, gentlemen, let's get back in there and get this thing over with."

The jurors were expressionless as the vying attorneys alternated between optimistic exuberance and sober concern. At times, the plaintiff's case appeared convincing, as when Hall exposed the record of several whom had not been required to submit alumni references and whose qualifications were apparently in question. One even dropped out of school.

Seeking confirmation, Edgar Hall, in cross-examining a college official, posed the fact that "These students were, of course, white."

"I—what do you mean?"

"They were not Negroes.."

"Of course not!"

Hall then proceeded to affirm the double standard by which the college apparently operated and emphasized the prejudicial and unfair treatment of the plaintiff. He pointed out that, while there seemed to exist no published policy against Negroes, Crestview State College did indeed advocate and practice discrimination—as proven by the clear examples offered.

Rob DeWitt, in the course of the deliberation, established the premise that it might appear that the college was administering a "double standard," but in fact the instances intimated were not "normal" and that there was no irrefutable proof that bias or bigotry was involved in the admission decisions of Crestview State College.

In their closing arguments, both attorneys maintained their unshakable stance—Hall emphasizing the need for his client to attend an institution which offered the specialized training he sought, that was conveniently nearby for economic necessity, and that this, in his opinion, was the boy's inalienable right, as a free American citizen, to attend the college of his choice. He stated that Joey Henderson's academic qualifications were beyond reproach and that only a technical impediment—a vague regulation not always applied—was being used to prevent the young man from obtaining an education he so justly deserved. According to the black lawyer, racial prejudice was all too clear and that, as decent American citizens, the men of the jury had no choice but to rule in favor of the plaintiff.

The assistant attorney general for the state took a cautious and considered approach in his summing up. He calmly "talked" to the men in the jury box as if he knew them intimately, as if they were neighbors gathered around a pot-bellied stove on a long winter's night. He even cracked a joke or two, even expounding the cowboy-philosophy of Will Rogers: "We're always sayin' let th' law take its course, when we really mean 'Let th' law take our course.'" He then related it to the boy's ill-advised attempt to exploit legal methods to obtain unwarranted goals. He questioned Henderson's ethical intent and personified him as a instrument of the NAACP. DeWitt denied that the college was biased in its practices and maintained the institution's constitutional right to operate in its best interests, including the freedom to apply whatever rules deemed appropriate to regulate the quality and acceptability of students.

"As you men know," drawled DeWitt, "to run a successful business, you have to have th' privilege of making business decisions that you feel are in th' best interests of that business and th' people involved. Now, that's exactly what we have here. Nothin' more. We're talkin' about the right of Crestview State College to enforce its regulations as it sees fit, for th' sake of th' college and all those who attend."

DeWitt walked slowly up and down in front of the jury. Referring to the twelve men before him, he asked, rhetorically, "Who do we have here? A planter, an insurance man, a shoe salesman.. Now, gentlemen, surely there comes a time when you make personal judgments in your respective businesses as regard the interpretation and application of certain principles of operation. Do you not think that a college deserves that same privilege, the freedom to accept on basic principles students who the academicians themselves know will meet th' standards of admission? Of course!"

Judge Grooms instructed the jury, admonishing them to omit from consideration what he termed "a plethora of red herrings" strewn in the path of these proceedings, and to concentrate on the central issue of litigation: whether or not the plaintiff's constitutional rights under the fourteenth amendment had been violated by being wrongfully denied admission to Crestview State College because of his race or color.

The jury shuffled from the box through an open door. Judge Grooms gaveled adjournment. The audience, standing, erupted into speculative chatter, and the lawyers gathered up papers. Joey stood alone. He turned to leave the courtroom with the Reverend Ellison.

CHAPTER 14

During the long weeks of the trial, Joey and the Reverend Mortecai Ellison shared a room in the home of Mrs. Blanche Wolfe, a widow and worker for the state headquarters of the National Association for the Advancement of Colored People. She lived in a brown, two-story house not far from the NAACP offices. She was a stout, congenial woman, who laughed a lot and was always on the go. She had received them graciously without compensation, but warned them that, because of her busy schedule, they would be strictly on their own, especially for meals.

After a long day at the courthouse, Joey and the reverend would usually pick up a hamburger—or, sometimes, simply buy a can of sardines, a box of soda crackers, and several bottles of pop from the corner grocer to eat in their room.

On weekends, Pastor Ellison would drive back to the town of Crestview, where he could fill his pulpit on Sunday and Joey might recount for his family the excruciatingly slow developments of the trial.

Evenings in the state capital were idle and restless for Joey, who would either walk the streets of the urban neighborhood or lie on their double bed, thinking, dreaming, hoping his effort would eventually bring success and happiness. Ellison conversed with him on occasion—reviewing the case and the day's proceedings, or sometimes the minister would reminisce about his life as a boy and as a man of God. But there were many quiet moments as well, moments when the reverend would read his Bible and the young man would ponder an unpredictable future. He wished fervently that this effort would eventually reward him with a life of promise, in which his parents and Abby might share his pride.

With the trial ending in the late afternoon of the fifth day of the week, they now faced a long, anxious evening as they awaited word of the outcome of their case. Hall had told them that it would be impossible to know how long the jury might be sequestered. So he advised them to stay at their rooming house until he telephoned. Then, they were to rush to the courthouse in time for a pronouncement of the verdict.

Now that the trial was over, Joey realized how truly exhausted he was. He sat on the edge of the bed, his head bowed, his back to Ellison. The preacher sat in a cushioned armchair on the other side of the bed, reading the Bible. Minutes passed. Because the boy sat still and quiet, his body slumped, his arms limp, Mortecai Ellison looked at Joey over the rim of his glasses and asked, "Anything wrong, Joey?"

Joey glanced over his shoulder. "No, suh."

"You're awfully quiet tonight."

"Yessuh. I jes' reckon there's nothin' to say."

"No, I suppose not. It's all over, now, and I guess there's nothin' to do but wait."

"Uh-huh, I reckon."

Ellison resumed his reading of the Scriptures. He read silently, but his lips moved. He had not read more than several verses when he heard Joey ask, "How do you think it'll all come out, Pastor Ellison?"

Mortecai looked up and closed the Book, his fingers holding his place. "Jus' like Mr. Hall tol' us—and I think he's right—we can be rightly pleased. I think we won th' case, Joey, I really think we did."

Joey turned and leaned on his elbow. "And maybe it'll mean that I'll be able to go to college, you think?"

"Of course! And soon, now, I'd say..!"

Ellison's optimism stirred a tentative feeling of elation within Joey. For one clear moment, it seemed that all the worry and waiting had been worth it. His wished-for ambition was being decided and soon, if the reverend was right, he would enjoy a triumphant verdict. Yet, doubt still lingered.

"I reckon it depends on that judge, now, don't it?" asked Joey.

"Th' judge? Yes, him and th' jury. But I cain't see them not decidin' for us. And when they do, that judge will prob'bly order th' college to take you in right away."

Joey lay on his back and stared at the ceiling of their room. What if it did happen? An anticipation envisioned the culmination of the campus experience, the awarding of his degree, the completion of a long-sought ambition. Life would have real meaning. He smiled.

He suddenly thought of Abby. He had missed her graduation. And then it occurred to him that, with his acceptance at Crestview State College, Abby might even be able to join him. Why not? How wonderful it would be to have her sharing college life with him—walking the campus, attending class, studying together.

Then, the reverend shifted. He put down his Bible and removed his reading glasses, and he said, "Guess we oughta turn in now, Joey. Better get as much sleep as we can, 'cause we don' know exactly what time they'll be callin'."

"Yessuh," Joey replied as he rolled off the bed and stood up, stretching. "How long do you think th' jury'll take?"

"Hard to say." Then, the minister said, "I think we ought to kneel down by th' side of this bed, now, and pray to th' good Lord to be with that jury, to guide them as they reach a decision, and he'p them understand our cause and what it means to us and to our people."

"Yessuh."

They knelt, each on opposite sides of the bed. And through his squinted eyes, Joey saw the Reverend Ellison clasp his hands and look upward, his eyes closed.

"Oh Lord God our Savior, we thank thee fer your presence during these days of trial, and we beseech thee one more blessin'. If it be thy will, see that justice is done and that your servant heah, Joseph Henderson, receives his just reward.."

Mortecai Ellison droned on, beseeching blessings upon the attorneys, the judge, and even Mrs. Wolfe. He omitted no one. And Joey's mind wandered, imagining moments of idealistic fulfillment to be shared with Abby some sweet day—and then, he heard the reverend arrive at his "amen."

As Joey arose from his knees, a cold shudder passed over his body. "Someone jus' walked over my grave," his mother used to explain it, after experiencing a similar tremor which always caused her to hug herself and smile sheepishly. He never really understood the feeling. Was it a sign of foreboding? He looked anxiously at Ellison, who was getting undressed.

"What if—we lose?" the boy asked.

The minister looked quickly at Joey, pausing as he pulled off his trousers. "Oh, I don' think that'll happen. Not with th' way things been goin'."

"But what if we did?"

Ellison said, "Joey, you mustn't think like that."

111

"But—"

"If we did, why of course there'd be an appeal."

"What then?"

"That's up to th' courts."

The Reverend Ellison saw the concern in Joey's face. He smiled. "We'll jus' have to trust in th' Lord, I reckon," he said, quietly.

Hearing the familiar phrase, an image of Uncle Nat flooded the boy's mind. He saw the old man seated on his cane-bottom chair, the faded denim of his overalls covering his outstretched wooden leg, and the black ebony of a gentle face reflecting a cautious wisdom. He saw the silver light on the white wool of Uncle Nat's head. And in Joey's mind he heard an aged voice and he felt his actual presence. He felt at that instant a sudden sense of sadness.

"Turn out th' light when you're ready," Ellison was saying as he crawled into bed.

After he had undressed, after the light was out, Joey lay still on his side of the double bed and listened to the reverend snoring. As weary as he was, he could not sleep. He tossed and turned restlessly. His mind, going a mile a minute, conceived mosaics of convoluted, confused thoughts, some positive, hopeful, many strange and fearful—all, spawned of recent events. It might have been a dream, for he did doze off sporadically. He thought he heard a telephone ringing, distantly, downstairs. Or was it part of the dream? He then heard footsteps padding up the stairs, a brief moment of silence, then pounding on the door, and Mrs. Wolfe's voice.

"Mr. Ellison, Mr. Ellison! You're wanted on th' telephone!"

Joey leaned over and shook the body beside him. Ellison snorted awake. "Wh—what?"

"It's Mrs. Wolfe..!" whispered Joey.

He heard her. "Mr. Ellison! Are you awake?"

"Uh—yes—yes!"

"They're on th' telephone, Mr. Ellison—can you come down?"

"Uh, yes—yes—I'll be right down..!"

Ellison struggled into his trousers and hurried down, barefooted. As Joey dressed, he heard the muffled voice of Reverend Ellison speaking on the telephone downstairs. This was it. Joey knew that the moment of decision had arrived at last and he wondered what truths would be revealed this night. Again, he felt a shiver run through his body. Was it dread or merely expectation? His lips curled into a half smile as he thought, "Jes' somebody walkin' over my grave."

It was slightly after midnight as they walked into the courtroom. Only a few people were present. They walked down the aisle to where Edgar

Hall and Avery Anderson were waiting, standing, beside the plaintiff's table. Hall saw them and stepped forward to greet them. He told them that he had not expected a verdict so soon—less than eight hours after the conclusion of the trial—and he hardly knew how to interpret the alacrity of the jury's deliberation.

Joey looked over and saw the principals for the college, seemingly self-assured and confident. Dr. Cartwright was standing, with arms crossed, listening as lawyer Hanson was apparently telling a joke. The assistant attorney general was seated, looking up at Hanson. As Hanson finished his joke, they laughed.

The almost empty courtroom seemed a strange and eerie place to Joey, and an old, familiar fear returned and beads of perspiration dotted his forehead. He sat next to Hall and beneath the table he nervously jiggled his knees.

The bailiff opened the court, the judge entered, and the jury filed in slowly. The faces of the jury appeared placid, weary, resigned. And as soon as they were seated, Judge Grooms asked if they had reached a verdict.

The foreman struggled to his feet. "We have, your honor."

He handed a folded slip of paper to the bailiff, who moved quickly to pass it up to the judge. Grooms looked at it for what seemed a long time. Looking over at the jury box, he asked, "What say you?"

"Your honor.." The foreman paused to clear his throat. Then he announced, "We find for—the defense!"

Eli Hanson, beaming, slapped Rob DeWitt on the back. Hall's head slumped dejectedly into his body, as Anderson, tight-lipped, sympathetically laid a hand lightly on Edgar's shoulder. Joey had no fix on his feelings, but to him it seemed as if this obviously was the end to it all.

Yet, it was not the end. In a swift, impromptu meeting, the attending attorneys for young Henderson announced that they would appeal the verdict. Joey was now aware that the struggle would continue, a prospect he did not relish. He left the courthouse feeling weary and downhearted.

CHAPTER 15

Back home, Joey Henderson began to absorb the full meaning of their failure. He looked about his simple surroundings and felt the walls closing in on his life. A longing to lift himself from the lifestyle of his youth had been dealt a disappointing blow.

He pondered how much longer he would have to endure the notoriety of being front and center of this daring endeavor. He had hoped that the struggle would have ended, that he would have been freed of the constant anxiety imposed by his participation. And he wondered if he could withstand the pressure, for the seemingly endless, agonizing pursuit had yielded little promise and the future looked bleak and foreboding. He thought maybe his pa might have been right, after all.

It was now Sunday. For the Hendersons, it was a typical Sabbath. It was church, of course, a chicken dinner, a long, languid afternoon of quiet ease or neighborly visits. It was another hot day. Elijah had removed his Sunday suit and, clad in clean overalls without a shirt, lay back on a blanketed bench beneath an old chinaberry tree. Hannah had tidied up the kitchen and left, dressed in her Sunday finery, to visit an elderly woman up the road. Joey, in blue jeans and a green shirt, fanned himself in the doorway and thought of Abby. He would be seeing her soon.

It had been arranged at church that morning. During the service, he had watched her as she sat with her family, across and a few pews from him. Once, while singing a hymn, she had turned to look at him and he had smiled at her. After the benediction, his eyes followed her as she arose and moved slowly toward the exit. He saw her pause now and again to exchange greetings or respond to friendly remarks.

Joey, in the opposite aisle, could not catch her attention. He was caught in a clot of worshippers who insisted on casual socializing and idle conversation. Managing to free himself at last, he arrived at the door, hastily shook the parson's hand and, leaping from the church stoop, executed giant strides to intercept Abby before she reached the family Ford. They talked. She told him she would be happy to see him that afternoon.

Now, as he approached her house, he saw Jonathan, Abby's older brother, sitting on the porch steps eating watermelon. Deep in the shadows of the porch sat two men. He recognized Horace, Abby's stepfather, who with Abby's elderly uncle was also eating watermelon and spitting the seeds over the banister.

Joey never liked Horace—possibly because Abby too was not fond of him. Remembering her own father with genuine affection, she could not accept him warmly as the paternal leader of their family. She refused to call him "papa"; instead, called him by name and treated him with indifference. Their estrangement was reciprocal, for he never treated her kindly. To Joey, he was a cold, unapproachable man.

As Joey came near the house, Jonathan looked up. "Hi, Joey. Whut's up?"

"Nothin', really. Jes' come over to see Abby."

Jonathan wiped his mouth with his sleeve, leaned back and called, "Joey's heah!"

The aged uncle, in a shrill, crackly voice, asked, "Is thet th' Henderson boy..?"

Jonathan shouted, "Yep, it's him, Uncle Tyme..I"

Uncle Tyme learned forward, squinting. "You sure have growed, boy!"

Joey ignored the remark and when the elderly uncle asked if he had been working, young Henderson answered affirmatively.

"He's workin' all right," muttered Horace. "Workin' to git himself into a peck o' trouble, messin' around wit' that ther' white man's college."

"Yeah, they kinda took your number in court, didn't they?" grinned Jonathan.

"Yeah, I guess," admitted Joey, meekly.

Uncle Tyme ignored the reference and asked, "You he'pin' yo' pa?"

"Yessuh."

"That's good. He needs yo' he'p, y'know."

"Yessuh, I know."

"I rec'lect," recalled Uncle Tyme, "when me and yo' pa broke thet new ground down by th' old Magnum Swamp. But I 'spect yo' were too young to remember. Lord, 'Lijah was somethin'..! He was plowin wit' an old brown mule, so strong it took two o' us to hold him..." He chuckled. "Yo' shoulda seen how thet mule tore into those stumps and roots, so hard it almost knocked him to th' ground..."

Joey was no longer listening. At that moment, he saw her standing in the doorway. Even in the dim light of the porch, Abby looked radiant. She stood there, trim, in a blue cotton dress, looking down at him. He watched her from the bottom of the porch steps. He longed to get her away, alone, away from the house. His smile reached up to her.

"Be back after awhile," she said lightly, as she skipped down the steps to join Joey and walk ahead of him.

"Preachin's tonight, Abby!" Horace reminded her in a loud voice, but she gave no hint of hearing.

The azure sky held a hot sun, its brilliance creating a sheen on the dark blades of the full-grown corn. They walked beneath its tasseled height and followed a narrow path to the main road. He still smarted at the snide remarks Horace and Jonathan had made about his effort to enter Crestview State College. He hoped Abby would be a little more sympathetic, helpful, for he so desperately needed encouragement and advice. The long months of disappointment had weakened his resolve and for the first time failure seemed imminent. He wanted very much to talk with Abby, to receive her solace, her sense of equilibrium, her understanding. But how? He knew her feeling, so how could he broach the subject?

He did not have to. She did it for him. "Too bad it turned out th' way it did," she said.

"Oh, th' trial, you mean?"

"Yes."

"Yeah, I thought we had a chance."

"So, what happens now?" she asked.

"It goes on, I reckon. Th' lawyers filed an appeal-—only—-I worry that it's takin' so long. And when it's over, all of this may not work out," he said, glumly.

They walked on in silence for a way.

"What if they turn you down ag'in, Joey?"

He looked at her and shrugged. "I don't know."

"Will you go away, git a job maybe, or will you stay here and work on your papa's farm?"

116

He took a deep breath. "I don' honestly know, Abby." In truth, without an achievement of his goal, he could not bring himself to consider other options. "Why?" he asked. "Why do you want to know?"

"Oh, I don' know.."

They had reached the road.

"I figgered that if you went away, I'd—jes'—miss you, that's all!" said Abby quickly as she rushed ahead up the grassy slope onto the yellow clay road.

Now, they were walking silently, apart, down the dusty, country road, its brick-colored swath curving to disappear behind towering trees of pine. In the distance, they saw a wisp of smoke curling from the flue of a curing barn, set in a sunlit field of wilting tobacco. They left the road to follow in single file a familiar, yet little traveled path through the woods.

Abby walked ahead of Joey. At length, she heard him say, "I'm sick of waitin', Abby. I never thought it'd be like this. I knew it wouldn't be easy, but—"

At his pause, Abby asked, "What are you going to do?"

"I don't know. I had hoped they'd work it out."

Glancing over her shoulder, Abby said, "At least you tried."

His white eyes rolled heavenward. "Yeah," he breathed. "I tried."

Then, he voiced anger as he asserted, "But it ain't right. They oughtn't be able to do this to me—to us—to all of us."

She stopped and faced him. "It'll be all right, honey—don' you see? Maybe it's for th' best."

"Naw," he muttered, disdainfully. "Nothin's good about it, if things stand as they are, if I don't git to go to college."

"But you will; I'm sure you will—one day."

He looked off, his jaw set. "But this was my chance—to do somethin' more than jes' git an education. I hate what they're doin' to us. Ever'time I think about it, it gits my goat. Who's to tell us, 'cause we're black, you ain't worth nothin', you don' deserve nothin', you don' git nothin'..! How long can we live like that?"

"It's—I'm afraid that's th' way things are, Joey," Abby said softly.

"But it don't have to be, Abby," snarled the young man. "Somebody's got to do somethin'."

Abby looked up at him. "Maybe. But it don't have to be you. Why have you got to risk your life for all this?"

"But Abby, darlin', I gave them my word. They're depending on me."

"I know, but—if it's for the best, you ought to quit."

"I cain't—we're almost there."

"Joey, you know as well as I do, they'll never let you in that college."

He held a limb for her to pass.

"But what if they did?"

Abby refused to parry with his persistence. They walked on. The wooded terrain sloped and followed beechwood and sweet gum down by a narrow, winding stream they called the "crick." The couple walked along its bank and saw the tiny tributary trickle into little rapids, sequined by the sun, then widen at other points into placid pools, where beetle bugs and flitting dragonflies marred its mirror surface. They paused a moment to gaze upon its wrinkled reflection of umber hues and green foliage. Joey picked up a stick and tossed it into the water, watching it bob among the expanding ripples. Abby leaned against the slanting trunk of a fallen tree.

"So nice and peaceful here," whispered the girl.

"Yeah."

He moved closer to her.

"You know, Abby, during the trial I kept thinking about you. I thought that if we did win th' case, it'd be possible fer you and me to go to college together."

"You mean—to that college?"

"Crestview, sure."

"Oh, no.."

"Why not?"

She shuddered and, hugging herself with crossed arms, shook her head slowly and said, "I'd be too scared."

"But why? If we won, it'd be all right. It'd mean colored people could enroll. They'd have to take me, and they'd have to take you, too. There'd be no problem. And think what it'd be like, you and me in th' same college, th' same class—th' two of us!"

Abby leaned forward to stand with her back to Joey. There was a pause before she quietly replied, "Only—you didn't win, Joey."

"I know," he said, sadly. "Not right now, but if.."

She turned to him. "I don't understand you, Joey.. Why do you feel so bound to these men, especially now that you know it's no use. You said you would do it, and you did—you tried—but now it's over. But they want you to keep on, and on, until one day ther's goin' to be a heap of trouble, and you're goin' to be in the middle of it all. Joey, somebody's goin' to git hurt real bad. And it won't be them. Don't you see?"

He recognized the truth of Abby's remarks. No longer could he dismiss her litany of concern. He had to listen.

"But what can I do?" he asked.

She looked into his eyes. "Jes'—give it up, Joey."

"But how?"

"Oh, Joey, jes' tell 'em that you've decided that—" She stopped, aware of the heresy of her suggestion. She looked away. "—That you don't want to go to college."

"But that ain't so," the young man maintained.

"I know, I know. But you can tell 'em that anyway."

Abby moved nearer and took his arm. "Don' you see, Joey, honey? If you can git out of this mess, now, maybe you'll find a way—to go someplace to college—to a Negro college—where they'll take you, where—you belong."

He winced. The phrase *where you belong* struck him full square and he felt the bitter abrasiveness of its meaning. And although Abby had intended it only as innocent advice, he recoiled at the offensiveness of a white man's cliche.

He wanted to rebuke her, yet he saw in her sincerity a simple devotion that defied his feeling of moral indignation. He bit his lip to restrain himself and focused the conversation on her.

"Ain't you goin' to college?" he asked.

"I—I don' think so," she replied.

"Why not?"

"Oh, too much to do 'round home, I reckon. Besides, I ain't as smart as you are."

"Shhhaw..!" he scoffed. "You'd study circles 'round me—you always did, and you know it!"

Their conversation was lighter now, exulting in a melange of experiences and memories the young couple shared. They became so engrossed that they were not even conscious of a summer cloud that came closer, until, suddenly, it was casting its shadow on the sylvan scene. The trees grew luminescent against a slate-gray sky. And then, Joey and Abby heard the rumble of thunder in the distance.

He smelled the rain and taking her hand, he tugged her after him. They ran through underbrush, as sapling limbs swiped at her blue cotton skirt. Her trim pistoning legs pounded the humus floor in the race to escape a downpour. But it was too late! Already, a clatter of drops sprinkled the leaves and, like open stops of an organ, ascended into a crescendo of rushing rain. They ran, recklessly, and at last reached the road.

Joey shouted, "Look! A barn! Let's go!"

So they dashed over ditches and through fields, splashing through the gray mirage of mist to arrive at length at the shelter. Laughingly, they embraced and—they kissed.

It was an impetuous moment.

119

Abby, having reached the haven of the overhanging shed, giggling giddily and out of breath, had whirled quickly, her damp skirt spiraling about her thighs. Joey had rushed in to scoop her up in strong arms and swung her around. She squealed. They were both laughing as he set her down. He held her closely, their faces a breath apart, and slowly, inexorably, their exultation dissolved into a stilled mask of intimacy. He lowered his face to her and, without hesitancy, she accepted his lips.

For both, it was time eternal. They were transfixed in a passion that erased all sound, all senses, all being.

Gradually, she became aware of the world and the rain drumming on the tin roof, the rivulet of spatter beneath the eave, the cool, dank air against her skin. She pulled away from Joey and, moving to a column post of the shelter, looked out at the falling rain. She hugged herself, as if chilled.

Joey, momentarily stunned by his emotion, gazed at the girl's back, measuring the curve of her body, seeing the silhouette of her legs through the cotton skirt, feeling an urge within his groin. Drawn by her image of sexuality, he eased over to her and tenderly encircled her waist. She leaned back against his cheek.

"Ever wonder 'bout us?" she whispered.

"Yeah," he breathed. "Like now." He nuzzled her and then he heard himself saying, as if from afar, "Abby, I want to be with you."

"You are with me," she answered, quietly.

"No, I mean—in bed with you."

"Joey!"

Her reproach was followed with "please!" as she extricated herself from his arms.

"Aw, c'mon, Abby. I meant no harm."

She had not been offended. And although she sensed Joey's embarrassment, she too shared his chagrin at having responded to that tingle of desire, the temptation, the need. At the moment, she hated the rigidity of her religious upbringing which made it difficult to do what passion dictated. It would have been so easy. An abandoned barn, a soothing rain, a serene Sunday afternoon—everything to assure privacy and encourage the fulfillment of lustful thoughts. For one brief moment, she wondered if she had been too hasty. She released a heavy, nervous sigh, which exuded both her humiliation and her regret at having denied herself the experience. She truly loved this man and would have gladly sacrificed her chastity for his sake.

She solemnly looked at the slanting rain and said, "Looks like it's never goin' to let up."

120

The afternoon waned as they waited for a lull, but the showers continued unrelentingly. At last, Abby broke the heavy silence. "Joey, I think we'd better go."

"But it's still rainin'."

"I know, but it don' seem like it's evah goin' to quit. And it's gittin' late."

He agreed. "Yeah, sure looks that way."

"It's late now," she emphasized. "Mama and Horace'll be settin' off fer church for sure—and I 'spect they's wonderin' 'bout me."

Joey seemed reluctant. "You sure? It's rainin' hard."

"I don' want to stay here."

He took a deep breath. "Okay. Let's go."

So, they left their shelter to shuffle through the slime of the field and pick their way between the puddles of the road. They walked steadily but unhurriedly. Being already wet through, they resigned themselves to the discomfort and misery and trudged on without talking. Abby occasionally slipped or stumbled, but Joey held fast to her arm and guided her along the treacherous clay road.

It was well after six o'clock when they saw the house. It was dark and still in the gathering gloom. For a moment, it looked windowless without lights. They ran the few remaining yards to reach it, clamoring up the porch steps to pause breathlessly before the screen door.

Joey heaved to catch his breath. "Looks like—like they've gone already."

Abby nodded. She kicked off her mud-caked loafers. "I'll light a lamp," she said. "C'mon in."

"I cain't."

She was holding the door. "Why not?"

"I'm muddy."

"Take your shoes off," she told him.

The screen door slammed behind her and Abby disappeared into the darkness of the room. Joey, balancing on one leg like a pelican, struggled to remove his shoes. He then stepped inside to stand, feeling the rain water drip from his jeans onto his bare feet. He saw light in the kitchen. Abby finally approached him, her face lit by the flickering glow of the two kerosene lamps she held, one in each hand. She handed one to Joey. Looking up into his glistening black face, she said, with a wry smile, "You look like a drowned rat."

He grinned. "You don' look so slick yourself."

She laughed. "Guess not. Well, we'd bes' git out of these heah wet clothes. You wait heah," she instructed, "I'll git a pair of Jonathan's overalls fer you."

He stopped her. "Abby?"

She turned.

"Maybe I'd better be gittin' home," he said.

"In this storm? You can wait a little while to see if it lightens up a bit. And right now, you bes' change, or you'll catch a death of cold."

And then she was away, walking across the room with the flickering lamplight casting dancing shadows about her. Holding the other kerosene lamp at arm's length, Joey watched her as she moved through a door into another room. He put his lamp on a table nearby and looked around him. A finer house than his, for sure—roomier, better furnished, neater perhaps. He noted how well Abby's stepfather had provided for them. But then, Horace was not a sharecropper. He was a mechanic.

Abby returned to toss a pair of faded, clean overalls at Joey. "Heah," she said, "now you can git out of them wet clothes. I 'm goin' in my room to change."

Joey, clutching the crumpled denims, watched her go. He watched her, saw her, even after the door closed behind her. For he had memorized her figure, her face, her dimpled smile, her warmth, her lips. And he felt urgently a need for her, looking for a long time at the closed door.

Slowly, he unbuttoned his shirt and shrugged out of the damp garment, dropping it on a chair. He stood there, looking at the door, feeling the moistness of his chest with unsteady fingers. He then moved ever so slowly toward the door, stopped, and studied its panels. He started to call her name, but no sound came from his parted lips. He nervously reached for the doorknob and twisted it quietly. The door eased open. He peered around it.

She was standing, nude, by the dresser. One leg was raised, the foot resting on the bed, as she dried herself with a towel. Suddenly aware of his presence, she straightened quickly and gasped.

"Joey..!"

She frantically tried to cover herself with the towel, her face showing shock, vexation, disappointment.

"I ... I 'm sorry," he stammered.

He stood immobile. And, clutching the towel to her, she watched with strange disbelief and detachment as the apparition appeared nearer, for he was not standing still, or leaving, but moving toward her. She wanted to cry out, to scream, to shout stop, go back, get out—yet, it seemed an abstraction, an unfocused dream, and she was bedazed and tongue-tied. She watched, hypnotically.

He hesitated and, with a vague, uncertain gesture, he motioned for her to come to him. Curiously, she did. But then, she stopped suddenly and he took the final step to close her into his arms. Their lips crushed and, as her hands released the towel, her arms reached around his naked shoulders to hug him tightly. The towel held, suspended between them.

She felt the hungry depth of his love as he pulled her greedily against his pelvic hardness, gripping the rounded, fleshy cheeks of her exposed body. They both were lost in this moment of ecstasy, but then, suddenly, she forced herself from him, pushing herself frantically from his bare chest with an urgency of alarm. Her face had changed. Her eyes were wide and pleading.

"No...no...!" she quaked.

His face had changed too. He gripped her arms and slowly, determinedly, forced her against the bed. She fell backward upon the purple counterpane, openly exposed to him. He encompassed her nakedness, his eyes fixed on the dark areolas of her breasts and following the curve of her young body to the patch of pubic hair. She made no effort to cover herself; instead, averted her face, covering it with her arm. He started to unbuckle his belt in order to lower his wet jeans. But, looking down upon her, he saw her abdomen heaving in a quick, erratic, undulating rhythm. She was sobbing. And beneath her arm, he saw a tortured mouth and a trickle of tears.

He turned, flushed, and felt his way from the room. At the door, he risked one more glance at the body on the bed. Then, outside, he leaned against the door, closed his eyes, and gritted his teeth in a seizure of abject humiliation. He felt the shame of having abused the honor of the one he deeply cherished.

He remained there, breathing heavily.

At last, he walked wearily to a chair and slumped into it. He leaned over, holding his stomach. His groin ached.

He sat there for some time before hearing the click of her doorknob and, turning, saw her emerge from the room. She was wearing a thin, flowered robe, which she held together at the neck. He could not face her, so he quickly looked away and lowered his eyes to stare at the floor. He heard her bare feet approaching him.

Abby came up behind him and put her arms around him. She leaned over his shoulder and placed her cheek against his. He smelled her gentle fragrance.

"I'm ...sorry...!" he said, his voice choking.

She did not speak. She could only hold him and sway with him, side to side, as one might gentle a baby. Her eyes brimmed with tears, as she vowed to herself that one day she would give herself willingly, fully, passionately, unfettered by conscience. And it would be a gift of total love. And it would be only to this man.

CHAPTER 16

One week after Labor Day, the United States Court of Appeals for the Fifth District convened in Atlanta. At the time, Joey Henderson was home harvesting hay on his father's farm. As he wielded his pitchfork, he thought of Edgar Hall and wondered how he might be faring at this advanced level of judicial review. Hall, even backed by the professional expertise of the NAACP, was after all an ordinary trial lawyer. And Joey knew that his future was inextricably assigned to Hall's success.

He paused to take a deep breath. It had been a long, agonizing struggle, to be sure, and many times he had speculated as to the value of the endeavor. It seemed so futile and at times so helplessly frustrating. "What chance have I got?" he spoke aloud. For he considered the appellate procedure, at best, a very long shot. He did not understand completely this process of litigation, but he did recognize the reality that there was only a remote chance of ever reversing the lower court's decision. And the more he thought about it, the more depressed and despondent he became.

He thought of Abby. He saw again her body, exposed, vulnerable—and there stirred within him the arousal of mixed emotions. He chided himself at having permitted his conscience to interfere with a natural biological urge. Yet, he respected her. He loved her.

He leaned on his pitchfork and, as he thought of her, he felt an itch within his groin. He tried to castrate the memory, to concentrate on developments which might significantly affect his life.

If he could but realize his goal, to be a responsible professional man of medicine, it mattered little if he could not achieve the NAACP objective. And yet, there was no choice. The two intentions were irrevocably linked.

He had to break down the color barrier at Crestview State College, if he was to receive an opportunity to fulfill his ambition. He wondered how Hall was doing.

Hall took his place first at the lectern before Appellate Judges McIntire, Petranoff, and Shelton, who, black robed and imposing in appearance, looked down from the bench with studied resolve. They had read the briefs filed by the contesting parties and familiarized themselves with the trial record, and now they were ready to listen to oral arguments which might lend a dimension that could either alter or corroborate the lower court's decision.

Judge Petranoff indicated to Hall, "You may begin, sir. You will have forty-five minutes for your presentation."

"Your honor, I would like to reserve five minutes of my time for a rebuttal."

"Granted."

Edgar Hall, bolstered by the knowledge and judicial cunning of the two NAACP attorneys supporting him, addressed the court and quickly summarized the salient points upon which the plaintiff had entered an appeal. He emphasized the issue of a procedure which he felt had been unfairly implemented by the institution to deny the plaintiff his constitutional rights. He assailed the motive of the college as prejudicial and he pointed out the injustice of the trial's verdict.

"The technicality which the attorney for the defense insists was the sole cause for denying the plaintiff's acceptance at Crestview State College, was, I submit, only a pretext to cover the real reason for refusing him. They did not want him as a student at this institution because he was a man of color!" declared Edgar Hall, the fat jowls of his face quivering from the stress of emphatic emotion.

Judge McIntyre asked, "Do you have proof of that allegation?"

Hall cleared his throat. "Your honor, the plaintiff has established adequate proof of his qualifications to enter college, a fact I believe my opponent would equally acknowledge. He met every standard required of prospective students, except one. And even that was met by the provision of the requisite number of references attesting to his good character and academic potential. The mere fact that these letters were not from graduates of Crestview—which obviously implies persons who are white—was the only basis for denying the plaintiff's application. Now, since this rule has been applied infrequently and without consistency, it is important to note that only in this incident of a black applicant has it ever been administered with such strict interpretation. Your honor, the conclusion is obvious. This is clearly racial discrimination."

For his turn, Rob DeWitt arose slowly and walked calmly to the lectern and, spreading several notes before him, looked up at the three judges. "Sirs, I will probably not take the full quota of my time, for you have the record before you and I do not see the need to prolong these proceedings. I simply want to reemphasize the validity of our position." He glanced at the plaintiff's table; then, looking at the judges, said, "I can understand the desperation of my colleague, but the truth of the matter is that it's impossible to link Crestview State College with any action of bias or deliberate distrust. There does not exist a policy, written or otherwise, which denies the acceptance of qualified Negro students. And the failure of the plaintiff to gain acceptance was due only to his failure to complete the specified application procedure to the satisfaction of the registrar and officials of the college. Nothing more. And I might add, your honor, it is the right of the institution to determine the qualifications of its student body."

Judge Shelton spoke up. "You are referring, of course, to that admission requirement which compels prospective students to submit six letters from former graduates of the institution, are you not?"

"Yes, that, and other regulations, which have been established to maintain certain standards of acceptance."

"I understand," said Judge Shelton. "But it is of course this requirement of references which is the sticking point."

"Yes, sir, it may seem so," DeWitt replied. "But it has been on the books for some time."

Judge Shelton: "But are we given to understand that this particular entrance requirement is not expected of all candidates who enroll at Crestview State College?"

DeWitt answered, "Why, no, your honor, and we have explained why.."

Shelton: "Yes, yes, I know. But if you can show leniency in some cases, why not here?"

DeWitt tried to smile. "Mr. Henderson, your honor, was an unknown," the attorney explained. "Much the same as countless other students who are also required to comply with this rule. It is important to understand, sir, that the purpose of this requirement is to obtain valid information to adequately identify the character and capability of any particular candidate for enrollment."

"But it is my understanding that the candidate did submit references attesting to character and academic ability," interjected Judge Petranoff.

"But sir, they were not satisfactory," said DeWitt.

"Why not?"

DeWitt explained, "None of the letters were from people known to the college as reliable, trustworthy respondents. It is for this reason, sirs, that in the case of doubtful candidates, such as Mr. Henderson, the college admission authorities deem it significant to have in hand certificates of character from loyal alumni."

Petranoff mused, "Well, isn't that stretching the point a bit too far?"

"Sir?"

"Most reference letters are written by respectable people, whether known or not," said Justice Petranoff. "Moreover, it is my feeling that any regulation not equally applied runs a risk of being discriminatory."

Shelton: "And it appears to me that if this rule is not effected for all, then the same element of human understanding—which the college obviously offers to many candidates—could certainly be extended to the plaintiff."

DeWitt did not answer immediately and Judge McIntyre declared, "Especially since the plaintiff is black and incapable of complying completely with what is essentially a demand predisposed to white students. Unless, of course, it was the intention of the college to preclude Negro students."

"Of course not!" DeWitt declared. "There is absolutely no evidence, as borne out in the trial itself, that Crestview State College is guilty of prejudicial judgment in the refusal of the plaintiff's application for enrollment. As we have pointed out many times, it was simply the failure of the candidate to meet the enrollment standards of the institution. And sirs—it should be accepted that a college does have the right to regulate itself, within the parameters of the state educational system. It is our state law..!"

In Hall's five minute rebuttal, he decried the fallacy of Crestview College's pretense and pleaded for an understanding of the need to abide by the Constitution and to restore the rights of the citizen, whether he be black or white.

When the hearing ended, Rob DeWitt sauntered over to the plaintiff's table to shake Hall's hand. He nodded at Thurgood Marshall and Anderson, saying, "Good case, gentlemen."

Even as he walked away, the Negro attorneys sensed the certainty in his demeanor. And they could not help but wonder of God's will in a white man's world.

Young Henderson was informed that it would take weeks, even months, before a ruling could be rendered by the appellate court. And although his lawyer and Ellison appeared hopeful, there was a gnawing doubt in Joey's mind that the lower court's verdict would ever be reversed. And he fully understood that even a favorable decision might not bring immediate closure to the process. Expected delays and legal maneuvering could extend the struggle almost indefinitely. Now frustrated and filled with angry impatience, Joey saw his life suspended in a vacuum of uncertainty.

He concluded he could no longer wait.

On a dark October night, Joey Henderson stood uneasily on Abby's porch. Having reached a difficult decision, he was anxious to tell her first. He knocked, stepped back and watched for a stirring in the house.

He heard footsteps and then the front door opened. She stood there, her slim figure silhouetted against the lamplight of the room. The illumination behind her cast its faint glow on the young visitor standing there and she recognized him.

"Joey..!"

"Abby, I—I've got to see you.."

"Come in!"

"No," he said, quietly, his tone grave, thoughtful. "I bes' not. I —maybe we could talk out here. Could you come outside fer a minute or two?"

"Joey, is there somethin' wrong?" she asked.

"Oh no, I—I'd jus' like to talk to you, that's all. Cain't we take a little walk or somethin', jus'—out in th' yard?"

She stared at him standing there, then, glancing over her shoulder she said, "Jes' a minute. I'll get a sweater."

In a moment she returned, struggling into a cardigan. He helped her. And together, they descended the steps into the yard. She carried a flashlight, which cast an eerie, erratic circle of light before them as they strolled slowly from the house.

"What is it, Joey?"

There was a pause before he answered. Then, he said, simply, "I reckon you've been right—all along."

He felt her puzzled gaze as he continued. "It's been a long time comin', I know—but I finally got it through my thick skull that nothing's goin' to

129

come of all this. I mean, it's now 1953. It's been a long time—over a year-and-a-half since I graduated from high school, and Abby, look at me! I ain't done nothin'! No school, no job, no nothin'! I cain't wait around no longer."

She felt the hurting in his voice. She understood, of course, but what could she say?

"God knows, I tried to bide my time, to wait it out, to do what they wanted me to do—but dammit, Abby, I cain't go on like this forever. It's no use! I've—Well—I've decided. Abby, I'm leavin'..!"

"Leaving?"

"I'm gittin' out."

"You mean—quittin'?"

"I'm givin' up. It's all over anyway, I reckon," he said, bitterly.

"Oh, Joey..!" There was empathy in her utterance, yet it hardly disguised her relief. For him it was an agonizing moment, she knew, but she could not help but be pleased that it would soon be over.

Then she heard him say, "Yeah, I've given it a lot of thought. I'm leavin' town."

This option surprised her. She looked at him. And for one dreadful moment, she felt a fear of losing him.

"But—why?" she asked.

He said, simply, "I got to git a job—somewhere. I got to git some money. I cain't wait around here, doin' nothing.. Besides, I don' think I want to face 'em."

"You're not telling 'em?"

"Naw, why should I?" said Joey. "They'd only try to talk me out of it. And I don' want be bickerin' with them lawyers. I'm tired of messing around. It's like you said it'd be. It was trouble from the start."

"I know how you feel, honey, but—you don't have to leave town, do you?"

"Yeah, Abby, 'fraid so. I got to git a job."

"But I thought you was he'pin' out on your pa's farm..!"

"That don't bring no money. And I need money."

"For what?" she asked.

He turned to her. "Look, Abby, I said I was quittin'—but that don' mean I'm giving up going to college, of maybe even someday bein' a doctor. I know it's a long haul, but I want to keep on until it's done. I've got to. I cain't go on spinning my wheels for nothing!"

They took a few more steps and Abby at last asked, quietly, "When are you leavin'?"

"Tomorrow afternoon, on th' two o'clock bus."

Her heart skipped. She had not expected a departure so soon. "So soon?"

Her voice was weak, wistful, and her intonation unveiled disbelief and disappointment. She reached for his arm as they strolled. And when he did not speak, she asked, "Wher'll you be goin'?"

"Upstate. Fairfield. It's a good size city, I hear, lots of big plants up there. Maybe I can git a job." And when Abby did not comment, he explained, "I got a cousin who lives up there. I 'll stay with him and his family 'til I can git on my feet."

"What do your folks say?" Abby wanted to know.

"I ain't told them yet."

"Oh?"

"I—well, I wanted you to know first," he explained. Her grip tightened as she acknowledged his thoughtfulness.

The beam of the flashlight splashed against the clapboard siding of an outhouse building. Abby moved toward it and opened the door. It creaked wide and she stepped over the threshold onto the concrete floor.

Her flashlight revealed a storehouse of old furniture and bric-a-brac. There was an old chiffonier, a small round table, a broken rocking chair, a shelf lined with Mason jars and stacks of bottles and assorted dishes. Against the wall leaned iron bedsteads, the coiled metal springs, and a mattress. Abby reached up to a shelf and set the flashlight on its end, its beam encompassing cobwebbed rafters and casting a glow of indirect lighting about them and the room. Then, she turned and paused, her shadowy figure before him.

"I'm—goin' to miss you," she said, softly.

He tried to smile and then, suddenly, she was in his arms. His strong arms enclosed her, eagerly, and he felt the warmth of her cheek. "Abby, Abby," he moaned.

It would have been so easy to pull down the mattress, to have it flop to the floor in a cloud of dust, to be the bed upon which they could consummate their sexual hunger. As he held her, Joey eased his hand beneath her cardigan and cupped a blouse-covered breast. There was a sharp intake of breath as Abby felt the pressure of his hand, but she did not resist. She even pressed forward, her breath quickening, and for a moment it seemed as if she had acceded to this suggestive act. But then, she pushed away.

"No, Joey, please," she whispered.

He appeared bewildered.

And fearful that she might have offended him, Abby hastily stammered, "I—I want to, Joey, darlin', really I do, only—"

131

"But Abby," he groaned. "I love you!"

And he heard her whisper passionately, "Oh Joey, darlin', I know, I know—only—"

"Only what?"

She paused before she said, "We cain't—not—not 'til it's right."

"I can make it right," he insisted.

"I know." she said.

He took her words to mean her willingness, and he released her to reach for the mattress. Her hand stopped him.

"No," she said quietly. "You know what I mean. We got to be married first."

"But—I'm leaving, Abby," he said, hoping she might recant and submit.

"If you don't go tomorrow," Abby told him, "we could then git married and—and we could go away together..!"

He shook his head. "No—no, I don't think that'd work."

"Why not?"

"Like I told you, Abby, I have no job, I don't have no money. We cain't git married like that." He pulled her to him. "But I need you, little girl; God, I want you..!"

"I know," she sobbed and he felt her tears.

He almost wanted to force her to yield to his uninhibited lust, to succumb to an overwhelming passion which seemed to encompass both of them.

Instead, he drew a deep breath. "I bes' go now," he said. "But I'll be back for you, Abby, honey, I'll be coming back..!"

"But—what am I going to do?" she asked.

He said, "Jes' think of me. Pray for me. Keep on bein' my girl."

He retrieved the flashlight for her. He leaned over and kissed her, then turned and stepped through the door into the night. And she stifled a sob as she watched him leave.

CHAPTER 17

The mud-spattered, rust spotted Dodge swerved from the red clay road into the rutted lane leading to the Henderson house. The face of the Reverend Mortecai Ellison behind the wheel was solemn and intense. He was deeply concerned about the future of his local NAACP chapter and wanted to inform Joey of a very important meeting he had arranged.

Worried that an inordinate delay by the courts in reaching a decision might cause many followers to lose faith and perhaps defect, he had asked Edgar Hall to speak to the group to explain the time-consuming and complicated legal procedure. With the meeting set, Ellison had notified the members and wished of course for the presence of Joey Henderson.

As his car approached the house, he saw Hannah on the porch. Reverend Ellison cut the ignition and got out. Walking slowly toward her, he tipped his hat.

"Good afternoon, Miz. Henderson!"

She nodded.

"I come to speak to your boy, Joey."

"Joey ain't heah," she said.

The reverend stood in the yard with his hands on his hips. He looked around at the fall scenery. "Nice day, ain't it," he said, casually. Then he asked, "When you 'spectin' Joey back?"

"We ain't."

"You—I—don't understand."

"He's gone."

"Gone? Where?"

"Joey left town last week."

"Left—town—?" Uncertain as to her meaning, Ellison took a few faltering steps toward the porch. He looked up at Hannah, anxiously. "What—what do you mean?"

"He jes' up and left. He talked to his pa and me. And he said—well, he tol' us that he was tired of waitin' fer somethin' to happen, and—well, he was goin' to go off and git a job someplace."

"Where? Where did he say he was goin'?" demanded Ellison, his voice strident with concern.

Before the woman could answer, Elijah appeared in the darkened doorway behind her and muttered, "Who you talkin' to?"

Hannah turned. "Pastor Ellison."

Her husband brushed past her and, not bothering to use the steps, he jumped off the porch and in one stride faced the visitor. "Whut you be wantin', Pastor Ellison?"

"I come to see Joey," said Ellison.

"He ain't heah."

"I know, Miz. Henderson jes' tol' me. She said he left town."

"That's right."

"But where? Where'd he go?"

Elijah leaned over to spit. He was dipping snuff. He eyed the minister. "Didn't th' boy talk to you?"

"No!" Ellison was visibly upset.

"I reckon he should have," acknowledged Elijah, his voice low, guttural. "He talked to us. He tol' us whut he was goin' do. He said he wanted no more of this college business and that he was givin' it up and leavin' town."

"But why? Where did he say he was goin'?"

Elijah hesitated before he asked, "Why do you want to know?"

"Look, Mr. Henderson," insisted Ellison, "your boy's important to us! He's important to ever'thing we're tryin' to do. He's got to be here. We need him!"

"Well, he's gone," said Elijah simply.

"But he cain't! He promised!"

Elijah shrugged.

Ellison was exasperated. "He cain't quit now—after all this, with us so close. And it ain't over yet!" The minister reached out to lay his hand on Elijah's arm. "Please, Mr. Henderson, he's got to come back. He's got to see it through. Too many people have done too much not to give us a chance. And you know what it means, for Joey, for all of us!"

"Yeah—you're damn right I know," snarled the stocky farmer, moving away from the hand. "It means a helluva lot of trouble fer all of us, and 'specially my boy!"

"Now, wait a minute—"

"No, you wait one damn minute—and hear me out. You got our boy into all this.. And I want to tell you right now, it ain't right." Elijah spit. "Now, I know, he said he'd do it, and I reckon he can be blamed.. But by God, it was a crazy damn thing to do, and I tol' him so all along. And I can tell you, Pastor Ellison, ther' ain't been a day when his ma and me ain't worried about whut was goin' to happen. And plenty's happened, all right..It's riled up ever' redneck in th' county, and on that one night—remember?—families fer miles around heah were skeered to death.. Uncle Nat, that God-fearin' man ever'body liked, got killed. All because of this damn idee of your'n that we can step over th' traces with white folks and git away with it. Well, let me tell you, preacher-man, I'm glad Joey had th' good common sense to see whut was happenin'. And he had th' guts to quit, and I'm glad. I'm glad."

Ellison looked at the man calmly. "I—know how you feel, Mr. Henderson."

"Do you now?" retorted Elijah.

"I've thought th' same thing—many times," said Ellison. "And I've prayed and prayed to th' good Lord to see us through, safely, and with good feelings that one day soon th' wolf shall dwell with th' lamb, that th' colored man shall one fine day mix with his white brothers, and that there be peace and understanding in our neighborhood and th' world."

Elijah grimaced. Just like a preacher, he thought, always sermonizing with idle quotes or parables from the Bible. But how can one preach away the reality of threat and fear, and the formidable dominance of a Caucasian universe? He was not about to sacrifice his son on an altar of idealism or future dreams.

"Don' expect Joey to be a part of it," Elijah told him.

"But we need him," said Ellison, quietly.

"I cain't he'p it, Reverend. Joey made it plain. He ain't comin' back."

"But..." Ellison paused, then looking Elijah in the eye, asked, "But won't you tell me where th' boy's at? I'd like to talk to him, even if—"

Elijah stated flatly, "I'm 'fraid I cain't he'p you, Reverend."

"Please."

Elijah turned to spit before dismissing Ellison's request. "No. My boy's done with all this."

"Please?"

"Look, pastor, I hope God forgives you fer all th' trouble you've done us. And don' be askin' me to give up my son jes' fer th' sake of whut you thinks bes' for yo'self..!"

That was it. Joey's pa turned and wearily ascended the steps of the porch, leaving the minister standing, speechless.

As Mortecai drove home, he felt despondent, helpless, confused. He saw his plan, his hope, crumbling, and he did not know what to do. He began to hate more and more the unconscionable stranglehold which white people held on the souls and minds of his race. But what he deprecated most was the cowardice and concession of his own people, who would fail to try, who would flinch and submit.

"Damn! "

The expletive expressed Rob DeWitt's shock at reading the judgment just handed down by the United States Court of Appeals. It had been seven weeks since the hearing and, to his astonishment and dismay, he was now being informed that the decision had been turned back to the District Court. He simply could not believe it. He read it again.

PER CURIUM

> Brought by appellee for himself and all Negroes similarly situated, against the administrators of Crestview State College, charging that they had denied him the equal protection of the laws guaranteed to him under the Fourteenth Amendment, by having refused to admit him to Crestview State College solely on account of his race and color, the suit was for a declaratory judgment and an injunction.
>
> The trial by jury, although dealing with the issues and findings of fact, did not, in the opinion of the Appellate Court, properly assess the effect of the college requirement of six alumni letters as being an unreasonable impediment denying the admission of the plaintiff. The Court takes judicial notice of the fact that the separation of the races is legally mandated by the state and that it is not customary for Negroes and whites to mix socially or to attend the same public or private educational institutions, and that therefore, by reasons of this presently existing social pattern, the opportunities for the average Negro

*to become personally acquainted with the average white person,
and particularly with the alumni of a white educational
institution, are necessarily limited.*

*To the extent, therefore, that the state institution, Crestview
State College, relied on the requirement of alumni certificates
and recommendations, Henderson was discriminated against
in violation of the equal protection clause of the Fourteenth
Amendment and was unlawfully denied admission to the
college.*

In conclusion, the decision remanded the case to the trial court for a
declaratory judgment and injunction.

DeWitt finished reading the document for the third time.

"Damn!"

DeWitt met with his superior, the attorney general of the state, and
also the governor. They were disturbed. The reversal as conceded by the
court of appeals was a surprising turn of events. It meant that the merits
of the case would have to be reviewed again and, despite an appellate
denial, there was hope that the college position might yet be advanced as
a reasonable resolve.

DeWitt, however, was reminded that it was a political imperative that
the suit be won at all costs, even if it had to be settled by the Supreme
Court of the United States. Under no circumstances, they declared, must
the state's educational system endure the onus of having racially-mixed
enrollments.

With this order in mind, DeWitt had his secretary put through a call
to President Byron McAndrew.

As Pastor Ellison entered the lawyer's office, a little winded, Edgar
Hall looked up, beaming. "Mortecai..! I been tryin' to reach you!"

Ellison gasped for breath. He had hurried up the stairs too fast. "I—I
must of been on th' road."

"Sit down, sit down. You look a little peaked. But just wait 'til I tell
you th' news..!"

Ellison wiped his brow.

"We jus' received th' appellate opinion and Ellison my friend, we
made it..! The justices considered the six alumni letter-requirement of the
college as discriminatory. They sent th' case back to the lower court for

137

an injunction. Mortecai, we did one helluva job and I think we've been successful..!"

The minister seemed benumbed as he stared blankly at the exuberant man seated at the desk.

The excitement in Edgar's face now faded. "Why—what's wrong, Mortecai?"

"He—Joey—ain't here no more," Ellison explained. Hall was puzzled. "What do you mean?"

The reverend swallowed. "He's gone."

"You mean our young man? Gone, you say? Where?"

"I don' know. They say he took a bus. Left town."

"For how long?"

"For good," was the weak response from the minister.

Edgar Hall struggled from behind his desk, his jowls quivering, his eyes enlarged by Reverend Ellison's unexpected revelation. "You know of course where he's at, I hope..!"

Mortecai Ellison shook his head. "I tried to find out, but th' Hendersons won't tell me.."

"Why?"

"I dunno," said Ellison, nervously. "I tried to get Joey's pa to tell me, but he won't say nothin'. He only said that his boy had decided it was no use, that he was wastin' his time, that he was tired o' waitin'."

"Waitin' for what?"

"For somethin' to happen, I reckon."

"But somethin' *has* happened!" exclaimed Hall, impatiently.

Mortecai Ellison nodded. "Yeah, but I don't reckon he knew."

Edgar Hall turned on his heel and stalked behind his desk, pounding his fist into his hand. "Goddam idiot! That jus' goes to show you—you cain't depend on kids like that. Why couldn't he wait? If he'd only let us know what he's thinkin', we could he'p him decide what's best. No, he's got to high-tail it off just when th' action's goin' our way." Hall slumped into his chair. "Hell, Ellison, do you know what this court decision means?"

Ellison thought he knew.

"I know there's still one more fence to jump, but th' lower court's got to agree to a reversal in judgment. Th' appellate court specifically noted that th' college policy was discriminatory. I think our chances are good for overcoming the original verdict." The attorney then shook his head slowly.

"But for this upcoming trial, if we cain't produce a plaintiff, we're up a creek. Do you understand?"

The minister understood.

The lawyer emphasized, "It's important, Ellison. Joey's got to be here!"

The Reverend Mortecai Ellison saw his responsibility and he now felt a little ill, uncertain, as if his life had been ripped from under him, leaving him bereft, bewildered, his goal unattained.

"What are we goin' to do?" Ellison weakly asked.

"You got to find him. Bring him back," stated Hall firmly.

At a hastily called meeting with the president of the college and Hanson, the advising attorney, DeWitt apprised them of the situation. He tried to be optimistic. The initial verdict might yet hold, he told them, if the alumni letter requirement for admission could be eliminated. "This, after all, was the principal crux of the appellate disapproval.

"Isn't this a little too late?" McAndrew ventured.

"I think not, Mac. If we comply by eliminating this issue, it might have some bearing on the outcome."

The president was puzzled. "But this was the basis of our defense," he insisted. "What are we to do now?"

DeWitt said, "At the moment we'll simply await the decision of the District Court. We can hope that the previous verdict will be sustained."

"And if it doesn't?"

"Well, Mac, we'll go forward with an appeal to the United States Supreme Court. If we do not receive a favorable verdict from the lower court, I will issue a writ of certiorari to gain a hearing before the High Court."

Hanson pondered the possibility. "But—what are th' chances, Rob? After all, they take only—what?—about two percent of th' cases brought before the court."

"About that. But I think we have a good chance," DeWitt answered. "Civil rights cases have occupied their docket quite a bit of late. I don't think they'll overlook th' significant implications of this dispute."

"But—what argument can we offer to support our case?" asked McAndrew.

DeWitt answered, "We'll have to find new rationale for refusing the young man."

With an edge of impatience, the president inquired, "And what might that be?"

DeWitt rubbed his chin, thoughtfully. "I think we need to delve into the boy's past. If we can uncover a few family skeletons, that might well justify our procedural action. You see, that would shift the emphasis of the case to character rather than color—then, we can vindicate our position."

President McAndrew nervously drummed his fingers on the table surface. His face was clouded in doubt. He sighed. "I don't know," he muttered, "I have a bad feeling about this."

Hanson said, "But I believe DeWitt has a point. We can't very well abandon what has been laid out as our principal argument. If we can find misconduct in young Henderson's background, that would certainly justify our concern."

It was quite obvious that the president was unhappy. The long, tense delay in settling the legal controversy had taken its toll. The college, the community, both the faculty and students had been affected by the protracted procedure of court litigation. And now, irked by what seemed a last-minute tactic of furtive deceit, Byron McAndrew found the struggle weak and tasteless.

"I hope to God this ends soon," he breathed.

Both DeWitt and Hanson looked at Byron as he sat, head bowed, an abject image of disillusionment.

DeWitt quietly said, "We all do."

So the meeting ended.

Meanwhile, a man moved inconspicuously through the town of Crestview, visiting the colored school, talking with community leaders, interviewing neighbors of the Henderson boy, under the guise of a national reporter. He was told that no one had seen the young man for several weeks.

CHAPTER 18

Dr. Charles Cartwright was offended. He had not been included in the president's called strategy session to determine a feasible college course following the appellate contravention. And he felt strongly that he should have been involved

. After all, who knew best the personality and tradition of their institution? He was the "old guard," who knew most intimately the Morton mystique. His advice would have been invaluable.

Charlie did not like McAndrew's approach to the crisis they faced. He felt the man was too free, too broad-minded, and he feared that Mac might yet give in to what Cartwright conceived a communist-inspired NAACP. And he was worried.

So now, he stood on the white, wide banister-encircled porch of Henry Hartley's home. And he was quite uneasy. Charlie had debated a long time before deciding to consult with the senior member of the Crestview State College board of trustees. And as he paused before the huge front door, he was not at all sure that it was the proper thing to do.

He lifted the heavy brass door knocker.

His mind mulled the consequences. After all, he was Mac's assistant and as such was expected to be loyal, trustworthy, and faithful. But he told himself that his allegiance to the college was far more important, that he could not stand by and witness the extinction of acknowledged social values of his beloved institution.

He took a deep breath. Old man Hartley himself opened the door. He seemed peculiarly cordial as he welcomed the college official. Charlie had telephoned earlier to find out if it would be convenient to stop by his home to discuss a rather delicate matter. And now, standing at the threshold, Charlie saw a colored woman enter the spacious foyer from a hall door behind the elderly man. She stopped when she saw Hartley.

"Oh, I see you got th' do'," she said.

"Yes, Albina, I got it."

She shrugged and retreated slowly as Hartley ushered Cartwright across the entranceway into the library. He muttered, "That woman. She's deafer'n I am..!"

The house smelled of furniture polish. Charlie was taken by the charm of the large, ante-bellum home with its clutter of antiques and bric-a-brac. Particularly striking was the winding staircase which curved upward to the second floor. And as he entered the library with the old man, Cartwright admired the elaborate tiers of book shelves crowded with dusty volumes and extending to the height of a very high ceiling. Henry Hartley tottered in, supporting himself on a cane, and indicated an overstuffed leather chair.

"Have a seat, Charlie."

Hartley took the seat opposite. But only after the old man had slowly, gingerly settled into his chair did Dr. Cartwright sit. Cartwright said, distinctly, politely, "I'm happy, sir, that you were able to see me today."

"Yeah, well, what's up?"

The familiar Hartley, thought Charlie; curt, decisive, to the point. No nonsense. And for one brief moment, the presidential assistant began to wonder if coming to see this man had really been wise. After all, he did not know how this crusty, old paragon might take his actions, or even if he might possibly report this breach of confidence to President McAndrew himself. As he was trying to decide, he became aware of someone else in the room and he looked up. It was Albina.

"Would you gent'men like a cup of tea?" she asked.

"That'd be nice," said Cartwright, smiling.

"Haw!" snorted Hartley, "I reckon ol' Charlie heah would like a little somethin' more'n that, somethin' that'll put hair on his chest—like a little bourbon, eh, Charlie?"

"No, that's all right. Tea would be fine."

"Sure?"

"Tea will be fine."

"Well, all right," conceded Hartley, and added, "Jus' make mine whiskey with a little branch water, Albina."

142

Albina turned away, but over her shoulder she informed him, "You'll git tea, too, suh, 'cause you know whut Dr. Ogden tol' you..!"

She was gone before Hartley could retort, and he grumbled, "I got to git shed o' that woman, 'fore she's th' death of me. I don't see how I tolerate such an uppity nigger in my house."

Charlie chuckled. "Because she takes pretty good care of you, I would imagine."

"Shaw!" snorted the old man; then, shaking his head, his eyes twinkled. "I reckon, I reckon."

Hartley fondled his cane and looked Cartwright straight in the eye. "Now. You said you wanted to see me."

Cartwright looked down at the Persian carpet beneath his feet. He coughed once, nervously.

"I didn't really want to bother you, sir, but—to tell you the truth, Mr. Hartley, I'm a little concerned."

"About what? Th' college?"

"Yes, sir."

"What about it?"

"This Nig-ra case has been a great strain on us all," Charlie began. "So it's kind of difficult to draw a bead on th' real problem."

"Come on, Charlie, you prob'ly know th' problem better'n anyone else—spit it out."

"Well.." Cartwright took a deep breath and began again. "Well, I'm—that is, we're—just a little worried about th' way this Nig-ra affair is being handled. Mostly, we're bothered by th' way certain people are thinkin'."

He paused and Hartley urged him on.

"I personally would like to see a more determined direction in our resistance to this threat. We can't afford to give in to this Nig-ra action. We got to fight it every inch of th' way. Now, it's sad, but I don't think that kind of feeling is present—not now—and that worries me."

"Are you talkin' about th' lawyers?"

"Oh, no, sir, I think they're doin' their best."

"Who then?"

Charlie hesitated. His mind rapidly searched for the right words. "I just feel that we should have more decisive leadership—"

He felt Hartley's penetrating eyes as he heard the old man ask, "From your president?"

Cartwright shifted, uncomfortably. "Well…"

"You talkin' about McAndrew?"

"Well—yes, but—"

"Nevah liked th' sonuvabitch."

143

Cartwright swallowed. Although Hartley's acidity was not unexpected, his candor came triphammer hard and Charlie immediately felt a tremor of unease. Be careful, he told himself. Watch what you say.

"It's not easy, mind you, and I'm surely not envious of Mac's job. He's kind of caught between a rock and a hard place. But I do wish he'd be a little more vocal and resolute in his response to this problem. I want to see him openly advocate our all-white policy."

"And he doesn't?"

"No, sir, not exactly, not in so many words. To tell you th' truth, it's hard to know what he thinks. And that has us a little worried. We're afraid he's goin' to give in without much of a fight. And that would be a disaster. All th' things this fine school was meant to be—well, it just wouldn't be anymore. And that'd—and that'd be a shame."

Hartley's knarled fingers nervously kneaded the polished head of his cane. His jaw set, as he muttered, "You don't mean to tell me that he wants to see niggers in our college..?"

"I—I don't know how to answer that, really," Cartwright replied.

"Why not?"

Charlie looked at Henry Hartley and was connected with the old man's piercing eyes. "Well, it's just that he won't vigorously oppose this dastardly action. He—I tell you, sir, he hasn't convinced us that he is strongly in favor of maintaining the college in th' way that it was founded. Or at least he doesn't confirm th' same feelings that we have."

"What are you goin' to do about it, then?" asked Hartley.

A brief, nervous smile flickered across Cartwright's face and quickly faded. "I—don't know, exactly," he said, uncertainly. "I thought it'd be best to let you know something about th' situation—you bein' a board member with a long-time understanding and love for th' institution. And I thought it would be good to know your thinking on th' matter, sir."

The old man leaned back in his chair. "Hmmf..! Well, I don't know... This news about Mac's attitude toward niggers, I find, is quite interestin', and a little disturbing, though not surprisin'." Then he added, "I don't like it. I don't like it one damn bit."

"I—sort of hate to tell you this, sir, but th' thing that worries me most is somethin' that I'm afraid President McAndrew is mixed up in."

"Yeah? And what's that?"

"I think he's—well, I think he may be—a communist sympathizer," whispered Cartwright.

"A communist!?"

"Yes, sir. I've tried to warn President McAndrew—a number of times, in fact—about th' clear and present danger of a communist conspiracy,"

And he has refused to conduct any investigations or organize any preventive measures to protect Crestview State College. Now, his failure to take an active role in combating this menace would lead one to believe that he's part of th' persuasion. I—honest to God, I hate to say it, but I fear he's part of th' threat facing Crestview State College..!"

Hartley glared at the man across from him. "Do—do you know what you're sayin'?"

"Yes, sir, I—I think I do. And it's only because of my concern for th' college that I dare suggest these things. But sir, it's obvious. It's affected his thinking—like in th' Nig-ra case, for instance."

"And what do you mean by that?" growled Hartley.

"Sir," said Cartwright, "I don't know whether you know it or not, but th' N-double A-C-P is a front organization of th' Communist Party. It's an established fact! And you can be certain that they're behind this colored boy tryin' to get into Crestview."

Hartley stared at his visitor coldly, observing Cartwright's passion and concern. Hartley suddenly straightened. Albina had entered the room with a tray. She set the tea pot and cups on a table between them. The conversation ceased until she had left the library. The old man, with a shaky hand, poured a cup of tea and eased it across the table toward Charles Cartwright.

"Go on," he said.

"I've tried to talk to Mac, repeatedly, about this whole business," continued Charlie, "but he absolutely refuses to take it seriously. And if somethin' isn't done—and soon—-th' N-double A-C-P's goin' to take over th' college and ever'thing that we've worked for—that Jasper Morton, God rest his soul, worked for—all that will be down th' drain."

Hartley rubbed his chin. This talk of the NAACP taking over, the likelihood of racial integration, and the imminent disintegration of hallowed Southern traditions galled the old man and his features hardened. All he could say was "Damn niggers."

"I tried to warn him, as I said, but he seems headstrong in doin' it his way, which means doin' nothin', look th' other way, or worse—accept this Nig-ra intrusion as somethin' normal, as somethin' ordained, as somethin'—that he actually *wants...!*"

"Bastard!"

Charlie shook his head. "I've—really, honest to God, I've tried to be loyal. I've tried to help and advise him, and, well, give him th' benefit of my experience at Crestview. But—truly—it's frustratin'. He's not a Jasper Morton, you know."

"No. No, that's for sure. That much is damn obvious." The old man rubbed his chin, thoughtfully. "What do you think we ought to do?"

"I—really don't know. I was jus' worried, and I thought you ought to know-. Bein' involved with th' college for so long. I thought you might have somethin' to suggest."

"Maybe we oughta get rid of th' sonuvabitch." The solution was simple, sudden, and not atypical of the old man.

Cartwright smiled, nervously. "Well—I don't know about that," he said, slowly, weakly.

"Well, what else?" snapped the old man.

"But who'd—replace him?"

Hartley observed his visitor with icy, examining eyes. "Now—now, that's a big problem, ain't it?" The old man pondered the prospect. "It'd have to be somebody who knows th' college, its traditions, its priorities and standards, its long-respected Southern heritage. My God, we cain't afford to buy a pig in a poke no more on th' basis of big degrees and a pseudo-Southern background. I want somebody in there I know, somebody we can depend on!"

Charlie's plastic smile quivered. The old man was talking about him, he thought, and he trembled in a moment of anticipation. Could Hartley and the board consider him as McAndrew's successor? But wait, he cautioned, be prudent, be not obvious or self-serving. Be hard to get. Be careful.

"But I don't think there's time," Charlie warned. "Crestview State College is teeterin' on th' edge of disaster. And while we cain't do much to change th' course of events we're now facing, by God we can be determined to resist, in all our power, th' evil influences threatenin' us."

"You're meanin' this—communist conspiracy you're talkin' about."

"That—and this colored encroachment."

Henry Hartley did not know how to measure this man or his problem. He knew of course of the nation-wide panic over communism, but he did not put much stock in the frantic concerns being perpetuated by many people, some in high places. Oh, he acknowledged the potential evil, but he could not somehow see a threat to this quiet Southern region, so innocently apart from worldly concerns. He did, however, feel strongly about the forfeiture of the long-heralded Southern ideals of white supremacy. And since Charlie Cartwright had linked the two issues, he felt compelled to listen.

"Well, Charlie—I'm glad you told me these things," said Hartley. "I think we ought to look into it."

Dr. Charles Cartwright had not known what to expect from this tete-a-tete with Crestview's venerable trustee. He was there because he feared

146

for the future of the college and he had boldly decided that only Henry Hartley could influence or alter that which he perceived as a pernicious course. Yet, he knew he was running a risk. But no matter. It was the noble thing to do, he believed. Loyalty to Crestview Sate College transcended any duty he owed to this man McAndrew.

Cartwright suggested, "We can't afford to wait until it's too late."

"I know," muttered Hartley. "But there's time. We got to wait to see what comes out in court."

Charlie was a little disappointed. He had hoped that Hartley would have taken more expedient action. But for now, he could only smile and say, "Thank you for seeing me, Mr. Hartley. I do feel it's important, you understand."

"Yes. Yes, Charlie," said Hartley. "I'm sure it is."

The old man was already struggling to his feet. And Charlie quickly arose to assist him, but Hartley waved him off.

"Uh Mr. Hartley, I hope that our little conversation will be held in th' strictest confidence," said Charlie.

"Hmm? Oh yes, yes of course."

Hartley leaned heavily on his cane as he moved slowly toward the door. And Cartwright, who had left his tea almost untouched, followed the man from the library.

Reverend Ellison heard the reverberate sound of the sanctuary door. He emerged from his small office to see a young girl enter his church and move slowly down the aisle.

"Come in, miss." As she approached, he said, "I'm Reverend Ellison."

"Yessuh. My name is Abigail Price, and I called to talk to you about Joey Henderson."

He indicated that she should have a seat in a forward pew. He sat nearby.

"What about Joey?"

"I'm worried, sir. You see, I've known Joey for a long time—and we've come to think a lot of each other. We've talked a lot about what's happenin', what he's doin' and th' like—and—-well, we both are a bit upset and a little scared."

"About what?"

"Th' trouble all this is gonna bring. He didn't realize it at first, I think, but now Joey knows that a lot of bad things can happen. And I think so, too. I don' want to see him hurt in any way. He——he could even get killed," she said in a voice that quivered slightly.. "Sir, he's gonna be blamed for startin' an ugly row between white people and us. What he's doin' is dangerous."

"Oh, I wouldn't think of it in that way. Remember, Miss Abigail, this is all bein' handled by the N-double A-C-P and th' courts. There'll be no trouble.

She was skeptical. "You cain't say that for sure. There are whites who don' like colored folk. Terrible things can happen. I know. You see, my pa was lynched when I was a little girl."

The minister looked at her and said, softly, "Oh.. I 'm sorry, my dear."

"I want you to talk to Joey. Cain't you? Tell him that he don't have to do this."

Ellison sighed. "But this is important, what Joey's doin'. He made a promise, and I figure he'll want to keep that promise."

"Please…"

"Besides, Joey knows what he's doin'——he volunteered."

"Please…"

The reverend saw the sincerity of her concern. He looked away as he quietly consented.. "All right," he said softly. Then, after a pause, he turned to Abby and said simply, "But Joey ain't here, now, is he?"

"No, sir. He left town."

"Do you know where he's at?"

When Abby did not say anything, the minister presumed that since she was close to the young man she must surely know where he was staying. He asked again, "Can you tell me where Joey might be?"

Abby felt that Joey would not wish her to divulge his whereabouts.

But then, Mortecai Elision suggested the obvious. "If I'm to talk with him, I'll need to see him. Won't you tell me where Joey's at?"

"I don't think he wants nobody to know," she said, quietly.

"But if you want me to talk to him——to see how he feels—you will have to trust me."

She paused. Then, she reluctantly told him.

Meanwhile, in Fairfield upstate, a young Negro found his existence lonely and disappointing. It had been several months without success. Employers shunned him at the hint of his participation in the NAACP

148

scheme to integrate an all-white college in Crestview. He was viewed with distrust and cold suspicion and was offered only menial jobs.

The cousin with whom Joey was staying one day confronted the boy. "I'm afraid this cain't go on, Joey. If you cain't get a job here, then I'm of a mind that you'd better be movin' on."

The young man agreed. He missed his family and most of all, he missed Abby. Then, to his surprise, he was contacted by the Reverend Mortecai Ellison. Ellison informed Joey that his girlfriend had told where he was for she was worried and wanted to see him. The minister urged him to return. Joey said he would think about it.

On a rainy afternoon, he boarded the bus for Crestview. And as the vehicle cut its swath over the wet asphalt road, Joey stared out the window at the steady drizzle and dreamed of a hopeful tomorrow, which seemed as dubious and as indistinct as the misty scenery outside.

CHAPTER 19

The year ended. It was now 1954.

The Negro problem—as many referred to it—ceased to be the main topic of conversation, and life took on a numbing routine of normalcy. In the void of pending developments, the people became somewhat indifferent. It would never come about anyway, they reasoned, so why worry.

But the problem was never far from mind. And curious individuals continued to discuss the probabilities, always inquiring of late news, always eager to compare and pass opinions. In Bobby Ray's Bar and Grill, there were lively conversations about consequences which might occur if—"If that nigger gits in, all hell'll break loose! I bet you anything that ever' last white student will up and leave school!" In Al's Barber Shop, speculation and rumor ran rampant. Even Ethel's garden club enjoyed their whispered concerns and conjectures. In some homes, talk of integration, its improbability, its effect, inevitably surfaced as suppertime discussion and lingered like a bad taste. But it was obvious, after many weeks and months without incident or information, people were tired of waiting for something to happen and were inclined to dismiss the affair as unlikely and of little consequence.

Not so in the administrative leadership of Crestview State College and its cadre of legal advisors. Rob DeWitt was given leave by the state attorney general's office to vigorously prosecute the case to a satisfactory conclusion.

He and his staff labored arduously to refine their brief in anticipation of a crucial appearance before the United States Supreme Court.

More and more, pressures experienced by President McAndrew seemed to grow and intensify. He received daily calls from regional businessmen and former Crestview graduates, demanding that the institution be kept "pure and untainted by mongrel races." He somehow felt adrift from his own associates and he tried hard to balance their beliefs with those tenets he held dear. He worked long hours, could not sleep at night, and was in constant conflict with his own conscience.

Florence felt sorry for her Byron. She tried to assure and encourage him, for she wanted to ease the treacherous path he had to follow. She worried about his health, his position, his integrity. She knew him well—a man of principle—and she wanted what he wanted. But she knew, too, that as president he was also expected to maintain the traditional facade of the college and the community. Would his ethics waver in the face of such universal intolerance? Flo wondered.

The phone rang. Albina moved to answer it. "Mistah Hartley's resdence."

After a few moments, she said "Yes'm" and put the phone down on the hall table. She shuffled into the library where H. P. Hartley sat, comfortably reading. She said, "A Mistah Parrish wants to talk to you, suh."

The old man looked up from his book. "Leon Parrish?"

The Negro housekeeper shrugged and he reached for the extension near him.

"Hello?"

It was a young lady on the line. "Mr. Hartley?"

"Yeah, speaking."

"Would you mind holding, sir? Mr. Parrish wishes to speak with you. He'll be right with you."

Hartley grimaced. "Hell, no!"

The lady was shocked. "Sir?"

"I'll be damned if I'll hold!" he snapped and slammed the phone down. He glared at it; then, he calmly picked up his book to resume his reading. He had read only a page when the telephone rang again. After about five rings, Hartley reluctantly reached for it, realizing that Albina had ignored the call.

"Hello!" he barked.

"Henry..! How are you?" This time it was Parrish himself. "I apologize for having my secretary put this call through first. Didn't mean to bother you, but—you just wouldn't believe how busy things are around here, and—"

"Look, Leon, if you want to talk to me, you call me directly yourself, you hear? I ain't got time to pussyfoot around with some hired help."

Leon Parrish, accustomed to Hartley's abrasive personality, was not surprised or put off by the brittle voice at the other end of the line. As a sharp-eyed industrialist, he could appreciate the old man's brusque, outspoken candor. He even admired the senior board member's crotchety demeanor, for it exuded a no-nonsense facade typical of any astute businessman. And he was a part of that. Moreover, Parrish was not in the least intimidated by Hartley's acrimonious approach. He felt secure in the trust tendered by the college hierarchy, who were indebted to his continuing philanthropic efforts.

Parrish was the owner and executive of a burgeoning tool and die company and, having accumulated considerable wealth, gave generously large subsidies in support of Crestview State College. Leon had been a long-time friend of the late Jasper Morton and one of his sons had even graduated from the institution. Because his endowments meant so much, all the college administrators and trustees naturally went out of their way to treat him with awe and respect. All, that is, except Henry Hartley. Hartley held to his contentious, petulant honesty, and Parrish understood.

Leon laughed. "Good God, Henry, you sound like you got up on th' prickly side of th' patch. How you doin', anyway, my friend?"

"Tolerable. But if you're so damn busy, then you sure didn't call to inquire about my health."

"No," said Leon, chuckling. "No, I can tell you're still fightin' fit. No, I called you to find out th' straight of this court case th' college is involved in. I don't like what I've been hearin' and—well, I figured you're th' one man who ought to know—or, at least, could tell it straight."

"What've you been hearin'?"

"Oh, I don't know, that things aren't goin' too well—that, in fact, you people down there are losin' th' fight..!"

"Where did you hear all this?"

Parrish answered, "Oh, come now, my friend, I'm no dunderhead. I keep my ear to the ground. You know how much I'm interested in that college of ours. I may be sittin' in this office a hundred miles away, but I know pretty well what's goin' on over there." He paused. "Now, what I want to know is—what's wrong?"

"Nothin' we cain't handle, Leon."

152

Leon chuckled, but he was a little annoyed. Just like Hartley, to be evasive, taciturn, cunningly concise.

"You mean to tell me you're not worried?" asked Parrish pointedly.

"Hell, Henry, we've never faced anything like this before. My God, who would've thought we'd be arguin' over whether or not to admit a Nigra!? Before, there was never a question..! And now, we're dickerin' over th' ungodly notion that this black boy's got *rights*—and from all I hear, those in charge of your damn institution are knucklin' under!"

"Simmer down, Leon," said Henry Hartley. "First of all, nobody's let a Nig-ra in—not yet. And I would remind you, Mr. Parrish, that a number of us run this college—includin' *myself!*"

"Parrish quickly relented. "Of course, Henry, I wasn't thinkin' about you. I was referrin' to that administration—especially your president. What do you think of him?"

"Ohh—I reckon he's caught between a rock and a hard place."

Parrish persisted. "But I hear he's a weak-kneed liberal who'd hand over th' whole damn place, lock, stock, and barrel, to that weaselin' little black bastard..!"

There was a pause and Hartley asked quietly, "Tell me, Leon, have you been talkin' to Cartwright?"

"McAndrew's assistant? Hell no! I don't trust him either," Parrish replied.

Hartley was relieved. It had crossed his mind that Charlie Cartwright might have attempted to ignite a ground swell of resentment against McAndrew. That would be decidedly unwise, thought Hartley.

"Well, jus' like I said, Mr. Parrish, there's nothin' we can do about anything at this point.." said Hartley, "..but bide our time and wait for th' Federal Court to act."

"I don't know, but I'm countin' on you, Henry. You're on th' board. Don't wait until it's too late. And keep me posted!"

Henry Hartley did not bother to respond. He just hung up.

Only a few people reading the Crestview Gazette recognized the full significance of a page one story sandwiched between a cornfield beating and a UDC meeting. It was a one-column account of the high court's settlement of Brown versus Board of Education of Topeka.

The ruling had been rendered on May 17, 1954. A unanimous decision by the United States Supreme Court held that de jure segregation in public schools was a violation of the equal protection clause of the 14th Amendment of the U.S. Constitution. It stated that racial segregation, no matter how equal the facilities, branded minority children as inferior, thus hindering their development. This reversal of the "separate but equal"

153

doctrine of Plessy vs. Ferguson was greeted with both trepidation and hope, as whites and blacks awoke to an important meaning of this landmark decision. This was the first fissure in an obvious and inevitable crumbling of a long-time rule of Southern law.

It angered many. Die-hard Southerners, deeply distressed and determined to protect what was perceived an unalterable order of life, arose to protest. Senator James O. Eastland (D.,Miss.) expressed his venom in a speech that said, "We're about to embark on a great crusade. A crusade to restore Americanism and return the control of our government to the people...Generations of Southerners yet unborn will cherish our memory, because they will realize that the fight we now wage will have saved for them their untainted racial heritage, their culture, and the institutions of the Anglo-Saxon race. We of the South have seen the tides rise before. We know what it is to fight. We will carry the fight to victory!"

In the face of the rising tide, 14 men met in Indianola, Mississippi, to organize resistance to what many called a "socialistic doctrine." In developing their protest against the Brown decision, these men of Sunflower County decided on a more dignified or "white collar" strategy and approach to accomplish their aim. They would, for instance, reject the crude and violent methods normally associated with hate groups. They would enlist middle class, respectable southerners through service clubs and civic groups, usually the finest representatives of any community. And while they would not exclude them, the newly organized group as planned would not be dominated by the nominally notorious "race haters". The organization would be called the White Citizens Council and its aim would be to apply pressure, both social and political, to alter in time a threatening trend toward desegregation. Soon, local chapters would spring up all over the South.

Now, in Crestview, a passive yet uneasy attitude prevailed. Spring planting became the focus of community activity and the stores of the town stocked the needs of the farmer. The segregated schools of the region busily concentrated on the final weeks of the term. And the citizenry said little about their local crisis, as they quietly awaited the final outcome of the pending court dispute. As for the Brown decision of the high court, most believed that its effect would be minimal, that everything would turn out well—eventually.

College administrators kept a close vigil with their legal counselors, seeking whatever solace or understanding they could receive as time tediously measured the lingering litigation. Rob DeWitt remained optimistic. He felt the decision of the court of appeals, while not encouraging, did not completely scuttle their chances. He felt that their case might yet be

154

upheld by the trial court—but, if not, it should be heard by the U.S. Supreme Court. Not on basis of racial discrimination, as the Brown case had concluded, but evaluated instead on the constitutional right of an institution to govern itself.

Charles Cartwright, meanwhile, was quite disturbed—not by speculation of any pending court verdict, but by a television program which he had seen only a few weeks before. On *SEE IT NOW*, Edward R. Murrow had critically examined Senator Joseph R. McCarthy, which exposed groundless, fearful tactics in the senator's unprincipled pursuit of communists in high places. Cartwright was now confused, disillusioned, uncertain. He could not abandon a belief that no threat existed. He felt strongly that the dreaded menace did indeed influence the problems they now faced.

On a farm near Crestview, a lean, strong, Negro man turned his mule at the end of the row and swung the plow into place. The mule paused and Joey wiped his brow with a soiled neckerchief. He leaned against the plow handles and took a deep breath. As so many times before, he was thinking of what life offered, what might happen if he succeeded, or, for that matter, failed. Once, innocence had created idealistic images of an exciting struggle which might end in a victory of retribution. By the depth of his dream, he believed that his action would ease tension and erase all animosity and a utopian world would exist for all people, black and white.

Now, he was not so sure.

CHAPTER 20

The Sumpter House was Crestview's lone hotel. Located two blocks from the courthouse, it was a white, two-story, wooden building, with smoke-gray shuttered windows. It was fronted by a high-ceilinged portico, which extended just over the cracked sidewalk and supported by four square columns.

Dr. Charles Cartwright parked his car a few feet from the hotel entrance and, glancing furtively about him, walked quickly to enter the building. He paused inside the lobby. As usual, there was no one around. A cluster of faded, overstuffed chairs and a couch were arranged around a coffee table containing scattered sections of a newspaper and several magazines. A tabby cat, uttering a series of mournful meows, slowly slinked along the counter top of the registration desk.

Cartwright sauntered to the desk and, seeing no attendant, rang the bell. In a moment, an elderly man emerged from an adjoining office and over wire spectacles peered at the visitor.

"'Mornin'," the man said.

Cartwright looked down at his watch. It was 1:15. "How do you do. I believe you have a Mr. Leon Parrish registered here. Perhaps you could give me his room number."

The old man started to consult the register, but then remembered. "Room 25," he said.

"Thank you."

"At th' top of th' stairs," the old man directed.

Cartwright took the stairs two at a time and paused before the dark brown door. He knocked and waited. At length, it opened and Charlie faced a stocky man in a rumpled white shirt, open at the collar, his sleeves half rolled. He wore seersucker trousers and suspenders.

"Cartwright! Come in, come in."

"Thank you, Leon, it's good to see you again," said Cartwright, as he stepped over the threshold to scrutinize the room. A briefcase lay open on the bed, with several papers strewn about its wrinkled counterpane. Clarlie also noticed a bottle of gin on the dresser. A damp towel had been tossed over the back of a chair. A window air conditioner hummed loudly.

"Damn racket," muttered Leon Parrish, indicating the air conditioner. "But I sure cain't do without it..!"

"It's hot, all right," agreed Cartwright.

"Have a seat," gestured Cartwright's host, as he quickly scooped up the towel.

Cartwright, with a sense of uncertainty, eased into the chair. He did not know why he alone had been invited to the hotel room of this important industrialist and benefactor of Crestview State College. If it had to do with the college, surely Parrish would have arranged a meeting in an office at the administration building. Yet, why would he wish to see him, Charlie wondered, if it did not involve the institution.

"Now, Charlie.. I want to know what'n th' hell's goin' on?"

The question, put directly, caught Cartwright off guard. "Sir?"

"You know damn well what I'm talkin' about—how'n th' hell did you guys screw up on this damn thing?" Parrish demanded.

"You mean..."

"Damn right! You guys must've had your fingers up your ass to lose that court case..! Now, what'n th' hell's goin' on?"

Charlie tried to smile. "Well, Leon, it's not over…Not yet."

Leon, standing, glared down at his visitor. "Over? What'n th' hell is it but over!?"

It was clear that curiosity, no doubt conceived of distrust and fear, had brought Parrish to Crestview. Cartwright now realized that he had been singled out as an informer, that Leon expected him to reveal the full particulars of administrative plans and action. It was still a puzzle to the presidential assistant why this man had sought him out. Why not more influential people? A board member, perhaps, the president, even DeWitt, the attorney in charge. Why had he selected him—alone, here, in this hotel room?

"Th' trustees met several days ago," Cartwright told him. "They talked about th' action of th' court and discussed a little of what might possibly be done."

"And...?"

Charlie wondered if Parrish was privy to the knowledge of what had transpired at this closed meeting. He hedged.

"Nothing conclusive was decided, really," Charlie said. "But we can be assured that th' fight's not over. They're not goin' to let that Nig-ra in, if they can help it.. I think you can count on that."

"You sure?"

"Of course."

"And how do you figure that?" Leon asked.

"There're ways," said Charlie, with a smile. "We can delay actin' on th' court's order."

"What'll that do?"

"Give us more time."

"For what?"

"Well..," said Charlie, his annoying smile still in place. "You don't have to be a lawyer, Leon, to surmise that if this thing's tied up in litigation for a long time, we'll eventually come out on top."

Parrish shook his head. "I—don't quite follow you."

"A lot can happen," replied Cartwright. "For one thing, th' boy might get fed up with waitin'—so much so he just might decide to drop th' whole thing, give up. Oh, I know that's a long shot, but we don't really know what'll happen if this thing drags on. A delay would at least give us more time to figure out new strategy—uncover new evidence, maybe."

Parrish seemed provoked. "Godammit, Charlie, who'n th' hell are you people tryin' to kid? You guys are goin' to fart around until we have a nigger sittin' up there in class like he owns th' sonuvabitchin' place..!"

"I—hope not," breathed Charlie, quietly.

"Well, if somebody don't get on th' stick, it sure as hell will happen—and pretty damn soon!" Leon paused, and took a deep breath. "I cain't understand how you folks got suckered into this situation in th' first place."

Parrish walked over to the dresser and poured gin into a glass. "Want a drink?" he asked.

"No, sir," said Cartwright, smiling. "A little early, I think. And besides, I got to get back to th' office soon."

Parrish plopped in several ice cubes and added tonic water. He tasted it. "Ahh," he said, approvingly, "Nothin' like a gin and tonic on a hot summer day." He then walked over to place the glass on the bedside table

158

and stretched out on the bed. He folded his arms. "I don't know, Charlie. I don't know about you guys. I wonder sometimes if you people actually know what'n th' hell's goin' on at that damn college. You're so damn caught up in high moral standards and academic respectability that you cain't see shit when it's smeared on your doorstep! Do you know what all of this is really about?"

Cartwright did not answer.

"Look, it means more than our college, you know!" Leon emphasized. "Hell, it means our whole way of life—down th' toilet. If that big-lipped bastard gets into your college, Dr. Cartwright, evah last vestige of common decency will be destroyed. There'll be no stoppin' 'em. They'll be able to do evah damn thing they want. They'll mix freely with whites, there'll be interracial marriages, there'll be hell to pay!"

He sat up.

"Now, I figure we cain't have none of that, no-siree—not now, not in our lifetime, not evah!"

"I agree," Cartwright hastened to reply.

"Well, then?" Leon Parrish looked down at his visitor with an incisive stare. "What'n th' hell you folks goin' do about it?"

Charlie now was not smiling. He resented Leon's implication that all administrators at the college were incompetent, unconcerned, or incapable of perceiving the problem. He, for one, knew exactly the social repercussions that would occur if a Negro was permitted to enter their institution. And he had fought it. He could not be blamed.

"Like I said," Charlie answered. "Wait it out."

Parrish snorted. "Hell, Charlie, we cain't sit on our tails and play by th' rules. Not now. I don't give a damn about th' courts, we jes' cain't let it happen!"

Cartwright shifted in his chair. He did not have his clipboard to feel or fondle and he missed it. So he kneaded his hands nervously.

"Like I said, I think we'll be countin' on th' court system to prolong th' ultimate outcome," he said.

"What about that outcome? What if, after all this finaglin', it don't work?" Parrish asked, pointedly.

Charlie shrugged.

"I don't like it," Parrish muttered. "I have a damn queasy feeling that little bastard's goin' to get in."

Charlie shook his head. "No, Leon, we're not about to give up. There're a lot of us who'll fight this thing down to th' wire."

Parrish drained his glass and slowly arose from the bed. He walked past Cartwright to stand before the dresser. As he tipped the bottle of gin to replenish his drink, he looked into the mirror at the presidential assistant. With his back to Cartwright, he asked, "What about McAndrew?"

Charlie frowned. He had not expected the question. He opened his mouth to answer but discretion delayed his response.

Leon turned and faced Cartwright. "Is he ready to do what it takes to keep that little jig out of Crestview?"

Cartwright conceived a weak smile. "That's a little difficult to answer," he said, circumspectly.

"Of course you can answer!" snapped Parrish. "You're his damned assistant, aren't you?"

"Well, yes, but—"

Parrish interrupted. "That's exactly what I'm talkin' about! You guys are pussyfootin' around like a bunch of pantywaist push-overs! My God! Not one of you know what'n th' hell's goin' on, and all you can do is hold each other's hand like old maids in a thunderstorm..! My God!"

Charlie was piqued. "Just a moment, Mr. Parrish, that's not exactly true! Quite a few of us know precisely what th' situation is and what's got to be done. But damn it, sir, knowin' and doin' it are two different things!"

Parrish leaned against the dresser and smiled. "So th' first thing you need is a little leadership—right?" was his silky observation.

"Well, yes, but—"

"And you're not exactly gettin' it from your president. Right?"

"Well.." Cartwright paused. He tried to be diplomatic. "It's a tough situation to be in."

Parrish took a few steps to stand in front of his visitor. "Tell me th' truth, Charlie. That McAndrew fella doesn't have th' stomach to put up a fight, now, does he? He'd jes' soon give in, call it quits, right?"

"I—don't know. I—I just have a feelin' that he's not too concerned, one way or th' other. If it turns out that we have to integrate, I believe he thinks it can be done without too much trouble."

"Damned idiot!"

Cartwright did not comment and Leon moved around to sit on the bed. The industrialist and benefactor of Crestview State College leaned forward. "You mean, it doesn't bother him one little bit to have a colored person in our college…?"

Cartwright swallowed. "It—might seem that way."

Leon Parrish stood up abruptly and began to pace the floor thoughtfully. "I appreciate your forthrightness, Charlie, in letting me in on what it's like around here. Because I'm—-darned worried." He paused and looked at Cartwright. "That's exactly th' reason I asked you up here. I didn't want to see McAndrew. I didn't want to listen to a lot of guff about what could or couldn't be done. I wanted to get th' straight story."

Charlie nodded.

"I jes' don't like th' way he sees things."

"Frankly," said Charlie, with a nervous chuckle, "I don't either."

Parrish folded his arms and shook his head. "We cain't go on like this, that's for sure. We don't need a president who won't do what needs to be done."

Cartwright smiled. "Well, he's no Jasper Morton, that's for sure."

Parrish nodded affirmatively. "Damn right. Morton—he'd sure know what to do." Suddenly, he turned to Charlie. "By th' way, what would *you* do?"

The question surprised Charlie. He chuckled lightly and shook his head. "Thank God I don't have to make that decision..!"

"But what *would you* do?" Parrish persisted.

"You mean—if I was th' president?"

"Precisely."

Cartwright paused to contemplate. "I—don't—really know. I sure as hell would fight it, tooth and nail—every inch of th' way, I think. And—I don't think I would accept Nig-ras, even if th' court ordered it..!"

Leon rubbed his chin. "I see." He walked slowly toward the window and looked out the dusty, sunlit panes. Charlie barely heard him above the hum of the air conditioner, as he said, "I think we ought to be gettin' a new president, if you ask me."

Charlie Cartwright was simultaneously unsure and heartened at Parrish's opinion, but he cautiously tempered his acceptance of the man's statement. Instead, he said, "Rather late, don't you think? Replacin' Dr. McAndrew's not goin' to alter th' outcome at this point, I think. And I don't think it wise to be stirrin' up extra trouble."

"Charlie, McAndrew's weak. You and I both know that. We need somebody who'll take a stand, who'll act in our own interest. Somebody we can trust. Even when this thing's over, there's th' future to think about and, by God, we need a traditionalist in charge. No, I don't think McAndrew's our man."

"That's pretty much up to th' board," said Charlie, forcing a smile.

"Not entirely."

Cartwright's smile weakened.

"Look, Charlie, I've done a lot for this damn institution. In fact, I was intendin' to build that gym they've been needin' for so long. My money, my vote, man, means somethin'. And by God, I think they'll listen if I tell those board members that we sure as hell need somebody to get this place back in line, to lead this college th' way that it was supposed to be run."

Charlie grinned knowingly. "As Dr. Morton ran it."

"Exactly!"

Cartwright unashamedly savored the prospect and for one brief moment felt a tinge of elation. He was smiling. Even if he was being disloyal, he felt it was all for the good. Byron McAndrew was unaware, incompetent, curiously indifferent to the vital issues affecting the future of Crestview State College. And it was better to be unfaithful to McAndrew, he thought, than to see the college destroyed.

"Well," said Cartwright, arising as if to leave. "I think perhaps it would be best if I were not personally involved in any such plan to—uh—-unseat President McAndrew. I'm sure you understand."

"Yes, of course," Parrish replied.

Cartwright moved toward the door. But he paused when he heard Leon suggest, "I—don't suppose you'd consider th' position, would you, Charlie?"

"I—don't know," he heard himself say. Then, he eased out the door.

The white citizens of Crestview lived the long weeks of July as if awaiting the other shoe to drop. The expected ruling of the U.S. District Court to sanction admittance of a young Negro into their all-white Southern college did not come immediately. A month passed without a word and it seemed as if they had been magically spared. And why not?

For them, it was difficult to presume that a segregated society could be altered without popular consent. After all, this was a free, democratic country, in which it was deemed that Americans controlled their destiny and, by the same token, Southerners possessed an inalienable right to preserve age-old traditions. Colored folk? Why, they were of a heritage that could hardly be classified as native American and therefore were not entitled to privileges of decision and choice. They did not vote. They could not expect equality. And so, it was assumed by many that such a drastic pronouncement would never come to pass.

But it did.

During the first week of August, 1954, Judge Grooms issued the expectant order. The long suspense was over. And while it came as no great surprise, the college administration found it difficult to accept. Yet, closure seemed at hand. Crestview State College was mandated to admit young Henderson as a full-time student for the coming fall semester.

CHAPTER 21

Bernice Tutwiler straightened her dress as she settled comfortably in a leather chair facing President McAndrew's desk. Near her was Dr. Charles Cartwright with his familiar clipboard. Also present was the dean of students, Ed Blair. Byron stood up and moved around to seat himself beside them in an informal circle.

McAndrew explained the called meeting. "I thought it best to communicate with you people directly, rather than try to explain this matter by memo." The president seemed weary and to Bernice, she imagined that he had aged much in recent weeks. Byron took a deep breath. "As you know, I opposed the decision of the trustees to postpone or ignore the court's order, for I feel their choice is truly indefensible. Rather than place this institution in jeopardy, I thought our only acceptable course was to abide by the ruling of the court and to cooperate in every way possible."

Jeopardy? Cartwright shook his head slightly as he stared at his clipboard. The college had already been placed in jeopardy. And giving in so readily, thought Charlie, was not going to improve matters.

But the president surprised Charlie by informing them that he had requested a deferment of the court's order. "As you know, we have less than four weeks before the start of the fall semester. That gives us little time to make essential preparations for Mr. Henderson's enrollment. There are many things to be done. We must orient the faculty and student body as regard the ramifications and meaning of this unprecedented event. We surely have to enlarge our campus security force and a plan must be worked out to accommodate on-campus housing for this new student."

Blair frowned. "You mean he's living on campus?"

"I'm afraid so."

Cartwright shook his head. "That could pose a problem."

"Possibly," Byron said. "But according to the injunction, we may have no alternative."

After a pause, Cartwright asked, "Did you say that you have asked for a delay?"

"Yes," replied McAndrew. "I've conferred with Mr. DeWitt, our attorney, to request a postponement of the court order. He agrees that we need more time to adequately prepare for the enrollment of this colored student and feels the court will grant us a stay until at least the spring semester."

Charlie was relieved. Good, he thought. Any delay was welcome.

So, as Byron indicated, Rob DeWitt communicated to Judge Grooms the necessity for an extension of the court order to enroll Henderson. The attorney pointed out that with only weeks to go before the young man's appearance, there would be insufficient time to accommodate indispensible actions to insure the safety of the college, its personnel, and indeed the young Negro himself.

Judge Grooms found feasibility in the argument and accepted a motion to suspend the injunction to register the young man until the beginning of the spring semester.

Rumors roiled the campus, yet a strange indifference engulfed the students. For the most part, they seemed incurious as to whether or not a black person might join the student body. Not that it was not discussed, but in general they seemed impervious to the pressure felt by the community and the college administration. No student seemed occupied by the issue. Except one.

Archie Blevins was thin, wiry, tall for his age. He was a third year law student at Crestview State College and he prided himself at being an activist for causes he felt important. As a campus politician, he made little effort to disguise his racist feelings; so, as the Henderson case culminated in a court decision for the plaintiff, Blevins vowed it would never happen, that he would fight to keep this interloper at bay.

It was a warm September day when Murdock Faison, having been invited to confer with some college kid he had never met, paused to peer through the store front window of Marylou's Diner. He could not see much, so he stepped inside quickly, closing the door to relish the air conditioned coolness of the room. As his eyes adjusted to the darkness, he saw two men seated at a back table. They seemed to be the only persons in the room and one of the men, obviously a young man of college age, raised his eyes in apparent recognition and motioned Murdock to join them.

As Faison approached, the boy stood up and smiled. He extended his hand to Murdock..

"Hi, Mr. Faison. I'm Archie Blevins."

Blevins was dressed in a white shirt and black tie, his sleeves rolled back, collar loose, his tie askew. Faison was impressed by the young man's confidence.

"And this is Miles Stone from Indianola, Mississippi."

The other man struggled to his feet and, with an expressionless face, shook Murdock's hand. "Mr. Faison."

"Let's sit down," said Blevins, and the three settled in Marylou's bow-backed restaurant chairs.

"Would you like coffee or a piece of pie?" asked Blevins. "Th' pie's quite good here, I understand."

"I can testify to that," offered Mr. Stone. "I jus' had a piece."

"I don't think so," answered Murdock Faison.

"Okay, then, let's get right down to it," said Blevins in a brisk, officious manner. He extracted a pen from his pocket and began toying with it, as he explained, "I called you, Mr. Faison, 'cause I was told that you'd be interested in what we're plannin' to do. And we need a lot of people's help. We're facin' critical times. As you probably know, our college is bein' forced to take in a black boy."

"Well, I know he's tryin'," said Murdock, "but what exactly is th' story?"

"He's in, Mr. Faison."

Murdock looked at the young man curiously.

"According to th' court," said Blevins.

"But I thought th' court had given th' college permission not to take him in jes' now.."

"Right—but only until next semester."

Murdock shook his head, sadly.

"Of course, now," Blevins continued, "we sure don't see it that way. He's actually not in yet, and by God he won't be if we have anything to say about it. Th' college has pussyfooted around too damn long and now they've let that black bastard get th' upperhand. That lily-livered president of ours and his weak-kneed cohorts have knuckled under! We cain't let them get away with this!"

Murdock Faison rubbed his beard, thoughtfully. He was not sure that he liked this young man. Too cocky, too sure of himself.

It's up to us!" declared Blevins. "Yes, sir, it's up to us.. We cain't sit around and let it happen. And that's exactly why I got in touch with Mr. Stone here. I heard about th' White Citizens Council he and a bunch of other true-blue Southerners started over there in Mississippi, and I said—why not?—why not here..!?"

Murdock was puzzled. "A—White Citizens Council..?"

"Sure. That's a group of citizens who—got together in Mississippi to—"

Stone interrupted. "I'd like to explain, if you don't mind, Archie.. You see, Mr. Faison, when those damn old men up there in Washington on th' Supreme Court made that God-awful rulin' sayin' we law-abidin' Southerners had to accept Nig-ras in our public schools, well, naturally we got beet-red, hoppin' mad. And we swore right then and there that it'd nevah be. But we figured we had to be clever about this thing, that th' old way of resistance—scare tactics, violence, burnin' crosses and th' like—jes' might not do it. We'd have to apply political pressure, gain public support, create a unanimous front to oppose this awful decision. So we got together, some of us in our small Mississippi town, and we started what we called th' White Citizens Council. Its function, of course, is to let people know exactly what th' evil forces of our government and justice system are doin' to dilute th' white Caucasian race and destroy our most hallowed principles of Southern social life. And so, through this organized effort, we've set out to stir up people, get them involved, to create a massive wave of citizen opinion against that which th' Supreme Court and many of our elected officials are doin' to ruin our lifestyle here in th' deep South..! But like I said, it would have to be backed by important, respectable citizens of th' community."

"And that's where you come in, Mr. Faison," said Archie Blevins. "We're goin' to set up a chapter here in Crestview and we need you."

"Me?"

"Of course!" exclaimed the college junior. "You think like we do, don't you? You hate what's happenin'—!"

"Yes, but—"

"Mr. Faison," said Stone, quickly, "you're a respectable citizen here in Crestview. You're a prominent business man, an active member of th' Chamber of Commerce and Rotary Club, I understand. And most of all, you're a deep down, dyed-in-th'-wool Southerner. Now, that's th' kind of

166

person we need. And if you believe in what we're doin', well, we'd consider it a real privilege to have you join us."

"Don't you see, Mr. Faison?" pointed out Blevins. "This is not a low-down, lawless organization, but a straightforward, honorable group of citizens of all types—some in high places—who are fed up with th' way we're bein' railroaded into mollycoddlin' these black sonuvabitches..! And by damn, th' Council is determined to maintain our freedoms and our culture and to fight, if we must, to protect our way of life. And please understand, you're not th' only fine citizen who'll be joinin' our cause. There're others. Right now, I'm workin' on th' mayor."

"Th' mayor?"

"Sure. He's thinkin' it over. And I think he'll come around," said Blevins.

Miles Stone added, "You got to know that a lot of people are upset by th' high-handed methods bein' used these days. We cain't depend on nobody. So we got to take things into our own hands. But we got to be smart, we got to be responsible. And that's how th' White Citizens Council's goin' about it. And that's why a lot of important people who don't like violence or physical force, but who don't like to see colored people runnin' things either, are joinin' us."

Blevins smiled. "Now, what about it?"

Faison lowered his eyes. "What exactly do you want me to do?"

"Get us members," said Blevins. "Get us some leaders in th' community. Get us some well-known citizens of Crestview who have clout, contacts, influence. That's what you can do. That what we need."

"Then what?"

Blevins grinned. "Well-1.."

Stone answered, "We're goin' to do what it takes to get things back on track. We're goin' to put pressure on officials and on th' Nig-ras themselves. We're goin' to let ever'body know that we got rights, too. And there'll be meetings—mass meetings—meetings open to everyone. Even though there'll be prominent people present, th' Council's open to ever'body—farmers, mill workers, whole families, ever'body. And there'll be speakers—important speakers—"

"And we'll turn this town on its ear!" promised Archie Blevins. "Crestview, th' college, th' whole damn nation'll know that we'll never give up our principles, our God-given rights, for some nigger-lovin' sonuvabitches in Washington..!"

Murdock looked around. He was glad that Marylou was in the back room with her kitchen help. These fellows were getting louder and more excited by the moment.

167

"When's your first meetin'?"

"Next week. Saturday, a week," said Blevins.

"Can we count on you?" asked Stone.

Faison did not answer immediately, but then he nodded. "I'll be there." As he stood, he said, "Jus' tell me where."

On the second Monday in October, the United States Supreme Court convened to begin a new judicial term. As its first order of consideration, the justices peremptorily adjudicated several pending civil rights cases, based on the Brown decision. Among those remanded was the Henderson versus Crestview State College case with the affirmation of the appellate opinion.

Counselors for the college had fully expected a year's delay in the deliberation of their case and were astounded at this sudden development. It was unprecedented and, to DeWitt's mind, unfair that the high court should summarily rule that, with the landmark Brown finding as a reference, their litigation needed no review.

As disappointing as it seemed, hope still held in the delay that they had achieved and possible consequences which might be derived from their clandestine investigation. With new evidence, a reversal might yet be attained.

It was Friday night, the eve of 1955. It was not yet midnight when Elijah Henderson stepped onto his porch and raised his 12-gauge shot gun to the black, starless sky, and pulled the trigger. The thundering explosion echoed and reechoed in the woods beyond. Elijah broke the gun and extracted the smoking shell. He then pulled open the door and stepped inside. He was smiling.

"Happy New Year," he said.

Joey and the family returned the greeting. As far back as Joey could remember, it had been his pa's ritual to shoot his shot gun on the eve of each new year. It was his father's mischievous way of celebrating, although Joey suspected that it was more than that. It was, as it were, an act of release—a footnote underscoring the difficult and often depressing twelve months previous, and no doubt a punctuation of hope for the coming season.

"Happy New Year," Elijah repeated.

When the gun went off, Joey trembled. Not at the explosion, but at the realization of what the year of 1955 might hold for him. His long struggle was ending and the goal was at hand. And it would be happening soon. In about a week, the spring semester was scheduled to begin at Crestview State College.

As Mortecai Ellison pulled his Dodge into a parking place, he cut the ignition and drew a deep sigh. He glanced at Joey beside him and asked, "Ready?"

Joey nodded and the two slowly got out of the car.

He heard the crunch of their footsteps on the gravel path as they walked a gauntlet of curious bystanders. Joey was uneasy, but Ellison plodded on with determination and a sense of mission. Inside the building, the minister inquired of two boys as to where he might locate an admissions officer. One awkwardly indicated an office at the far end of the corridor. A young girl, standing nearby, flashed a weak but friendly smile. Joey was nervous. He felt apprehensive and out of place. The reverend started down the hall, but stopped when he saw her.

Someone had alerted Miss Tutwiler and she was hurrying to meet them.

Her smile was strained and she looked edgy and unsettled.

"We—we didn't expect you—today," she said.

"Yes'm," said Ellison. "But today's th' day Joey's s'posed to register, I think."

"Yes, well—" She glanced about her.

She saw students waiting in the corridor watching her.

"Let's go in here," Bernice said and walked quickly ahead of the two black men. They entered an office.

It was the office of several secretarial assistants, but Bernice Tutwiler, conscious of the unseemly sight of Negroes in the building, anxiously approached two girls who were laughingly conversing. They looked up, startled, to see Miss Tutwiler followed by the two black men.

"Ladies, can we use this office for a moment?" Bernice asked.

"Oh—uh why, yes'm," one girl replied.

"Privately, if you don't mind."

"Well, yes, of course."

As the two girls departed, Bernice Tutwiler closed the door behind them and indicated some chairs. "Have a seat," she said.

169

Joey started to sit, but the reverend quickly tugged at the boy's arm. Ellison frowned and Joey realized that they should wait until the woman had taken her seat. As she sat, they slowly settled onto the wooden office chairs.

Bernice observed the polite, expectant faces before her and she thought how much she hated her job at this moment.

"I'm—sorry that you had to make this trip over here this morning," she said.

"No trouble at all, ma'am," answered the Reverend Ellison with a gracious smile.

"No, you don't understand," Bernice continued. "I wish you had contacted me first. I could then have informed you that it wouldn't have been necessary. Something's come up, I'm afraid."

Joey swallowed. Ellison eyed her quizzically.

"As it so happens, we cain't register Mr. Henderson as we intended," she said, quietly.

Ellison was shocked. "You cain't—?"

"I'm afraid not."

"Why not?" asked Joey.

Both Ellison and the registrar looked at the boy. It was the first time he had spoken—and even Joey himself was a little surprised to hear his own voice. But his query had emerged instinctively out of an impulse of fear and disappointment.

Bernice, fidgeting with a typewriter eraser and avoiding eye contact with her visitors, attempted to explain. "It apparently has come to the attention of the college that Mr. Henderson has, in the past, done certain things which reflected upon his character and has created considerable doubt as to whether or not he can meet the moral standards expected of our entering freshmen."

The two black men stared at her. Neither understood.

"What do you mean?" asked the Reverend Ellison.

"I believe that your brother, Mr. Henderson, is in the state penitentiary now serving a sentence for a crime committed some nine or ten years ago," suggested Miss Tutwiler.

Joey answered slowly. "Yes'm, but—"

Ellison wondered aloud, "What has this got to do with Joey?"

"At the time, you also were involved in this felony, I believe, were you not?" she asked, looking at Joey.

Ellison protested, "Now, wait a minute—!"

"Were you not?" persisted Bernice.

170

Joey nervously glanced at Ellison, then at Miss Tutwiler. He weakly, reluctantly replied, "Well, yes'm, but—honest to God, I didn't do nothin'!"

"It is my understanding, however, that the records show that you were arrested and actually arraigned in court," Miss Tutwiler informed than.

"What's she talking about?" asked Ellison.

Joey shifted fidgetingly in his chair. "My brother—it was a long time ago!"

"What'd he do?" Ellison asked, pointedly.

"He—he robbed a store once—a man was shot—-but they let me go—-I didn't do nothin'!"

"But, you were—involved," insisted Bernice. "And under the circumstances, the college cannot possibly accept your application—without a thorough investigation into this matter, or of course, a receipt of the specified references required by our registration policy."

"Now, wait a minute!" Ellison declared. "You cain't do that! Th' court order!"

Miss Tutwiler shook her head. "As much as I would like to make exceptions, I am required by the college to follow the rules of admission."

"But th' court—!" croaked the reverend.

"I'm sorry. It's my understanding that the college will be making a petition to the court."

For an instant, no one said anything. Then, Joey asked in a pitiable, unsteady voice, "You mean—I don' get to go to college this year?"

Bernice tried to smile, sympathetically. "Not this semester. Not-here, I'm afraid."

Mortecai Ellison's face contorted in repressed anger. "Let me tell you, ma'am, y'all won't git away with this..! No, suh!," he stated firmly.

To Bernice Tutwiler, it sounded as a threat. And she didn't like being threatened by a black man. But she said nothing. She understood.

Mortecai Ellison left the building in anger. He reached the parking lot and, across the hood of his Dodge, stared at Joey Henderson and demanded, "What was that all about?"

"It happened a long time ago," Joey declared, his voice pitifully thin and unsteady.

"What happened?"

"It was my brother, he got into trouble," explained Joey, weakly.

Joey felt the minister's hard, steel-like stare. "Git in," ordered the reverend.

Joey opened the door of the Dodge and slid onto the seat beside the man who obviously was very annoyed. Joey cautiously eyed the man as he

171

hunched over the steering wheel. He did not immediately start the car, but simply stared through the dusty windshield at the emptiness of the parking lot.

Ellison was despondent. He wished Edgar Hall had been present to deal with the situation. But Hall had a court commitment in the state capital and had asked the minister to accompany the young man to the college to be registered.

"Now, I want to know exactly what happened."

"It happened a long time ago," Joey repeated.

"You said that before, but what?," the reverend snapped. "You ought to've tol' us!" Then, quietly, he asked, "What exactly did happen?"

Joey swallowed. "Derek got caught stealing. And the man fought my brother and Derek's gun went off and th' man was shot."

"A man was *shot..?*"

"Yessuh. He started to grab my brother and—well, th' gun went off," said Joey.

"And you were there!?"

When Joey did not answer, Ellison repeated, "When it happened, were-you—*there?*"

Joey paused. "Not exactly. I was outside. Derek wanted me to warn him if anybody came around."

"But you were there when your brother—shot—this man," Ellison declared, as if to corroborate the accusation.

"But he wasn't killed..!" the boy insisted.

"They arrested you?"

"Yessuh," admitted Joey, solemnly. "My brother and me."

"And what happened then?"

"They let me go. They said I was underage. I was only nine. And I really hadn't done nothin'."

They drove in silence for the next few seconds. As they entered Main Street, Joey furtively glanced at the driver and uttered a plaintive, "I'm—I'm awfully sorry."

The minister saw the pain in the young man's face and said, sympathetically, "Well, we'll see how it turns out. We'll talk to Hall and see what he's got to say."

CHAPTER 22

With Joseph Henderson's denial to enroll as ordered, the court ruled that the college had to show cause why they should not be held in contempt. Rather than being troubled by this mandate, Rob DeWitt welcomed an opportunity to introduce new evidence which he had just obtained. He felt it would support their position and compel a court's reversal as to the outcome of their case.

A hearing was scheduled in March on Monday of the month's first full week. On that day, the litigants of the long struggle once more faced each other.

All rise! The District Federal Court of the Fifth Circuit is now in session—the Honorable Harvey Grooms presiding..!

Edgar Hall was confident that they had now reached a final showdown, that the college could no longer evade the inevitable, that a hard-bought victory would soon be realized. Yet, he knew also that Rob DeWitt held a trump card in the discovery of the youthful indiscretion of his client. How his opponent would play this hand and what impact it might have in the judgment of the court, Hall could only guess.

Edgar felt a clamminess in his hands as he extracted papers from his worn, leather brief case. He wanted to do well. For one thing, Thurgood Marshall was present. He had made a special trip from New York to witness a successful conclusion to this significant case.

Standing now, they watched the magistrate enter to take his seat in the large, high-backed, black leather chair. They noted that Judge Grooms was not as brisk in his actions as usual and that he appeared particularly wan and weary-looking. Yet, his voice was strong as he sounded his gavel and announced, "Case number one-five-eight-seven-one."

He then asked, "Mr. Dewitt, are you prepared to answer the charge of contempt pending?"

"I am, your honor. I intend to put forth before the court new and indisputable evidence which validates our decision to reject the plaintiff as an unfit candidate for admission into Crestview State College."

As Edgar suspected, this would be an effort to introduce events of Joey's past to substantiate their claim as to the inadmissibility of the young man's application. Still, Hall felt this subterfuge would be dealt with expeditiously and the hearing would once again be placed in proper perspective.

He had tried to prepare himself for this eventuality by spending long hours interviewing Joey Henderson about the events leading to his brother's arrest. He went over every instance, covered every detail, considered each moment, determined every action, its motivation, its significance. And in the process of the interview, Hall learned of Derek.

As a child, Derek had been active, energetic, bold. Except for the birth of a brother and a sister—-one who had died at birth, the other at age two from a severe case of measles—Derek had been an only child until Joey was born eight years later. As he grew older, Derek became more determined and independent. He was the source of much anger and frustration for his family as his precipitate personality led him into many wild and irresponsible activities. At first, only frivolous forays—stealing watermelons, taking hub caps, playing pranks on teachers.

At fifteen, there emerged a more serious proclivity in Derek's behavior. He began consorting with a few delinquent Negro boys, began drinking, staying out late at night. And then, finally, he found himself joining in escapades of minor felonies.

Derek always considered himself as good as anyone. And he deeply resented the inferior role in which Negroes had been cast. He therefore saw justification in his surreptitious acts of crime, particularly if his victims were white. He found satisfaction in what he perceived as revenge for the humiliation and suffering his race had endured over the years. Not that Derek possessed a social conscience; no, his object was purely personal, and no less instigated by greed and incorrigibility.

On that fateful afternoon, Hall had been told, Derek had decided to leave the fields without telling his father. He needed money for a night out and he thought that it would be a rather easy task to take it from a small gas station-grocery on Tarboro Road. It was operated by an elderly white man and Derek reasoned that under threat he would gladly hand over the contents of his till.

Unable to contact his usual cronies, Derek persuaded his little brother to assist him. Joey was unsure, unaware of the risk, but he was intrigued by the thrill of the adventure. He did not know then that Derek carried a pistol. So he went along with his older brother, a willing and trusting participant.

It was a quiet, hot afternoon as they approached the gray, wooden building and its two gas pumps out front. The premises appeared deserted. Not knowing whether the owner was in the store or in his small house out back, Derek and his small brother left the road and paused at the corner of the building. As they stood beneath a large tin **ORANGE CRUSH** sign tacked to the building, Derek told his nine-year-old brother to watch carefully and if anyone should appear he was to give instant, shrill whistle as a warning. "Wait here," he instructed.

When Derek departed, young Joey stood alone, uneasily peering around the corner at the road beyond the gas pumps. It was ominously quiet. He heard a dog bark and the occasional whine of a passing vehicle. But no one came and Joey grew impatient. He tried to whistle a tune to himself, quietly, but his lips were dry. It was exciting, but he wished Derek would hurry. The thrill was being throttled by fear.

Suddenly, an explosion! Joey jumped. Something had gone wrong; he wanted to run. But he couldn't move. He clung to the wall of the building, his heart beating madly. Then, Derek brushed by him and, without stopping, cried, "Git! Let's git out of heah!"

Joey, stunned, watched him flee—and then quickly followed, stumbling after him, breathlessly frightened.

What went wrong? What happened?

At twilight, the sheriff, in hobnailed boots, clumped onto the Henderson porch. He and his deputy were there to make an arrest. A white man had been shot, they said, and a witness had seen and recognized the two Henderson boys running from the gas station. In the trial, it was revealed that Derek, while attempting to rob the premises at gunpoint, had been grabbed by the elderly owner. In the scuffle, the pistol had discharged. The old man dropped, wounded, and almost died. But fortunately, he recovered and was able to tell the story. It did not take long for a jury of twelve white men to convict Derek and subsequently sentence him to twelve years in the state penitentiary. Joey was arraigned before juvenile authorities, but because of his age and indirect involvement was released.

It had been a pivotal point in young Joey's life. It was for him a sobering experience. He saw the error of Derek's ways and under the tutelage of Uncle Nat, he found the goodness of a righteous life, an appreciation of truth and honesty. His father, meanwhile, deeply hurt by Derek's dishonor, became very stern in his parental control of Joey. Elijah avowed that no member of his family would ever again stray from his firm, hard working, religious principles. And Joey responded, working diligently by his father in the fields, steadfastly studying and making good grades in school, attending church regularly, and always showing respect for his family and others. Joey proved himself different from Derek, but Elijah was never fully convinced.

Now, as Joey sat stiffly beside his lawyer, watching the courtroom activity, his thoughts were of his papa. He thought of Elijah's struggle to survive as a simple farmer and of his profound feelings of shame when Derek besmirched his good name. And of the hope his father held for him. And of the uncertainty and worry he had caused his father when he decided to join the NAACP scheme to gain admission to Crestview State College. Now, the ultimate disgrace. Joey now realized he-as the son in whom his father possessed such faith and promise—was about to be subjected to uncompromising scrutiny which would bring further humiliation to the Henderson family. He became conscious of the courtroom again as he heard the judge say, "You will have that opportunity, Mr. DeWitt. But I would like to hear first the prosecution's version of events which induced this action. Mr. Hall?"

Edgar Hall arose and summoned Bernice Tutwiler to the stand.

Bernice was expressionless as she moved through the balustrade gate, which was held open for her by the black attorney. Without granting him a glance she strode past him and took her seat on the witness stand. She hated the process and wondered how many more times she would have to be subjected to an interrogation by this Negro.

After being sworn in, Miss Tutwiler eyed the attorney coldly as he began. "Miss Tutwiler, is it not true that on the day of spring registration, January 9th of this year, the plaintiff, Joseph Henderson, presented himself to you to be admitted as a fulltime, qualified student as per order of this court?"

She paused before answering quietly, "He—was there, yes."

"And did you not, at the time, refuse to process his registration?"

Bernice Tutwiler hesitated. She was about to open her mouth to answer when a sudden, strange sound drew all eyes to the bench. A collective gasp greeted the sight. Bernice had turned to see Judge Grooms, half risen from his chair, his hand clutching his robe, his face white, constricted in a glazed

176

look of agony and shock. He slumped forward on the blue blotter surface of the desk and slid down behind the bench. Bernice put her gloved hand to her mouth. Someone screamed.

The clerk and bailiff rushed immediately to the magistrate's aid. Hall stood transfixed, his hand suspended in a still life gesture. His witness stared at him in stunned, wide-eyed bewilderment. An anxious murmur emanated from the assembled group. Finally, the bailiff, obviously shaken, stood up from behind the bench and shouted, "Get a doctor!"

The terrible tableau had taken only minutes, but it seamed an eternity before an ambulance rescue squad arrived. As they assisted the stricken judge, attorney Hall sidled next to the state's assistant attorney general and asked, "My God, what now?"

"Who knows," answered DeWitt, bedazed.

"God," muttered the black lawyer.

It was ascertained that Judge Grooms had suffered a heart attack; how serious, no one seemed to know. The court was adjourned until further notice and the stunned participants moved silently into the hall.

Later, it was determined that Judge Grooms' heart attack was not as severe as first imagined. It was decided that if he responded to several weeks of rest and recuperation, he would be able to resume as the presiding justice. The hearing was therefore continued until the second week of July, 1955.

The mayor of Crestview, Lonzo Butler, stopped by to see his good friend, Dr. Neal Ogden. It was after hours and the reception room was empty. The door to the doctor's office was ajar and the mayor surreptitiously looked in to see Ogden slumped in his chair, asleep, his spectacles askew. While Lonzo was debating if he should disturb the weary physician, Ogden aroused himself and mumbled, "Oh, hello there."

"Howdy, doc," saluted the mayor. "You must have had a tough day."

"Ah, yes, well—what time is it?"

"After six. Six-thirty to be exact," the mayor informed him.

"Must have dozed off."

"I think you've been working too hard, Neal."

"Well, I was tryin' to wind up some reports here. It's been a long day. I got only four hours of sleep last night. I was up until 4:30 this morning tendin' to th' Morley family. Her daughter's got diphtheria, you know."

"Neal..?"

"Yes?"

"I'm ...scared."

"You? Scared? Of what?"

"This ...Nig-ra problem. It's attractin' more attention than a two headed mule. What am I goin' to do? I'm th' mayor, I ought to do somethin'. But I don't know—what to do, Neal."

When the doctor didn't reply, Butler looked off and muttered, "This place is swarmin' with newspapermen, radio and TV reporters—not jus' from here, but the world over. There's a broadcaster here from London, England. Can you believe that!? And this damn mess is making us look bad, real bad."

"Yeah," agreed Neal, "It's an important story, I reckon."

"I wish to God we could get along!" lamented the mayor, and sadly related a story about his youth. "I remember playin' with a little colored boy when I was little. We had a lot of fun together—-we were friends! And then, when I got older, I learned that I wasn't supposed to mix with that sort of person. But you know, I still remember him and th' times we had, wrestlin', playin' football, kick th' can, hide-'n'-go-seek, things like that. And I never thought for a moment back then that it was wrong, that he was different from me."

"I feel as you do, Lonzo," said the doctor.

"I know you do. That's why I stopped in to see you—to get your opinion and advice. I tell you Neal, I'm worried. I had a visitor today."

"A visitor? Who?"

"Some college kid," said Lonzo Butler. "He tried to get me to join an organization he was startin' called th' White Citizens Council."

Dr. Ogden seemed incredulous and asked, "White Cit—what's that?"

"He said it was a politically active group made up of outstanding citizens who were intent on preserving our Southern way of life."

This euphemism for racial segregation was all too clear to the good doctor. He pulled out a cigarette, lit it, and asked, "What did you say?"

"I told him I needed to know more about it and what they hoped to accomplish. He tried to tell me, but I knew already I wasn't interested. When he left, I had a sinking feeling that this was th' beginning of real trouble. Neal, I tell you ... I 'm scared."

Some citizens of Crestview saw their world of white domination disintegrating, but one person who refused to accept a collapse of segregation was Archie Blevins. He worked hard, made speeches, canvassed the community for insurgent support. He tried to organize his fellow students into vocalizing violent disapproval of blacks and to protest the acceptance of a Negro at Crestview State College. Either because of timidity or troubled conscience, few members of the student body, however, seemed willing to follow his bigoted course.

Archie, of course, dismissed student apathy as immature and unenlightened, and devoted most of his energy to the growth and effect of the White Citizens Council. This, he saw, was the grass roots upheaval of genuine Southern concern. He tirelessly expanded the attendance of each meeting, and now, on this June night—only weeks away from the resumption of a court hearing which many thought might decide the issue—Archie Blevins eagerly arrived for his most important meeting of the White Citizens Council. He had carefully organized what he deemed an effective program.

A large crowd filed into the white high school auditorium on this warm, summer night, talking, laughing, resolute in a belief that a white man's Armageddon was near. If true, they were equally convinced that white authority would triumph, that a tradition of race separation would remain indelible, their destiny secure. And as the shuffling people moved toward the entrance, some seemed solemn, thoughtful, and many conversed in low tones of deep distrust. But the majority seemed jovial, filled with an exuberant expectancy, as they apparently anticipated an evening that would restore their faith in the infallibility of white supremacy.

It was a curious mix. Overall-attired farmers and mill workers in blue jeans entered shoulder to shoulder with business men in linen trousers and sport shirts. There were families—mothers herding small children, some with tiny babies, rushing to keep up with eager husbands. The mass of milling people pushed forward and there was a scramble for seats.

Mic Purvis rudely brushed by a young woman to capture an empty seat by a man who glanced at him with disdain. Observing the grubby individual beside him, the man quickly turned away to talk to the person on the other side. This obvious act of contempt did not faze Mic. Purvis nudged him.

"Sure a big crowd, ain't it?"

The man looked at Purvis coldly, grunted, and turned away again. Mic shrugged and watched the overflow crowd contest for the few remaining seats. Those too late to locate a seat had to stand with others against the wall. Some sat on the floor in the center aisle. And looking over the heads of the people in front of him, Purvis observed the lighted stage. It was barren save for six chairs arranged in a semicircle. At center stage, there was an upright lectern with a standing PA microphone beside it. The backdrop was a huge Confederate flag.

The sweltering auditorium undulated with the pendulum motion of rapid fanning, as the hot, restless crowd awaited the start of this significant meeting of the White Citizens Council. The drone of their loud chatter suddenly erupted into cheers and applause as six men emerged from the wings and walked slowly to take their seat on stage. One of the six moved directly to the microphone. He held up his hands and the shouting and the applause soon subsided.

The public address system squealed as Archie Blevins started to speak. He stopped. Some in the audience sniggered. Blevins began again. "I'd like to call on th' Reverend James T. Morehead of th' United Methodist Church to give th' invocation."

A man, distinguished by his white hair and dark suit, stepped to the microphone. "Let us pray," he said.

There was a rustle as the audience settled into an expectant silence, marred only by an occasional cough or the crying of a baby. They bowed their heads as the minister intoned, "Our God Almighty, we beseech thy blessings upon these, thy servants of th' Lord, and lead them through this valley of th' unknown. Give them strength to decide th' purity of their race, as God intended, and to resist those voices of evil which cry out against our righteous way of life. Be with those who speak this night and see that these devoted followers return safely to their Christian homes. We ask this in th' name of our Lord and Savior, Jesus Christ—amen."

A murmur resumed and, even as Archie Blevins paused for quiet, it did not abate. Suddenly, he screamed, "Are we nigger-haters!?"

The audience erupted instantly, yelling, clapping, stomping their feet. It took a while to silence them. Over occasional catcalls, he proclaimed, "I tell you, folks, this ain't no place for nigger-lovers!"

Laughter and cheers greeted Blevins and rhythmic clapping began, building in tempo and volume until it reached a sustained and mighty crescendo.

He held up his hands. He was smiling.

A fever of excitement had engulfed the group. They were standing. Mothers, clutching babies, screamed approval and men, waving fists in the air, thundered their defiance and unrelenting prejudice. It was everything Archie Blevins had hoped.

Anxious to accelerate the momentum, he shouted, "Are we goin' to let niggers take over..!?"

More than three hundred voices responded as one, "Nooo!"

"Are we goin' to put th' bastards in their place!?"

180

"Yeahh..!"

"I cain't hear you!"

"Yeahhh..!" shrieked the gathering.

The banter continued, intensifying, echoing its exuberance in this crowded hall of screaming fanatics. It was like a revival meeting or a pep rally. And caught in this flood tide of emotion, men and women and even children raised their voices to protest and assail the menace they imagined was upon them, poised to strike. Archie Blevins played upon their fears, their insecurity, their uncertainty. He manipulated them like puppets. And they responded with vigor and an unrestrained passion of inherited hatred.

At last, Blevins endeavored to guide the emotion toward a more solemn and serious consideration of the issue they faced. He calmly spoke to them about the imminent threat that existed and the need to coordinate a concerted effort to resist the growing pressure from high places.

Then, he called upon Ben Stanley, a local pharmacist, to introduce the principal speaker of the evening.

William Howard, state senator, then stepped forward to deliver his address. He began by telling the story of the hare and the tortoise, of the overconfident rabbit conceding a headstart to the slower and inept turtle, only to find that the tortoise had duped him into losing the race. He gave th' tortoise an inch—and he took a mile!" explained Senator Howard, and added, "So it is with Nig-ras..!"

He spoke sneeringly of the NAACP's campaign to integrate schools. He said, "What's th' real purpose of their campaign? I'll tell you! It's to open th' bedroom doors of our white women to Nig-ra men..! And what'll happen if their campaign succeeds? Th' Nig-ras then will see to it th' nation gets a Nig-ra vice president..! And after that happens, what's to prevent them from assassinatin' th' President and makin' th' Nig-ra our President!?"

The audience groaned and shouted their anger and dismay. The senator continued, projecting loudly his theory with a warning. "You say it cain't happen here, but I say it can—and will, unless we stand up and fight!"

"Yes!" shouted one man, standing, and around him arose the throng, as if ready then and there to wage battle for country and the protection of white womanhood.

The state senator praised the White Citizens Council as the force of the people to keep the country on an even keel and to make sure that righteousness prevailed as regard preserving the decency of a white society. He indicated that strong measures were in store for those who defied the laws of the South. "Not killing, as was done in th' past, but a slow, sure, effective means to convince all colored people that they have no choice but to acknowledge that they are now, and forever will be—secondary citizens. And they must, and will, abide by our laws and our customs."

The audience reacted with approval. As the shouting and applause faded, William Howard suggested that the White Citizens Council would put the Negro "in his place." The purpose of the organization, he proposed, would be "to make it difficult, if not impossible, for any Nig-ra who advocates desegregation to find or hold a job, to get credit, or even renew a mortgage!"

The crowd cheered and applauded and businessmen nodded with smug satisfaction. The senator concluded his speech by urging his audience to do everything 'in their power "to protect th' purity of the South..!" And Archie Blevins bounded to the front of the stage, waving his hands, shouting scurrilous epithets about "niggers," and once more whipping the people into a frenzy of emotion.

Long before the meeting had ended, a lone figure slipped out the door of the auditorium and departed into the night. Lonzo Butler, the mayor, had been standing in the rear of the hall, having entered late. He was wearing dark glasses and nobody recognized him. He had stood there, uneasily observing the spectacle and hearing the booming, sound-reinforced threats and racial slurs. He shuddered and, removing his dark glasses, he eased out the door. No one saw him leave.

CHAPTER 23

It was the usual Saturday afternoon gathering of mill workers, farm laborers, and drifters, as they shared camaraderie and drink in the dimly lighted bar area of Bobby Ray's Bar and Grill. They solemnly fondled bottles of brown brew and discussed sundry concerns—crops, prices, politics, and personal perceptions of the "Nig-ra problem."

"Ought to ship th' whole damn kit 'n' caboodle back to Africa, I say, wher' they come from!"

Some heartily agreed, a few were amused, others simply ignored the comment as a commonplace gibe.

Mic Purvis chortled, "Yeh."

Purvis was straddling a chair, gripping a bottle of Budweiser. His drinking money had been earned during a week helping Aldo Fenrick unload his plumbing supply truck. But even without money, Mic often frequented the bar in the hope that babitues of Bobby Ray's would offer drinks. And they usually did, for they thought he was funny when he got tipsy.

Across the small table from Mic Purvis on this particular afternoon sat a thin, tall farm boy, wearing a John Deere cap. Although he was younger than Mic, he was friendly and not put off by the older man's inane actions or talk. Drink had bridged the generational gap and the two soon found themselves immersed in a warm glow of mutual comradeship.

"That was one helluva meetin' last night," slurred the half-drunk youngster in the John Deere cap.

"Yeah, but I want to see th' good part start," snorted Purvis.

"What d'ya mean?"

"All talk," declared Mic Purvis. "Hell, I want to see some action!"

"Like whut?"

"My God, man, they ain't goin' to let that nigger git away with this..! Hell, no! And when they start rippin' his ass, I want to be ther'!"

The summer Saturday afternoon slipped past its prime and the pendulum wall clock chimed 4:30. While some lingered, a few left and others arrived. Finally, the boy in blue jeans and the John Deere cap decided he needed some air. Mic Purvis stood unsteadily and staggered after him. Bleary and blinking, they stumbled into the glare of the bright sun and, motioning to the young man to follow him, Purvis headed across the railroad tracks and along the tire ruts of a sandy road. Clutching a bottle of cheap bourbon whiskey, he walked on silently. Their breathing was the only sound as they strode the stillness of an airless, torpid afternoon.

Bernice was sitting in her velvet chair, knitting, and talking with the Negro girl who had just come in from the kitchen *to* ask about the pot roast for dinner. As Bernice talked of flowers and cooking, Abby stood beside her twisting the oven cloth in her hand. The girl responded with her usual polite "Yes'm" and offered an occasional comment when it was deemed necessary.

Abby was about to turn and walk back to the kitchen when they both felt her presence. They had not heard her enter but there she was, standing still at the threshold, her arms folded and her demeanor as precise as a porcelain figure, her icy eyes penetrating the girl at the far end of the room.

Bernice's brief smile of recognition quickly dissolved as she stammered, *"Why, Ethel, what's wrong?*

"It's *her!* That's what's *wrong!*" proclaimed Ethel, pointing at Abby.

This sudden indictment left both Bernice and the girl stunned. Abby swallowed and stared at the angry woman before her. She tried to speak but no words came.

"I want that girl out of this house!" Ethel shrieked. .

"But—but *why..?"* Bernice cried.

"She knows very well *why,*" declared Ethel. "And to think how we've trusted this little snip all these years!"

Abby was shaking her head, disbelievingly, her eyes stinging from the painful, piercing words.

"Sister!" snapped Bernice. "What in the world are you talking about..!?"

"I'm talking about her! And what she's done!" Ethel, who had been glaring at the girl with undisguised dislike, now turned to Bernice. "She's been spying on us..!"

"Spying? Whatever—"

"She's a friend of that despicable boy—did you know that? They're thick as thieves! And she's been in our house all this time, listening, spyin', taking down everything we said and knew and telling him, his lawyer, and lord knows *who* else."

Bernice looked at Abby. "Abby, is that true? Do you know him?"

The girl glanced at the portly sister with doe-like eyes of despair. Her lips quivered. "Yes'm." Then, she quickly said to her accuser, "But I didn't tell him nothin'..!"

"Oh, fiddlesticks, she'd say anything now," scoffed Ethel.

"But how do you know this, Ethel?" asked Bernice.

"That's just it," said Ethel. "I've never been so mortified in all my life! I had to—it was terrible—-I had to be told by two ladies at the UDC luncheon today. They had heard, they knew—-that we were harborin' a little conspirtor, a little sneak!"

"No ma'am," pleaded Abby, "I ain't told him nothin'!"

"Oh yes, you did! Don't deny it, young woman..! And that's exactly how he won in court and why we're bein' forced to take him into our college!"

"But Ethel, he hasn't been admitted yet..!"

"Don't be a fool, Bernice! He's practically there!" She glared at the girl. "And she did it! And as far as I'm concerned, young lady, you're through! We don't want any part of you! You can get out of this house right now!"

Abby's wide eyes trickled tears. "But ma'am, I—"

"Go!" ordered Ethel. "Get out!"

"Ethel!"

Abby, nervously twisting the oven cloth in her hands, suddenly turned and ran from the room. And Ethel called after her, "You little vixen!"

Bernice, still shaken by her sister's onslaught, made a brief gesture to intercept the girl, but let her hand fall limply as Abby disappeared through the door. She turned anguished eyes on the woman beside her. "Oh, Ethel..!" she groaned.

"Oh, I know, you're going to take up for her," sighed her sister. "But Bernice, you've got to understand how I felt. Imagine! Having some of the more important ladies in this town questioning our sensibilities—our stupidity, really—by employing anyone who would fraternize with that Nig-ra upstart. I was ashamed. I was ashamed."

"But right now, you didn't think much of Abby's feelings, did you?"

"I couldn't care less about anyone who would be so underhanded as not to confide in us that she knew th' boy—and what's more, was intimate with him..! Why, it's no tellin' what we might have said while discussin' th' court case in front of her."

"Nevertheless, I think you were unduly harsh with her," said Bernice. "After all, she said she hadn't told him anything.."

"And you believed her? Ha!" snorted Ethel. "Dear sister, you should know a little bit more about Nig-ras. They're all shifty, and practically none of them can tell th' truth."

"Ethel, really!"

"All right!" exploded Ethel, angrily. "But that certainly doesn't excuse her from putting us in a very embarrassing situation!"

Bernice drew a nervous sigh. "I cain't let that girl go like that. I simply cain't. I'm going after her." And she turned.

"After the humiliation she's caused, don't you dare bring that girl back into this house!" Ethel commanded.

Bernice did not find her in the kitchen. The pot roast had been removed from the oven and covered. Abby had lingered only long enough to put things in order and then, apparently, had departed quickly.

Bernice hurried through the screen door onto the verandah. She moved around the bend in the porch to see the young black girl start down the steps. She called. "Abby, wait!"

The girl turned and looked up. Her cheeks were streaked with tears. She paused, respectfully, as Bernice approached to stand at the edge of the steps above her. Bernice then gingerly sat on the top step and indicated Abby to join her. The Negro girl slowly climbed the steps and, at the white woman's invitation, sat beside her. Abby rubbed the tears from her eyes. "I didn't do nothin', Miz Bernice, really I didn't."

"I know, I know."

Bernice put her arm around the young girl.

"You mustn't mind sister. She's upset. She really doesn't mean a lot of what she says. It's just—you know, it means a lot to us what people think. And this trouble which this young man has stirred up—well, has everybody on edge."

"But I didn't do what she said, Miz Bernice, honest!" Abby sobbed. Bernice gave her a little hug. "I know, I know. But she'll soon forget those things she said to you, and everything will be all right."

Abby sniffled. "I don' know.."

"Oh yes, everything'll be all right. You'll see."

There was silence for a moment. The afternoon sun filtered through the full foliage of the magnolia tree, glinting its full, exposed leaves. The serenity of the garden seemed to accent the hum of the bee, the rustle and twitter of birds among a canopy of shadows, a sense of tranquility marred only by an incongruous hoot of a distant diesel locomotive.

Bernice asked, quietly, "Do you know this young man well?"

The girl answered tentatively, "He's my boyfriend."

"I see." Bernice released the young girl quietly and looked out across the bed of flowers and beyond the picket fence to the shade-dappled, dirt street that ran by the house. "You know, I really don't think it's wise of him to be doin' what he's doin'."

Abby said, "I know, I tol' him. I said—lots o' times I said, Joey, it's too dangerous, you cain't do this and git away with it. But, honest to God, Miz Bernice, he don' listen."

"Yes," sighed Bernice, "young men his age can be awfully set in their ways. But I think you ought to talk to him again, Abigail. Tell him that, for his sake, he oughtn't be doing this, not now, not at this time. The time may come, maybe, someday, when it'll be proper and accepted. But right now, I really don't think it's advisable. You must talk to him. Tell him. You do understand, don't you, Abigail?"

"Yes'm."

"If he cares anything at all about you, Abigail, he'll have to listen. Talk to him, talk some sense into him."

"I'll try," Abby promised.

"Otherwise, I'm afraid his life's going to be ruined. Now, nobody wants that, now, do they?" Bernice told her.

"No'm."

"You talk to him."

Abby nodded.

"And, as for Miss Ethel, I'll talk to her. Don't you worry. I'll straighten things out," said Bernice.

Abby looked down the verandah in the direction of the kitchen. "I'll git your supper on th' table, if you want," she offered, starting to rise.

"Oh no," Bernice replied, "that'll be all right. You go on home. I 'll take care of supper."

"But I'll be glad to—"

"No, that's all right," Bernice told her. "With Sister Ethel feelin' like this, perhaps it would be best for you not to be around this evenin'. You run along home. And be back tomorrow. Everything'll be all right, you'll see."

Bernice raised herself slowly to stand. She looked at Abby, who was already standing, and said, "Don't you fret, child."

And then Bernice Tutwiler started walking slowly along the verandah. Abby watched her, saw her disappear around the corner of the porch, and thought how very old the lady seemed. Abby turned and moved lightly down the steps to the gravel path below. As she reached the picket fence gate, she looked up into the glare of the setting sun and surmised that there might be enough daylight left to take the shortcut home—across the railroad tracks and through the mill yard.

The two men left the road, jumped a narrow ditch, and stumbled through a grove of trees and underbrush to come up on the open expanse of a small saw mill. There were rows of stacked lumber and slabs and, a few yards away, an open shed. Behind the shingled shed one could see a pyramid pile of saw dust.

Purvis led the way. Clutching his bottle of bourbon, he stepped heavily over watery ruts past logging equipment which was red-caked with mud and rust. Ten feet behind him, the young boy in the John Deere cap followed limply in an unsteady line. He was humming to himself.

At the shed, they staggered in, stumbling, and sat on the log carriage near the gleaming circular saw. They were short of breath and their nostrils stung with the acrid smell of turpentine and pine sap. Since it was Saturday afternoon, the mill was deserted and they relished the quietude of their rendezvous. Purvis removed the screw-top and lifted the bottle to his lips. He swallowed, coughed, and wiped his mouth with his sleeve.

"Cain't I have a swig?" asked the young man.

Mic Purvis grinned. "I tho't you was drunk enough."

The boy sniggered. "You cain't git too drunk on a Sat-dy night."

Purvis laughed. "You're damn right 'bout that!"

They sat and drank and talked about people and places they knew, about their experiences, about the scum of the black race and the need to once again put the "colored" in their place.

"What'd th' bastards want?" the boy wanted to know. "God, we're good to 'em; we give 'em ever'thing they need. What'n th' hell they want?"

"Evah Goddamn thing we got, that's what!" growled Purvis.

They were silent for awhile, with Purvis lounging on his elbows listening to the staccato sound of locusts and the passing caw of several crows. The setting sun left a cooling earth with lengthening shadows and a suspended glow of solitude.

But the sun still shone brightly on the young Negro girl who strode briskly by the stacks of weather-gray lumber, her cotton skirt swirling about trim, shapely thighs. Her breasts swayed provocatively as she took long strides in the blaze of the burning twilight. And this was the vision of the two men who watched from the mill shed. Purvis saw her first.

"Ooeee, looker ther'!" he whispered, licking his lips.

The young man was replacing the cap on the bourbon bottle. He looked up. "Yeah," he breathed. "You know who that is?"

"Who cares," drooled Mic Purvis. "That's some black meat!"

"She's *his* girl..!"

"Who?"

"Him! Th' nigger who's been stirrin' up all th' trouble! That's his little piece..!"

"How'n th' hell you know?" challenged Purvis.

"Oh, I know her," said the boy in the John Deere cap, smiling. "She's worked on th' Oliver farm where I done some plowin'. I seen th' two o' 'em together."

"Look at them legs," mused Mic, admiringly, as salvia oozed from his crooked smile.

"Yeahh.."

Purvis looked at the young man. "So she's his'n, y'say?"

"Damn tootin'."

"Well, hell, what're we waitin' fer? C'mon!" hissed Purvis, as he scrambled over the log carriage. The tall teenager was jolted into action and he quickly followed.

Abby, meanwhile, unaware of the menace, moved among the stacks of lumber, tightening the hold on the shoulder strap of a cloth purse which swayed to the rhythm of her stride. Her mind was consumed by her disturbing encounter with Miss Ethel and the crisis seemingly created by the one she cared for most. How could she convince Joey that his quest was not worth the struggle, that success or failure was certain to leave a tremor of lasting trouble? And yet, she wondered if she should even try, for she burned with anger and resentment at Miss Ethel's impertinence.

The sun, full in her face, was hot, bright, and blinding. She smelled the pine rosin of recently cut lumber and she glanced up at the towering pile of planks. She hurried on, unaware of anything amiss. But then, suddenly, she was accosted by two silhouettes which loomed quickly between her and the sun. The apparition, haloed in the glare of the overwhelming

189

light, frightened her. They were upon her and terror overwhelmed her. She screamed.

Then, it quickly happened.

A callused, sweaty hand covered her mouth and smothered her cry of shock. Octopi tentacles tore savagely at her body, wrestling her to the ground. Her shrill shriek, though stifled, seemed to linger as a vibration in the trembling air.

Struggle as she might, she could not move, for she was pinned by Purvis. And his foolish grin looked ghoulish in the glimmer of twilight through the trees. Her vision dissolved into a haze of humiliation, as she felt her dress being torn and her body exposed.

She almost fainted.

The determined boy in the John Deere cap knelt quickly between her legs and rudely pried unwilling thighs. He leeringly ignored the awe-stricken eyes which pleaded for deliverance as he licentiously leaned down upon her body. She felt the excruciating force, the crushing weight, the hot, foul breath which offended her face.

Then, pain!

And shame became a companion of fear, as she fought the infamy of her predicament, that unholy feeling of desecration. She was ill. Groaning, sobbing, her head spasming from side to side, she struggled to resist.

"Git 'er, boy; git 'er good!" goaded Mic, his saliva-slick mouth distorted in a salacious grin.

And the world spun in a blinding, bitter malaise as the tall boy responded, thrusting deep, his breath coming faster, faster, until, with a groan, he shuddered in release. He slowly raised himself from the trembling, inert body beneath him.

Her eyes were squeezed tight to hide from sight the ignominy of the violation. She lay hurt, harboring anger, resentment, regret. And through a prism of tears, she saw curious lights and color. There was red—and—and yellow—-the purple of hate—and the black of darkness which defined her distress.

"Oh God, you got 'er good," praised Purvis, as the boy in the John Deere cap stood unsteadily and assumed an arrogant pose, breathing hard, buckling his belt.

"Now, it's my turn," giggled Mic.

As Purvis awkwardly lowered himself over the prostrate figure, the young man snapped, "You better make it quick. We sure as hell don't want to git caught..!" And, glancing about him, the boy adjusted his John Deere cap.

Mic Purvis eagerly groped for the girl, but she was limp. She had mercifully fainted. But unmindful, he struggled, grunted, and withdrew. "My God," he said with surprise, "She's bleeding!"

Abby slowly conceived consciousness. No one was about. She was alone. In the eerie silence of dusk, she shivered with tortured thoughts and terrible pain. She lay in a fetal curve, trembling, sobbing.

The day was now ending. The sun had set.

CHAPTER 24

Joey ran through the night, jumping ditches, crossing fields, rushing madly through slashing blades of corn to enter at last the dirt road leading to her house. Breathless with emotion, he gulped for air as he widened his stride.

The terrible news relayed by a neighbor had reached him that same night. And he was almost in tears as his muddled brain embraced the horrible image of Abby's ordeal and agony. He had been told that she had struggled home, weeping, distraught, and nearly collapsed at the front door. Between stifling sobs, Abby reluctantly revealed that she had been brutally ravished by two white men.

It was now late, almost midnight. Joey, apprehensive, paused briefly to catch his breath, but anxiety urged him onward. He ran as fast as he could toward the house, which he now saw dimly outlined in the brightness of a full moon. As he approached the porch of the building, he pulled up short, for there in the shadows he thought he saw a dark figure. It was a man seated on the porch steps.

"Is that you—Jonathan?"

The man did not answer at first. Then he said, menacingly, "Don' come no closer. You ain't wanted 'round heah..!"

Joey did not understand. "Jonathan, it's me!"

"I know who'n th' hell it is," the man growled. "And I'm tellin' you, Joey Henderson, you ain't wanted 'round heah..!"

"But Jonathan, I heard 'bout Abby and I came straight over!"

"Well, you can turn right around and go home."

Joey was puzzled. "But I want to see Abby! I heard what happened."

"And whut happened was all your fault."

"I don't know what you're talking about. I had nothin' to do with it."

"Oh no? You caused it all by doin' whut yo're doin'. Cain't you see? You're causing trouble fer all of us!"

Jonathan's accusation hurt. Joey did not reply, but brushed by the young man to climb the steps. Jonathan grabbed his shirt sleeve. "Go home!"

"No! I've got to see Abby!" said Joey between clenched teeth.

"Dammit! I said—"

Jonathan tried to force young Henderson back, but Joey whirled quickly and Abby's brother slipped from the steps to the sandy ground below. He raised himself on his elbow and shrieked, "Bastard!"

"Whut's goin' on out ther'?" The voice came from a dark figure standing behind the closed screen door, framed in lamplight. It was Horace, Abby's stepfather.

Joe hurried onto the porch.. "It's me, suh. Jes' me—Joey."

Horace seemed not to recognize him.

"Joey," the boy repeated. "Joey Henderson."

"Oh, you. Well? And whut do you want?"

"I came to see Abby."

"She's not able to see nobody," Horace informed him, curtly.

Behind Horace, Joey noticed a white man with a satchel. It was Dr. Ogden. It was not unusual to see him in Negro houses. He often offered his services to assist the one colored doctor in town, despite the criticism he received from white patients and the people of the town. But Dr. Ogden took the Hippocratic oath to heart and conducted his practice on his own terms. And although the white citizenry of Crestview fumed and complained of Dr. Ogden's "indiscretions," the physician was nevertheless held in high esteem—by both races.

Joey said, "But suh, I'd appreciate it if I could see her—for jes' a minute. I heard what happened and I came right over. Cain't I see her?"

"I'll tell her you dropped by," Horace told him.

"But.."

"Look, she's been through a lot!" declared Horace, irritably. "She cain't see nobody right now..!"

Joey heard Jonathan's voice behind him. "Least of all, *you,* Joey Henderson!"

"Keep your voice down, Jonathan!" ordered Horace. "My Lord, she might hear you..!"

Apparently she had, for even Joey heard her weak call from the bedroom. Joey even thought that she had said his name, but he could not be sure. He saw the doctor put down his bag and hurry off toward the sound.

Horace also saw Dr. Ogden leave and, irked, turned his attention to Joey. "Now, go on home, boy, you're jes' upsettin' ever"body."

"But—couldn't I jes' see her—jus' fer a minute?"

"No. You know whut happened. We got to deal with it."

At that moment, Joey heard Jonathan's taunt. "First, it was Uncle Nat—and now, by God, it's our Abby—you ain't fer shit, Joey Henderson!"

Despite an urge to anger, Joey said nothing. He was deeply troubled. He wanted to speak to Abby. He had to tell her that he never intended this to happen. He wanted her to see that he was sorry, truly sorry. With Jonathan's accusation searing his mind, he wanted her to know that he was ready to do whatever she wished regarding his participation in the NAACP plan.

"Please..?"

It was a plaintive plea, but Horace responded with a sneer as he snapped, "No. It'll do no good. Jonathan's right, you know. You've stirred up a helluva mess and until you can git a little sense in yo' haid, nobody wants a damn thing to do with you, boy. You're big trouble, that's th' long and short of it." He paused, then said quietly, "You bes' go home now."

Joey swallowed hard.

"You go on home," Horace repeated.

Joey then heard Abby's door close, and the doctor walked over to Horace. Dr. Ogden spoke in a low voice, but Joey heard him say, "She wants to see him."

"Who? Him?" asked Horace, glancing over his shoulder at the young man who still stood there on the porch. Horace frowned. "I don' know 'bout that. I don' think we want this fella 'round heah. And I think you know why, Dr. Ogden. You bein' a white man, you ought to know better'n anybody."

Dr. Ogden said, quietly, "I only know what's good for my patients, Horace." He glanced back at the bedroom door. "And that young girl in there," he continued, "is anxious to see this young man. And under the circumstances, her state of mind means more than anything else. It's entirely up to you, but, as her doctor, I would suggest that you let him see her—just briefly—for that's apparently what she wants. And—to deny her—well, could very well complicate her recovery from this terrible ordeal."

"But I thought you said she needs rest..!"

"She needs peace of mind, too."

Horace looked out at the young man still standing on the porch and, glancing back at the doctor, shrugged, then turned and walked away into the room. Dr. Ogden, accepting his action as approval, moved to open the screen door. He said to Joey, "I gave her sedative, she needs rest. But—you can see her, young man, but only for a minute."

Joey stepped inside to sidle past Horace and the doctor and move quickly before the paneled door of Abby's room. Seeing her door, he felt a familiar tinge of shame and a touch of embarrassment as he remembered entering that time and saw her unclad. He paused to look back at the two men. The doctor nodded. Joey turned the door knob slowly and quietly entered.

She was lying still, her back to him. A kerosene lamp, turned low, cast an eerie glimmer of light and shadow about the room. He moved around the bed quietly and craned his neck to see if she was awake. Her eyes were closed. And for several moments, he stood there, gazing at her tenderly, not daring to move or make a sound. Then, her eyes fluttered and, in a blur of recognition, she smiled tentatively and whispered, "Joey.."

He quickly dropped to his knees by her bed, his face close to hers. He touched her cheek gently. "Oh, Abby, Abby," he breathed.

She tried to smile, but tears welled in her eyes. She half hid her face in the pillow and her form trembled as a current of silent sobs surged within her.

"I'm—sorry. So sorry," he said, his eyes glistening with empathy and regret.

She did not raise her head or speak.

"It's goin' to be all right now, honey, honest it' ll be," whispered Joey. "I've been such a fool. But—but I never thought anything like this would happen. God knows, I never wanted anything to happen to you—especially you!"

From beneath the sheet covering her, her hand reached out for his and he took it. And she squeezed. And still, she could not speak, even though her heart seemingly had much to say.

"I want you to know, Abby, I've decided," said Joey quietly, a quaver in his voice. "Just like you wanted, I'll give it all up. I've been a fool."

She squeezed his hand.

"It's late, I know, but I'll set things straight—you'll see," he promised.

She struggled to lift her head from the pillow. Obviously drugged, her voice was weak and slurred. But she forced herself to ask, weakly, "Can—you —still—love me?"

He looked at her strangely. "Oh God, yes! I—of course I do..!"

Her cheeks were damp and her face mirrored her misery. Her moist eyes searched his for a confirmation of truth, as she murmured, "But—after—this—!"

He leaned over and kissed her cheek. "Of course I love you," he told her. "You're my girl..!"

"Oh, but Joey, how—can you—now..!?"

Her concern confused him. He could not truly translate her pain, or recognize the ache of her mental trauma. He did not see that she felt hopelessly defiled, indecent, unvirtuous, unworthy of his caring. He saw only the scars of his own guilt.

"I'm—I'm sorry, darlin'," he said. "Oh, God, I'm so sorry. If I hadn't been so damn stubborn, none of this would've happened. Oh, God, I love you..! And I'll be tellin' them tomorrow that I'm droppin' out, quittin', that I don't want no part of their scheme, that I don't give a damn if I ever get to college! I'll be tellin' 'em, Abby, I'll be tellin' 'em tomorrow!"

"No..!" Even in her feeble voice, she tried to be emphatic.

But he persisted, "Don't you worry none, I'm through with all of it."

"No," she repeated. "Please.."

She felt weak, weary, but she had to make him understand. "I want you --to keep on.. Keep at it, do it! I want you to do it now—-"

He looked into her wan, weary face, bewildered.

"For me," she said, weakly. Her voice trailed—"For me."

"Maybe you'd better not talk no more," Joey said.

"No, please, Joey," she pleaded. "You've got to hear me—you've got to go to that college like you said you would..!"

"You don' mean that, honey; you said all along that—"

She whispered, hoarsely, "I—I was wrong."

"I—for God's sake, Abby, I don't understand..!"

"It's different now.. After what happened tonight, I hope to God—!" She sobbed, and Joey held her hand tighter. "They cain't treat us like this, Joey, it ain't right. It was my daddy—and now it's me..! You cain't quit, not now, not ever..!"

"But Abby—"

"No! I want you to do it! For yourself and—for me!"

He reached out and gently touched her cheek and felt her tears. And he saw in her dark eyes the obstinacy of her decision.

"Promise me," she begged.

He did not speak at first. He did not know what to say.

She squeezed his hand again. "Promise me," she persisted.

He paused. Then, he said softly, "I promise—if—if it's really what you want." And he stood up, slowly, but her hand still held his.

He bent over to hear her faint, strained words "Oh, Joey, it was—so—awful… I feel so dirty—so—ashamed."

"I know, I know," he said, tenderly, "But Abby, don't you be worrying none about what happened tonight. Just know that I still love you..!"

She could not explain her anger, her dismay, her deep remorse at being denied the privilege of giving herself first to this man.

"Now—it's too late," she muttered.

Not really understanding her torment, Joey assured her, "You jes' get well and everything will be all right."

"You'll—keep on—lovin' me?"

"Yes..!" he whispered, feelingly, and with his finger wiped a tear from his own cheek.

Joey heard the door behind him and turned to see Dr. Ogden standing there. "I think you'd better leave now, son," the doctor said.

"I was just goin'," said Joey, quietly.

The young man leaned over to lightly kiss her once again. "Don't you worry 'bout nothin'," he said and, straightening, strode quietly from the room. As he passed the white man, he said briefly, but with deep sincerity, "Thank you, sir..!"

News of this abhorrent act even pricked the conscience of the white community. Most were duly shocked. Even if it was a colored girl—which some assumed she might have brought upon herself—it was a foul and evil offense which no respectable Southerner could condone.

No one was more bothered than the Tutwiler sisters. They harbored an agonizing guilt that they may have been responsible, indirectly, for the young girl's misfortune. If Ethel had not driven the young lady from their home, thought Bernice, Abby might never have been subjected to this brutal attack. And Ethel, as well, sensed an uneasy association with her action, although she would never admit to it.

Noticeably absent now was their customary comradeship and doting sisterhood. They followed their usual routine, went their separate ways, but when together they had little to say and a telling tension marred heir daily life. Bernice worked her hours at the college admissions office, then hurried home to prepare the evening meal. Ethel hovered politely at the periphery of their relationship, gently probing for understanding, and seeking to say small things she hoped might ignite a conversation. But her efforts were usually fruitless. Bernice remained taciturn and distant.

197

It was several weeks when, one evening before supper, Ethel stepped into the kitchen as Bernice removed a tray of biscuits from the oven. "Can I help?" she asked.

"No, dinner's 'bout ready," Bernice replied.

"I'm not helpless, you know."

Bernice ignored the remark and gingerly emptied the tray of hot biscuits onto a platter.

Ethel glared at her. "All right, sister, let's have it out."

Bernice looked at her, then turned away to retrieve a broiler of steaming butter beans from the stove.

"You've been acting quite snippety these days," accused Ethel, "and I'd like to know why..!"

"I think we'd better eat while th' biscuits are hot," quietly answered Bernice.

"I want to know *why!*" demanded Ethel.

"Now, sister, I do think we ought to eat while the food is hot," Bernice maintained.

"Bernice, you are exasperatin'! And I demand to have it out with you, here and now, once and for all..! Do you hear what I'm sayin'?"

"Mercy me, Ethel, you don't have to shout..!"

"Well, *listen!*"

Bernice rubbed her hands upon her apron. "I am, but I really think we ought to—"

"For days now, you have treated me with deliberate disdain. You have not talked or been very cordial. You certainly have not treated me as your blood and kin—and—and it's unfair. I want to know why."

Bernice did not answer.

"Why!?" Ethel demanded. "Is it because of that snip of a colored girl who used to be in our employ—is that it? Since when did my dear sister come to be a lover of Nig-ras, so much as to turn against her own kind?"

Bernice gripped the kitchen table for support. "Oh, Ethel, I didn't turn against you. I only felt sorry for Abby—for what we did to her, for what happened."

"We—didn't—do anything to her," emphasized Ethel. "It was those horrible men! They did it. It was a horrible, hateful thing, but they did it..! And we had nothin' to do with it! Cain't you see that?"

Bernice almost choked as she said, "All I know is we drove her from the house—and it happened..!"

"We did..! You mean I did!"

"Ethel," said Bernice, twisting her apron, "We *both* are to be blamed for that poor girl's misery. And no force on earth can restore her life of

198

decency! Her life has been ruined! And so young..! I cain't—help—but feel for that poor girl. Call it what you like, but I feel for our Abby and—and I'm so dreadfully sorry that we were so unfeeling as to force her from our home, as we did."

"But we didn't know anything like that was goin' to happen, now, did we?"

Bernice nodded

Ethel added, "Probably wouldn't have, if it hadn't been for that boy..!"

"But—it did happen," said Bernice, sadly.

"Well, we're not to blame. And besides, Nig-ras are always gettin' into that kind of trouble."

"Ohh, Ethel..!"

"I know, I know. It was a terrible thing, I admit, and I'm sorry for the girl. But—there's no reason for you to feel bad about us. Our little run-in had nothing to do with what happened to her. It happened, and it's over, and there's not much we can do about it."

Bernice said, quietly, "I don't happen to feel that way."

"What exactly do you mean, Bernice?"

"Ethel, it was rape."

"So?"

"The violation of a woman."

"A Nig-ra woman," Ethel reminded her.

Her eyes glistened as Bernice bitterly stated, "Not just a Nig-ra woman, my dear sister, but a betrayal of all women—white or black. And we cain't allow it to happen—-to her, to no woman on this earth. Th' authorities cain't do as they've done in th' past——look th' other way, ignore it, drag their feet, do nothin'—simply because she's a colored girl. We cain't let that happen! She's a woman, Ethel.. She's a woman—like you, like me!"

But a black woman, thought Ethel, and there is a difference. How her sister could become so emotionally affected by the plight of a simple Negro girl was beyond her. It had been a deplorable act, of course, one to be ashamed of, to denigrate. But, after all, it was a Negro.

"But Bernice," muttered Ethel. "It's up to them—th' law—"

"No.."

The stout one wheeled, scooped up a ladle from the table, and waving it as a threatening fist, proclaimed, "It's up to us! It's up to we women—we Christian, white, law-abiding ladies of this proud community..! It's up to you, sister,. . .and those important club ladies of yours! Yes, it's up to those fine, fastidious ladies who feel so proud to be Southern—to stand up for Southern womanhood! This is an act against all of us! And you must see to it that your ladies are incensed and angry and as concerned as we are..! No! We cain't leave this to th' indifference of white law enforcement."

"Ber-nice..!" gasped Ethel. "I've never seen you like this..!"

Bernice turned her back on her sister. "There's never been anything like this."

Ethel was a bit shakened by her sister's stance. But she now understood more clearly Bernice's concern and her resolve. And the younger sister had certainly struck a vital nerve. Ethel took pride in her various womens' organizations to which she belonged, believing in their social esteem and integrity. But she liked to think also that they stood for more than mere social prestige—important as that might be in a small town like Crestview—but served as well to influence civic and moral standards of the community. Ethel appreciated, above all, their advocacy of womanhood and, in particular, their devotion to the respect and sanctity of Southern femininity. Now, this principle was being challenged. And Bernice was right. All women, including the respectable white ladies of the community, should rise and remonstrate against this ghastly crime—even if it was a young colored girl who had been made the symbol of this evil act.

"What do we do, then?" Ethel asked.

"Do? We let everybody know what we think of this despicable attack on this young innocent girl. We'll write letters to the editor of the paper. We'll raise a stink!"

"Really, Bernice. An *issue*," she corrected.

Bernice was twisting her apron. "We cain't let them sweep this thing under th' rug, dear Ethel, we simply cain't. Those men must be brought to justice! And I have a feeling they won't be, unless we—and all th' women folk of this town—absolutely demand it. Now—will you talk to your friends? Will you explain why they should be concerned, too?"

Ethel eased toward the door of the kitchen, but over her shoulder she said, "I think we'd better have supper, dear."

"Ethel?"

"Yes, yes, of course I'll speak to them. Now, let's eat."

Bernice sighed. "Th' biscuits are cold," she said, glumly.

Sheriff Fisher strode indifferently into his office and was about to move around his desk to take a seat when his deputy, Corny Evans, informed him, "A reporter from th' local paper was lookin' fer you."

"Yeah? Whut about?"

"I think he wants a progress report on th' investigation into that rape case."

"Whut case?" asked Jethro Fisher.

"You know, that Nig-ra girl."

"Oh, that. Well, that's under th' jurisdiction of th' city police," answered the sheriff. "Did you tell him that?"

"Uh..no, but—"

"Well, you should have. He'll have to see them," Jethro growled.

"He did talk to them," said Corny, "But they said it was a joint investigation."

Fisher muttered, "Bastards," and eased into his chair. "Hell, what do I know? My God, ther's more to do around heah than chase after some nooky-hungry black bastard. Hell, how do we know it was rape? You never know, she prob'ly opened her legs like pinking shears and swallowed his dick like a snappin' turtle..!" He laughed.

Corny did not laugh. "But they said it was a white man who done it."

Jethro's joviality faded. "Who says? Nobody's got no proof! Hell, it could be any black man.. Ain't they th' ones with th' big pricks? Besides, she could have asked for it. You know how loose them nigger gals can be.."

Corny Evans turned to leave. "Well, anyway, he's comin' back."

"Okay," said Sheriff Fisher, as he ruffled through some papers on his desk. "I'll be waitin'."

Jethro was diffident. He wondered what he might tell the reporter, what he might say to pacify his prying interest. He had not put in much time on this particular case, he knew, for he put little credence in the girl's story—even in spite of Dr. Ogden's corroboration. What did the doc know? The doc was too liberal, too lenient with Negroes to offer a reliable opinion, anyway. We could do without the likes of him and those who coddle these worthless people, thought the sheriff. And what about all those letters to the editor? My God! What do those bleeding-heart ladies want? Southern womanhood..!? Hell! This was a colored girl!

CHAPTER 25

Joey Henderson had not slept well. On the morning of July 12, 1955, he awoke to the sound of a cooing mourning dove and a vague realization that this was the day of an ambiguous beginning. He turned over in bed and stared at the ceiling. He had dreaded the sunrise and yet, somehow, was thankful of its coming. It had been a restless night.

He eased his legs over the side of the bed and looked through the murky panes of his bedroom window at a pink and purple sky. He had to dress, for soon the Reverend Mortecai Ellison would pick him up for the journey to the state capital. This day marked the resumption of the seemingly never-ending court case. But this time, Joey sensed a foreboding which had hardly affected him before. His name, his family, were on trial.

A brief thought of Abby crossed his mind. He had seen her only the night before and they had talked of this day and what it meant. And when he told her that he was nervous about the outcome, she assured him that everything would turn out well and that she would be anxious to hear the news after it was all over.

Later, at breakfast, he sat silently with his father and absently toyed with his bacon and eggs. Elijah had delayed leaving for the fields to see his son off and to wish him well. And when Joey heard Ellison's car pull up outside, he quickly hugged his mother and nodded farewell to his father. As they drove away, Joey looked back to see his father wave.

As the car sped along the asphalt road, a familiar panorama of fields and gray, weather-beaten barns and tenant houses slid past. The Reverend Ellison was unusually quiet. After a brief conversation before entering the highway heading out of town, he said little and concentrated on his driving. Joey respected his reticence and remained silent himself. Once, noticing Joey's nervousness, the reverend had said, "Don't you be worryin', boy, ever'thin's goin' to turn out all right. Today's th' day!"

As so many times before, Joey entered the Federal court building with awe and an edgy uncertainty. Inside, he sensed even more an air of strained expectancy. There were low murmurs as lawyers casually moved about, busying themselves with last minute details, conferring, laughing, joking. Joey turned in his chair to watch a few people find their seats in the courtroom.

Suddenly, the loud voice of the bailiff bade the audience to rise and give notice. Judge Grooms quickly entered and bounded up the steps of the riser to take his seat behind the bench. All eyes scrutinized him carefully for any sign of poor health, but his sharp features belied any evidence of debilitation or weakness as a result of his recent heart problem. He cleared his throat and asserted a firm demeanor which described a determined intent to bring this process to a speedy and definitive conclusion. He gave a brief, curt apology for the delay he had caused in the fulfillment of the scheduled hearing, and he promised that everything would be done to expedite a fair and reasonable verdict. He called on the prosecution to present its case.

Edgar Hall, glancing at his support team of Marshall and Anderson, almost reluctantly arose to approach the bench. He called to the stand Bernice Tutwiler.

After the usual amenities of identification for the record, Hall issued his ultimatum. "You would not accept my client as a bonified student on the day of registration for the spring semester—is that not correct?"

"Yes," said Bernice weakly.

Edgar Hall spoke up, "I beg your pardon?" And he cocked his head as if he had not heard.

Bernice was annoyed. "I said yes!" she blurted out.

"On what basis, Miss Tutwiler?"

"He was not qualified," she answered.

"Really? On whose authority?"

"On—mine," Bernice replied. "The college has set definite guide lines, *which* I follow."

"But—in this case—what was the basis of your decision?" Hall asked.

"Moral turpitude."

Hall acted surprised. "Moral—turpitude?"

"Yes, I believe he has a family record which would make him an unfit candidate for admission into Crestview State College," she stated firmly and convincingly, she hoped.

"Oh?" Hall paced several steps and turned. "And what family *record* do you presume to base your denial of this young man?"

Bernice shifted uneasily in the chair. "He has a brother currently serving an extended sentence in our state penitentiary."

"So?"

"So—" Miss Tutwiler paused. "Well, he—this young man, I mean—was involved as well."

"You're referrin' to th' plaintiff?"

"Yes."

"And how was he involved?" asked Hall. "Was he tried and convicted for any alleged felony?"

"He received a suspended sentence, I believe," said Bernice.

"Th' truth of th' matter, Miss Tutwiler, is that th' young man whom you've refused entrance into Crestview State College was only nine years of age at the time of this particular incident—and that he was only indirectly involved because of the peer pressure of his brother. He was reprimanded and released by the juvenile authorities. Now, he has not caused any trouble since and for ten years now Joseph Henderson has been a reliable citizen and a model student. I ask you, does that one misdemeanor prove sufficient cause to deny this person his constitutional right to receive an education?"

Miss Tutwiler replied, "He's not being denied an education."

"Oh, no?"

"He's just being denied admission to—our college, that's all."

"But why..!?"

Bernice looked him in the eye. "He could go to a Negro college, I suppose, if he wanted," she said.

"I see," said Edgar Hall. "So then th' basis of your decision was *race!*"

"No! Not at all!" exclaimed the registrar, trying to indemnify her unfortunate remark. "The fact remains is that he has a record and a background which warrants careful consideration. And it's our prerogative to refuse admission to anyone we deem doubtful, no matter who he is..!"

Hall smiled. "I understand." He paused. "Miss Tutwiler, I would assume that you are a religious woman.."

She eyed him curiously. "I try to be."

"Do you believe in Jesus Christ?"

Bernice was taken aback by this personal and presumptuous query. "I-I—-of course!"

"Your honor!" interrupted the opposing attorney, Rob DeWitt. "I must protest this line of questioning. Miss Tutwiler's religious beliefs have little to do with the issue at hand. She is governed by the precise rules and regulations of the college—and is only carrying out a mandate imposed by her office."

Judge Grooms leaned forward. "I must confess, Mr. Hall, I too am puzzled by your approach. Can you clarify your objective before you go any further with questions that appear, to say the least, impertinent and irrelevant?"

"Gladly, your honor! I was about to allude to the fact that we have all sinned and that our Lord Jesus forgave us and said go forth and sin no more. My client has done just that—he sinned once, yes, but he has led a responsible and irreproachable life since..!"

"Mr. Hall!"

"Yes, your honor?"

"Confine your questioning to the facts of the immediate issue. We will not engage in a philosophical discourse, is that clear?"

Hall wiped his forehead with a wide, white handkerchief. "I understand, your honor, but I beg you to accept my point as pertinent and germane to our case. It's an obvious fact that the witness and th' officials of this college cannot, in good conscience, reject th' application of this young man merely on the basis of some minor, youthful indiscretion, which even th' juvenile authorities at th' time thought it excusable under the conditions of th' offense. I—was only making my point in terms of th' religious principles of my witness."

The judge stated firmly, "There's no need to belabor the point, Mr. Hall. Let's get on with it."

"Yes, your honor," said Hall, quietly, and turned away. But he glanced back at Miss Tutwiler to say, "That's all, ma'am, thank you."

When Edgar Hall attempted to call several character witnesses, Judge Grooms again intervened and this time summoned the lawyers to his chambers for a conference. They did not bother to sit as they entered and Judge Grooms turned to them and spoke bluntly .

"Gentlemen, I know what's going on here—and I'm not about to sit through a lot of worthless rigmarole reiteratin' what we already know. Let's get this thing over with. If you've got witnesses who can add anything new, let's get 'em on and off, but I'll be damned if I'm going to prolong this procedure much longer. Let's not forget why we're here. Th' court's already ruled that this damned college cannot refuse this young man. And yet it did. Now, by God, you'd better get on th' stick, Rob, and justify their actions, or you're goin' to be hit with one helluva contempt citation. Let's hurry things up. And don't you be giving me any more of that evangelistic crap, Edgar, and forget about character witnesses. I've got my own ideas as to what this Henderson kid's like. I simply want to hear all th' testimony. … But it better be *pertinent* testimony. Do I make myself clear?"

The two men nodded and the trio trekked back into the courtroom, and the hearing resumed.

The assistant attorney general of the state reviewed his roster of witnesses and decided that he should continue as planned. He called upon the juvenile authority present at the time of Joey's arraignment. The official detailed the circumstances and suggested that, had it not been for the young boy's age, he would have been in serious trouble as an accomplice and no doubt would have received something more than a mere reprimand.

Hall, in cross-examination, tried to minimize the indictment, but the juvenile officer maintained that the offence had been grave. He again reminded the lawyer that being underage had been a determining factor in Joey's release.

Then, DeWitt introduced testimony to characterize Joey's brother as unconscionable and incorrigible. He called to the stand an elderly Negro, who shuffled through the balustrade gate and awkwardly raised his hand to take the oath.

"Take a seat," instructed DeWitt. "Your name, please?"

"Ol Suggs."

"That's—Oliver, isn't it?"

"Yessuh, but they all calls me 'Ol'," he said with a slight smile.

"You've lived in the community near the Hendersons for quite some time, is that correct?" DeWitt asked.

"Yessuh. Jes' about two—no—three farms over."

"Then you know the Hendersons."

"Tolerably well."

Joey strained for recognition. He could not place the man. Hall leaned over to Joey. "Who'n th' hell is he?" Joey frowned and shrugged.

And then, a sudden glimmer of recall made Joey sit up straight. He remembered now that his papa once had a falling-out with a man over some borrowed farm equipment which one or the other had not returned. It had been a brief but bitter encounter and the two never spoke again. Joey had not known the man, but he felt sure that this must have been the person Elijah so angrily despised.

"Then, you know the plaintiff's brother?" DeWitt inquired.

"Derek?" The man chuckled. "Ever'body knowed Derek."

206

"How? In what way?"

"He was a bad'n, all right," muttered the man, shaking his head.

Joey hastily scribbled something on a piece of paper and shoved it in front of Edgar Hall.

"He was always stealin' or gittin' into all sorts of mischief," added Suggs.

"And was the plaintiff with him whenever he did these things?"

"Oh, yessuh, I seen th' two of 'em pallin' around together."

DeWitt wheeled. "That'll be all, Mr. Suggs"

Suggs had half risen from the chair when the firm, deep voice of Edgar Hall halted him. "Mr. Suggs..!" As the lawyer approached him, Oliver Suggs watched him warily. "If they palled around as you say they did, then it's more'n likely th' older brother had a lot of influence on th' young one. Wouldn't you say that?"

"I—I don' know.. I reckon," Suggs replied, uncertainly.

"How many times did you see them together?" Edgar asked.

"Ohhh, I don' know—lots of times, I think."

Edgar Hall looked at the Negro intently, as the old man wrung his hands nervously. "Is it not true, Mr. Suggs, that you had a dispute with the plaintiff's father four or five years ago over some farm machinery and that you've not spoken to Mr. Henderson since?"

Suggs looked surprised, perplexed, as if his memory had escaped him. Hall, not waiting for an answer, pressed on, relentlessly. "The fact is, you don't really know the Hendersons very well, do you?"

"I know thet Derek was a devil!"

"You know what other people told you about him, what was generally known, but you never had any direct dealings with Derek, now, did you?"

"Well..."

"Or, for that matter, with Joey Henderson here. In truth, Mr. Suggs, you know very little about th' Henderson family, about this young man—especially this young man—how he distinguished himself in school, how he's become a model citizen with a fine reputation. All you really know, I dare say, is that you still hold a grudge against Elijah Henderson, th' plaintiff's father. That much is obvious and I think we've heard enough!"

Oliver Suggs was angry, flustered. He tried to protest. "Wait a minute, I—"

"Dismissed!" snapped Edgar Hall and turned his back on the witness.

Suggs was standing. "Wait one damn minute!"

A sharp crack of the gavel preceded Judge Grooms' curt command, "That'll be all, Mr. Suggs—you're dismissed—thank you."

Rob DeWitt was obviously disappointed. He had debated a long time the advisability of placing Ol Suggs on the stand. He knew that he was not very intelligent but, being black, DeWitt thought Suggs might be an ideal counter to any character testimonials the prosecution might offer in behalf of the plaintiff. He could have been most effective in presenting what might appear an unprejudiced perception of the Hendersons and the notoriety of their offspring. Unfortunately, he did not fulfill these expectations and his appearance as a witness was a failure.

Okay.. But Rob DeWitt had other cards to deal from his deck, so he stood up and summoned Professor Walter T. Timonds to take the stand. The assistant attorney general for the state was convinced that his testimony would do better for their cause.

"Would you state your name, please?"

"Walter T. Timonds," the man replied.

"That is—*Doctor*—Timonds, true?"

"Uh, yes—I have a Ph.D. in psychology from the University of Virginia and I am currently on the faculty of the state university."

"That's—our state university, you mean," prompted DeWitt.

"Yes, of course—here in the city."

DeWitt looked up at Judge Grooms and declared, "I might add, for the record, your honor, that Professor Timonds is one of the leading clinical psychologists in the country, and that he has conducted considerable research and written extensively in the area of behavioral psychology, particularly as it pertains to criminality."

The magistrate acknowledged this and muttered, "Continue."

DeWitt turned back to the little man on the witness chair. "Dr. Timonds, I believe you have conducted some studies with regard to family inheritance of criminal traits.."

"Yes, I and others have researched the probable chance of such tendencies being passed from one generation to another in a given family," said Timonds.

"And—your conclusions?"

"It can and does happen."

"You mean—-let me get this straight—-that if a member of a family is an incorrigible, conducive to criminal activity, then it is likely that other members of that family might also be assigned a similar fate?"

"There is positive evidence of that, yes."

"Like—in the genes—or something."

"Yes."

"Then, in the case of the plaintiff, there is a likelihood of inbred tendencies as exemplified in his older brother, a convicted criminal..?"

"There is—that possibility," Dr. Timonds replied.

"Objection!" Hall followed with the simple view, "Speculation."

"But your honor," said DeWitt quickly, "this is more than mere speculation. It is based on research!"

"I—find this a rather interesting theory," said Judge Grooms. "I will allow an explanation before deciding its significance and applicability. Continue, Mr. DeWitt."

"You said, sir, that there was a possibility. Would you not say that it is, in truth, a *strong* possibility?" asked DeWitt.

"Oh, my, yes."

"Something that would justify caution in the consideration of this young man?"

"Yes."

DeWitt smiled. He turned to his perspiring opponent. Your witness."

Hall approached the professor slowly. "You—would not dare suggest that this occurs in all families, now, would you, Dr. Timonds?"

"Well, no—I—"

"It is true, is it not, that an offspring can be unaffected by such tendencies, that members of a particular family can be different as night and day in ther moral make-up and personality?" pressed Hall.

"Of course, but—"

"And in this case," challenged Joey's attorney, "is it not possible that this young man, who has had absolutely no encounters with the law since his early youth, when he was so vulnerable and under the peer pressure of his older brother—is it not possible that he is truly an upstanding individual, incapable of committing any wrong, that he is not subject to this theory of 'inheritance' of which you spoke?"

Timonds paused before he answered. "Possibly," he said and added quickly, "But this would be an exception and not the rule."

Hall persisted, "But this could be the circumstance, could it not?"

"Yes, it could be. But research supports the likelihood of generational inheritance of these tendencies."

"But, as you've said, it isn't always true in every instance, is it?"

"No."

Hall turned away and, over his shoulder, uttered indifferently, "That's all."

Judge Grooms recessed the court for lunch.

Now, at length, the hearing was entering its final phase. Judge Grooms had expedited the procedure and now it was up to the competing attorneys to prevail. Edgar Hall arose and charged that his adversary had deliberately laid down a "smokescreen" to hide the indefensible actions of the college. "But it's a hopeless tactic, I tell you!" Hall shouted. "It's clear, it's obvious that it's a last-ditch effort to deny this young man his constitutional right!"

Edgar Hall, plump, big jowled, and perspiring, stalked the floor in front of the bench with the intensity and frustration of a caged animal. Part of the smokescreen, he pointed out, had been the unwarranted warning of trouble. If trouble came, he maintained, it would be because of the recalcitrance of the white community. "I'm not saying it will be easy," Hall declared, "but I am saying it is *right!*" Hall cried out that the decision had been long ago established by the courts and any delay in activation was an injustice, that the ruse of refusal of Henderson was ill-conceived and improper and without legitimate rationale.

"Th' very idea that a youthful indiscretion could be used to besmirch th' proven reputation of my client is ridiculous and inexcusable. It is a dirty, unforgivable trick. It's a red herring!" screamed Hall.

As Rob DeWitt stood up, he was smiling. "I can appreciate the passion of my opposing colleague, but facts are facts. His client is the product of a lawless family, the subject being involved in something more than what my opponent has dared to call—what was it?—'youthful indiscretion'?" DeWitt maintained that the scientifically accepted theory of inherited criminal tendencies made the young man a decided risk and therefore offered ample basis for the college to reject him—-"on grounds applicable to all present and prospective students," he added. "Your honor, we feel completely justified in opposing the order of this court in the honest belief that, when the full facts were learned of the applicant, his background, justice would be amended and the verdict reversed." He again argued that the college had every right to decide its own course "for the benefit and safety of all concerned." DeWitt walked over and looked down at the Negro attorneys. "My colleague here," he said, indicating Edgar Hall, "would have the court believe that this is a simple process—that a Negro can overnight be admitted into the all-white environment of an American college and expect a peaceful, uneventful transition." He looked out over the court. "I caution you! I caution the court! Let us not reap chaos and destruction! For either the college, the community, or the individual..!" The assistant attorney general then turned and slowly approached the bench. Looking up at Judge Grooms, he pleaded, "For God's sake, don't create a situation in which we will regret a needless loss of human life!

210

I'm not saying that integration of our institutions of higher learning is not proper, I'm merely cautioning that it is simply not wise at this time. It must be a slow, orderly process. There must be restraint in the enforcement of this decision. Otherwise, it must be said, don't be surprised if we have blood on our hands!"

So ended the hearing.

The judge was not swayed. In his ruling, later, Judge Grooms issued an order that Crestview State College would forthwith admit the plaintiff, Joseph Henderson, at the commencement of the fall semester, 1955, or otherwise be held in contempt. "This is a final judgment in this case," the judge asserted. "Under no circumstance can this decision be altered or reversed."

CHAPTER 26

The Crestview State College board of trustees, even in the face of this entrenched judicial decision, was unable to accept their contentious future. E. Braxton Edwards called a meeting closed to the press and media, but included the governor and certain members of the college administration.

As Byron prepared to leave for the meeting, Florence knew he was bothered.

"What's the good of this meeting?" she asked. "It's all been decided, hasn't it? The court has ruled and they must certainly comply—isn't that so?"

"You would think so. But these people have minds of their own."

"If they resist, what happens?"

Byron answered, "They run the risk of a contempt citation."

"Which—," said Florence hesitantly, "—would involve you as well."

He looked at her. "Yes, I suppose so."

Florence McAndrew turned her back on her husband and walked slowly, thoughtfully, across the room. She turned.

"What will you do?"

"Now—or eventually? I don't really know. I will of course try to convince them that it will be most unwise to defy the order of the court."

"But—" She paused, then observed, "They'll not listen, will they?"

"They must."

Wearily, he sat down in a wingback parlor chair. He leaned over and covered his face with his hands. "I don't know how this will turn out, Flo. I did try to do my best—only—"

He looked up at her. "I regret that I didn't confide in you more. I simply did not want to worry you needlessly. Yet, I know now that whatever happens is crucial to both of us. It involves you as much as me."

She smiled and moved toward him.

"I shouldn't worry. You have truly done your best," she assured him. She then knelt before him, resting her arms on his knees, and he looked deep into her eyes. She whispered, "I'm sure everything will turn out all right."

"But you must understand, my dear, this is a critical point in both our lives. It could affect our very existence, certainly my career."

Florence said softly, "We'll survive. You know that."

He glanced at his watch. "Goodness, look at the time."

"You're leaving now?"

"Yes."

"Why so soon?"

"I decided I'd walk tonight," Byron explained.

"But why? I could drive you," his wife offered.

"That's good of you, my love, but—I've got to do a little thinking," he said as he walked with her into the hall with his arm around her waist. "I need some time to myself. I've got to sort out a few things. The long walk to the building will give me a chance to do just that."

"Aren't you taking a raincoat?"

"No."

"Why not? I heard on the radio that a big storm's headed this way," she told him.

"Yes, I heard. But it's not expected until tomorrow morning. And even if it does blow up, I can always get someone to bring me home."

He then pulled away, saying, "I'll see you later tonight." With long strides, he was at the front door.

She watched him and, as he placed his hand on the doorknob, she ran quickly to him. She fell into his arms and hugged him tightly, her head against his shoulder. He smelled her hair, her faint perfume, and he heard her say, "I do hope it goes well, darling." She looked up into his eyes. "I'll be with you in my thoughts every minute..!"

He stooped to kiss her, a gentle peck. And he smiled.

"I'm glad. That's nice to know."

The air was heavy with a scent of the approaching storm. The radio had reported winds of hurricane force off the coast of Georgia and had issued warnings that the turbulence was turning inland and might approach Crestview about noon or early afternoon of the following day. Already, as Byron McAndrew walked, the trees above him trembled. The air seemed charged with expectancy.

But Byron, deep in thought, did not concern himself with any likelihood of a predicted storm, for his fretful mind leafed quickly through pages of his past, recalling particular moments: his graduate days, his first date with Flo, their wedding, their struggle of married life in the Massachusetts university town of Cambridge while studying for his doctorate. He remembered his first academic position, his first classes. He thought of his service in the navy and those long war years away from his wife. And his return to academia, his first exposure to administration at Bowling Green, Ohio, his yearning to return South and the eventual opening at Crestview—quick reflections which reinforced his feelings and asserted the validity of his beliefs. He had to measure the meaning of tonight's determination in terms of his own character, his own conscience.

He had not been wrong. Looking back, he would not have changed a thing in the evolution of his career. And when he applied at Crestview State College, he knew and understood the difficult challenges awaiting him. He expected to walk in the wake of undiminished idolization of his predecessor, Jasper Morton, and to constantly feel that his every move, his every decision, would be matched against the presumed faultlessness of the former president. But this had not bothered him. He felt secure in his position. And he felt he knew the territory, the people, and that he had the patience to endure their impatience and their continuing scrutiny.

That is, until now.

Now, he found himself at a decisive crossroad where his life, his career, was on the line. And while he never reckoned that integration would become an issue, he did somehow foresee its advent and had tried to warn the board and members of his administration. But cloistered as they were in their bastion of bias, they had refused to listen.

In the twilight of these thoughts, he emerged from the gravel path bisecting the circular drive fronting the administration building. He saw immediately the large white van with the multicolored peacock symbol and the block letters **NBC Television.** It struck him. National coverage!

He saw a number of automobiles parked around the curving driveway and noted the limousine which no doubt had brought the governor. Yes, undoubtedly, this momentous event had attracted widespread attention— and he felt queasy at the thought that he might be a central figure in this imbroglio. As he turned and started up the steps, McAndrew was suddenly accosted by a man in a blue suit who thrust a microphone in his face.

"Hi! I'm Ed Winston of CBS..!"

Byron paused.

"President McAndrew, do you think this meeting will achieve the objective you're seeking?"

"I beg your pardon?"

"The trustees are seeking a consensus to defy the court's order to admit that young Negro boy—is that not correct?"

"I know nothing about that," said Byron. "As far as I know, this meeting is merely to discuss recent developments and decide a possible course for our institution."

"But you would agree, President McAndrew, that certain members of your college board are quite vocal in their prejudice against Negroes," insisted the CBS reporter.

Byron blanched. "I would not care to characterize any person serving on the Crestview State College Board of Trustees. They're honorable, dedicated men. And now, if you'll excuse me, I must hurry inside."

Winston hurriedly said, "What do you think about a Negro in your college?"

Byron smiled. "Anyone qualified is certainly acceptable as a student in our college." He glanced quickly at the entrance beneath the portico of the administration building. "Now, I really must be going," he said and hurried away.

"But President McAndrew!" called Winston, but Byron did not hear.

As he reached the door, someone touched his arm. It was Al Spivey. Spivey indicated the horde behind him. "Nosy bastards, aren't they?"

Inside, McAndrew turned. "Well, I guess they're doing their job," he said.

Leaving Spivey, the president quickly entered the conference room. He saw Bernice Tutwiler, already seated, obviously as far from the head conference table and its lectern as she could possibly be. She was alone.

Near the head table, the governor was standing, talking to several board members. He saw President McAndrew and waved to him. Byron smiled and acknowledged him with a small gesture, but he walked over to where Bernice was seated.

The president spoke to her. "Good evening," he said. "I see they've brought everybody together tonight."

Bernice looked up at him and asked, quietly, "Do I really have to be here?"

215

"I suppose so, Miss Tutwiler. What happens tonight concerns us all, I guess. It's good to have you with us, for your good sense, I think, will mean a lot to help us reach a reasonable decision. I'm glad you're here."

He smiled at her and she thought how very kind and considerate he was. She admired him, despite the dichotomy and confusion regarding his perceived view of racial matters. She watched him as he walked away to shake the hand of the governor and engage him in a cordial, animated conversation. Then she saw Dr. Cartwright.

Charlie Cartwright, obviously pleased to be involved, had taken a seat up front. Although he was discomforted at the thought that his institution might lose its longstanding policy of segregation, he saw little hope in this final, feeble effort to resist. Dr. Cartwright would have normally given credence to a continued struggle, but his resolve of recent had been weakened. He had been shakened by the repudiation of Senator McCarthy at the end of 1954. With diminishing interest now in communism as a threat, the cause celebre of Cartwright's obsession seemed wanting, leaving him unsure and bereft of his beliefs.

The men filed into the room and, chatting noisily, took their places at the table. The chairman of the board, E. Braxton Edwards, stood before the speaker's lectern. He gaveled the meeting to order.

"Folks, our meeting will come to order. As you know, we, th' trustees of Crestview State College are meetin' tonight to discuss and hopefully decide a most crucial course for our institution. Now, this is a closed meeting, for I didn't want any of us to be intimidated by the presence of outsiders and especially th' press. However, we do have with us several invited people who are not members of th' board, or who, as ex-officio members, meet with us only now and again.

"These people have been involved with this issue, either directly or indirectly, and no doubt can give us good counsel and advice. We're especially pleased to have with us th' governor of our great state, th' Honorable Wilfred Eggerton..!" The governor smiled and nodded. There was a sprinkling of applause. "Governor, sir, would you say a few words?"

The governor stood. He was not smiling as he said, "I'm privileged to be with you this evening. But let me say at the outset that I'm only here because of the gravity of the situation. What is decided here tonight will undoubtedly affect th' future structure of higher education in our state. Other than that, I would not care to express any opinion at this time. I truly understand the seriousness of your responsibility, but in no way am I here to influence your decision. You must decide what is best by your own conscience. You must do what you believe is right for Crestview State College."

A few people clapped as the governor sat down. Edwards responded: "Thank you, Governor Eggerton. Now, it's time for us to evaluate our situation and arrive at some official decision. Your participation is welcome, please speak your mind."

He then reviewed the long process of court deliberation and its apparent outcome. And he called upon the assistant attorney general of the state to assess their case as he saw it from a judicial vantage point. DeWitt was not optimistic. He felt that everything had been done to alter the legal course leading to racial integration and that little remained but to abide by the court's decision.

"My God," muttered B. H. Bellinger, dejectedly. And the sense of his reaction reverberated throughout the room, as faces of other members of the board reflected disappointment and dismay.

Al Spivey's hand shot up in the air. "Mr. DeWitt!" He quickly got to his feet, his thick jowls burnished with untempered rage. "I cain't believe that we're even sittin' here discussin' this damn business like this—like it's done for and settled, like we got no other choice but to take that—that black kid into our college! Hell, don't tell me that there's no way we can keep this thing from happenin'..! We don't live in a po-lice state; there ain't no storm troopers forcin' us to do somethin' we don't want to do, that we know ain't right. By God, there's bound to be some legal recourse. There's got to be a way.. There's—there's just-—*got* to be..!"

"Yeah..!" echoed McCall.

"I think.." Bellinger's bass voice thundered above the gathering murmur of disgruntled board members, and he repeated, "I think Al's got a good point there. I mean, we cain't abandon a position we've held all along. We said we'd never give in."

The murmur now erupted into concerned chatter, as Edwards tried to gavel the meeting to order. "Gentlemen, gentlemen, please!" The sounds of dissent gradually ceased.

The chairman then said, "We have invited the assistant attorney general of our state here for the sole purpose of providing his expert opinion as to whatever legal alternatives we have left—and—if I understand you correctly, Mr. DeWitt, you say there are none."

DeWitt cleared his throat and, standing beside Edwards at the podium, declared, "None that I can see. Not with the case that we now have or the evidence we're able to offer."

The chatter increased. They simply could not fathom the finality that loomed large and conclusive. They refused to accept what seemed inevitable. Yet, there was the staunch immutability of the elder member of the board. They had to take heart in the hope of Hartley's determined stand: "It cain't evah happen! We cain't prejudice our position..!"

The attorney explained, "You have to understand that this is the final ruling, as clearly stated by the judge himself, and that any departure from his declared mandate will result in a citation of contempt."

Contempt? "And—what does *that* mean?" asked Russ Carver.

The lawyer replied, "It could mean anything. Judge Grooms did not specify any particulars.. It could mean a heavy fine, or even the incarceration of the people named in the indictment. Or both."

"You mean—arrest our president!?" exclaimed Al Spivey.

"I'm afraid so, Mr. Spivey," said DeWitt. "And," he added, "—even you as well. Th' board of trustees was also named in th' arraignment."

Miss Tutwiler was shaken by this revelation, for her name too had been included in the bill of indictment.

Bellinger chuckled. "Come now, Rob, let's be reasonable. That judge wouldn't go to that extreme, now, would he?"

"He could, and he would," DeWitt assured him.

The assembly erupted into a bedlam of bitter reaction. E. Braxton Edwards held up his hand and hastily rapped his gavel. The excitement finally subsided into a troubled undertone as the men shook their heads in confused dismay.

Over the murmur, Bellinger again spoke without moving from his chair, his deep voice filling the room. "I, for one, don't like to be threatened. I only know what's right—and one thing more—if this thing happens, it'll be th' end of our college. And that's a fact—th' absolute end! And I mean in more ways than one! No self-respectin' S'uthern parent's goin' to be sending his kid to this place after we start lettin' colored people in. You all know that! If and when we do this, my friends, this place'll be nothin' more than a pile of red brick. It'll be over, believe me. But as bad as that may seem, there's something else that bothers me even more. Gentlemen, if that black man sets foot on this campus, th' whole thing's goin' to explode, blow up in our face. Believe me, you won't ever see th' likes of what's goin' to happen..! It's goin' to be God-awful! Lives are goin' to be put on th' line, a lot of people are goin' to be hurt—and we're not goin' to be able to do a damn thing about it!"

You could hear a pin drop. Everyone looked at the paunchy face of the Crestview banker. They were mesmerized by his vivid account of life which might hold if they acceded to the court order. But what could they do?

"In view of the court's mandate, Rob," posed Edwards at the podium, "what can we possibly do?"

DeWitt slowly shook his head.

"Do!? Dammit, we do what we have to do!" exploded Bellinger. "I don't see how any system of justice can let this happen, considering what's at stake..! I mean, my God, th' law's here to protect us—right, DeWitt?"

Eyes searched out the wrinkled, congenial face of Rob DeWitt as he eased slowly to the lectern. "Th' law's here to protect th' rights of all people, Mr. Bellinger. It relies on proof; it is based on what exists, not jus' what could be or might be. If what you suggest did happen, th' law would certainly act to settle the issue based on th' situation."

Bellinger grumbled, "Well, we all know it's goin' to happen, all hell's goin' to bust loose, no matter what."

To no one in particular, Jim McCall said aloud, "My God, it seems like we ought to be able to run this place th' way we want to!"

"What about states' rights..!?"

Everyone turned at this outburst by Jeremiah Swazy, farmer, land owner, philanthropist. "Since when did we give up all our rights to th' Fed'ral government!? We been scrappin' about constitutional rights; well, hell, th' Constitution, by God, says somewhere that some rights belong to the states—and to th' *people.*"

"Yeah..!" breathed Spivey, and almost under his breath demanded, "What about *that....!?*"

For one moment, it looked as if they had found an answer to their dilemma and their spirits soared in a rumble of speculative discussion. Chairman Edwards rapped his gavel for order and turned to Governor Eggerton. "Perhaps th' governor could speak to that," he suggested.

DeWitt stepped aside for Governor Eggerton to take his place at the lectern, but the state executive spoke from where he was seated. "That's an interesting idea, certainly worth pursuing, I'd think. What do you think, Rob?"

DeWitt paused, then said, "I don't know." He arose to stand at the lectern. "It's a matter of interpretation, I suppose, but you must understand that the Federal Constitution and its provisions take precedence over laws and jurisdiction of the states—and the courts are required to uphold that principle. Now, the court has already concluded that this young colored man has been unfairly denied his rights under the Fourteenth Amendment. I—I really do not believe that we have sufficient grounds for rebuttal under a theory of states' rights." He paused. "I'm sorry," he said and sat down.

An intimidating silence held, as no one seemed to know what to say. Swazy looked across at Henry Hartley. He leaned over to the person next to him and whispered, "Wonder what he's thinkin'?"

219

Henry Hartley sat quietly by, immovable, enmeshed in a veil of uncertain thoughts. Around his stolidity and elderly poise eddied the troubled confusion of desperate men.

Then, someone spoke.

"What if—we admitted him—and then—expelled him?"

This drew all eyes to Clayton Smith, a newly elected member to the board, who had ventured this speculative opinion.

"On what grounds?" asked Hanson.

Smith shrugged. "He—I don' know—he—he jes' don' belong here."

Hanson snorted, "That's a helluva reason."

E. Braxton Edwards shook his head. "No, gentlemen, unless we can think of some real substantive cause to alter the decision of the court, then, I'm afraid we're right back where we started."

"But what about th' trouble it'll cause!" thundered B. H. Bellinger. "Hell! Don't you guys even care..!? Hell, th' trouble this'll bring to our town will be—terrible. There's—there's got to be a way..! There's got to be—a way. . ." And as his voice tapered into a tomb of thought, the room was instantly engulfed in a nausea of doubt. Suddenly, it became too apparent: the struggle was lost—it was over.

The room grew old, oppressively warm, and there followed an eerie, awesome silence as seeking eyes wandered aimlessly, hopelessly. Bellinger chewed his cigar, while Eli Hanson drew endless circles on his desk pad. The pencil broke.

"Damn..!"

He threw it. It skidded across the polished table top to drop to the floor with a small clatter.

What went wrong? Where went the heart and soul of the secessionist, the strength and will to fight? Where went the spirit of rebellion, the battle cry, the mentality of do-or-die? Why? Against all odds, would they surrender, give in so readily?

As one last hope, deeply disturbed eyes sought out the man hunched at the head of the horseshoe-shaped conference table. They beseechingly observed Henry Hartley, for he was their Gibraltar, the solid rock of a Southern age, who would stand steadfast against this intrusion upon the consecrated course of Southern tradition. They knew he would mince no words in manifesting their deliverance.

The old man sat quite still and the stunned air of the room still held an electricity of pending hope. There was no sound, only his breathing. For a moment, he returned their gaze with a glimmer of sympathy. Then, his fingers contracted and, with an effort, he drew himself up. As he arose, everyone watched—and feelings found wings!

Now!

They watched.

Now, he would tell them in concise, brittle oratory to take heart, to persist, to take issue with those who would dare distort their future. And afterward, long after this time, this place, the glory of this inspiring moment would be told and retold—how, in the face of certain defeat, Hartley had risen to the challenge and tradition had been preserved!

But then, an awful moment...

Mist clouded his composure and a chagrined group saw tears topple across a cracked face. The trustees stared at the horrible tableau. The governor had half risen, but Hartley waved him away. For one brief, bad moment, the titan of Crestview could not speak. And, in that brief moment, the world came to an end for the men in that room.

Then, driving his fist into his hand, Hartley cried, "You know how I feel..!" He swallowed. "...about this damn nigger business!"

They knew, they knew!

And they watched, bewildered, as the old man awkwardly, angrily, brushed the tears from his cheek. He declared in a brusque and broken voice, "When I was admitted to th' bar more'n fifty years ago—hell fire, I took an oath—and God help me, I cain't go back on that now... I—I cain't see no other way. We got to uphold th' law! ..Th' bastard's won...th' bastard's won...!"

And he slumped into his chair, his final words a hoarse whisper barely audible. The distressed gathering, shocked, stared disbelievingly at the pitiable figure before them. Now, the feelings with wings wilted as his meaning rang clear.

A vote was not even necessary, for the die had been cast.

CHAPTER 27

Now Monday dawned, September 5, 1955. And Joey Henderson awoke to his day of days. A day he feared might never come. And yet, now that it had, now that it was here, he felt strangely uneasy, uncertain, unsure of himself.

As he dressed, Joey recalled the occasion of his registration. By special arrangement, he had been enrolled early. He remembered the trembling expectancy as he accompanied his lawyer and the Reverend Mortecai Ellison to sign up for classes. This time, however, it was accomplished without objection.

College representatives and several campus police politely but surreptitiously ushered the group through a side door into a private room for the enrollment ritual. Hall took note of the procedure and complained that his client should not be treated as an intruder, that he should be given the freedom and courtesy of any qualified student. The college officials tried to allay his concerns by explaining that, due to the high profile nature of the event, a clandestine approach was considered practicable and necessary. Undue publicity, they reasoned, could be disruptive and detrimental to their mutual goal. Edgar Hall acquiesced and accepted the procedure as suitably wise.

He did, however, vigorously protest the institution's failure to provide dormitory quarters for the new student. After all, insisted Edgar Hall, the court ruling implied full privileges which, he said, would of course include on-campus accommodations for his client. But Ed Blair, the dean of students, maintained that the court order had been issued too late to reserve a dormitory room for Henderson and the best he could do would be to furnish a rather confined basement room next to the boiler furnace in the administration building.

This, Hall and Ellison agreed, was totally unacceptable. It was tantamount to in-house segregation. But rather than risk a probable postponement of Joey's admission, the men grudgingly gave in and decided, temporarily at least, that young Henderson should commute.

On this morning, Hannah seemed overly solicitous as she hurried about her kitchen preparing Joey's breakfast. Her pride in her son was obvious as she made sure that he was well fortified with an ample helping of sausage and eggs and grits.

As he ate, he tried to imagine what the day would hold. How would he be received? What would it be like? He cleaned his plate and, with a sense of anticipation and a degree of intimidation, he awaited the arrival of Ellison's car.

Dr. Charles Cartwright viewed this day with a degree of disillusionment and dismay. It was not so much that an admission of a black man was his primary concern, as it was the unmistakable belief that the college was being forced to follow an uneasy course leading inevitably to ruination. It was clear that this unprecedented event would not pass without incident and Cartwright feared the consequences.

He hearkened back to the idealistic days of Jasper Morton's reign, when sound reasoning dictated a policy that was irrefutable. The college at Crestview then was operated as an educational institution which observed the social ethos of the region and was administered with ingenuous independence.

Now, with the present issue *fait accompli*, Dr. Cartwright could do little but assist in preparations for young Henderson's first day of classes. Weeks before, he saw President McAndrew organize arrangements and mete out administrative assignments with the dispatch of a commanding general. Ed Blair was instructed to supervise the interrogation of prospective new members of the campus police. "Above all," Byron pointed out, "be sure that these candidates harbor no deep-seated prejudice against Negroes." He added, "Their main assignment will be to protect one."

Bernice Tutwiler was asked to inform the secretarial and maintenance staff of the impending development. And the president requested Dr.

Cartwright to assemble the faculty as early as possible for an orientation meeting.

It was hoped that everything was in order for the opening of the college semester—and for the strange, unpredictable experience that awaited them.

As Ellison's Dodge pulled into the parking lot, two uniformed officers of the campus police stepped off the curb and approached the automobile. One officer stooped to look into the car window at the young Negro boy seated beyond the driver. He asked, "You Henderson?"

The reverend answered for the boy. "Yessuh, this heah's Joey Henderson."

"Well, we've been ordered to take th' young man to his first class," the officer explained.

"Anything wrong?" Ellison asked.

Ignoring Ellison's query, the other officer told the boy, "You jus' come along with us." And he turned to lead the way toward a cluster of buildings which appeared to Joey an intimidating site of his future.

As Joey emerged from the automobile, he quickly surveyed the campus. It looked quiet, peaceful, unconcerned. He saw students hurrying or idling across campus en route to class. Nothing seemed amiss. To Joey, everything appeared normal as far as he could tell.

Ellison started to follow Joey and the accompanying policemen, but one of the officers turned and said, "We'll take it from here. You don't need to come."

The minister paused, reluctantly, as Joey nodded and smiled. "I'll be all right." And Ellison watched them walk away, up the gravel path toward the humanities building.

As they came near the building, Joey noticed a group of male students waiting by the entrance. And as they approached, one, Archie Blevins, stepped forth and spoke curtly, "Where you think you're goin', nigger?"

The invective was unexpected and it stung. One of the officers flanking Joey stepped in front of Blevins. "C'mon, now, knock it off. Let's not be startin' no trouble."

Archie pushed against the thick chest of the policeman and yelled, "It's th' Goddam nigger who's causin' th' trouble!"

"Yeah, go home, nigger!" someone shouted as the group edged forward.

The other officer grabbed Joey's arm and guided him quickly up the few steps and through the door. Inside the cavernous entranceway, the campus cop paused and released Joey's arm. He looked back to see his partner slam the door and move quickly beside them.

"Wild bastards," he muttered.

Joey was beginning to perspire. He felt strange in the company of the two white officers. This sudden hostile greeting had startled and surprised him, but he now trusted the mission and responsibility of his two companions. The trio moved past several young men and women who stood in the hallway. Joey heard them conversing in low tones as they unobtrusively eyed the curious procession of police and a young black boy. At length, Joey and his escort arrived at the door to his first class. It was open and Joey carefully peered into the classroom. He saw the instructor, standing, leaning over his desk arranging a few papers and books. Some students were already there, seated in pairs or apart among many unoccupied student desks. He entered slowly, prudently, as his teacher straightened, smiled, and came forward to greet him.

"You're Mr. Henderson, of course, and we're pleased to have you with us. My name is Christian Knowles—Professor Knowles—and I'm your instructor for this course, English 101. Until we can work out a seating arrangement, you may take any seat." He then turned to the officers. "Thank you," he said.

One of the officers nodded, but they still lingered, standing there, arms folded.

Professor Knowles cleared his throat. "I think it would be best if you left us," he told the police, and added, "Thank you."

The officers looked at each other uncertainly. Then, one of the officers turned. "We'll wait outside," he said.

Joey turned up an aisle between rows of empty desks. He moved by a young blond coed, who looked up and even smiled as he passed. He felt awkward, afraid; he felt out of place. He found a desk-seat near the back, away from the others. He slid into the seat to bide his time until class began. He heard two boys whispering across the room. Other students tried to ignore his presence. Obviously, it was a strange, uncertain atmosphere. It was uncannily quiet.

As class time neared, more students bounded into the room to noisily take their seats. One male student started to select a desk near Joey but, seeing the Negro, hastily retreated to another seat. A couple of students, having heard that a colored person might appear, looked in at the open door, paused, and then departed. As Professor Knowles stood to open class, two other students, who had already seated themselves, quickly gathered

225

up their books and left the room. Joey looked around him. There were a lot of empty seats.

"The first day of any class is quite important," Knowles began. "You must realize that class procedure and assignments are discussed at this time and only at this time. The information is vital to your success in this course. And to see that we obviously have a number of students absent is of course of considerable concern to me."

Joey listened attentively to what the man said, but he was also aware of the eyes upon him. Without looking, he could feel each gaze, furtively measuring his presence. And he wondered in a warmth of embarrassment and self-consciousness what the eyes beheld—pity, animosity, regret? With nervous fingers, he felt tiny beads of perspiration on his brow. He earnestly wished for the class period to end soon, so that he could be released from an agony of excruciating unease and the probing eyes of the room.

The class ended early. And as the class members exited quickly, no one even acknowledged Joey's presence. Except one. One boy smiled as he passed the young black boy, and said quietly, "Hi," but he was gone before Henderson could return the greeting. But even this gesture of cordiality made Joey feel all the more strange, different, in every sense an interloper.

He entered the hallway and discovered, to his astonishment, that his police escort had left. They had disappeared. He suddenly felt quite vulnerable and a little frightened. He neither expected nor wanted trouble on this first day of college, and yet..

He moved toward the entrance and looked through the glass panels of the heavy doors. If he had seen any of the belligerent students who had accosted him en route to class, he would have retreated hurriedly in hopes of managing a desperate escape. He looked very carefully, but saw no one. He decided to risk it. Cautiously, he pushed open the door and stepped into the sun.

As he walked toward the science building for his next class, freshman chemistry, he nervously glanced about him. Although he had assumed there might exist bitter feelings, this sudden acrimonious encounter had left him unsettled and apprehensive. It hurt. His mind still rang with racial slurs which had been leveled at him. It left him weak and vincible and filled with disappointment and doubt. For these were not ordinary rednecks..! *These* were students!

As he rounded the corner of the building, a figure suddenly confronted him. Joey gasped. He was petrified. Less than six feet ahead of him stood Archie Blevins, his feet planted apart, his arms akimbo, his face a snarling grimace.

226

"Where you goin'—nigger?"

Behind Blevins, four or five burly men, athletic in size, advanced slowly. Joey swallowed; he was frightened. He bolted and ran.

And, as he sprinted, he heard them giving chase. He also heard them shouting for him to stop. Breathing hard, clutching his books, his legs pistoning at a frantic pace, he turned from the gravel path onto the grass and started streaking beneath the trees of the campus. He heard their heavy footsteps coming closer. He tried to run faster.

Suddenly, a weight hit him just below the knees and he toppled in the grip of his tackler. His body hit the ground hard with a thud, skidding on the grass, his books flung into the air. He was stunned. Hands were clutching at him and yanking him to his feet. He was pushed back against the trunk of a tree, as two young men held him tightly. Joey's eyes, white and wide, darted from one person to the other. His brow was damp with perspiration, his lips quivered, and he heard himself whimpering.

Blevins now approached, swaggering, trying to catch his breath. He stood in front of his captured prey and grinned. He reached out and grabbed Joey's tie and yanked it. It began to choke the young Negro boy.

"Look, you little bastard, you don't belong here. You understand what I'm sayin', nigger?"

Joey tried to nod, to speak, but he couldn't. The tie was choking him. It was hurting. The others relished the indignity of the moment and they were giggling.

"If you know what's good for you, you'll git your ass out of here—for good!" yelled Blevins. "There ain't no place for dirty, smelly, black sonuvabitches like you—you hear me, nigger!?"

Then, a voice thundered beyond them. "Hold it there!"

They turned. The two campus policemen were approaching at a trot. One of them yelled, "I tol' you, we don't want no trouble..! You jes' leave that boy be!"

As they arrived, Blevins released Joey's tie and shouted, "Th' bastard don' belong here!" Joey almost collapsed as he bent over, gasping for breath. His white shirt was torn and soiled with grass stains. He felt sick.

The campus police led him safely away.

Abigail Price, home alone, had finished drying dishes when she heard the knock. And wondering who could possibly be at the door at this hour, she opened it to see a disheveled apparition, a forlorn figure with his white shirt wrinkled and soiled, grass-stained and torn.

"Joey!" she cried, "What on earth—!?"

He smiled sheepishly and replied, "I jes' been to my first class in college."

It was really no joke. And as they sat on the porch swing holding hands, that fact became painfully clear as Joey related the horror of his harrowing encounter. He described in fearsome detail the ordeal and Abby's face reflected abhorrence and hate. He then explained how the campus police had delivered him safely to the administration building. It was the dean of students who had offered to drive him home. But as they neared the house, Joey asked to walk the rest of the way and Blair let him out of the car. Instead, he came directly to Abby's place.

She sat sideways on the swing, looking at him, listening. Once, she gently caressed his bruised cheek and murmured, "Oh dear, dear."

"I needed to talk to you," he told her.

The girl squeezed his hand. She asked, "What are you goin' to do?"

"I don't know. That's just it. I knew it'd be hard, but I never thought it'd be like this. I never did."

"You cain't keep on now, can you?" she pointedly suggested.

"I don' know," he said, uncertainly.

"It's too risky, Joey; give it up," she advised.

"But I thought you said—"

"I know, I know," she bemoaned. "But I was mad enough at th' time to want you to keep on, to fight them. I felt like you did, it was time to stand up to be treated fair and equal like other people. But I was wrong. I should have known. We cain't ever expect anything but what we got. Colored people don't count. That's th' way it is—and ther's no changin' it."

As if in a trance, he muttered, "Don't say that."

"But I have to. And what's happened jes' proves my point," Abby emphasized.

"But I cain't—quit," he said softly.

"You've got to."

"Look, Abby, I won th' right to go to this college. It's my right! Now, I know it don't set well with ever"body, but I cain't be scared off like this. I got to face up to it. Besides, it's up to th' college to make it right."

"Oh, Joey, I—I don' know about this. I don' want you to git hurt," she said.

He forced a smile. "Don' you worry. I think I can take care of myself."

She did not reply, and a few moments of silence enveloped them. Only the creaking chain of the porch swing was heard as they swayed gently to and fro. Then, suddenly, they heard the staccato exhaust of an approaching automobile. They watched the road. As the car came into view, Joey recognized Reverend Ellison's Dodge. He arose quickly.

"Who is it?" Abby asked.

Joey, not answering, started down the steps. Ellison was already out of the car and walking toward the house.

"Joey! Thank God you're here..! I was at th' college to pick you up and they told me what happened. And when I got home, you weren't there—and I was worried! I stopped by your folks' house and they said you'd likely be here. Thank God you're safe and I caught up with you. We'd best be gettin' home. You're stayin' with me."

"Why?"

Ellison answered, "Cause it'll be easier for me to take you to classes ever' day."

"I don' know if they'll let me now," said Joey.

"Th' college? Oh, they'll let you. They'd better," stated Ellison firmly.

"But look, Reverend Ellison, after what happened today—!"

"Listen, Joey, I know it was rough on you. And Lord knows, you know I wouldn't want anything to happen to you. So I talked to th' president of th' college, and he said they'd handle that bunch of white guys who attacked you. In fact, they're goin' to suspend classes until they can sort things out. When they do, President McAndrew said I should bring you straight to his office and they'd see to it personally that you get to go to classes without any more trouble. He really seemed upset 'bout what happened, so I don't think we'll have much to worry about from here on out."

Joey looked back. He saw Abby standing at the bottom of the porch steps, her arms crossed, her eyes on them.

"Get in," said Ellison. "We got to go."

"Just a minute," said Joey, and he walked back to where Abby was standing. He stopped before her and said, "Don' you be worryin' now."

"You know I will be," Abby told him, with a slight twinkle in her demeanor. "I want you to be careful, very careful, now, you hear me?"

He leaned forward to kiss her. But she threw herself into his arms and he felt the pressure of her lithe body as their lips met. He felt the need of her.

CHAPTER 28

The incident had incensed the staff of the institution. Never before in its history had there been an act of violent behavior as this and the professorial members were perturbed. They fervently felt something should be done, that there should be an adequate explanation—so they welcomed a special convocation called by the president.

President Byron McAndrew watched his faculty file into the small auditorium. Seated on stage, flanked by E. Braxton Edwards and Dr. Charles Cartwright, he heard their concerned chatter as they speculated the significance and outcome of the meeting.

Once, McAndrew leaned over to hear a whispered comment from Edwards and answered him quietly with a slight smile. But as he moved to stand before the speaker's podium, the president's face was sallow and solemn. He looked tired. The one hundred-fifty faculty members settled into silence as their president cleared his throat and prepared to speak.

Looking out at the faces before him, he then spoke without notes. "Greetings and welcome to all of you. I have called this convocation of our faculty because of the recent occurrence on our campus which has disturbed all of us and made it imperative that we address the implications of this most grievous problem. I am referring in particular to that unfortunate scuffle yesterday which has placed our institution in grave jeopardy and which, if not dealt with promptly and effectively, may threaten our work and our future. Because it specifically affects you, the faculty, it is important that we act collectively to counter all negative aspects of this situation and maintain a normal atmosphere in which this institution can operate effectively."

He continued: "To review briefly those circumstances which have led us to this decisive point, let me remind you that the court case which reached its final adjudication only this summer had been in litigation almost three years. During that period, the board of trustees sought all legal means to maintain the historic tradition of racial division which they conscientiously believed to be in the best interests of all concerned. Their personal beliefs were confirmed by similar sentiment apparently felt throughout the state. Hence, as servants of the state, as well as in their individual capacities as citizens, the members of the board of trustees felt they had an obligation to strive through all proper means to uphold those customs which are older than the institution itself—an institution which, proudly I say, has been in existence for more than a hundred years."

Charlie Cartwright shifted and crossed his legs nervously as he sat on stage and watched the back of Byron and, beyond, an audience of attentive faculty members. Charlie wondered if these educators shared his concern for the college and, of course, the man who spoke as their leader. He tried now to concentrate on Byron, as the president continued his explanation.

"The legal battle, having been decided adversely, left two alternatives for the board of trustees—either yield to the court's decree, or defy the law," declared McAndrew. "Now, as you know, several members of the board are members of the legal profession. And they, upon entering that profession, had taken an oath to uphold the laws of the land—federal, state, and local. They, as well as other members, felt they had no choice but to comply with the court's decree. Accordingly, the board voted to permit the litigant to enroll here at Crestview State College."

President McAndrew added, "Another factor in this decision was of course the conviction that no institution of higher learning can afford to defy our laws and thus set an example of lawlessness for its students—past, present, or future.

"Therefore, this was the stand which the board of trustees of Crestview State College took when it made its decision to permit Joseph Henderson to enroll as a student."

There was a rustle and a low murmur among his audience, but Byron McAndrew continued. "In the light of the board's decision, which I believed met the approval of both our faculty and the student body, you can scarcely imagine how completely surprised and disappointed I was to find a group of students who accosted Mr. Henderson yesterday as he attempted to attend his first class and physically harassed him. Such behavior cannot be condoned. And I think you will agree that disciplinary measures must be imposed if we are to maintain control to assure the safety and well-being of our campus."

The auditorium erupted into applause and Cartwright shifted his legs again. Mac was making a good case for himself and his principles. But Charlie wondered once more if these faculty members truly understood how weak McAndrew had been in any effort to preserve their "tradition." It wasn't that he did not empathize with McAndrew's awkward position; merely, he was convinced that a superior person like Jasper Morton might have approached the matter differently and would have lifted this institution from its morass of problems.

"We have appointed a special faculty committee to make a prompt and thorough investigation into this unfortunate incident," the president told his Crestview faculty. "I am sure that all of you are aware that the world is looking upon our actions with a critical eye and that we must meet every standard of human justice and equality of judgment in order to resolve this problem for the benefit of all. The incident of yesterday does not—I say, does not represent the character and feeling of this institution. And I say to you, we must do everything we can to alter any antagonistic view which might accuse us of being against the inalienable rights of any individual, black or white. The suspension—"

A brief scattering of applause caused Byron to pause and begin again. "The suspension of classes today was only an immediate, temporary measure to provide us the time to evaluate our position and to rally our collective feelings as to future attitudes and action. Classes will resume tomorrow and, God willing, will continue uninterrupted for the remainder of the semester, hopefully in the tranquility to which we are accustomed here at Crestview State College and which, I might say, is so essential for us to perform our proper mission."

"Mr. President!"

Byron looked out to see a hand waving and a figure arise from the group. "Yes?"

"President McAndrew, how can you expect us to continue when our routine has been threatened? How can we be sure that our classes can be conducted without interference or even possible violence!?"

Someone else stood up and shouted, "Yes! Our campus police are obviously inadequate!"

Byron held up his hand. "Please..! It is the responsibility of this institution and the state to do all that is necessary to make the campus safe for all students and faculty."

There followed a few disgruntled remarks and then another faculty member asked, "Does that mean that the state militia will be called out? Or, at the very least, the state patrol? Is this not an imperative to make it possible for our college to function?"

McAndrew answered, "If necessary, of course. But please, let us keep a level head about the events which have taken place. Let's try not to exaggerate the situation or overreact. As I explained to you, the unfortunate incident yesterday was but an isolated demonstration involving only a few students. To call in the guard, or in any other way arm this campus, would only serve to exacerbate the problem and nationally publicize our failure. I do believe it's best, therefore, to be as patient as possible and try to resume a normal routine."

Professor Knowles stood and Dr. McAndrew recognized him. "No matter how much you might try to minimize yesterday's disturbance, President McAndrew," he said, "the fact remains, it was a threatening act which unnerved everyone, especially those close to the incident. Now, 'normalcy' cannot be expected on this campus as long as such abusive acts continue. Even if it's no more than verbal abuse, the atmosphere for serious study and teaching has been violated and the function of this college unequivocally impeded." He sat down as many faculty members applauded.

Byron McAndrew paused as if pondering the professor's comments. He nodded. "I understand precisely what you are saying, Dr. Knowles, and I quite agree that we find ourselves in a most unwarranted predicament. But all we can do, at this point in time, is move as cautiously as possible and await developments as they unfold. If, for any reason—"

"Sir!"

The president had been interrupted by Eugene Bayside, a political science professor, who declared, "Surely you don't mean you'd wait until tragedy strikes before you'd contemplate any action of protection..!"

The comment ignited instant reaction from the assembly as a concerned murmur grew into a crescendo of excited discussion.

"No, certainly not!" exclaimed Byron above the melee. He seemed a bit flustered and he quickly added, "I was about to say—please—I was about to say that under no circumstances would we ever tolerate any activity which might place your lives, or anyone else's lives or property, in danger. But as I mentioned, this incident, although not insignificant, was relatively minor—"

"Minor!?" shouted Professor Bayside. "It was certainly serious enough to suspend classes!"

"I didn't mean that it was not serious," insisted McAndrew, firmly. "I merely meant that it was a small, first-time incident involving a few misguided students. At the moment, I would not consider it consequential enough to establish the sort of threat to which you seem concerned about. But in no way am I trying to minimize your apprehension. I, too, share your anxiety. At the same time, I feel that I must reassure you that the process of integrating this young Negro man into our system will be watched very carefully and that all essential measures will be taken to make certain the safety of everyone here."

Professor Bayside was already side-stepping in front of his seated colleagues in the row as he moved toward the aisle. He was waving a sheet of paper in the air as he loudly requested, "I have a motion to make and I'd like to use the microphone!"

President McAndrew hardly knew what to say. He did not want to appear dictatorial and yet he sincerely hoped the meeting would not become ensnarled in faculty wrangling or parliamentary debate. He really wanted to adjourn the convocation as soon as possible, but, as he saw the professor rushing down the aisle, he realized that he could do little else but allow the man an opportunity to speak. Byron stepped aside for Bayside.

Dr. Eugene Bayside clutched the mike. He was breathing hard. "Fellow faculty members, I should like to offer a four-part resolution. I move that, one, we as the faculty of Crestview State College condemn the bigotry in evidence on our campus, and two, that it be acknowledged that this institution cannot continue to operate under any further threatening conditions; three, that the faculty call upon the president and those in authority to immediately provide adequate police protection, either civil or military, to assure the safety and well-being of the faculty and students; and finally, four, that if no such assurances are given, the faculty declares here and now for the suspension of academic functions."

Before he had completed the reading of his resolution, the audience stirred in noisy, restless reaction. As he ended, there followed scattered applause and a few exclamations of protest.

President McAndrew stepped back to the microphone and held up his hand for silence. "You have heard the motion on the floor. Is there a second?"

Someone out front raised his hand and yelled "Second!"

"It has been moved and seconded," said Byron, and then added, "But before I invite discussion of this resolution, I should like to offer my own reaction. The points of the resolution are well-taken; they make sense and they obviously touch on the concerns of everyone. But as I've tried to explain, this one incident does not in any way imply an outbreak of hostilities or violence or widespread protest. And while it is prudent that we take every precaution, we must guard against actions which are based on fear and which might give an impression of panic. I quite agree with your condemnation of bigotry and I would of course respond immediately to any action that might involve or threaten anyone. But until such occurrences warrant such drastic action, I would urge patience. Let me say.."

Byron paused as he heard the rustling murmur in his audience. "Let me say," he repeated, "that you represent a most dedicated group of educators, who I believe to be the most loyal, understanding, and intelligent faculty one could possibly know. And as we face what may prove to be difficult decisions, I can only hope that I have your studied thoughts, your abiding respect, and your prayers."

A faculty member stood for recognition. President McAndrew acknowledged him. "Sir, I move that we adjourn," he said.

This suggestion was immediately greeted by several loud complaints, and the president said, "I'm sorry, but we have a motion on the floor."

Another faculty member arose and quickly declared, "I move that we table the motion on the floor until such time as might seem expedient..!"

"On the motion to table, express by saying 'aye'."

Wearily, gratefully, the faculty responded with a thunderous "aye!" And with a few scattered "nays," the motion was tabled. The vote for adjournment carried and the meeting ended.

Ed Blair brushed past the startled secretary and, without comment or consent, quickly entered the president's office. A surprised Byron McAndrew was seated at his desk. He looked up. Something was wrong.

A few hours before, the dean of students and a campus policeman had escorted the young black student to his class in the science building. This was the day academic activity had resumed at the college and, from all appearances, life appeared normal. The campus was calm.

Yet, now, Ed's expression revealed a pending dilemma. He blurted out, "All hell's about to bust loose, Mac!"

"What do you mean?"

Blair was breathing hard. "A gang of mean-lookin' rowdies have gathered in front of the science building. They're out to raise hell because of that Nig-ra boy..!"

"Students?"

"Hell, no! This time they're outsiders—millworkers, farmers, who knows? And I think many of them are from out-of-town. I tell you, Mac, it looks bad; we're in for big-time trouble!"

"The boy..!?"

"He's okay. For now," Ed replied. "Th' campus cops and I got him safely into the building this morning. There were a few curious students about, but nothing like what showed up a short time later. It looks bad, I tell you, Mac, 'cause if they decide to force their way into that building— well, I don't know if anybody can stop them."

"But the campus police are there, aren't they?"

"Oh, sure, but what can they do? They're blocking off th' building, but for how long, well, is anybody's guess."

"I'd better get over there," Byron declared, standing.

"Now, wait a minute—are you sure?"

"Why yes. Why not?"

"It's risky, Mac. This whole affair could turn out nasty,"

McAndrew was moving around the desk to retrieve his coat. "If it's as serious as you say, I need to be there. If they're shutting off the building, then classes won't be meeting. And we can't afford to suspend classes, not again. We simply cannot afford to have our schedule disrupted like this!"

Solemnly, Ed said, "I don't know if we can do anything about it."

"Is Cartwright there?" asked the president.

"Yes."

"Has he tried to disperse the crowd?"

Blair snorted, "Hell, what can Charlie do? You cain't get to first base with a mob like that."

"Then, I need to be there. Let's get going."

Ed drove his car around to a side service entrance of the building. As they emerged from the automobile, they heard loud sounds, shouting, and taunts reverberating at the front of the brick edifice. The two men hurriedly entered the service door and made their way through a storeroom into a corridor, then strode quickly by classrooms in the direction of the lobby. But before they reached the end of the hallway, a uniformed officer confronted them. The campus policeman nodded in recognition of the college president.

"Where's th' young man?" Byron demanded.

The officer answered, "I think he's upstairs, sir, waitin' in one of th' chemistry labs."

"Anyone with him?" asked Ed Blair.

"One of th' teachers, I think."

McAndrew asked, "What does th' situation look like?"

"We need help, sir," the officer said.

Byron asked, "What about th' town police?"

"They're out there. So's th' sheriff.

"Well?"

"They say they cain't do nothin' 'til somebody breaks th' law."

"Breaks th' law!?" Byron exploded. "What'n th' hell you think they're doing now? They're trespassing! They're disrupting classes! They're interfering with th' operation of a state institution! They have to be arrested!"

The man shrugged. "I'm—afraid we cain't."

"Why not!?"

"Ther's— Ther' jus' ain't enough of us to do that, sir," the campus cop explained.

McAndrew was frustrated. He uttered an oath beneath his breath. "Where's th' chief?"

The officer jerked his thumb toward the lobby, where a group of men stood waiting, cautiously watching the scene outside through heavy glass paneled doors. As Byron hurried to confer with the director of campus police, he was intercepted by Charlie Cartwright.

"Mac..!"

"What'n th' hell's going on here, Charlie?"

"I don't know, Mac, but—really—I think our campus police are doing th' best they can."

"I want order restored here," McAndrew demanded.

"I know," said Charlie, "but that's not going to be easy. You have to realize that it's a crazy bunch out there. They're not about to listen to anybody."

"Well, something's got to be done. We can't stand around and wait. Have you tried to talk to them?"

"That group out there? Oh, yes—yes, I tried. But it's no good." Cartwright shook his head. "I don't know how it got this way. It started out a simple demonstration, but I'm afraid it's now an angry protest."

"But we can't tolerate this," insisted the president. "We've got to do something—and now! What about local law enforcement?"

"They're not responding," muttered Cartwright, glumly.

"My God..!"

Cartwright glanced nervously at the door and saw the undulating movement of the restless crowd outside. He said, "Mac, those men out there don't give a damn about th' law—about us, th' college, about anything other than getting their hands on that dark-skinned kid. That's what they want—and that's what they mean to have. I'm just afraid that if we don't give in, they'll tear this place apart."

"Well, we're not giving in."

Charlie pursed his lips, doubtfully. "Okay, if you say so."

Byron moved away in the direction of Chief Nealy, who managed the small staff of campus police

"Nealy! I wondered—"

"Oh, Mr. McAndrew, glad you're here..! I've ordered th' men to shoot if anyone tries to force themselves in."

"What!?"

"I tell you, President McAndrew, we're not a force big enough to deal with that mob if they start gittin' violent..!"

McAndrew was shocked. "I don't want any shooting!" Byron proclaimed.

"Jus' over their heads—at first."

"Look, there's not going to be any shooting.. Is that clear? There's not going to be any violence," McAndrew informed him. "I don't think they'll try anything foolish. So I want you to rescind that order immediately. We certainly don't want any trigger-happy officers making matters worse..!"

Nealy said, "I don't think you understand, President McAndrew. If those men out ther' git rough—!"

"No shooting!" Byron snapped. "You understand..!?"

Nealy nodded. "If you say so—but if they do git nasty, I don't know what we'll do."

McAndrew peered through the glass-paneled door at the jeering men who crowded the steps, waving fists in the air and mouthing threats. He turned to Nealy.

"I'll try to talk to them."

"Them?"

Nealy's shocked response riveted McAndrew.

"I cain't let you do that, sir," stated the chief.

"I've got to.."

"No, that crowd out there will stop at nothin'."

Byron saw through the door's glass panel the seething, restless group outside, looking very much like a herd of cattle awaiting an approaching storm—roaming, standing aimlessly about, edgy with uncertainty and foreboding.

McAndrew reconsidered and quietly admitted, "Maybe you're right."

Nealy nodded. "I know I'm right."

"Okay," Byron said to Cartwright and everyone. "Then, we've got to get that young boy out of here—and *now!*"

"But how?" someone asked.

"We've got th' car in th' back. We'll sneak him out of here without those people knowing..!"

Cartwright was uneasy about the maneuver and questioned, tentatively, "Mac..?"

Nealy warned, "Kinda risky, ain't it?"

Ed Blair stepped forward to add, "Suppose it don't work, sir?"

"Yes, and also, Mac—why should we risk our lives for—well, for him?" asked Charlie. "I know he's a student, but he's also a—"

Cartwright stopped short of his intolerant observation and Byron remarked, "We have to make it work. Go get him, Charlie."

A few moments later, Cartwright and Joey Henderson descended the stairs. The young Negro was obviously frightened. Byron instructed Blair to check out the car to make sure that none of the rednecks were around and that it was safe. At the end of the corridor, Ed at length motioned for them to come quickly.

The president said, "Let's go..!"

At the car, Ed Blair glanced nervously about him as he seated himself behind the steering wheel. The president, his assistant, and the boy climbed into the back seat of the sedan. As Ed gunned the motor for departure, he did not see the denim-jacketed man with a stubbly beard emerge from behind a red pick-up truck. When the man saw the black boy being spirited away, he excitedly yelled, waved his hands and pointed in the direction of the disappearing car.

His compatriots sprang into action and the pickup, with its four-wheel drive, leapt away with a screech of rubber to give chase.

As Ed's car entered the road leading away from campus, he breathed a long, deep sigh. It had been touch and go, but he felt relieved at last.

"Where to now," he asked.

Byron answered, "Keep going into town. We'll stop at Grayson's Drug Store and I'll telephone Reverend Ellison from there." Turning to Joey, he asked, "You're staying at his place, aren't you?"

"Yessuh."

The weak reply betrayed the young man's discomfort. He felt uncomfortable seated between the two white administrative officers, as if bracketed by bookends.

Charlie cautioned, "We'd better not linger long in town. We don't want to be seen. And when you call Ellison, Mac, better arrange for him to meet us some place outside of town."

"Good Lord!"

McAndrew sensed the alarm in Ed's voice. "What's wrong, Ed!?"

"We're being followed!"

CHAPTER 29

Blair floored the accelerator in an hopeful attempt to evade the approaching threat. But being in town now, he slowed to negotiate a sharp turn into a side street. He turned quickly into another narrow street.

"I think we lost them..!"

"Thank God," breathed Charles Cartwright.

But then, suddenly, as they entered another street, they came face-to-face with the red pickup. The truck bore down on them recklessly in unconscionable abandon and headed straight for Ed's car. Ed cut his wheel sharply and gunned the motor. Miraculously, they slipped by the pickup with only inches to spare. This breathtaking maneuver created even more frightening results. The car rocked back and forth dangerously, teetering on two wheels at a time, until finally regaining its equilibrium.

"Oh, my God..!" wailed Cartwright.

In the quick instant that the red pickup flashed by them, they saw, all too close, a nightmarish moment of malicious faces. And ringing shrill in their ears was a half-second of screaming taunts hurled at them as the pickup passed. This chilling, bloodcurdling instant left the occupants of Ed's car shaken and weak.

"We cain't stop at Grayson's Drug Store, not now!" Ed shouted as he turned back toward campus.

"You're right! Take us to my house!" ordered McAndrew.

"No! Not your house!" declared Cartwright.

"Yes."

"But—we cain't..!"

"Why, Charlie, why?"

Cartwright glared at him. "Mac, my friend, consider the consequences."

"Hellfire, we've got to go someplace!" shouted Blair, as he gripped the steering wheel and pushed his foot forward to induce greater speed.

"It'll be safer there," insisted McAndrew.

"But my God, man, think of the impropriety of having a—having this man in the president's mansion... "

"I can't be worried about that, Charlie. It's our only chance. It'd be the last place they'd think to look for him."

Joey, seated between the two men who were talking as if he was not even present, sensed the import of his predicament. He was no simpleton. He instantly recognized a concern regarding the decorum of admitting a black man into a white man's house. A lump settled in his throat and he tried to swallow. His life, clearly, was on the line and he was afraid.

Florence had heard the car drive around to the back entrance and she hurried to the kitchen. "I'm sorry, dear," said Byron, as he entered. "All sorts of things have erupted on campus and we've got to keep Mr. Henderson here until th' police get things under control."

Her face mirrored concern. "I heard it on the radio," she said. "I was worried. What happened?"

"Oh, an angry mob formed in front of th' science building this morning and it was a very threatening situation," Byron explained. "Charlie, Ed, and I had to sneak this young man out of th' building—and they nearly caught us. I decided it would be best to bring him here."

"Yes," she agreed.

Charlie thought he saw doubt in her face, even revulsion.

But then, to Charlie's surprise, Florence smiled at Joey. "Of course," she said and, turning to the others, added, "I suppose none of you've had a thing to eat."

Byron suddenly realized that it was now almost four o'clock in the afternoon. In the excitement, no one had been aware of the time. They of course had not eaten lunch.

Flo turned to Albert, who was standing behind her in the kitchen, and directed him to prepare sandwiches and iced tea for the visitors. "If you will, Albert, please serve us in the sun room."

241

"Yes'm."

Cartwright quickly said, "Young Henderson can have his sandwich here at th' kitchen table. You don't mind, do you, while we go in and try to sort things out."

Byron said to the boy, "We won't be long."

"Take care of him, Albert," said Florence as she led the way toward the front hall. The others followed.

Joey slid onto a chair by the kitchen table and waited. He watched Albert as he busied himself at the counter cutting ham. Then, as he was spreading mayonnaise on slices of bread, the Negro houseboy, with his back to Joey, said, "So." He then glanced over his shoulder at the young man. "You be th' one, I reckon, who's causin' all th' trouble."

"Me?" Joey took a deep breath. "I reckon."

Albert asked, "Ain't you a little scared?"

"Maybe. A little."

Albert layered ham on slices of bread. "Why you doin' all this, boy? I mean, it's awfully chancy—what you're doin' ."

"I reckon. I know. But it was a way to go to college," Joey answered.

The houseboy turned to face young Henderson. "But you know you ain't got no business in a white college."

"I know, but th' court said I could."

"Yeah, but they's a lot of people 'round heah who don' like it."

"I know."

"And not jes' white folks," said Albert, as he placed a sandwich in front of Joey. "They's a lot of colored folk who say you're makin' it hard on them and all of us. 'Cause when you stir up trouble like this, it don' jes' stop at your doorstep."

Joey looked up at him. "Don't you think I ought to be doin' this?"

"I don' know. It's a pow'ful risk," said Albert, as he gathered a tray of sandwiches and tea and pushed open the kitchen door. He paused a moment to suggest, "This could be one helluva mess you're gittin' us all into!"

Then, he was gone.

Joey wondered, why couldn't blacks understand his motive, for it was more than a personal quest for achievement. It was also an honest desire to conquer oppression which his race had endured over the ages. Could they not see the value of this effort in terms of their own salvation? He told himself repeatedly that it was the right thing to do, that he would soon he vindicated, that it would be accepted as a well-advised crusade. He wanted to think of it in those terms.

Even so, he could not subdue the trembling anxiety which emphasized the uncertainty of the next few hours.

Florence led the men along the library toward the sun room. They never bothered to glance out the side panel of the front entrance.

But Cartwright did. And what he saw made him gasp. Stunned, he stammered, "My God!"

They stopped to look back at Charles Cartwright. McAndrew asked, "What is it?"

"It's th' red pickup!"

"Where!?"

"There!"

Sure enough, parked on the street near the entrance to Byron's driveway stood the same vehicle which had given chase. A man in a farmer's cap and leather jacket leaned against the cab door, smoking a cigarette, conversing with someone inside. Two other men had climbed out of the bed of the truck and were standing at the rear of the vehicle.

"What do you make of it?" asked Blair.

Byron said, "They obviously followed us. And...now..."

"Now what?" Charlie asked.

"Now, they're waiting for the rest of the mob," Byron surmised.

As predicted, they came. They came in pairs, in groups of four or eight, alighting from vehicles parked haphazardly on the street fronting the president's mansion. And the Crestview officials nervously watched through curtained windows as the bold and angry assembly gathered on the front lawn. They appeared not to have weapons.

At first, they seemed indecisive—milling about, talking. Several, the apparent leaders, huddled in a discussion of strategy. The others simply waited.

"Come on," urged McAndrew, "We've got to get that boy out of here!"

"What do you mean?" asked Cartwright.

"We've got to get him away from here—*now*, while we have a chance...!"

"Are you sure about this, Mac?" asked Ed Blair. "Do you think we can manage it?"

"We have to," said Byron firmly.

"But how?"

"Yes," echoed Charlie, "How?"

The president said, "While they're in front here, we'll get Henderson out the back way. But hurry, we'd better do it quickly..!"

"But will he know what to do, where to go?" asked Blair.

"One of us will have to go with him," Byron replied.

"One of us? Who?" asked Charlie, tentatively. "And do you think it's necessary, Mac? I mean, wouldn't it be safer if he was alone?"

At that moment, Albert entered the front parlor with a tray of sandwiches and tea. Florence told him that the situation had changed and to return the sandwiches to the kitchen. "Yes'm," he answered and turned to leave.

"Albert."

He stopped and looked back at Mrs. McAndrew.

"I think we'll be coming back to the kitchen now—and—perhaps you could put some of those sandwiches in a sack to be taken out."

"Yes'm."

He then departed and McAndrew explained, "No, Charlie, it's an obligation of the college to assure this young man's safety. So it's urgent that someone accompany him to make certain his well-being. But let's not waste any more time, we must act now."

Charlie was uneasy. "Who'll it be then? Who'll go with him?" he asked.

Blair interceded. "It cain't be Mac, that's for sure."

Cartwright was confused. "But why not, if the college is being represented?"

"Look, Charlie, he needs to be here to protect his house and his wife. It's got to be either you or me, my friend. And if you ask me, I think it might be better to get away with the boy than to face that mob out there. Be less dangerous. We don't know what that crowd will do."

"Enough talk," declared Byron, "We've got to get moving now!"

The three men and Flo hurried to the kitchen. As they entered, Joey Henderson was at the back door. Albert had a hand on his arm as if trying to restrain him.

"What's going on here?" asked McAndrew.

"He was tryin' to leave;. I told him not to," Albert emphasized.

"Certainly not—not yet!" enunciated Byron.

"But sir," pleaded Joey, "If they catch me, they'll kill me!"

"I know," acknowledged the president. "And that's why we're going to help you get away. One of us will leave with you."

Dr. Cartwright surprised them by saying, simply, "Mac, I...I'll go with him."

The two men were astonished at Charlie's willingness to undertake the mission. Perhaps Ed Blair's opinion that greater danger existed in facing the mob had persuaded Charlie that to escape with the young man was the lesser of two evils.

"Are you sure, Charlie?"

"Yes, I'll do it. I don't like it, but I'll do it."

McAndrew took a deep breath. "Well, you'd better get going. And remember, stick close to the house until you're even with the outbuilding. Then beyond the building you'll come to a dirt road that leads into town."

Charlie nodded and said to Henderson, "Come on, ready or not, let's go."

As the pair eased out the back door, McAndrew said, "Good luck."

Florence whispered "God bless" and watched the two as they disappeared into the dusk of a waning day.

Byron, Ed, and Flo then moved into the front, where Blair watched from a window.

"What's happening?" McAndrew asked.

"Not much," Ed replied. "They just seem to be standing around."

Byron then said, "I'm going to call Nealy. We need police protection."

"Maybe you won't have to," said Ed. "That looks like th' sheriff out there now."

"Alone?"

"I think so."

Byron joined Ed at the window to watch Sheriff Fisher step from his car and swagger indifferently down the drive. He appeared nonchalant, even elated, as he cordially greeted these men who stood in clustered groups. To the amazement of the two men inside the house who observed the sheriff, they saw him embrace individuals and exchange cheerful repartee.

The sheriff laughed and joked with the men, seemingly indicating that if things did not get out of hand they had the right to protest peacefully. And with that, he turned to leave as one man escorted him to his car.

"So much for police support," bitterly muttered Blair.

Suddenly, the front door bell chimed.

"They're here!" hissed Blair.

They hurried into the front hall. But before Byron could open the front door, Ed cautioned, "It might be a trick, Mac."

"I'll be okay. I want to talk with them."

"Be careful."

245

Byron opened the door and stepped out to face a portly man in a sweater and denim jacket. Beside him, in a wrinkled white shirt open at the collar, his black tie sagging, was the familiar figure of Archie Blevins. And behind him stood a gaunt-faced, unshaven individual in blue jeans and a sweat shirt.

"Good afternoon, gentlemen."

"*Gentlemen!*" The gaunt man sniggered. "Sure is a good judge of character, ain't he!"

Archie Blevins ignored the gibe. "President McAndrew?"

"Yes?"

"We've come for that Henderson fella."

The portly man said, "We don' want no trouble, but we seen you bring him here. And we figger you ought to know better'n that. For one thing, you ought to know better'n to bring a jig into a white man's house.."

Resentment seethed within Byron, but before he could retort, Blevins spoke. "Sir, it'd be best if you'd let us take him off your hands."

"No," said Byron quietly, and added, "Now, if you will quietly leave these premises, I promise there'll be no trouble."

The portly man said, with a grin, "Oh, ther'll be trouble awright, if'n we don' git our hands on that black boy..! Better to turn him over—now!"

McAndrew tried to be as firm. "I hope you understand that you're going to be in deep trouble if you don't leave," he stated, and added, "This is private property—it's state property—and the laws for harassment and trespassing can be severe."

Blevins smiled. "You think that bothers us? Naw.. Besides, we ain't broke no laws.. So far, this is jus' a friendly visit."

The gaunt man behind them stepped forward to say, "But it could git nasty if you don' cooperate."

Byron felt blood rush to his face. He felt feverish. "I can have you all arrested!" he cried. "And as for you, young man, you're risking being expelled from college—do you understand that!?"

Archie grinned. "Maybe I don't want to be no part of this nigger lovin' institution..!"

Byron started to reprove this young upstart, but he bowed to discretion. He would await an opportunity to thwart this impertinence at another, more opportune time.

Then he heard: "Like we been sayin', we ain't lookin' fer no trouble.." It was the guttural voice of the gaunt-faced man, who jammed his hands into his pockets in a contemptuous pose. "But somebody's gonna git hurt if that coon ain't long gone from heah shortly. Now, I figger you bein' a college pres-i-dent and all, you got to be purty smart. So, you oughta know whut's best. And I figger you're goin' to make th' right choice. Now, who's it gonna be? Who's gonna git hurt—th' nigger—maybe you—or—your wife?"

The threat hit its mark. "Now, listen," said McAndrew between gritted teeth. "We will not be threatened..!" Then, in a more conciliatory tone, he said, "Listen to reason, men. You can accomplish what you're after without resorting to this despicable mob action..!"

The portly man said, "That's whut we've been tryin' to tell you..! Turn th' nigger over to us and ever'thing'll be hunky-dory."

"No," said Byron, "I can't do that."

"You cain't?"

"No, because.." Byron paused. "Because—he's not here."

"Th' hell you say—I seen you drive him here," growled the gaunt-faced man.

President McAndrew tried to assume a staunch, authoritarian presence. "I can have you indicted for trespassing, you know! If you know what's good for you, you'll tell that crowd to go home."

Blevins said quickly, "Wait a minute... Th' boy—you say he's gone?"

"Yes."

"When? How?"

The portly man snarled, "He's lyin', Archie. Hell, he'd say anything to save that damn nigger."

"You wouldn't lie to us now, would you, President McAndrew," offered Blevins soothingly with a wily smile.

"Certainly not," returned the president. "The young man left the house shortly after your people appeared. He's gone. And now, it's useless for you to continue this lawless action. I demand that you disperse this gathering immediately."

The portly man admonished the president, "I don't believe you for a moment, mister, and if you're lyin'—"

At that moment, he was interrupted by the distant sound of sirens, which quickly came closer with the sight of two state patrol cars careening into the driveway and screeching to a stop before the president's mansion. McAndrew wondered if Blair had telephoned for help. The officers got out and hurried up the steps. One immediately recognized the president and said,

"Are you okay, sir?"

"Yes, I'm all right."

"Okay, let's break it up!" demanded the trooper.

Blevins said, "We're leaving."

247

CHAPTER 30

Dr. Cartwright and his Negro charge hurried along the dirt road in the gathering dark. And when Charlie could not keep up, the youthful Joey moved quickly ahead. The college administrator was breathing hard and at last slowed and stopped, calling out, "Wait!"

The young man turned to see his escort stagger onto to a grassy knoll beside the road and slump to the ground. Joey tentatively retraced his steps. Standing over the man he asked, "Are you all right, sir?"

The man gasped, "I'm—okay—but let's—let's catch our breath a minute..!"

Together, they stood silhouetted against a graying sky as gradual darkness enveloped them. In the distance, an aurora of town lights seemed inviting.

"But sir, don't you think it best that—we keep on?"

"Yes, of course," Cartwright agreed. "But we're in th' clear now, I think. We've got time. Let's—let's sit a spell and talk this thing over."

"Yessuh."

Resting his arms on his knees, Dr. Cartwright looked up at the young Negro who still stood above him. "How do you feel?" he asked the young man.

"Okay. I'm okay."

"I mean ... about what's happened.."

"You mean about all those people... Well, sir, it was kinda scary, but —I think we'll get by."

"For now, maybe," agreed Cartwright, "but this is not the end of it all, you know."

"Yessuh, I know."

"Don't you feel, given the circumstances, that you should—-well, reconsider your position?"

Joey hesitated.

Charlie pressed his point. "Cain't you feel that it's really unwise to buck the resistance that's so adamantly against your entering this college?"

Joey thought a moment and then he said, "Maybe, sir, but it's my chance—and—I really do want to go to college. And I've been told it's my right and th' right of anyone to better himself—if it's possible."

Cartwright was impressed by the young man's self-assurance.

"True enough, but being pragmatic about it, you've got to understand that your goal faces formidable odds. To achieve your hope, you face a risky future."

Joey looked off at the lights of the town in the distance and considered the uncertainty of what this college leader had made all too clear. He knew that his safety was a priority. And he anxiously eyed the road ahead and felt the need to be moving.

"Don' you think we'd better be goin', sir?"

Cartwright sighed. He slowly raised himself to his feet. "Yes, yes, I reckon we should." Together they commenced walking, side by side.

The narrow road now emerged into a bumpy back street where houses appeared more frequently. And although a few were separated by vegetable gardens or vacant lots, it was becoming more populated as the town became more evident. Crestview's main street was only a few blocks away.

They remained silent now as they moved quickly by the dark houses with their dimly-lit windows. A dog barked. With wide-eyed apprehension, Joey imagined that the vicious men who had threatened him during the day might well reside in these very houses.

Dr. Cartwright apparently shared the same concern, for he quietly advised Joey that they should no longer talk as they strode stealthily through the neighborhood.

One fear Charlie deeply felt was that if they should be seen together, both he and the young man would be in decided danger. For any perception that a white man was assisting a Negro—particularly an impudent black person who had violated social standards of the community—would certainly put their lives in jeopardy.

At the street outside the president's mansion, Archie Blevins leaped into the bed of a pickup truck and waving his arms, demanded the attention of the departing throng.

"Look, follow me! And when I stop, gather around—I have a plan!"

He started his car and the caravan of redneck cohorts followed. At length, he pulled to the curb. He got out and motioned for them to assemble before him. He spoke to the group.

"Men, men!" he screamed. "We ain't through with our nigger tonight!" Several reacted with approval.

"We're gonna git him! We're gonna string his ass up!" shouted Blevins, his voice strident, emotional. "And whether we git him tonight or not don't make a damn; we're gonna git him!"

There was gleeful laughter, acclamation and applause.

"But I think we can git him tonight," Blevins informed them. "In leavin' th' president's house, he probably headed for town. And by God, if he's here we gonna git him!"

The group roared their approval.

"So, what we're gonna do is stage a demonstration right here in th' middle of town. We're gonna show ever'body we mean business! And most of all, our actions tonight will strike fear into th' black heart of that bastard! Are you with me!?"

Blevins was greeted with a thunderous shout, and the milling group turned to embark on a new crusade.

Archie implored them. "Wait! We'll meet at the head of Elm Street. We'll park our cars and start from there!"

Someone suggested that if they created a disturbance it might flush out their quarry.

"Hell yes!" emphasized Blevins, "Let's turn this place upside down!"

"Let's go!"

Motors gunned as the vehicles took off for town.

The two figures hurried into the shadows of a brick building. Charlie and Joey leaned against the brick wall, breathless, too exhausted even to speak. Charlie glanced to the right to see an intersection lighted by a street lamp. He was breathing hard.

"I—" He gasped for breath. "I think we made it."

Joey mumbled quietly, "Yessir."

It was obvious that the black youngster was numb with fear as he searched the incertitude of their possible fate. For several moments they said nothing. Then, Cartwright, gripped by apprehension, suggested, "You can make it from here. You won't need my help now. Just cross over Main street and th' railroad tracks, and you're home free. Just be very careful and hurry!"

At the thought of being released on his own, of having to face the unpredictable prospect of gaining safety alone was a disquieting decision. And while it had been an uneasy experience to move in the presence of this college official, Joey appreciated his assistance and his advice.

Joey reluctantly acceded with a tentative "Yessir."

For several seconds, neither moved. They stood with their backs to the brick wall, breathing deeply, pondering unpredictable moments ahead. They had taken great care to skirt the courthouse square, to avoid the center of town. At last, the young Negro boy turned to leave. But the man touched his arm.

"Wait."

He had heard an approaching automobile. He looked toward the dimly-lit intersection and saw a passing police car, its whirling roof-top spotlights flashing a kaleidoscopic brilliance of red and blue. He froze. He did not trust the police. Then, too late, he saw that it was not local but the state police.

They stood there for a long minute, listening. Most of the stores had closed and, except for the occasional sounds of night, the town was eerily silent. No one seemed to be stirring and Cartwright, eager to end his assignment, whispered, "All right now, go! Just be careful."

Joey turned, but a hand again restrained him.

Cartwright had heard the sound. Joey heard it too. It seemed, faint and far away. But it soon became a distinct, blaring, menacing blend of turbulent voices moving nearer. Cartwright clutched the young boy's arm, now out of fear. They were coming! That angry mob, now jubilant in their quest, were marching down Elm street toward them. Both Cartwright and the boy trembled at the thought that they had been discovered!

The undulating, awkward parade of redneck rowdies marched stolidly down Elm Street. With grim determination and buoyant spirits, they noisily advanced to the beat of a scurrilous chant:

Nigger, nigger, black as night

You know we'll keep our college white..!

And marching jauntily near the front of the group was Mic Purvis, grinning, wearing a grimy baseball cap and clutching a borrowed rifle. Someone had unfurled a large Confederate flag, which swirled in the breeze above this army of white separatists. It was for them a field day, asserting their challenge against a brazen sacrilege of Southern values.

Leading the group was the student instigator, Archie Blevins, who strode confidently before the gathering of millworkers and farm laborers. He enthusiastically waved his arms and joined in the chant. And when several people, curious about the commotion, stepped out on the sidewalk to watch the demonstration, Blevins glowed with personal pride.

Like foxes before the hunt, the two people cowered in the darkness of the building, waiting, anxiously wondering what to do. The boy wanted to break and run, but Cartwright urged caution, pleaded with him to stay hidden until' they could determine the route of the approaching mob. It sounded as if they were coming down the street to their left; if so, the young man and he would sneak across the intersection of Main Street at their right.

As they paused, excruciating fear coursed through Cartwright's tight, tense body, causing his knees to buckle and vibrate. He stayed close to the Negro boy, holding onto Joey's shirt. His mind was a profusion of tormenting possibilities. He knew not what to do. To separate himself from the boy now would still leave him vulnerable and exposed to danger. And yet...

Joey suddenly asserted, "I'm leavin'!"

"No, I—wait!"

"You can stay heah if you want, but I'm leavin'..!" Joey firmly stated, as he pulled himself free of Cartwright's hand and started to move.

"No, I'm coming with you," croaked the frightened presidential assistant.

They eased along the brick wall, glancing edgily about them, eyeing hopefully the lighted area of Main Street. Beyond that, they knew, were the railroad tracks, the depot, and the dark night of freedom. Yet, as they neared the corner of the building, they hesitated.

They heard the approaching clamor of the mob. The sound seemingly cascaded down Elm Street, overwhelmingly louder and more threatening. And then, quite suddenly, the noise veered away from Elm Street and for a moment was muted by the building. Had they turned back?

Cartwright's mind searched frantically for a solution to their—no, his plight. Should he now leave the young man and return to the McAndrew home? Obviously, the mob had abandoned the siege on the president's mansion and it must now be a safe haven. But his tortured mind mulled over the prospect of attempting the dark, uncertain trek through unknown neighborhoods alone. He decided to stay with the young man. Later, when they were safe, he would telephone Byron and the campus police and someone would escort him home.

With a furtive look at each other, a decision was quickly made and the two fugitives moved slowly, cautiously across the intersection beneath an overhanging street light. They had taken only a few steps beyond the curb when the rioters, having crossed from Elm to Main Street, suddenly burst into view.

"Look! It's him!" screamed someone in the crowd.

For an instant, Joey was paralyzed. Then, he tried to bolt and run, but Cartwright panicking grabbed him. In a callous act of betrayal, the college official screamed to the crowd, "I've got him, I've got him!"

But Mic Purvis misinterpreted the struggle. He saw a white man being attacked by a black person. And before the eye could blink, the night was slit by two loud explosions. The successive reports sounded like the cracking of tree limbs, and the sharp, piercing sound echoed between the buildings of the town. With a gasp, the surging group stopped, stumbled back and, shocked into silence, stood gazing at the fallen figures which lay crumpled in the middle of the street.

As Purvis heard the reverberation of his gun shots diminish into a terrifying quiet of infinite darkness, he shuddered. What had he done? He felt a shortness of breath as he stood, staring, gripping the rifle. He knew! He had been the first to respond to an unconscionable act of a white man being bludgeoned by a black. No one could fault him for that!

And yet, he had committed violence. He looked down at the rifle he held and, with angered regret, flung it aside. It clattered to the pavement. Then, as if in a trance, he started walking slowly toward the grisly scene.

At the sudden and unexpected firing of the gun, the crowd had recoiled. And Archie Blevins, realizing that his ethnic rebellion was being aborted, leaped to the front of his shaken followers and shouted, "Wait! It's all right, it's all right! We warned th' nigger! It's all right!"

Purvis, without looking behind him, shuffled closer to the victims and saw two figures in cruciform, one sprawled over the other. The Negro was on top, face down, his hands outstretched.

For what?

No less a dream.

And beneath him was the white man, his upturned face frozen in surprise. His open eyes stared blankly at the dark heavens above. His mouth was open.

But he was not smiling.

Blood of the black man and the white person intermingled, oozing in a widening pool on the pavement around them. And the street lamp glinted the stain so that it seemed silvery light and shadowy dark. But as Purvis stared, stupefied, he could see that the blood was neither black nor white.

It was red.

CHAPTER 31

The bleak night bled into a psychedelic dawn as morning delivered the stark and tragic news. Over breakfast in white pristine Southern homes, a stunned citizenry read the morning paper and digested the grim details with mixed emotions. The bold, screaming headlines emphasized the horror and disgrace which cast their community upon a glaring, critical light of international attention. The evening Gazette emphasized the tragic death of a prominent educator, who, in company with a Negro boy, had been shot in cold blood. The people of Crestview as indeed the nation were left uneasy and apprehensive.

A few felt the white man deserved his fate. If, as it seemed, he was assisting an irresponsible black youth prevail against a legitimate white protest, he was indeed culpable. Many surmised that it was the fault of the Negro, for he had challenged white authority and had offended the principles of Southern ethics. For some, the college administrator had been an innocent victim of an occurrence which had shamefully branded their town as a hotbed of racial bigotry and violence. And there existed among many the agonizing feeling of self-reproach and humbled pride.

Today, decades later, if you returned to the community of Crestview, the town might seem the same. As you entered by the old state capital road by the Marathon station, you would move along Main Street between the Coast Line railroad tracks and the familiar facade of sidewalk stores. You would pass Bobby Ray's Bar and Grill (it's still there) and, turning up Elm

Street by the courthouse, you would of course see Marylou's Diner and, fronting the town square, the sheriff's office. These remembered sights hearken a sense of the familiar, the commonplace.

But it is not quite the same. Time has transformed this place. Some changes are evident. The old picture show just off Main Street is boarded up now, having been replaced by a three-cinema movie house at the new shopping mall on the edge of town. And the Sumpter House, in need of repair, has been up for sale.

To look at it today, one would hardly suspect the cataclysmic event which catapulted this town into an arena of public notoriety some forty plus years ago. Its aura of quiet gentility, its cloistered, neat, well-cared homes along magnolia-shaded streets exemplify an easy, peaceful existence. But in these residences reside painful memories of an epoch of horror. The respectable white families who live there hardly ever discuss the past. They try to face each new day with gentle optimism, with a hope that time will eventually erase a lingering legacy of ignominy.

Life goes on. The club women of Crestview continue to pursue social status with the same dedicated sense of dutiful discrimination. Dirt farmers and mill hands still move in a common circle of concerns, where talk of crops, the economy, or social welfare tend to dominate their perception of the future. Men still frequent the barber shop or Bobby Ray's Bar and Grill. And on the edge of town, yet a world away, a cultural dichotomy exists in the essence of a college which is now known as Crestview State *University.*

So, Crestview has changed—especially at the outer limits of the town, where passing time has brought new trends, new influences, even new people. Farming is still vital of course but, with evidence of advanced agricultural technology, most small farms have practically disappeared— as, indeed, the tenant farmer and the sharecropper. And no doubt this would be the most telling transition of all.

Elijah Henderson eventually came into his own acreage. And Derek, at his release from prison, came home to assist his father and together, with the help of Elijah's other sons, managed to successfully operate the expanding farm. Derek soon married and, at Elijah's death some ten years ago, took over the tract of land. Derek's brothers departed for other places, other professions. Emma lived nearby with her family. They, with Derek, cared for their mother, who, although frail and wizened at 87, was still a sturdy worker around the house.

And today you would immediately perceive a clear though subtle change in attitude toward minorities. The community once observed a rigid social ethic which espoused racial separation. Now, however, there seems

256

a common bond among most citizens, black and white, and the ancient taboos of discrimination have virtually disappeared. And whereas the transformation culminated in the convulsive civil rights movement of the sixties, a full understanding of the struggle had been realized much earlier in Crestview. Although slow coming, one could now see a more active participation of Afro-Americans in the public sector of the community.

It might surprise you to learn that the current sheriff of Coplin County is black. It happened in 1981 when a young Negro attorney, Cole Adkins, decided to run for sheriff, an office hithertofore restricted to white men only. Adkins was known as an industrious, fair-minded individual. His candidacy brought about an astonishing black voter turnout. But his election signaled something more significant in that it demonstrated an optimistic view of race relations in Coplin County and Crestview. Cole Adkins was fully aware that he could not have been elected without the support and approval of the white citizenry of the region. People appeared to be looking forward to a more hopeful future.

Jethro Fisher, of course, would always be remembered. His arrogant attitude was hard to forget—-or to forgive. The shock of the tragic racial incident of 1955 left many people upset at the lack of law enforcement and control within their community. Sheriff Fisher's apathetic approach to the crisis was scorned by many citizens, including prominent members of the town. Even those who held strong views against Negroes were disappointed at the sheriff's incompetence. Fisher's diffidence in defining reasonable resistance in defusing the riot was criticized. Most were quick to reproach the man for having placed their town in publicized disgrace. A movement immediately arose to remove him from office.

Fisher had laughed off his critics, confidently feeling smug and certain that his redneck constituency would justify his actions, that inevitably he would be supported and ultimately exonerated. He stubbornly refused to step down.

"No nigger-lovin' bastard'll be running this county, that's fer sure," he defiantly declared.

But, to his surprise, he was soundly defeated in a subsequent election and another white man took over as sheriff of Coplin County.

As the years of the civil rights revolution evolved, the responsibility of law enforcement became a sensitive and difficult task. It was then that people of the region accepted Cole Adkins as their law enforcement officer.

Not all Crestviewians were as tolerant or unprovincial as others, and there were those who found tenets of the past hard to relinquish. Ethel Tutwiler refused to alter her opinion that blacks were decidedly inferior, even though she conceded that any oppression of Negroes was wrong. Even after her sister Bernice died in 1978, she continued her staid existence in the big house, participating in club activities, and holding firm opinions about the dissolution of the human race. Her only act of sentiment, it seemed, was a weekly visit to her sister's grave in the Crestview Memorial Cemetery.

Bernice, of course, had resigned her post as college registrar following the tumult of the Henderson incident. She obviously had been deeply affected by the tragic affair. And after confiding her feelings about the death of the young Negro student to her elder sister, Ethel's only acerbic reply was, "Well, my heavens! Don't you feel anything for the white man!?"

To the surprise of many, Bernice left in her will a tidy sum for the perpetuation of a scholarship which she had already quietly established for qualifying minority students to attend Crestview State University. Ethel was furious. She felt that this had been an unprincipled decision on the part of her late, departed sister; an unforgivable act which had brought eternal shame to their family name and an acute embarrassment to her life and reputation. She simply could not understand how colored people could be accepted or indulged in a segregated South. At first, she was quite vocal about this affront to the dignity of white people; then, said little.

In the late eighties, Ethel was committed to a nursing home, where she received frequent visitors from the Crestview club women she knew so well. In December of 1989, she died in her sleep.

To everyone's amazement, her will bequeathed a further and very substantial sum to be added to the scholarship already established by her sister. Furthermore, she demanded in her will that the endowment be named *The Bernice Tutwiler Memorial Scholarship in Memory of Joseph Henderson.*

And what of Mic Purvis? On the night young Henderson and Dr. Cartwright were killed, Purvis was apprehended immediately and arraigned for manslaughter. The leaders of the protest riot saw to it that Purvis was represented by a good defense lawyer. All were convinced that no local jury would convict this man for killing a Negro. But the attorney was circumspect. He cautioned that they should not presuppose an outcome, for the case was complicated by the fact that it also involved the death of a white man—and, regrettably, a prominent and respected educator. Mic's simple mind, of course, sensed no foreboding, and he entered the trial with a grinning, child-like demeanor of innocence, totally unaware of the actual dimension of his predicament. He even appeared giddy at the prospect of being the focal point of an important public trial. He sat, glancing about the courtroom, glorying in the acknowledgment that he was the center of attention.

His compatriots were concerned. Obviously, the trial was not going well for this mentally retarded, inept individual. And they feared involvement. But his attorney entered a plea of insanity, which Mic Purvis did not understand and accepted with a vacant smile. The jury adjudged him guilty and committed him to the state asylum for observation. As he departed, Mic Purvis felt a sense of elation and triumph, for he believed that be could not be held responsible for the victimization of anyone so obviously "inferior". As he was led from the courtroom, he smirked and waved to the crowd.

During the trial, a tall, thin man sat in the back row of the courtroom and not once removed his John Deere cap. He watched silently with interest and at the end of each session slipped quietly away. He knew well the defendant and was curious as to how the trial might turn out. He feared he and others might be involved, yet he anxiously awaited the verdict. He had been present that fateful night, had witnessed the shooting, but in fear he ran. And now, as he sat listening to the unraveling dialogue of indictment, he tried to look inconspicuous and unobserved. He did not wish to be associated with this man on trial.

It was easy for this itinerant farm hand not to be noticed. He was a country boy with undistinguished features and a personality that was notably bland. As a farm hand, he was nominally quiet and moved from farm to farm, working diligently but saying little. On his nights out, however, he became an entirely different person. He frequented the bars and roadhouses around town and, fortified with drink, became bold and talkative. At such times of intoxication, he usually said too much. On several occasions, he proudly announced that he had raped a young black girl. The incident had been years past, but people remembered. And someone reported him.

To the surprise of many, Sheriff Cole Adkins reopened the case. The investigation soon linked Mic Purvis with the man in the John Deere cap. Purvis implicated his friend.

Reluctantly, Abigail Price was led into a room for a police line-up. She disliked the unsavory prospect of seeing her attacker. Although it had been a long time since, the bitter memory of that baleful event burned like hot coals in the recesses of her mind. She tried to steel herself to the task, but she trembled within.

And then, when the man in the John Deere cap stepped forward, the wretched scene with its remembered pain suddenly engulfed her again and the fear and humiliation resonated within her quaking body. Her head bowed. She covered her face. And she broke down in tears.

The man in the John Deere cap later confessed. The case was closed.

The effect of the Crestview incident was far-reaching, but never so fateful as the future posture of what would soon be Crestview State University. Dr. Byron McAndrew was greatly affected by the tragedy, both personally and professionally. In addition to his acknowledged deep personal loss, there was the disillusionment at his failure to cope with the controversy. And Byron found himself facing serious criticism. Many felt that the president had been too slow to react to the impending problem, while others assailed him for his lack of understanding of the region. Some contended that President McAndrew had been too weak, too indecisive, not forceful enough to deal with the crisis. But most were simply disappointed, hurt, and a little ashamed that their town and their institution could be reduced to such depths of disgrace in the eyes of the country and the world.

Aware that his professional status had been inalterably injured by the incident and its violence, Byron McAndrew, after consulting with his wife and the board, tendered his notice several weeks later. Little was said or done to persuade him to stay. So, a year later, he said goodbye and left to accept the chancellorship of a small institution in the northeast.

The university under new leadership quietly continued and with deliberate determination tried to overcome the stigma which persisted after the racial tragedy that had created damaging publicity. The reputation of Crestview State University as a fine, effective educational institution prevailed, nevertheless, and growth and development was in evidence as it entered a new era.

In its coeducational concept, it now accepted minorities, so it was now a commonplace sight to see dark faces of promising Afro-American or foreign students walking the campus or attending class. Contrary to ancient fears, this inmixture of young people proved to be a salutary influence—not only for the institution, but for the community at large. The region, perhaps reluctantly at first, now accepted integration in the spirit of its rightful purpose, the equality of humankind.

Not that tension did not exist. Racial and religious prejudice, like a disease, remained a threat and afflicted the minds of many individuals *who* stubbornly persisted in a notion of subjacent citizenry—the Jews, the blacks. Ghosts of the KKK and other pockets of resistance still lingered, although far less effectively and with less eminence than before. Archie Blevins, who had been expelled from the college for his insurgent actions against the institution, tried to keep alive the Citizens Council movement and traveled the state, speaking, exhorting, urging the people to rise up and declare their loyalty to "white Caucasian values." But his frantic message became a weary tirade of hatred which soon fell on deaf ears. His audiences became fewer in number, then almost nonexistent. Blevins found his cause fruitless. So, he disappeared. No one has heard of him since.

In June, 1971, a thirty-five-year-old woman with a beautifully dimpled smile became the first Negro graduate of Crestview State University. Four years before, she had applied, had been accepted, and she received the Bernice Tutwiler Scholarship. It was with a fullness of pride, a feeling of exquisite triumph, and no less a sense of vindication she felt as she stood on that commencement stage to receive her degree. She looked out at the regimented pattern of mortarboards, heard the ovation, then drew a quick, nervous sigh, and said a silent prayer to the one she knew had made it possible. She hoped that, even in Heaven, he would hear her name being called loud and clear by the president of the institution. And it reverberated within the large room, as if repeating a challenge forever—*"Abigail Price..!*

EPILOGUE

This story does not end with an end to bias or bigotry, for this incessant evil still pervades the province of all humanity. And be not tempted to point blame or give mouth to indict intolerance exclusively as a regional ill. Know that it knows no bounds and can be found at all compass points, even this day and until the end of time. But be comforted by the notion that, even as prejudice persists, there is today the favor of a new tradition of brotherhood and equality.

This legacy of hope can be credited to figures of note—Martin Luther and Coretta Scott King, Thurgood Marshall, and countless others.

Yet, let us not forget the measure of a simple sharecropper's son. And if in your thinking, you imagine that he failed—observe and ask: what if this young man had not dreamed and dared, persevered and prevailed?

THE END

ABOUT THE AUTHOR

In a 40-year career in broadcasting, Emeritus Professor Robert LeRoy Bannerman wrote and directed more than 300 hours of dramatic and documentary programs for radio and television. Six of these presentations received national honors and one program an international citation. He contributed programs to the major networks, most notably the prestigious (CBS) Columbia Radio Workshop. Educated at the University of North Carolina and the University of Alabama, Professor Bannerman has written a number of articles and several books, both fiction and nonfiction, including the highly acclaimed biography of Norman Corwin, noted writer-producer of classic radio programs during the era of World War II. Having researched radio's Golden Age, he is an accepted authority of this aspect of broadcast history.

Printed in the United States
65121LVS00003B/94

9 781425 943912